Dream Lover

He'd intended to teach her a lesson. He'd determined to kiss her thoroughly, completely, and heartlessly, with all the skill he'd learned in a hundred brothels from here to Shanghai. He'd planned to ignite her senses until she begged for more, then walk away, leaving her weak and wanting.

His plan went badly awry.

He covered her mouth, driven by a passion that came out of nowhere. She tasted sweet—God, he'd forgotten how sweet. He cupped her face in both hands and tilted her head to deepen the caress. With the innocence of an unfolding flower, she parted her lips, tantalizing him, intoxicating him.

For years he'd lived on the pale memory of her kiss. He'd tried to forget it a hundred times, but it always came back to him in hopeless dreams and wishes.

But this was no dream. . . .

MIDNIGHT MISTRESS

Books by Ruth Owen

MIDNIGHT MISTRESS
GAMBLER'S DAUGHTER

RUTH OWEN

—

MIDNIGHT MISTRESS

BANTAM BOOKS
New York Toronto London Sydney Auckland

MIDNIGHT MISTRESS
A Bantam Book / January 2000

ISBN 0-553-57746-8

Published simultaneously in the United States and Canada

Bantam Books are published by Bantam Books, a division of Random
House, Inc. Its trademark, consisting of the words "Bantam Books" and
the portrayal of a rooster, is Registered in U.S. Patent and Trademark
Office and in other countries. Marca Registrada. Bantam Books,
1540 Broadway, New York, New York 10036.

PRINTED IN THE UNITED STATES OF AMERICA
OPM   10   9   8   7   6   5   4   3   2   1

MIDNIGHT MISTRESS

PROLOGUE

London January 1, 1800

A new century!

Cathedral bells all over the City, from St. Peter's grand chimes to the slow bells at Aldgate, pealed a welcome to the new hundred years. The palace Horse Guards paraded in front of Pall Mall, while mummers and mountebanks gave free shows for the children in Hyde Park. Earlier that morning, several hot air balloons had risen into the clear dawn skies, the impressive but impractical inventions of the last century delighting and astounding the celebrating throng. Pugilists staged exhibition matches for the masses, and there was a prime bang-up at the Bell Tavern over whether the favorite's mendozy punch was a flush hit or a hum concocted by their two managers before the fight. All in all, it was a glorious day, and the cold, crisp winter day rang with the sounds of celebration. And why not? There was much to celebrate.

The unpleasantness with the Colonies in America was over and done with. The war with France continued, but with the anticipated surrender of Malta, and the recent signing of Russo-Turk alliance, the devil Napoleon was at least temporarily at bay. With the new century had come astonishing advances in science, such as Joseph Priestley's machine for producing electricity by friction, and Humphrey Davy's incredible "column of electric light" from a battery. And Newcomen's coal-powered pumping engine, first developed almost seventy years ago for the Cornwall mines, had been redesigned by a young engineer named George Stephenson, who was using it to power a loud, impractical but still fascinating invention called a steam locomotive.

Almost seven hundred new books had been published the year before, and magazines such as the *Morning Post* and the *Gentleman's Press* were now being read by the upper class, though such rarified pursuits were, of course, far beyond the limited intelligence of the general public. Advances in medicine and social hygiene were reducing the City death rate from disease from one person in twenty to half that figure. But most impressive of all was the fact that the glorious British Empire stretched across the entire world, from India, to Australia, to the West Indies. And almost every ounce of cargo that came from the mighty empire, whether it was rum from the Indies, gold from Africa, jade from the Orient, or stone obelisks from the desert graves of Egypt, was brought in through the immense and sprawling network of piers, roads, tunnels and warehouses known as the London docks at Wapping, one of the largest ports in the world.

Yes, there was much to celebrate, and on this day of days everyone in the City, from the most pampered lord down to the most low-born chimney sweep, put away their quizzing-glasses, riding crops, mops, brooms, and shovels and joined in the revelry.

Everyone—save one.

Eight-year-old Lady Juliana Dare sat on a tea crate on the Execution docks near Limehouse Cut, watching her father's newest schooner, the *Swallow*, floating along the bright waters of the Thames. Her father owned many ships, along with a number of profitable estates and holdings, for the marquis of Albany was a rich and powerful man. But all his riches hadn't mattered a whit three weeks ago, when Juliana's delicate, beautiful mother had died of influenza. And all of his power couldn't help Juliana find a way out of the dark, hurting place inside her, where all she could think about were the stories her mother would never read her, the kisses she'd never feel on her brow, and the warm arms that would never be there to hold her.

"Lord, are you crying *again*?"

Juliana looked up into the handsome, irritated face of her cousin Rollo Grenville. Ten years her senior, Grenville was Juliana's closest relative besides her father. Lord Albany had brought the young man down from Oxford because Grenville had lost his own parents years ago and he'd believed her cousin would be a comfort to her. What Albany failed to realize was that Grenville had never cared much for his parents and was only marginally put out by their loss. He'd never much cared for Juliana, either.

Being saddled with a mewling baby in the midst of all this merriment was more than Rollo could handle. He looked at his silver pocket watch and determined that Albany would not be back from his business meeting for another three-quarter hour. And the buxom tavern wench who was throwing glances his way did not look as if she was prepared to wait that long. "Listen, I want you to promise to wait right here. Right here, mind you. I'll be back in ten min—" Grenville stiffened as the wench lifted her skirt to display a very immodest expanse of calf, then disappeared behind a stack of barrels. "All right, fifteen minutes. Wait here."

Her cousin's absence meant nothing to Juliana. Her world was just as cold and empty with him as it was without him. She used to love sitting on the docks and listen to her father tell of the wonderful, exotic places he'd visited. Juliana had been so excited when he'd said she and her mother would join him on his next voyage. But now her mother was gone, and the thought of taking an adventure without her only made the loss more painful.

"Why so glum, Princess?"

Startled, Juliana turned around. The speaker was a wharf rat—one of the orphaned children who lived off the scraps and leavings on the docks. She guessed he was twelve or thirteen, though it was hard to tell from his filthy clothes and half-starved appearance. Yet despite his deplorable state he held his head high, and his striking sky blue eyes met hers without a hint of uncertainty. "I'm not a princess," she admitted with strange reluctance. "And I'm crying because my mother died."

A haunted look shadowed his eyes. "Cor, that's a blow. Me own mum weren't much good to me, but I still miss her sore. Right here," he said, pointing to his thin chest. "Like someone carved out my heart and forgot to sew it back up."

"Yes, that's it exactly," Juliana cried in amazement. "Father says I must be brave and keep a stiff upper lip. But I keep feeling my lip and 'tis ever so soft. And Grenville says I'm a baby for crying. Do you think I'm a baby?"

The boy stared at her, as if amazed that his opinion would matter. "I think that anyone what loves enough to hurt ain't no baby."

"And do you think my upper lip will ever be stiff to please my father?"

The boy's gaze traveled to her mouth. A strange vulnerability shook his confident expression. "Your lips be fine. In fact, you're . . . perfect." Clearing his throat he took a step away, and touched the forelock of his muddy blond hair. "I'd best be going."

"Oh, don't. Please. Here, I've got a penny."

The bright confidence in the boy's eyes died. He stuffed his hands in his pockets and backed away. "I ain't no charity. I never asked for coin."

"But your clothes are so awful and you're so thin—"

"I ain't no charity!" The boy still held his chin high, but there was a gleam of shamed tears in his eyes. "I'm Connor Reed and I make my own way, see. Always have. Always will."

Juliana watched the boy stalk away, struggling with emotions too deep for a young girl to understand. She'd promised her cousin that she wouldn't leave this spot. She'd promised her father that she'd listen to Grenville. But she also knew that talking to this boy had made her feel more alive than she had in weeks. Somehow he'd touched the hurt inside her, and for an instant she hadn't felt empty or alone. *Magic*, she thought as she gazed after him. Like one of the heroes in the stories her mother used to read to her. A magical storybook hero.

She jumped up off the crates and ran after the boy. "Connor Reed, come ba—"

Her foot caught in a stray rope. She lost her balance and toppled over the side of the dock into the river.

The freezing water drove the air from her lungs. She struggled to the surface and tried to cry out, but her words came out as a choking whimper. No one saw her fall. No one knew she was drowning. She heard the celebration on the docks above her, the loud revelry that overpowered her faint cries. She flailed helplessly as the water closed over her a second time.

Her clothes felt like lead. Treacherous eddies pulled her under. With the last of her strength she clawed her way back to the surface and gulped much-needed air. She looked up and thought she saw Grenville watching her from the pier above. Then the water closed over her again, and as she lost consciousness she imagined a white-winged angel coming to take her to heaven.

But when she opened her eyes she saw that her savior wasn't an angel, but a half-starved, blue-eyed wharf rat, drenched to the skin. "You lie there qu-quiet-like, Princess," he said through chattering teeth. "Everything's gonna be b-bang-up prime."

And as she saw her worried father arrive, and watched

him lay his hand on Connor's thin shoulder, she knew that somehow things really were going to be "bang-up prime" after all.

London January 1, 1808

For the second time in her life, Juliana Dare felt as if she were drowning.

She sat in the shadowed corner of her father's study and watched her world come to an end. Her father, Frederick Dare, the marquis of Albany, stood behind his desk, his strong, stout shoulders bent in despair. And in front of the desk, with his back to her, stood the tall, rigid figure of Connor Reed.

"I want the truth, boy. By God, you owe me that much." The marquis rammed his hand through his graying hair and leaned forward, his broad, usually smiling face pale and drawn. "Connor, why did you do it? Why did you take the money?"

Juliana gripped the chair arm, feeling the pain in her father's voice stab through her. Eight years ago Albany had pulled Connor from the filth and squalor of the London docks. He'd raised the boy as his own, and no father could have loved his son more. Connor had become a part of Juliana's family, and had been her protector and companion during her father's fabulous seafaring adventures. She'd lost count of the number of times he'd saved her from the perilous situations her childish curiosity got her into. He was her hero—

"Why, damn you?"

Albany slammed his fist on his desk, sending quills and papers flying, and teetering the single candle that provided the room's only light. For an instant, the erratic flame shimmered through Connor's dark blond hair, turning it into an angel's halo. But the moment passed, and the ominous shadows closed in again. Connor bent his head and clasped his hands tightly behind him, as if the iron manacles were already on his wrists. "You have my confession, my lord. Why should my reasons matter?"

"Why, *indeed*." A shape uncurled itself from the shadows beside the desk. Mr. Rollo Grenville, Juliana's second cousin, stepped into the small circle of light. At twenty-six he was only five years older than Connor, but his elegant coat of plum-colored superfine and his polished manners made him seem like another breed entirely. "He has admitted to taking the five hundred pounds from your strongbox. 'Tis more than enough to send him to Newgate. I say we send for the magistrate and be done with the cur."

Rollo's words dripped with disdain. Juliana watched as Connor's hands balled into hard fists, and felt the ghost of a smile flicker across her lips. There had never been any love lost between Connor and her pompous cousin—Lord knows there had been times when *she'd* longed to pummel the smug Grenville for the insults he'd made at Connor's expense. But her father's old first mate, Tommy Blue, had told her to pay the dandy no mind. *It's deeds what makes the man, not words spoke by some silly popinjay.*

Of course, Tommy's words lost much of their comfort when she recalled that Connor's most recent deed was stealing five hundred pounds.

"I'll not send for the magistrate."

Lord Albany's pronouncement brought shocked gasps from Grenville, Connor, and Juliana. She pressed her hand to her heart. Connor wasn't going to prison. Her father had seen that somehow this was all a terrible misunderstanding—

"I'll not send for the magistrate if you resign your commission and are out of London by tomorrow's dawn and out of England by week's end."

Juliana's relief shattered. In exchange for his freedom, her father was stripping Connor of everything he possessed—his career, his shipmates, the country he loved . . . and her.

"Well, boy, do you agree?"

No! Juliana wanted to scream. *Do not agree. Say you*

didn't steal the money. Say you never saw it. Say anything, just don't leave me—

"I agree."

Like a man who'd just been handed a gallows sentence, Connor backed away from the desk and gave a nod of respect to the marquis, then a swift, unreadable glance at the smirking Grenville. As he turned toward the door, Juliana finally glimpsed his eyes, his brilliant, sky blue eyes that had always gleamed with easy laughter. The laughter had died. In its place was the lost, hopeless expression that Juliana had seen only once before, on the long ago day when she'd first seen him on the London docks—a filthy, starving beggar boy who'd been too proud to accept her coin. With a soft cry she reached out to comfort him. His mouth hardened at the sound, but he passed her by without a word. He slipped out of the room, leaving behind a whisper too soft for anyone else to hear. "I'm sorry, Princess."

The sob that had been building inside her finally broke free. Eight years ago he'd saved her from an icy grave in the Thames. He'd saved her from the loneliness of her mother's death, and in the years that followed they'd become the best of friends. When Connor had left three years ago to join the Royal Navy, not even distance could break the bond between them. He had remained her best friend, her trusted confidant, and her hero. Until last night, on the eve of the new year, when he'd become so much more. *I'm only a second lieutenant now, but in a few years they say I'll be promoted to commander. After that 'tis only a short jump to captain, and a man can support a wife on a captain's pay—*

A shadow fell across her, wrenching her thoughts back to the present.

"You should have listened to me," Grenville purred as he loomed over her. "I knew that wharf rat would show his true colors one day. Perhaps next time, my dear, you will not be so foolish as to entertain the attentions of a man so far beneath you. Why, he probably laughed about your *tender feelings* with a woman of his low and vile class—"

"That's not true!" Juliana bolted from the room before he could see the hot blush of shame stain her cheeks. Rollo was wrong. Connor loved her. Whatever else he had done, he loved her.

By the time she reached her bedchamber, she had a plan. The marquis of Albany was a man of passion and daring, and his daughter was cut of the same livery. Growing up on a merchant ship traveling to all manner of strange and exotic foreign ports had given her a nature both bold and practical. She opened her wardrobe and shoved aside the beautiful gowns that her doting father had lavished on her, and pulled out an ugly but sturdy oilskin from her seafaring days. She shrugged on the old coat and twisted her thick red-gold hair into a serviceable bun easily concealed beneath the hood. Efficiently masked, she opened her jewel box, removing the emerald necklace and earrings that she'd inherited from her mother. She breathed a silent prayer to the long-dead Anna Dare. *I know you wanted me to pass these on to my children, Mama, but Connor will need the money the gems will bring until he gets back on his feet.*

She penned a quick note to her father, telling him not to worry and promising to write soon. More than that she dared not say, not until Connor and she were safely wed. Then, without so much as a twinge of regret, she turned her back on her world of wealth and privilege and slipped out into the raw January night toward Connor's lodgings.

It was a foul evening, with a cold drizzle dripping down from the starless sky. Yet to Juliana it was like walking through heaven. She was on her way to join the man she loved, the man she believed in with all her heart, no matter what he'd supposedly done. Together they would put right this dreadful mess and clear Connor's name. He needed her love and support now more than ever. And he would have her support—

for richer and for poorer, in sickness and in health, till death do us part.

She raised her hand to her lips, recalling the soft kiss Connor had brushed across her lips to seal their engagement. It was the first time she'd ever been kissed. Connor's mouth had been warm and gentle as a South Seas trade wind. Just thinking about it started a sensation like a whole flight of butterflies fluttering in her stomach. In that single instant she felt a whole new life open up to her, a life that was as full of possibilities as the exotic cities she'd visited as a child— enchanting, mysterious, and more than a little frightening.

. . . laughed about your tender feelings with the woman of his low and vile class . . .

Juliana's steps slowed. She tried to tell herself that Rollo's words meant nothing, but the truth was she was less than confident about Connor's romantic feelings for her. Too tall, too thin, and with a bothersome spray of freckles across her nose, she could hardly be considered a beauty. Besides, she was sixteen and barely out of the schoolroom, while Connor Reed was a man of twenty-one who had spent almost three years sailing under the king's flag from one port to another. She'd spent enough of her childhood visiting such ports to know what went on in such places, far more than young ladies her age were supposed to know. Far more than she *wished* to know.

She had loved Connor for longer than she could remember. She had no doubt that he loved her—as a friend. But until last night he had never touched her in anything except a brotherly fashion. And the possibility that he might have touched other women differently filled her with a chilling ache that had nothing to do with the cold January wind.

She turned under the stone arch of the courtyard of the building that housed Connor's second-story rooms. Looking up, she could see his window, brightly lit and covered with the rose-embroidered curtains she'd made for him during her finishing-school needlework lessons. The chill of uncertainty left her when she recalled how he'd handled the amateur efforts as if they were the finest silks, vowing that he would treasure them always because *she* had made them. She remembered the look in his eyes—sure, strong, and so full of love it made her heart skip a beat.

She lifted her skirts and dashed across the cobbled courtyard as if she had wings on her feet. Grenville was wrong. Connor had not been unfaithful to her, any more than he had taken the money from her father's strongbox. She believed in him. If the whole world turned against Connor, she would *still* believe in him. And no matter what anyone accused him of, she would never stop loving him.

Shadows crossed the window. Against the backlit screen of Juliana's lovingly embroidered curtains she saw the tall, broad-shouldered silhouette of Connor Reed wrap his arms around another woman.

1

—🍃—

The earl of Morrow's New Year's ball was one of the most glamorous events of the year. The house, designed to ape the fashionable Argyle Rooms, was decorated in the Grecian motif, with magnificent Corinthian pillars, life-sized statues of fawns and nymphs, marble floors inlaid with glittering gold and jade, and hanging brass lamps, all of which put one in mind of a temple. The carefully selected guests came dressed to the nines in their most elaborate finery, in silks, satins, and velvets of every hue in the rainbow, and cascades of jewels that shone and sparkled as they whirled across the sweep of the grand ballroom floor.

But not all of the guests had chosen to deck themselves out in regal opulence. One lady in particular had arrived in a simple white dress cut in the classic style, unadorned save for the plain gold ribbon at her high waist and a spray of tiny white blossoms in her red-gold hair. It was a scandalously plain dress in the midst of the gaudy riot of fashion, and more than one lady clucked behind her fan at its inappropriateness. But those same ladies were also making mental notes to rush to their mantuamaker in the morning and have the same dress made for themselves. For the woman wearing the dress was an acknowledged leader of the beau monde, one of the most sought-after guests of the Upper Ten Thousand, and the lady who was poised to be the sensation of the upcoming Season—the honorable Lady Juliana Dare.

Juliana ignored the sidewise looks and settled with unhurried ease onto the gilt and brocade settee in the earl of Morrow's side parlor. Languidly, she unfurled her pearl and ivory fan and fluttered it eloquently beneath her chin as she declared, "The rest of the city might stand on their heads for this Archangel fellow, but not I."

A chorus arose from the group surrounding her, momentarily drowning out the music from the nearby ballroom. The celebrated Lady Juliana had been the toast of London for the last two Seasons, and it was anticipated that she would be just as popular when the next official Season began in March. She was beautiful, accomplished, and arguably one of the wealthiest heiresses in the country, and her style and wit set the bar by which all the other ladies of the *ton* were measured. But her comments about the mysterious privateer known as the Archangel, who was to make his first public appearance at Morrow House later that evening, were without precedent.

"But how can you say such a thing?" the impressionable Miss Millicent Peak uttered, her turquoise headdress of ostrich feathers bobbing with every other word. "The Archangel and his ship have run the French blockades dozens of times, bringing badly needed supplies to our soldiers in the Peninsula."

"For a pretty price," Lady Juliana replied.

Mr. Hamilton shook his head so firmly that his new wig slipped askew. He patted the lapels of his elegant bottle green velvet waistcoat that had been tailored by the fine and fashionable Mr. Weston in Conduit Street, and which Juliana suspected concealed a Cumberland corset under its well-turned lines. "Well-paid or not, you must own that the man showed uncommon courage. True, he sails under a letter of marque and gains a share of the cargo he captures in the prize court, but that is hardly the point. Three times he has put his bannerless ship between Boney's cannons and our defenseless merchant vessels."

"More likely 'twas just an ill-timed shift of the wind," Juliana drawled as she rose from the settee. "Or an unfavorable current. La, I suspect there is more buffoonery than bravery in his actions."

"Extweemly well spoken," Lord Renquist exclaimed in his fashionable lisp. Languidly, he twisted a curl of his raven hair, stylishly greased and tortured into the latest Brummel fashion. "I agwee with Lady Juliana."

"You *always* agree with Lady Juliana," Hamilton muttered.

"Well, I still think the Archangel is splendidly heroic," Millicent offered. "There was an account of his foiling of the French attack on the northern shore of Sicily. It seems he brilliantly anticipated the enemy's every move—"

"There was nothing brilliant about it," Juliana interrupted. "The French had only one choice. The channel currents run strong and deep in that part of the Mediterranean. Any tar worth his barnacles knows that the only way a ship can approach Portabello harbor is from the leeward si—"

Juliana's words dwindled to silence as she realized the others were staring at her. *Bilgewater and barnacles!* Her seafaring past crept out at the most inauspicious times. She raised her fan, fluttering it coquettishly in front of her reddening cheeks as she added, "Or so I have heard my father say. Not that I understand a word of it."

The censoring frowns turned to wry chuckles. Mr. Hamilton patted her arm. "Of course you don't, my dear. Such talk is for men of business, not pretty young ladies like you. I'd forgotten that the marquis of Albany had a ship."

"Fifty ships," Juliana murmured, unable to completely eliminate the pride from her voice. "My father owns the Marquis Line, a shipping concern second only to the East India Company in trade routes."

Lord Renquist reached into the pocket of his plum-colored waistcoat, which had also been tailored by Weston, but which had no need to conceal a corset. If anything, Lord Renquist was a bit on the narrow side, and his wiry frame had given him the reputation of a fencer of some note. Personally, Juliana could not imagine the languid lord wielding anything heavier than the silver snuffbox he pulled from his pocket. "Yes, I'd heard your father dabbled in *twade,*" he intoned as he deposited a pinch of snuff on the back of his hand and gave a bored sniff. "An eccentwic pursuit, to be sure, for a twuly cultivated gentleman is indiffwent to such common twivialities. Still, such failings may be forgiven in so distingwished a gentleman as Albany—especially one with such a lovely and remawkable daughter."

Juliana barely stifled the urge to ask the pompous gentleman how he could look down on the shipping trade when the merchant captains risked their lives to supply the spices for his food, the tea for his breakfast—indeed, the snuff for his snuffbox. But such a social breach would have made her a pariah in the rarified social circles of the *ton.* She could not afford such censure, not for her father's sake. Only last week she had received a letter from him in the Caribbean, saying how proud he was of the accomplished lady she had become, and how he was certain she would become as much a credit to the Albany family as her beautiful, refined, and immensely popular mother had been. He would be so disappointed in her if he heard that she had given Renquist a set-down like an angry sailor. *Even if he deserved it.*

Gritting her teeth, she gave Lord Renquist a glittering smile. "La, sir, you make my head light with such compliments. A poor creature such as I cannot bear the weight of so much acclaim."

Renquist leaned his dark head closer and dropped his voice to a fervent whisper. "That is not all I wish you to bear, dear lady. Have you given more thought to our pwior conversation, when I asked you to be my w—?"

"The minuet!" Juliana exclaimed, cutting off the lord's inquiry. She turned to Millicent and Mr. Hamilton and flashed them a brilliant, apologetic smile. "Heavens, I promised this dance to Commodore Jolly and he will be absolutely *devastated* if I do not seek him out. If you will excuse me . . ."

She slipped out of the parlor before the others could protest.

Once she was out of sight of the others she slowed her pace, lingering behind one of several large potted ferns that lined the grand ballroom. Her dance with Jolly had merely been an excuse to leave Renquist's proposal behind. She had few qualms about deserting him so abruptly—despite his lofty title, the man was an ass, and she had little doubt that his *tendre* for her was based less on affection than on the fact that he owed a small fortune in gambling debts. Besides, his was not her only proposal. She had received three offers of marriage, one from a viscount she felt had a true regard for her. But when she had opened her mouth to accept him, the words had stopped in her throat. It made no sense. She longed for a family, and for children of her own to love and cherish. *What is the matter with me? I am past twenty— nearly on the shelf. Yet when a fine man offers me marriage, I turn him away like all the rest.*

"Farthing for your thoughts?"

Juliana's frown smoothed into a sincere smile. "Meg, you minx. How could you leave me alone with the likes of Lord Renquist?"

Margaret Evangeline Evans's usually sober expression turned to one of pure mischief and the eyes behind her spectacles gleamed. "My attendance would have made scant difference—the man treats me with all the regard of a stick of furniture. But I paid for my desertion. For the past quarter hour I have been fending off the attentions of the Very Reverend William Hardy, who has informed me that God has called me to join him in his work among the heathens in India." She winced, pushing back the tight brunette curls that never seemed to stay in place. "Honestly, Julie, just because I am as poor and plain as a missionary's wife does not mean I want to be one."

"You are not plain," Juliana stated. Dark and petite as her Welsh ancestors, Meg Evans may not have had the cream complexion and the statuesque beauty that were the rage of the London set, but her heart was as true as a champion-aimed arrow. "And as for not being wealthy . . . I daresay there are plenty of men who would jump at the chance to marry a lady of rare intelligence and fine spirit, even without a fortune."

Meg gave her a smile that did not quite reach her eyes. "I fear you are beginning to believe those Minerva novels we used to purchase in the bazaar when the commodore wasn't looking. But I can assure you, if I ever do marry, it will be to a staid, stuffy and boring businessman who will set me up in a cozy little parlor and keep me warm and safe."

Meg's fine voice was as lyrical as a Welsh song, yet Juliana picked out the wispy thread of bitterness weaving through the bright tones. Meg's father, an itinerant actor, had dragged the girl and her gently bred mother through nearly every rural town in England in his quest for fame. The gypsy lifestyle had been hard on his young daughter and devastating on his wife, who died of consumption when Meg was barely fourteen. Griffin Evans had carted his daughter along with him for a few years more, but his interest in the girl lessened as his disappointment in his flagging career grew. In the end he had deposited her on the doorstep of Commodore Horatio Jolly, an old friend of his dead wife's family, and left without a backward glance.

Jolly and his mother took her in as a companion for their other ward, the daughter of the seafaring marquis of Albany, who had been in their charge almost since she left the school-room. Far more canny than her son, Mrs. Hortensia Jolly was well-connected in the right circles, and though circumstances had forced her to abandon social pursuits, she still was known for launching young ladies properly into society and securing them advantageous matches—which, of course, was the soli-tary goal of every well-bred young lady. Since they both came from such unusual backgrounds, the two girls had become fast friends, but despite their closeness Meg had never spoken of the years she spent alone with her father. Meg had been half-starved when she had been abandoned, and a year later, when her father had been killed in a drunken carriage acci-dent, Meg had not shed a single tear. Juliana, whose unusual upbringing had given her a very ungenteel knowledge of just how cruel the world could be to young women, surmised that the girl had lived through hell.

"You *will* marry," Juliana promised. "And he shall be the finest, bravest and most handsome a gentleman in the land. I will see to it."

Meg's smile deepened. "Well, if anyone can arrange such an impossibility, you can. But I doubt he shall be the finest and bravest gentleman. After all, *you* have already set your cap for the Archangel."

Juliana unfurled her fan and began to wave it under her chin with little of the grace she had shown before. "Heavens, where did you procure such an absurd notion? I know that half the unmarried ladies in London—and a few married ones as well—have made a proper cake of themselves fawning over the man. But I am not so easily enamored. He is a sailor like my father. I am curious about him in an entirely de-tached sort of way—like a botanist studying a rare kind of plant. Nothing more."

Meg's grin turned sly. "Like a plant, you say. Then why have you pored over the news accounts of his exploits like they were holy writ? Why did you practically swoon at Al-mack's last month when we heard the rumor that he might have been killed while defending Sicily? And why did you practically browbeat dear Jolly into attending the Morrows' party tonight, when you can barely stand the haughty earl or his equally insufferable friends?"

"All right!" Juliana snapped shut her fan and glared at her friend, dropping her voice to a clandestine whisper as she continued. "Perhaps I have followed the man's adventures closely, but 'tis because I admire his courage and nautical prowess. Pray, do not lump me in with the other foolish, fainting females who grow starry-eyed at the mere mention of his name. I am most emphatically not enamored with him."

"Perhaps you should be. I have heard he is handsome as the devil."

Juliana had heard much the same, but she had assured herself that it didn't matter. "He could have one eye and a wooden leg for all I care. It is his skill I admire, not his appearance. I know the waters he sails. They are some of the roughest, most treacherous seas in the world, yet he navigates them with a master's skill, a skill I have not seen since—"

Juliana bit her tongue. She'd shared much of her past with Meg, but not all of it. No, definitely not all of it.

After that fateful night, Connor Reed's name had never been spoken in her house or on the marquis's ships. Her father had forbidden it, and the one servant who had thoughtlessly done so had been sacked on the spot. The few officers who had been friends with Connor seemed just as anxious to forget the man's existence as her father. As for Juliana, she'd thought she would die of the pain of Connor's betrayal. She'd prayed to die. But her young, healthy body betrayed her as surely as Connor had. Instead of wasting away, she grew stronger. Life went on. She went back to finishing school. She made new friends. She grew into an admired and accomplished young lady. She even fell in love a few times, just to prove that she could. In time, the memory of the boy who had broken her heart faded like a transitory whitecap on an ocean wave, until the only time she remembered him at all was in dreams of the carefree days of their youth, when they would outrun thieves in the back streets of Madagascar, or climb like monkeys through the rigging of her father's ship, or play on the beaches of Tahiti. . . .

"Julie?"

The concern in Meg's voice snapped Juliana back to the present. She looked around at the swirling dancers, the gossiping guests, the blazing chandeliers, the music, the laughter, the anticipation. There was no room in her crowded life for ghosts. She squared her shoulders and shook off her past like a bit of dust on her sleeve. "I admire the man," she repeated as she glanced at the velvet-curtained entryway where the Archangel was to make his appearance. "I admire anyone who makes the seas safer for my father and other captains. But the Archangel is still a privateer. He sails for money, not honor. And I learned long ago not to put overmuch faith in heroes."

"What?" a nearby voice demanded. "What's all this about 'haste in heroes'?"

A big man with a wide smile loped toward them through the crowd. With his graying temples, commanding figure, and liberally decorated naval uniform, Commodore Sir Horatio Tiberius Jolly looked the picture of uncompromising authority, but there was a pleasant befuddlement in his grin that suggested otherwise, as if the world were a chess game where he was always one move behind.

"Not *haste* in heroes, Jolly dear," Meg explained as she stepped forward and twined her hand through her guardian's arm. "*Faith* in heroes. Juliana has her doubts about our guest of honor, the Archangel. Have you met him yet?"

"Me? Odds fish, no. Dunno a thing about the blighter, save that he's quite a devil with the rapier. Like me in my younger days, what?"

Meg and Juliana shared a smile. Commodore Jolly might have had the size and strength to be an accomplished swordsman, but his kind heart would have made him useless in a fight. Though he made friends easily and had moved steadily up the ranks of the Admiralty, there was little evidence that he had ever been in a battle. Currently, he worked at Whitehall in an office with a large window and a small desk, where he did, in the words of Juliana's father, "as little as humanly possible."

But while some may have disputed Commodore Jolly's wit, there was no one in the Upper Ten Thousand who doubted his heart. What he lacked in cleverness he made up for in compassion, and as Juliana watched he gave Meg's hand a fatherly pat. She thought how lucky they both were to have such a kind-hearted guardian, even if he was somewhat vague on facts. *A devil with a rapier, my eye. The dear man couldn't harm a beetle.*

A commotion on the far end of the room caught her attention. The music died and the dancers stopped midstep, looking perplexed until they saw the velvet curtain begin to part. The Archangel had arrived! Commodore Jolly and the two girls stepped toward the curtain along with the other guests. As they advanced, the crowd pressed around them, pushing and jostling the trio with an almost stifling closeness. Jolly tried to squire his charges through the throng, but the crowd closed around him and cut him off. Meg and Juliana pushed after him, but at the same time a tipsy, rotund gentleman stumbled forward and fell into Meg's back, knocking her so violently that her spectacles fell off and clattered to the wooden floor.

"No!" the girls cried in unison, for Juliana knew Meg could not see a foot in front of her without her glasses. Juliana glanced around for Jolly but she saw only patched and powdered strangers in various stages of dissolution, who dismissed her entreaties with an irritated shrug as they hurried toward the parting curtain.

Breathing a sailor's curse, Juliana urged Meg to stand still and knelt down, prepared to brave the stomping crush of well-polished bootheels to retrieve her friend's spectacles.

But before her knee touched the floor she felt a firm hand grip her arm and draw her back to her feet. "Leave me be. I must—"

Her protests died as a figure dove down and scooped up the spectacles. As he straightened, Juliana got her first good look at the fellow. He appeared to be in his late twenties and wore the gaudy gold livery and stark white wig of the earl's footmen. But while Morrow's servants were generally clean-shaven as polite society prescribed, this man sported a bushy, black, and exceptionally well-groomed mustache. The comical image of the dark mustache contrasting with the snow white wig brought a smile to Juliana's lips, but the smile changed to a surprised frown as she watched him lift Meg's hand with a very unservantlike familiarity and tenderly place the glasses on her open palm.

Meg gave a delighted cry. "Oh, thank you."

The footman held her hand a moment longer than was absolutely necessary, then stepped back and gave a smart bow. "*Je vous en prie,* my lady," he replied, then disappeared like quicksilver into the crowd.

Meg put on her spectacles and searched for a glimpse at her savior. "Julie, did you hear? He was French."

"Yes, and too forward by half. If I see him again I shall give him a piece of my mind. No *English* servant would have taken such liberties."

"I am hardly ruined," Meg replied dryly. "The man did me a kindness. Honestly, sometimes I think you are growing as stuffy as old Mrs. Jolly."

Was she? The commodore's bedridden mother had once been a high stickler of the first stare. Iron was less rigid than her opinions on class and social custom. Juliana had originally scoffed at her absurdly proper notions of how a lady did and did not behave, but she had to own that it was largely Mrs. Jolly's tutelage that had made her the darling of the *haute ton.* By following the older woman's instructions, Juliana had gained a place in the politest of polite circles, a position of prominence that had made her father proud and would no doubt secure her a satisfactory alliance. But in her heart, Juliana knew that her prominence was a sham. No matter how hard she tried to become the poised and elegant creature whom so many worshiped and admired, there was a secret part of her that longed to strip off her expensive silks and run barefoot on a stretch of sun-washed beach. Sometimes she felt as if two entirely different people lived inside her, each pulling in an opposite direction. Sometimes she wondered if she would ever find a place where she truly belonged.

Meg gasped. "Look, there he is!"

Two men had stepped out from behind the curtain—the portly earl of Morrow and a taller, younger man. He wore a dark coat and a plain white shirt bereft of the lace and jewels that normally accented a gentleman's clothing. Yet he seemed more suited to the role of command than any at the privileged gathering. He stood with his feet apart and his hands clasped behind him, his lean, powerful form as out of place in this fashionable assembly as a fox in a henhouse. No wig adorned his ragged, sun-bleached hair, and no powder disguised the long scar that scored his cheek. He made no attempt to hide what he was, no attempt to apologize for his ruthless appearance. He surveyed the crowd with the disdain of a king for his lesser vassals, and his pale blue eyes were as cold and pitiless as the northern sea.

Meg gave Juliana a nudge. "No eye patch. And there is not a peg leg in sight. I daresay he is one of the handsomest gentlemen I have ever seen. It appears you were quite wrong about his looks, my dear."

Juliana didn't answer. She could hardly breathe. She had been wrong about the Archangel's appearance, far more wrong than even Meg imagined. There was no mistaking the tall form, the bright hair, and the deep-set eyes that had once looked into hers with so much love. There was no mistaking the face that had turned her dreams to nightmares.

Connor Reed.

2

"It cannot be. God in heaven, it cannot be."

Meg craned her neck to get a better view and glanced at Juliana in annoyance. "Stop whispering. I am trying to hear Morrow. I believe the earl just said that his name was—"

"Reed," Juliana supplied dully. "Connor Reed."

"Do you know him?"

"I did. When I was younger. He—" Juliana bit her lip, barely able to stifle the unexpected sob that rose in her throat. She had put Connor and his betrayal behind her long ago. Until that moment she hadn't known whether he was alive or dead, and she'd been certain that she didn't care either way. Connor Reed was no longer a part of her life.

So why did she feel as if someone had fired a rifle ball straight through her heart?

Panicked, she grabbed Meg's arm and started to pull her away from the crowd to the front vestibule. "We must leave. At once."

But Meg planted her slippered feet on the floor. "Don't be silly. The only reason we came to this affair was to meet the Archangel, and now that we know he is your friend—"

"He is *not* my friend. Years ago he worked for my family, until he proved to be the most deceitful, lying jack who ever lived. I have no intention of meeting him now, or ever. He . . . broke my father's heart."

"Your *father's* heart," Meg repeated slowly. Pushing her spectacles up on her nose, she gave her friend a thoughtful look. "Of course we shall leave if you wish it. In truth, I am not so keen to meet this Archangel now that I know he is so thick with the likes of Morrow."

Juliana was having some difficulty pairing the two as well. The Connor she knew would sooner have embraced a bushel of week-old cod than a pompous dandy like the earl. But then, the Connor she knew would never have stolen money from her father, or pledged his heart to her while keeping a mistress on the side.

She shook the memory aside. "We will ask one of the servants to find Jolly for us. I'll say I have a sick headache—Lady Woolrich used the same excuse last week at Vauxhall and everyone thought it was quite the thing. We'll be out of here before anyone discovers we have lef—"

"Lady Juliana, suwrly you are not leaving!"

Renquist. Juliana stiffened, but continued walking. "Alas, I fear I have come down with a bit of a headache. Miss Evans was kind enough to offer to accompany me home."

Lord Renquist glanced at Meg as if she were a fly that had landed in his custard. His gaze returned to Juliana, taking on its veneer of adoration. "But my deaw, this is the event of the Season. You will never fowgive yourself if you leave before meeting the Archangel. And I shall never fowgive myself if I let you."

And with that he gripped her arm in a surprisingly firm hold and steered Juliana back toward the crowd.

—————

The admiral is going to pay for this, Connor thought as he shook the hand of yet another simpering lord. Slack-jawed lobcocks, every one of them. And all gaping at him as if he was a puritan at a prizefight. God's teeth, he'd rather face a ship with full cannons than this rum-togged bunch. But everything depended on his being in this place, on this night, at this moment.

"Allow me to introduce the duke of Peasford," Lord Morrow announced at his side, giving him a smile that managed to be both obsequious and patronizing at once.

Connor did not return Morrow's smile. There were some things he wouldn't do, not even for the admiral. He shook Peasford's well-manicured hand and wondered if his aristocratic admirers would be so eager to meet him if they'd known he'd grown up fighting wharf rats for scraps of meat. Probably add to his carnival attraction, he thought grimly.

For an instant he recalled the shame he'd once felt at their genteel and refined rejection. But the once-unbearable pain meant nothing to him now, a tiny pinprick lost among so many newer, deeper and far crueler wounds.

"Baroness Fairvilla," Morrow intoned.

The baroness pressed closer than convention demanded, giving Connor an ample view of her stunningly displayed bosom while she breathlessly described her adoration. Connor's heavy mood lightened considerably. A gentleman might have looked away discreetly, but Connor was no gentleman. And, from the low-cut gown and the wordless but unmistakable invitation in the woman's eyes, he suspected that the baroness was no lady.

On another night he might have acted on the tempting overture. But tonight he was playing a game, far deeper than any of the powdered and patched swells imagined. For four years he'd been through every kind of risk and danger, but he'd never stood closer to the gallows' noose than he did at that moment. He looked out over the assembly. *Raoul should have finished by now. Where the hell is he?*

"Lord Renquist."

Still searching the ballroom, Connor barely glanced at the lord who stood before him. He was vaguely aware of the man's tedious, lisping speech and didn't even realize he was being introduced to the lord's companion until she was shoved in front of him. His attention elsewhere, he noted only that she was too tall and too thin, or at least she seemed so after the substantially endowed Lady Fairvilla. If her name had been announced, he hadn't caught it.

Dutifully Connor took her hand, intending to bow over it and drop it as quickly as possible. But something unexpected happened. Her slim fingers felt like ice, but they sparked a strange heat inside him. Puzzled, he raised his eyes, taking in the narrow waist, the elegant carriage, the sweetly rounded shoulders, the swanlike column of her throat. Memories stirred inside him, weaving together into a taut pattern that ached with beauty and with pain. Like a man in a dream he lifted his gaze to her face, knowing even before he saw it that her hair would be the color of sunset and her eyes would be as green as the sea. A softness he hadn't felt in four years and several lifetimes touched his lips as he said, "Hello, Juliana."

Four years had gone by, four years that had changed her from an impressionable girl to a cultured and celebrated woman. And yet, as she watched his mouth curve into a ghost of his laughing smile, and felt his hand possess hers with its strength and surprising gentleness, she felt the years drop away. Once again she was sitting beside him in her father's moonlit garden, listening to him profess his undying devotion, her heart so full of love for him that it nearly made her weep.

But his voice shattered the spell. Rough and ragged, it was as far from Connor's light, breezy lilt as night from day. Juliana's spine went stiff as she recalled the rest of her memories, none of them tender in the least. The man was *beyond* redemption. He should have appeared contrite. Or made at least a halfhearted attempt to pretend not to know her. Instead, his pale eyes took in every detail of her form, then met her own with a bold, completely unrepentant familiarity.

All at once she was glad that Renquist had dragged her here despite her protests. It gave her an opportunity to tell Connor Reed exactly how much she despised him. She squared her shoulders, intending to deliver a set-down so brilliantly stinging that it would be repeated at garden parties for months to come, but Morrow spoke first.

"Why, do you know our Lady Juliana, Captain Gabriel?"

Gabriel? Juliana glanced around, wondering if another naval officer had joined them. But the earl still looked straight at Connor. "But Lord Morrow, his name is not—"

"Not one the lady expected to hear at tonight's party," Connor finished quickly as he stepped between them. "We have known each other for years, but I fear my identity is as much a surprise to her as it is to the rest of you. I can only plead that I was under orders not to tell a soul. Come, forgive an old friend his deception."

Connor's icy eyes were bright with unspoken warning. But if he thought a mere look would silence her, he was very much mistaken. Four years of anger boiled up inside her, four years of buried humiliation. "*Friend?*" she repeated, seething. "How *dare* you? How dare you even speak to me after what you did? I'll have you in irons—"

Her words ended in a yelp as Connor tromped on her foot.

"Heavens, look what I've done," the captain said, though to Juliana's ears his distress sounded as false as his name. "Lord Morrow, could you fetch a doctor? I fear I might have injured this poor lady."

The poor lady feared it as well, but she wasn't about to let Connor get the upper hand. Balanced on one foot and biting her lip against the pain, she growled, "Reed, you slimy son of a—"

"And delirious, too," Connor interrupted. "She believes I am someone else. Quick, Morrow. Fetch the doctor!"

The earl scuttled off to find help. Juliana turned to the rest of the crowd, determined to tell *someone* who this man really was, but Connor scooped her up in his arms and carried her behind the curtain. He called over his shoulder to the people who hovered nearby, saying the lady needed some breathing room. Alarmed, Juliana saw the crowd back away before the heavy curtain fell behind them and blocked her view.

Beyond the curtain was a narrow, deserted hallway that led to the rear of the house. Connor carried Juliana to the servant's stairs, where he deposited her on the bottom step. "Did I hurt you?"

" 'Tis a bit late to be asking that," Juliana fired back, barely able to speak. She'd thought his detestable actions of four years past were beyond compare. Apparently she'd been wrong. He'd compounded his already unforgivable behavior by stomping on her foot, sweeping her up, and carrying her off like a common barmaid. Had the man no shame? She bent forward and nursed her injured foot, burning with an emotion she told herself was simple fury. "I would not be surprised if you have crippled me for life."

Connor's hard mouth ticked up in relief. He'd wounded her pride, but nothing more. "No doubt," he agreed as he sat on the step just below her. He drew up a knee and leaned back against the wall, taking an unaccountable pleasure in watching her fuss over her abused foot. "It is your own fault. You should have heeded my warning glance."

"Captain *Gabriel's* warning glance," she corrected. "Where did you come upon such a ridiculous name?"

"It suits my purpose as well as any. Here, you are only making your foot worse by doing that. Let me."

Before she could protest, he took her foot, stripped off her flimsy slipper, pushed her skirt up to a scandalous height and started to massage the injury. Juliana wanted to jerk away, but she couldn't deny that his ministrations made her feel better. Much better. His strong, gentle hands seemed to magically draw the pain from her body. Anger and propriety told her to pull away, but her practical core reminded her that if she did so, she would be the one in pain, not Connor. With great reluctance she allowed him to minister to her ankle. At least, she told herself it was with great reluctance. "I am allowing this only because I fear permanent injury."

"Of course," he said as a hint of his old humor crept back into his voice. "You were not so angry the first time I stepped on your foot. Do you remember?"

How could she forget? She had been ten and Connor fifteen when her father had put into the Indian port of Bombay for repairs on their ship. Bored by the stuffy English children she'd been sent to play with, she'd stolen away to explore the back streets on her own. Wide-eyed, she'd wound through the narrow alleys, piling wonder on wonder as she took in the festive sights and rich, mysterious smells of the exotic Hindu city. Somewhere in the midst of the adventure she'd come nose-to-nose with a hissing cobra. She'd stood transfixed in horror as the creature rose up and unfurled its killing hood.

Then, out of nowhere, Connor appeared. He put himself in front of her, inadvertently stepping on her foot while driving the snake into the shadows. Afterward it did not matter to Juliana that her toe was black and blue for a week or that the cobra turned out to be a harmless family pet, or that her father had to bribe the owner to keep Connor from being handed over to the authorities for reckless mischief. All that mattered to her was that Connor had again risked his life to save hers.

She shut her eyes, fighting a stab of pain that had nothing to do with her injured foot. "That was a long time ago, and it was entirely different from your *cowardly* action tonight. Be assured that I still mean to tell everyone who you really are."

"Indeed," Connor commented, looking far too calm for

Juliana's liking. "And exactly what will you tell them? That their guest of honor, one of England's most worshiped and triumphant heroes, is really a beggar boy who got caught with his hand in the till? Do you think Morrow or his friends will thank you for the knowledge? Do you think the highly placed officials who have spent so much time and trouble to bring me here will thank you?"

Juliana swallowed. " 'Tis the truth."

Connor leaned closer, his eyes narrowing. "No, my innocent, 'tis *war*, and truth is always one of the first casualties. The Admiralty wouldn't care if I had robbed a dozen men and murdered a dozen others. I am their victor, their conquering champion, their highly publicized and carefully promoted hero of the hour. The few who remember me in Whitehall have already been cautioned to keep silent about my past. If they'd known you would be here tonight, you would have been told the same."

"I would not have agreed," she said firmly.

"You *will* agree. Not because it is right, but because no one wants to hear anything else. They don't give a damn about who I was—they only care that I am winning battles in a war where others are winning too few. Right now England needs all of her heroes, Juliana. Even tin-plated ones like me."

She wanted to tell him he was wrong. She wanted to scream it. But his winter gaze bored into her, freezing her speech, her breath, her thoughts. She looked in his eyes for a trace of warmth, for the bright humor that had once overflowed from his soul. She saw only ice and desolation. For the first time she looked at him without the memories of the past, seeing the harsh, unforgiving set of his jaw, the bitter line of his mouth, the red, livid scar that cut his cheek from his left eye to his throat. She wondered how he'd gotten that scar. She wondered if he'd killed the man who gave it to him. If he'd killed . . .

This man wore Connor's face. He had Connor's memories. Once he'd even borne Connor's name. But the pitiless eyes that riveted hers were the eyes of a stranger. Suddenly she was aware of the strength in the hands that held her foot, how they could snap her ankle like a bit of kindling. She was alone in a deserted hallway with a powerful, dangerous man, out of the earshot of anyone who might help her, and incapable of running away. She was at the mercy of a man who had no mercy.

"My dear, there you are!"

Commodore Jolly bounded down the hallway with Meg, Morrow, Renquist, and a man carrying a physician's satchel. Relief poured through Juliana, until she remembered her immodest pose. Hastily she pulled back her foot and was surprised to find the slipper back in place and her skirt discreetly arranged around her ankle. She glanced at Connor, but he was already on his feet with his hands clasped behind him.

Meg reached her first. "You poor darling. Are you all right?"

"I am fine," Juliana assured her, and twirled her foot as proof. "Captain Re . . . that is, Captain Gabriel was most helpful."

Was that a flicker of gratitude she saw in his face? She couldn't be sure, for no sooner had the words left her mouth than her view of Connor was blotted out by the solicitous Lord Renquist. "My deawr, I was so dweadfully wowwied for you."

"So was I," Mr. Hamilton stated emphatically as he pushed in beside Lord Renquist.

"And I," chorused another one of her suitors.

Suddenly the narrow hallway was stuffed with people. Juliana pressed back against the stairs, struggling to find the grace to deal with both the embarrassment of attention and with the less than gentle ministrations of the physician. She tried to catch a glimpse of Connor, but he had disappeared. A few minutes later she heard someone in the crowd mention that the captain had left Morrow House entirely. The man had gone without so much as a by-your-leave. Not that she expected one. Not that she *wanted* one.

Finally, with the commodore's assistance, she was able to make her way through the bevy of ardent suitors and limp to the carriage. She settled against the brocade cushions, with the concerned Jolly sitting across from her and Meg's arm clasped protectively around her shoulders, and watched as Morrow House faded into the shadows. The pain in her foot faded as well—by morning it would be quite fit to walk on.

In time, she told herself, this night would become no more than a curious memory in an otherwise sane and pleasant life, a life that did not include the disreputable Connor Reed. He would return to the sea, and she would return to her parties, picnics, and country weekends. Their worlds were as far apart as heaven and Hades. It was highly unlikely that she would ever see him again.

She clutched the carriage's door handle, determined to take pleasure in the thought of never seeing Connor again. Just as she was determined to ignore the ache that had suddenly twisted her heart.

He'd walked for hours. With his shoulders hunched against the night damp, he'd wandered through the dark streets like a ship without a compass, not caring where he was bound. He walked past shop windows without a look, traveled over the Thames bridges without seeing the eddying river beneath, passed the glorious facades of Mayfair and the rickety hovels of the East End with the same lack of interest. Somewhere after midnight it began to drizzle, but he hardly noticed that, either. It wasn't until dawn's first light that he turned his steps toward the London docks and his ship.

She should *not* have been at Morrow's. Weeks ago he'd learned that Lord Albany was in the Caribbean. He'd expected Juliana to be with him. Or away in the country. He'd expected her to be anywhere but at a party of fops and dandies, in the company of a simpering lord, wearing a dress that might have looked fine on some, but left far too little of her figure to the imagination—

"Hell," he growled as he slicked back his rain-damp hair. Four years ago she'd turned her back on him, just as everyone else had. He had to remember that. Even if her skin still smelled like summer. Even if the memories they'd shared had made him smile for the first time in only God knew how long. Even if the edge of fear he'd seen in her eyes had made him feel ashamed of the man he'd become, the man he'd *had* to become in order to survive.

Protecting Juliana wasn't his business anymore. Protecting his own skin was. He was walking a tightrope as it was, and the last thing he needed was to start worrying about a woman he hadn't thought of in four years. Well, perhaps not in *four* years, but at least a year. Well, over a month. "Bloody hell."

He reached the Upper Pool, the stretch of the Thames below Tower Bridge where ships had docked since Roman times. He walked across the wide docks to where his ship dipped and rolled gracefully against the pier—the sleek, shadowy lady that had become the only place he could even begin to call home. He walked up the gently swaying gangway and waved to the solitary lookout, then climbed down the narrow plank ladder that led to the captain's quarters. Wearily, he pushed open the door to the dark cabin and headed for the wall berth, pausing only to kick off his wet boots before he fell onto the covers fully clothed. At least he could grab a couple of hours of sleep before he met with his partner. And if he was lucky it would be a dreamless sleep, where he wouldn't have to think about sunset hair, or sea green eyes, or that long-ago time when his future had stretched out before him like a boundless, sun-swept ocean—

Connor's thoughts froze as he heard the tiny scrape of a boot against the wooden floor-planks. *Christ!* He bolted to his feet and leapt for the door, but it was already too late. Before he'd taken a step, his legs were swept out from under him. He toppled backward, hitting the floor with a force that knocked the air from his lungs. He landed a hard kick against some part of his assailant's anatomy, and was rewarded by a raw curse. Connor started to launch another kick, but his attacker dropped down beside him and pressed a knife against his throat.

"One move, *mon ami,* and you are a dead man."

3

Connor swallowed—a difficult thing to do with cold steel biting into his flesh. "So . . . you intend to kill me?"

"*Absolument,*" his attacker promised. "Such an *imbécile* does not deserve to live. He does not search his quarters. He does not check to see if his door has been tampered with. He does not even light a candle! Even for an English he is a fool."

"Perhaps," Connor said slowly. "Then again, perhaps I'm not so much a fool as you think."

"Ha!" His assailant's mustache bristled with irritation. "Brave words, English, but *I* am the one who holds the knife. Give me one reason why I should not slit your throat right no—"

The Frenchman's words died as he felt the nose of a pistol pressed into his gut. "*Merde.*" He rolled back on his haunches and glared fiercely at Connor as he stuck his knife back in its sheath. "This time you are lucky, English."

Connor sat up and rubbed the bruise on his backside where he'd hit the floor, feeling far from lucky. "Honestly, Raoul, couldn't you have just reminded me to check my cabin in the future instead of attacking me?"

Raoul St. Juste, vicomte d'Aubigny-sur-mer rose to his feet with all the grace of his aristocratic ancestors, then gave a shrug with all their indifference. "Ah, but where is the sport in that? Besides, now you shall think twice when entering seemingly deserted quarters, even if they are your own. *N'est-ce pas?*"

Connor grimaced. He hated it when Raoul was right, and in the three years he'd known him, the Frenchman had rarely been wrong. St. Juste was only a few years older than Connor's twenty-five, but he had been at this game for almost half his life, and it showed. He was a clever strategist, a courageous soldier, a poet, a cook, and a thief, as the situation demanded. There was no one Connor would rather trust his back to in a fight. But St. Juste was also one of the most egotistical men he'd ever met, and there were times Connor would have dearly loved to plant his fist squarely in the middle of his partner's smug face.

Now was one of those times. But before he had the chance to even consider acting on his impulse, the door to his cabin was thrust open, and a dark-haired boy of about eight barreled in. "Captain!"

Connor crossed the cabin and set his hand reassuringly on the child's shoulder. "What are you doing up at this hour, Jamie? All hands should be in bed."

The child answered in a gruff voice, as if unused to speaking. "Heard noises. Thought maybe watch had let someone by . . . maybe a thief or the like." He lifted his chin and looked at Connor with a courage that would have been hard to find in a man three times his age. "Nothin's gonna happen to you while I'm here. That's a promise."

"I am pleased to see that *someone* on this ship has his wits about him," Raoul commented, giving Connor a pointed look. "Now off with you, boy. The captain and I have business to discuss."

Jamie made no move to leave until Connor gave him a nod. " 'Tis all right. Besides, someone's got to keep an eye on Barnacle to make sure he doesn't wreak havoc on the breakfast." He stood looking down at the boy, every inch the stern captain, until his mouth edged up in the barest smile. "That will be all, mister. See to your post."

Jamie grinned from ear to ear at the formal dismissal, then gave a sharp salute and scooted out of the room without another word.

"That boy worships you," St. Juste said as he walked over to the map table and lit the lantern standing on it. "But it is a precarious life for one who is so young."

" 'Tis better than living like a rat on that godforsaken wharf in Cairo. If we'd left him there he'd have died of hunger—or worse."

"Yes, but we are not in Egypt now. You should look for a home for the boy. *Pourquois pas* with the mademoiselle Rose?"

"Jamie is no farm boy. He'd run away before the week was out."

"Well, perhaps you are right in that. But there are many good people in this country."

"And more bad ones," Connor countered as he stalked to his desk and rested his hip on the corner.

The Frenchman stroked his mustache thoughtfully. "So you have said. Many times."

For some reason Raoul's tone irritated Connor. "I'm sure you didn't come here to discuss Jamie. Out with it. Did you get the papers?"

"But of course." In the flickering light, St. Juste removed his greatcoat, revealing the gaudy footman's uniform he still wore underneath. He pulled out a worn leather wallet, which he placed on the desk beside Connor. "The Majorca papers.

Records of British ships and troop movements throughout the entire region. The officers and gentlemen of Whitehall will look like foolish old women when they find out their plans have been stolen. You did well with your diversion, my friend. And I did well too, *n'est-ce pas*? To counterfeit a lowly servant despite my noble bearing. The Admiral will be pleased."

"I don't give a damn if he's pleased or not, as long as it suits our ends," Connor growled as he studied the papers. The "diversion" of the Archangel's appearance had allowed Raoul to meet secretly with the Admiral's Whitehall source and receive the stolen papers. But it had cost Connor dear—in ways he could not begin to explain to his friend. Wearily, he ran a hand over his face. "Christ, I wish we were back at sea."

"With cannons firing on us and ships trying to ram us." Raoul took the chair across from his friend. "Ah yes, I wish for that too."

" 'Tis at least a clean fight, not this secret playacting for a man we barely know, and who never shows us his face."

"That is because you still have a sense of honor." The Frenchman sighed, as if Connor had contracted a fatal disease. "I am fortunate that the trait was removed from my makeup during the Revolution, along with our lands. In any case, I have news that shall lift your spirits. We have had double luck tonight, my friend. When I was still posing as a servant, this was handed to me to deliver to you."

St. Juste pulled out a cream-colored letter, which he pushed across the table. Connor stared at the note, feeling an inexplicable sense of foreboding. "What is it?"

"Since you ask, and since I have already taken the liberty of reading it, I shall tell you that it is an invitation to dine this evening at the house of one of the gentlemen from the ball . . . an officer who happens to be highly placed in the Admiralty."

"The Admiralty!" Connor grabbed up the note, his weariness vanishing. Luck was right—they'd thought it would take him weeks to break into the confidence of the truly powerful of the country—not just the circles traveled by foppish aristocracy like Morrow. Yet here it was, just a day after Connor's arrival, and he already had his foot in Whitehall's door. He leaped off the desk and paced the room. "What do you know about this Commodore Jolly?"

"*Zut*, I have been aware of this only a few hours," Raoul complained. "I shall find out all we need by evening. There is one thing I do know already—he has a very pretty ward. *Une jeune femme, très jolie* with hair like brown silk. Not striking, perhaps, but behind her spectacles her eyes are like—"

"Raoul, I'm not interested in the girl, just the officer."

St. Juste shook his head. "English, sometimes I think you are a race of very foolish people. In any case, the man has another charge who might be of more use to us. I heard from one of Morrow's serving maids that the girl's father owns many ships. While he is away, the daughter stays with the commodore. She is a great favorite of the gentry, quite rich, and pretty enough, for a tall woman. You might have noticed her. She has hair like—how you say—*coucher du soleil*?"

"Sunset," Connor supplied dully. He stopped pacing, and leaned against the wall, then threw back his head in a harsh laugh. "Of all the invitations to all the dinners in all the houses in London, why did it have to be hers?"

"You know this *femme rousse*? But this is wonderful!" Raoul rose from his chair and walked to the cupboard, where he pulled out a bottle of fine French brandy and two glasses. "With her help I am sure you can win the trust of this Commodore Jolly, and perhaps others in the Admiralty as well. We shall be done with our task before the month is out. Come—let us drink a toast to your lady."

"She is not my lady," Connor growled. "And I guarantee she is the last person who would help me win anyone's trust. Not that it matters. I will not see her, tonight or any night. I'm turning down the invitation."

Raoul sloshed the brandy he was pouring onto the desk.

"Are you mad? We thought we'd have to wait weeks, perhaps months, for an invitation from an officer of Whitehall. You cannot turn it down."

"Watch me." Turning his back Connor shrugged off his coat and began untying his cravat. "Now, if you'll excuse me, I need some sleep."

"You need a kick in the head," Raoul fired back.

"Probably. But I'm still turning down the invitation. I won't use her, Raoul. She was . . . important to me once."

Raoul set down the bottle and studied his friend. Then he walked across the cabin and picked up his coat and hat. "The invitation said that dinner was to be at eight, so I shall be here at six with my report on the commodore."

Connor glared at the Frenchman. "Didn't you hear me? I'm not going."

"I believe that you will," Raoul replied as he fingered the brim of his hat. "I never asked you of the life you led before we met. But I do know the burden we both carry, the debt we both owe." He settled the hat on his head, and turned for the door. "You will go tonight, English, because it is the only choice your sense of honor will allow you to make."

Connor stood for a long time, wrapped in silence, his only movement the gentle rise and fall of the deck beneath his feet. But inside him a battle raged that was every bit as fierce as the one he'd waged near Sicily. He'd resolved never to see Juliana again—he refused to involve her in his dangerous deceptions. Yet every time he made the decision, a picture flashed through his mind of a day two years before, when he'd lain wounded on the deck of a ship, choking on smoke so thick that he could barely breathe, hearing the crash of the cannonballs splintering the hull and the screams of dying men. And overhead, barely visible through the fire and smoke, fluttered a torn and useless white flag of truce.

Through the smoke he'd caught the gleam of a rifle barrel, and he'd steeled himself for death. But a split second before the gun fired a man stepped between him and the rifle, taking the bullet that had been meant for him. It was only after the smoke cleared that he saw who that man was. . . .

Two years ago he'd held the body of the man who'd given him back his life and promised to avenge his death whatever the cost. It was only the second promise he'd ever made that he gave a damn about keeping.

"Guests?" Juliana looked up from her mirror vanity and stared in surprise at her abigail. "Lucy, you must be mistaken. The commodore said nothing to me about any guests tonight."

"Beggin' your pardon, my lady, but the commodore don't always say what he means to," the maid remarked as she arranged Juliana's thick tresses and secured them with a pearl and ivory comb. "And sometimes even when he says it, he don't say it, if you catch my meaning."

Juliana caught her meaning all too well. The commodore was famous for forgetting to mention guests, dinners, or any number of social events. Once he had invited the entire cabinet office over for dinner and completely forgotten to mention it. The kitchen crew had nearly staged a mutiny. Sighing, Juliana took up her powder puff and began patting the inconvenient spray of freckles on the bridge of her nose. "So who are these guests?"

"Dunno, my lady. The commodore only mentioned it to Cook in passing, and she told Ruby the parlormaid, who told me. But I gathered that he's a seafaring gentleman."

Splendid, Juliana thought grimly. *More pompous bureaucrats from the Admiralty.* She glanced down at her dress, a rather plain gown of French gray bombazine trimmed with black gauze and a black satin ribbon. She considered changing into something more elaborate and flattering, but decided not to bother. The only thing the commodore's associates ever seemed interested in were horses, cards, and the latest betting opportunity at White's. She could have worn a flour sack for all the notice they would pay her. "I appreciate the warning, Lucy. That will be all."

Surprisingly, the girl hesitated. "My lady, beggin' your pardon, but perhaps you shouldn't attend. You've been lookin' a mite pale and sickly all day. And you keep gazing off like, as if you were thinkin' of something or someone far away. I know it ain't my place to say, but—"

"No, it is not your place," Juliana replied tersely. "You may go."

Lucy's face froze to stone and she started to leave the room. Instantly, Juliana regretted her sharp tongue. She had no reason to behave so coldly to her faithful abigail—no reason except that Lucy was absolutely dead-on about her behavior. "Lucy, I had no right to speak to you in that manner. Pray, forgive me. I have been . . . distracted much of the day."

As the mollified Lucy left the room, Juliana turned back to her dressing table. She had indeed been distracted for much of the day and for much of the previous night as well. And much as she hated to admit it, the reason for her annoying listlessness lay squarely at the well-polished boots of Connor Reed.

All through the day, questions that she had never asked him assaulted her mind. While she was drinking her morning chocolate, she caught herself wondering why he called himself the Archangel. During her visit to the silk mercer in Bond Street, she found her attention wandering from the merchandise as she contemplated how he had come to acquire a ship and a crew. As she joined Meg and the Misses DeBary for afternoon tea at Grosvenor House, her thoughts strayed to the question of why he sailed without a flag. And just before Lucy arrived to arrange her hair, she had gazed into her vanity mirror and fingered her cheek, wondering what horrible battle had given him his evil-looking scar.

Bilgewater and barnacles, I am acting like a grinigog!

Irritated, she rose from her vanity and squared her shoulders. Connor Reed had stolen from her father and betrayed her with another woman. He was despicable. Contemplating anything about him was as—well, as her father's old mate Tommy Blue used to say, "as bottle-witted as storing sea water in a sieve." She left her bedchamber and strode down the hall with a sailor's bravado, barely remembering to moderate her walk to a more fashionably modest cadence before she reached the drawing room. Pasting an equally fashionable smile on her face, she pushed open the door and entered the room.

The Jollys' drawing room was pleasant and well-appointed, with polished oak paneling and conservative mahogany furnishings that sported none of the faddish sphinx and crocodile carvings that had been the rage for the past few years. Books lined the walls, most of them worn and well-read. Slightly faded velvet curtains framed the large windows, but few noticed because of the wonderful view of Berkley Square across the way. The Jollys were far from the wealthiest family in Mayfair, but they always used what money they had with taste and good sense.

Unfortunately, that good sense did not always extend to their friendships. "My deawr Lady Juliana!"

"How pleasant to see you again, Lord Renquist," she commented, her smile hardly wavering. She glanced around the room. "I see my uncle invited quite a few guests."

"Yes, we have impowrtant business to discuss," the lord intoned grandly, apparently unaware that Juliana knew that his position at the Admiralty required almost as little effort as the commodore's. "How does Mrs. Jolly fair?"

"Oh, quite well, though she has a headache today and could not receive callers."

"Dweadful," the lord replied with a veneer of sympathy. It was no secret that Mrs. Jolly considered the lord's purchased title "new-minted." "But what of you? Is yowr ankle quite well?"

"My ankle? Oh yes, quite," she replied as she looked past Renquist's shoulder. Near the pianoforte stood Lord and Lady Marchmont, a pleasant but vague couple who rarely spoke of anything but the weather. Nearby, Mr. Feathergill and his wife chatted with some other officers, and though Juliana could not hear them, she was quite sure that Feathergill was again expressing his dissatisfaction at being passed over years ago to become the Vice Admiral of the Blue.

Over by the bookcases stood two plump officers who were named Rice and Caldwell, whom Juliana always thought of as a matched set of pleasantly overstuffed armchairs. And near the window, the commodore and Meg stood with another man whose dark, lean shape was silhouetted against the window. Juliana peered closer, trying to make out who it was. Instead, she saw Meg glance toward her, looking miserable.

Miserable?

The stranger turned. Juliana froze as she recognized the bleak, hard lines of his profile.

Her smile disintegrated. She wished she could run away and hide for a century. She wished the earth would open up and swallow her.

She wished she'd worn her prettier dress.

"There she is!" Commodore Jolly bounded up to her. "Look who I invited, my dear. Captain Gabriel—the man who was so helpful to you when you hurt your ankle."

"Helpful?" Juliana's word came out as sputtered gasp. "Commodore, he is the man who *caused* me to hurt my ankle."

The guests began whispering among themselves. The commodore's usually befuddled expression became positively perplexed. "But I thought . . . I imagined . . . oh heavens, this is a tangle."

"A tangle of my making," Connor admitted, stepping

forward. "Commodore, I confess that I accepted your invitation under less than forthright circumstances. I saw this as an opportunity to beg Lady Juliana's forgiveness."

Forgive him? Juliana thought. She'd rather be keel-hauled! Years ago Connor Reed's duplicity had nearly ruined her life, and she'd be the fool of the world to let it happen again. Yet as she looked up into his face, she found herself hoping, almost desperately, that somewhere underneath those cold, pale eyes and ruthlessly self-assured smile lived the boy she'd grown up with, the boy she'd always depended on, always trusted, always loved. . . .

Grinigog!

She turned away, angrier than ever that he'd managed to undermine her resolve yet again. She considered storming out of the room, but something far more cutting came to mind. With a practiced eloquence she lifted her hand to her mouth and gave a bored yawn. "Of course I shall forgive Captain Gabriel. I have always believed it is charitable to pardon the slights of the lower . . . that is to say, of *gentlemen* such as yourself."

Connor sucked in his breath as if he'd been struck by a bullet. For an instant his composure was stripped away and he stared down at her with the stark pain she'd seen in his eyes as a child. But within a second he regained his control. His jaw pulled taut and his eyes turned to opaque mirrors, reflecting her own indifference back at her. Then his mouth edged up into a smile that held every ounce of the cold ruthlessness that had made him the most notorious privateer on the high seas. "The lady is too kind," he stated, giving Juliana a bow of mock deference. "Commodore, I thank you for your hospitality, but I fear I have another engagement and must take my leave. Good evening."

The captain left the room leaving the still befuddled Jolly and the other guests in his wake. The Feathergills stared. Lady Marchmont murmured something about winter weather having ill effects on one's nerves. Only Lord Renquist seemed perfectly satisfied with her actions. "Oh, well done my deawr," he commented in a low voice only she could hear. "Nothing wong with tweating them as equals, but it never hurts to put them in their place."

He might have said more, but Meg stormed up to her and gripped her arm, making a perfunctory apology to the guests as she herded Juliana out of the room. She pulled her friend into the empty dining room and glared at her. "How could you be so monstrously uncivil?"

Juliana stiffened at the censure. "Meg, you do not understand. This man—"

"—was a guest in this house. The commodore invited the captain here as a kindness to you. You should have at least been civil to the man for Jolly's sake, if nothing else. Yet when you arrive, you treat him as if you were an ill-mannered termagant."

"Well, what if I did?" Juliana shot back. "He deserved it. You don't know what he did to me, how he treated me—"

"I saw how you treated *him*. Julie, I saw the look in his eyes. You wounded him—deeply. No human being deserves such treatment, no matter what he has done. You owe the captain an apology."

"Never!" Juliana lifted her chin stubbornly. "The sea will turn to freshwater before I apologize to that scoundrel."

"Then you had best pray for a deluge, because I believe you need to apologize to him, for your own sake, if nothing else. You know that a sister could be no dearer to me than you are. But since you started running with Lord Renquist and his smart set you have become more cynical and cutting. It has made you fashionable and popular, but it is at the expense of your natural kindness. And if you do not change your path, I fear you will become no better than those empty-headed dunderheads at Morrow's party."

Without waiting for an answer, Meg returned to the guests. Juliana joined them a few minutes later, slipping easily into Meg's explanation of momentary fatigue. For the rest of the evening she was the picture of elegance, acting as the perfect hostess to all the commodore's guests. But while the ever-cheerful commodore and his vapid officers droned on about several completely insignificant events at the Admiralty, Juliana thought on what Meg had said.

The butler, Roberts, arrived, announcing that dinner was served. During the soup course, Juliana dismissed the girl's observations as pure fancy. But by the time the fish arrived, Juliana realized that if her friend had seen changes in her, then she must have changed. By the time the mutton chop was served, Juliana had to own that Meg's observations were at least partially correct.

The veneer of arch sophistication had made her one of the most celebrated ladies of the *ton*. She had dozens of friends, scores of admirers, and more marriage proposals than she could turn down in a lifetime. Though still young, she had achieved a position that put her in the same circles as the incomparable Lady Jersey and the revered Mrs. Drummond-Burrell. She had earned her father's pride.

Lady Juliana Dare was a complete success, but she knew full well that such acclaim would never have come to a gangly, eager girl who had spent her early years climbing through a ship's rigging, trading ribald jokes with sailors three times her age, and seeing far more of life than a modest, well-bred lady was supposed to. If the full truth of her upbringing was known, she had no doubt that both her popularity and her devoted suitors would disappear like silver minnows snapped up by a hungry barracuda.

In truth, she was as mortified by her past as Connor was by his.

It seemed an interminably long evening, but eventually the guests left. Meg retired immediately to her bedchamber, barely saying good night. After the commodore settled in his study to read the latest humor magazine and racing form, Juliana headed to her own bedchamber. Pride was a hard dish to swallow, and of late she had had little practice at it. But as she turned the situation over in her mind, only one solution came to her—at least, there was only one solution that would not cost her another sleepless night. So she wrapped herself in her most concealing cloak, and padded down the hallway to Meg's chamber door.

4

"I cannot believe that you talked me into this," Meg said as she stepped gingerly around an evil-smelling basket of fish innards.

" 'Tis your own fault," Juliana countered over her shoulder. "You were the one who encouraged me to apologize to Connor."

"Yes, well, I imagined you might send him a nice note, not spend the night traipsing around the London docks."

"We are not traipsing—the harbormaster gave us excellent directions. We shall find the captain and be back home by eleven, I assure you."

"Perhaps," Meg replied as she gave a wary glance at the fog-shrouded docks ahead of them. "I only hope that you know what you are doing."

Juliana hoped the same. Ever since she had left the hired carriage and set foot on the docks, she began to have doubts about the wisdom of her plan. When she was a child, this place had been like a second home to her. The river had been the lifeblood of England's commerce since Roman times, and most of the successful shipping concerns, including her father's, had their offices here. But it had been almost seven years since she had visited those offices. And as she peered into the murky gloom, intermittently lit by lanterns and torches, and saw the dark forms of ships rise and fall on the rolling Thames like a fleet of ghosts, she began to wonder if a pleasant note might not have been the best solution after all.

Then she remembered the pain in Connor's eyes, pain she'd purposely caused. Any note she sent would likely be torn to bits before it was read. No, she had to face him when she apologized, to make sure he believed her. She wasn't entirely certain why it mattered so much to her,—she was sure that Connor was nothing more to her than a notorious scoundrel—but she did know that if she didn't try to make amends, she truly would be no better than Renquist and the rest of his shallow set.

"Look!" Meg's cry cut through her thoughts. She pointed directly ahead, toward one of the shadow vessels. " 'Tis the one, I'm sure of it. It has no name painted on its bow."

Connor's ship. It was a fine snow, a two-masted vessel used in trade and war. Juliana appraised the silhouette with a sailor's eye, taking in the sleek hull built for speed and maneuverability, and the high-set guns designed to fire at masts and rigging. *French design, and a real beauty,* she surmised as they approached the vessel, but her admiration was almost instantly replaced by a perplexed frown. It was hardly unusual for a privateer to be sailing a captured ship—often that was the only way they could acquire one. But usually the vessels were old and outdated, unable to outrun and outfight their more modern attackers. This frigate was nearly brand new, surely no more than a half dozen years out of the French shipyards. How in the world had Connor managed to win such a prize, when four years ago he'd left London with little more than the clothes on his back?

"Who goes there?"

Juliana started at the barked demand. She looked up and saw a man glaring down at her from the railing of Connor's ship. He had one eye, no neck, and arms like ham hocks. He looked as if he'd slit her throat for a penny. "We—ehem—we've come to see Captain Gabriel."

The large man leaned to his left and spit a wad of tobacco into the water. "'Ooh wants 'im?"

Make that a ha'penny, Juliana thought as she pulled her concealing hood closer around her face. Her reputation would be in tatters if news of this visit became public—though keeping her good name seemed the least of her worries at the moment. During her years at sea she'd learned that some rough characters were rock-hard on the outside but gentle as lambs on the inside.

This man looked as if he were made of stone clear through.

However, she'd come too far to turn back now. Gathering her courage, Juliana straightened her shoulders and spoke with as much authority as she could muster. "My name is of no consequence. I wish to speak with Captain Gabriel. Would you be so kind as to tell him that he has a visit—"

Her words died as a gummy wad of tobacco hit the wooden dock not six inches from her slipper.

"Shove off. The captain chooses his doxies, not the other way 'round."

"Doxies! Now see here, we're not—I mean, we aren't—my good man, if you just inform the captain of our arrival, I'm sure he will—"

She ducked as a well-aimed chaw sailed over her head and spattered against the shed behind her.

"Well, that could have gone better," Meg commented dryly as she looked from the spatter to the disappearing hulk of the sailor. "What do we do now?"

What indeed? In her younger days, Juliana would have stormed the gangway and yelled at the tobacco-chewing son of a packet rat until he was forced to take her to Connor, but those days were long gone. Such behavior would almost certainly attract the attention of the night watch—and assure her a front-page headline in tomorrow's *Tattler*. The Jollys would be mortified. Juliana had little choice but to give up and go home. "But I cannot go home, not yet," she breathed, speaking more to herself than to Meg. "There must be some way I can get on that ship and see Connor—"

"He ain't there."

Juliana and Meg whirled as one and stared at the large wine cask that had apparently developed speech. Juliana stepped closer. "Who said that?"

There was a scuffling noise and a child stepped out from behind the cask, a boy of eight or nine with curly black hair that needed combing. He stuffed his hands into the pockets of his oversized pea coat and glared up at Juliana with curious, wary eyes.

A strange feeling of recognition washed over Juliana, though she was quite sure she had never seen the boy before. She glanced at Meg, but the look of surprise on her friend's face showed that she was as astonished by the child's appearance as Juliana was. She took a step toward him. The boy darted out of her reach like a wild animal.

"Captain's over to the Bell," he said grudgingly, as if regretting his decision to reveal himself.

The Bell was a tavern on the docks that had been serving strong ale and few questions to seafaring men since the reign of Elizabeth. It took its name from the brass bell hung over the entrance, which was rung every time a ship went down. Juliana had visited it once, smuggled in under Tommy Blue's coat like a piece of contraband cargo. She remembered it as a raucous place, full of strong drink, laughter, fistfights, and pretty ladies with painted faces and old eyes. She'd had the time of her life until Connor had found them. Honestly, she'd thought he was going to skin poor Tommy alive.

Meg laid a hand on her shoulder. "Julie, the boy."

Juliana looked around and saw that the child was backing away into the shadows, poised to run. "Wait!"

Her cry tethered the boy. He looked up at her, his dark, hunted eyes showing that he was as puzzled as she was that her words had stopped him. "Crikey, what is it, lady?"

"I—" Juliana paused, inexplicably tongue-tied. After spending years in the rarified society of the *ton*, where rhetoric was an art that strove for complexity and cleverness rather than truth, she was at a loss for honest words. There was so much she wanted to know about the boy—where he came from, how he knew Connor, why he had helped them. Most of all, she wanted to know why she felt a strange ache in her heart when she looked into his suspicious eyes. "I . . . I am Lady Juliana Dare, and I want to thank you for your kindness. You are a true gentleman."

She wasn't sure where the words had come from, or why she'd said them, but the results were astonishing. For an instant, the boy's wariness vanished, and his face blossomed into the delighted pleasure of an innocent child. He faded into the murky fog, still smiling.

"What an unusual child," Meg commented. "Do you think he was telling us the truth?"

"I would bet my life on it," Juliana stated, staring at the empty place where the boy had been. She knew now why he'd seemed so familiar, why he'd brought an ache to her heart. His eyes were dark, not pale, and he was a child, not an adult, but such discrepancies hardly mattered. The wary, haunted look of a hunted animal was exactly the same.

The boy had Connor's eyes.

Juliana tapped her gloved fingers impatiently on the stained wooden counter. "Well, of course you must have heard of him. Captain Gabriel's name has been all over the papers. He's the Archangel."

"Never 'eard of him," the barkeep repeated as he con-

tinued to dry a mug with a less than pristine rag. "I got customers, lady—paying customers. Either order up or be on
your way."

Juliana glanced around the noisy, crowded taproom that
stank of smoke and sour beer. Leaving seemed like a grand
idea—except for the fact that she had not yet found Connor.
And she had far too much of her adventurer father in her to
be turned aside by an unexpected squall. "Oh, very well." She
glanced at Meg. "We will have two lemonades."

The barkeep looked at her as if she'd just sprouted wings.
"And I suppose you'll be wantin' some tea and biscuits, too,"
he snarled as he turned his back on her. "Shove off."

It was the second time that evening that someone had
rudely ordered Juliana off and she was getting heartily sick of
it. She opened her mouth to tell the barkeep exactly what she
thought of him and his wretched establishment, but Meg
stepped between them.

"We h'ain't no cunning shavers, guv'nor," she said in perfect cockney. "And we won't pass you no swimmers, neither.
Give us a cup of the creature and a dram of diddle and we'll
call you a Jemmy Fellow, aye?"

"Well, why didn't ya say so right off?" the barkeep said as
he turned and lumbered toward the bottles at the far end of
the bar.

Juliana bent to Meg's ear. "What exactly did you say?"

"I am not entirely sure," her friend whispered back. "They
were lines in one of my father's plays—*Murder at Midnight,* I
think. Worked like a charm, though, did it not?"

"Indeed," Juliana agreed with no little admiration when
the barkeep returned with their drinks. Juliana glanced over
her shoulder and squinted her eyes, attempting to pick out
Connor in the closely packed alehouse. It was a daunting
task. There were over two hundred people in the room, and
at least half of them looked as if they'd sell their mothers for a
shilling. She and Meg could spend an hour looking for
Connor and still not find him—if indeed he was here at all.

The boy could have sent them on a wild goose chase. Or Connor might have already left to go somewhere else. *Or with someone else,* her mind whispered as her gaze fixed on the fancy women at the end of the bar. She shoved aside the uncomfortable thought. "He must be here somewhere, he simply *must* be."

"Well, if he ain't, maybe I'll do."

Juliana spun around. At the bar beside her stood a stranger who was thin almost to the point of gauntness, wearing a fancy linen shirt and an expensive coat that had obviously been tailored for a wider man. The fine clothes hung on his frame like rags on a scarecrow.

"Name's Mortimer Sikes, and I'd be pleased to offer my services to you ladies."

He was harmless, of course. A man his size could not have beat up a butterfly. Nevertheless, something about the gleam in his too-small eyes made her feel . . . well, it made her feel a little like a fat chicken being eyed for the dinner table. Instinctively she drew away, anxious to put distance between them. "Erh, many thanks for your offer, sir, but we are . . . waiting for someone. No need to trouble yourself."

"Oh, no trouble," the man oozed, returning to her side. "Got what you want, I do. Make your dreams come true." He moved closer, whispering into her ear. "You got needs, don't ya, dearie? Needs that come to ya late at night, in the dark, in bed . . ."

Sikes's words were unbelievably forward. A proper lady would have pulled away immediately. But Juliana *had* had dreams such as Sikes described, dreams so intimate that she'd never shared them with anyone, even Meg. Dreams that woke her in the middle of the night, dreams of a man who wore Connor's face.

"Tell me you don't think about 'em. Men. Not the pouf nobs you run with. I'm talking about a real man—a strong young buck who could take you to heaven. I can get it for ya, dearie. Pleasure beyond imagination—"

Sikes's words ended in a yelp. He was jerked back, and
eld in midair like a flailing marionette.

"Leave her alone," Connor growled.

Startled, Juliana saw him holding Sikes by his collar. With
ffortless strength, he shook the man until his teeth rattled,
hen dropped him on the floor like a sack of old clothes.

"Now get out," he said, his words fierce with anger.

Sikes scuttled backward like a crab. Once out of Connor's
each, he stood up, his eyes narrowing to threatening slits.
This hain't the end of it," he promised. "No one meddles
vith Mortimer Sikes. And them that does is sorry they was
ver born."

Good riddance, Juliana thought as she watched the unsa-
ory fellow disappear into the crowd. "La, what a dreadful
nan," she commented as she waved her handkerchief under
er nose as if to be rid of an unpleasant odor. "I suppose I
hould have expected such ill-mannered individuals in a
lace like this, but—"

Her sentence ended as Connor grabbed both her and
Meg by the arms and dragged them to an empty table in the
orner. He deposited them in the chairs like a pair of unruly
hildren. Then he put his leg on a third chair and leaned for-
vard, glaring down at them.

"What the *hell* are you two doing here?"

Juliana's recently regained composure dissolved like sand.
'acing Connor's anger was bad enough, but as she dropped
er gaze, unable to endure his condemnation, she unwit-
ingly focused on the boot he'd propped on the chair in front
f her. The polished black Hessian hugged his muscular calf
ke a second skin. Her gaze slid over the gleaming surface up
o where his dark breeches hugged the rest of his leg. The
abric stretched taut over the coiled strength of his thigh,
utting her in mind of a finely carved Greek statue. But
Connor was no statue. And after the interlude with Sikes and
he disturbing dreams he'd made her recall, she had admit to
he fact that she wasn't one either.

"Well?"

Juliana's head snapped up. Unfortunately, meeting his fierce gaze only added to her distraction. "We were . . . um, that is to say we were . . ."

"We were looking for you," Meg finished, perplexed by her friend's apparent lapse of memory. "Juliana has something she wants to say to you."

Meg nudged Juliana in the ribs. She might as well have been nudging stone. For the second time that night Juliana was caught in a spell. She stared into Connor's eyes, wondering why she'd never noticed how the flickering torchlight filled them with glorious light, like sunshine breaking on new snow. She drank in the harsh, lines of his face, the ragged crown of his hair, and the energy that seethed just beneath his ice-hard countenance. He was all angles and edges and ruthless power, yet there was a part of her that yearned to seek out the gentleness that had once existed inside him, that might still exist under the anger, and the muscled body that made her feel like . . . like . . .

She ripped her gaze from his and pulled her hood down to hide her embarrassed blush. "I came here to apologize," she said stiffly, afraid her breathlessness might betray her unseemly thoughts. "I behaved rudely when you came to our home this evening. It was no way to treat one's . . . guest. Please accept my regrets."

There, she'd done it. Swallowed her pride. Admitted her error. Feeling quite noble, she lifted her hood, expecting to see a thaw in his winter countenance.

If anything, the ice grew thicker.

"So, you come in here like Lady Bountiful, dispensing empty apologies like Christmas coins and expecting me to be grateful for it."

Juliana's jaw dropped. "It wasn't empty! It took a great deal for me to come here."

Connor gave a skeptical snort. "Spare me the disruption this visit caused to your busy social schedule."

"That's not fair," she cried as she bolted to her feet. "I came here to prove how genuinely sorry I am for what I said this evening. I know how much it hurt you."

Connor leaned closer. "I've faced pirates, shipwrecks, French fortresses, and Spanish cannons. I've stared down death's gullet and barely escaped with my life. I've done more, seen more, and loved more in the last few years than you could in a lifetime. Do you really think I give a damn about the opinions of one useless, spoiled society chit?"

His words cut her pride to ribbons. She'd come here to offer him a heartfelt apology—but it was nothing to him. *She* was nothing. She sat back in her chair, feeling gauche, awkward and horribly embarrassed.

"Coach is here, Captain."

She looked up into the well-scrubbed face of a hansom cab driver. She saw Connor place enough coins in his hand to take Meg and her to China. "Get these children out of here," he growled as he turned his back on them. "Now."

She didn't argue—there was no reason to stay. She allowed herself to be hustled out of the Bell by the coachman, who immediately launched into a long-winded story about his adventures as a cab driver. Juliana barely heard him. Instead she glanced back, watching Connor until the smoke and noise of the crowded room swallowed him. He never bothered to turn around to see that she'd left safely. It was as if he'd already forgotten that she existed.

Useless, he'd called her. Useless as a person, as a friend . . . and as a woman.

It was last call at the Bell. Most of the crowd had thinned out, leaving only the most raucous or the most quiet behind. Outwardly, Connor Reed was the latter. Inwardly, his emotions raged like a hurricane. He raised his arm for the barkeep. "Another."

"That makes four, my friend," Raoul commented from across the table.

It made five, Connor thought, but who was counting? I
wasn't enough. It wouldn't be enough until he could n
longer remember how she'd looked at him, how her confi
dence had crumbled to dust when he'd told her he though
she was a spoiled socialite. He'd been angry—angry at her fo
risking her safety to come to a place like this and angry a
himself for caring. Most of all he was angry for giving a dam
what she thought of him. He wanted to hurt her as deeply a
she'd hurt him. And he'd succeeded, just as he won all hi
battles, with ruthless disregard for his opponent.

And he'd give ten years of his life to take the crue
words back.

"You are sure she made it home safely?"

"*Zut alors,* have I not told you three times already? Yes,
followed the coach as you asked. Yes, I kept out of sight—
though the brown-eyed *fille* looked my way more than once.
almost believe she knew I was there. . . ."

"But is Juliana safe?"

Raoul sighed. "I watched the commodore collect them i
his arms and take them into the house. Perhaps you woul
have wished me to go inside and tuck the lady into her bed."

Connor's mouth twitched. "Not bloody likely."

"Ah, I am glad to see that you have some wits left. Hold o
to them, English. You will have need them tomorrow, whe
you tell the Admiral how you managed to ruin a chance a
scaling Whitehall. The girl is sure to turn her guardia
against us—"

"She'll say nothing."

Raoul shook his head. "It is a woman we are speaking of
my friend. What any of them do is a mystery, even to the fa
more intelligent men of my country."

Connor stared into his mug, but it wasn't the murky ale h
saw, but a long-ago moonlit night. His grim mouth gentle
with a smile. "Have you ever been in love?"

The Frenchman stroked his mustache. "But of course

Only last month there was that *très magnifique* tavern wench in Gibraltar who—"

"Not *that* kind of love. I mean the kind the poets write about—when your life is consumed by wanting one woman. When you live for her smile. When you die when she cries. You would do anything, be anyone, risk everything to keep her safe. And you would give up your soul just to hear her say, one more time, that she loves you."

Raoul stopped stroking his mustache. He stared at his friend for a long while, then shook his head. "No, I have never been in love like that. I do not think I should want to be."

"You won't. But when it happens, you won't have a choice. Hell, you won't even know what hit you. The first time I saw Juliana . . .". Connor gripped his mug and downed the rest of the sour-tasting liquor in a single gulp. "I was an idiot, a boy in love with a dream. Now she has only contempt for me. But she won't talk—pride alone will keep her from admitting that she was bested by an inferior. She'll go back to her balls and parties, and forget she ever met me again."

Raoul raised an eyebrow. "And you, *mon ami*? Can you forget her so easily?"

"Think I can't? Ha!" Connor pushed his chair back, feeling a pleasant, fuzzy confidence begin to glow inside him. "I'll forget her before first light—see if I don't. There's plenty of women in the sea. Blondes. Brunettes. No redheads. All willing and winsome. Not spoiled. Not stuck-up. Can have my pick. Can have—"

He stood up and the world began to wobble. "Maybe I shouldn't have had that last drink."

"I warned you," Raoul said as he placed a steadying hand on his arm. "*Mon Dieu*, your head will ache like the devil tomorrow."

Tomorrow? What about now? His temples pounded like the stone under a mason's hammer. But better his heart than

his head. Not that his heart ached. Not over her. Plenty o
other women in the world—including the well-endowed bar
maid who gave him a wink as Raoul helped him to the doo
Cheered, he grinned at his friend. "She fancies me. And she
blond. Told ya—can have my pick. Already forgot the othe
one. Already forgot Juliana's name. Let her have her partie:
Let her marry one of those pompous asses. Don't car
Wasted half my life protecting her. Not anymore. She's o
her own from now on. She's—"

The bell sounded. Everyone in the room went still as th
tavern keeper cleared his throat and called out the name c
the wrecked ship. "The *Lady Anne*, out of Kingstown boun
for Southampton. All hands lost."

"Poor devils," Raoul muttered, crossing himself. H
looked at Connor's face and saw that it was alabaster white
"My friend, a shipwreck is a terrible thing, but the crew i
past our help. Indeed, we have problems of our own. Th
Admiral—"

"To hell with the Admiral," Connor growled, sudden
sober. "That ship was Albany's. God in heaven, it belonged t
Juliana's father!"

5

It was a bonny winter day, with the sun glancing off the new blanket of snow like a thousand diamonds. Chickadees lighted on the sill outside the windows where Juliana sat, chirping merrily, leaving tiny, bold footprints in the untouched snow. On another day, Juliana would have been delighted by their antics, but on this afternoon she barely saw them. She leaned her forehead against the cold pane and stared out the window, the bright world blotted out by the terrible sorrow weighing down her heart.

Father would hate me to feel this way. The marquis of Albany had loved life, and had bit it off in huge, risky, joyous hunks. During their last voyage together he'd stood at the wheel with his daughter beside him, with the wind at their backs and the cold, crisp spray in their faces. "If I ever don't make it back to safe harbor, I want you to remember me this way," he'd said as he cheerfully steered the ship into the fighting waves. "Remember that I lived my life doing what I loved, and no man can ask for more than that. I expect you to keep people from saying too many silly things about me, and to see that my bonny ships stay clear of reefs and shoals. Most of all, I want you to marry up with a good man and have a bunch of fat, happy children. Never waste a minute of your life on regrets, Julie. Not a minute. And I expect you to shed not one tear for me."

As always, Juliana's father had expected far too much from her.

During the two weeks since the news of the *Anne*'s disappearance had reached London, she'd received a flood of notes and letters, most of them from people who barely knew her father, who said many things that the marquis would have considered very silly. She had no idea how his "bonny ships" were faring. Indeed, since she'd learned of the fate of the *Anne*, she'd hardly left her bedchamber. Marriage to any man, good or not, was not even on the horizon. And as for not shedding a tear—well, during the last fortnight it seemed as if she had done little else. . . .

"My dear, I do not believe you have heard a word that I have said to you."

Juliana turned from the window and met the gaze of the elderly woman who sat propped against an expanse of satin pillows, her Irish lace cap tied under her chin with military precision, her expression one of profound rebuke. "I'm sorry, Mrs. Jolly. I was not attending."

"I can see that," Hortensia Jolly commented as she put down the letter she'd been reading aloud. "Apparently the prime scandal between Mrs. D. and the young lieutenant is lost on you. Well, perhaps it is for the best," she acknowledged as she laid the letter onto a pile of correspondence by her bedside. "It lacks barely a half hour until your father's will is to be read. Though I think it is unfortunate that the disagreeable Mr. McGregor must do the reading instead of your father's regular solicitor. The man has a reputation of squeezing a farthing till it screams."

"How did you know that Mr. McGregor—?" Juliana stopped midsentence, her eyes lighting on the stack of letters on the nightstand and the larger pile on the vanity. Mrs. Jolly had been bedridden for a good portion of her life, but she had turned her disability into an invaluable asset. Born into the well-connected Sommes-Fitzgerald family that could trace its bloodlines back to Eleanor of Aquitaine, she had grown up in the heart of London society—a position strengthened when she married the much-decorated, if somewhat dull, Captain Sir Robert Jolly. Her bedchamber was as well appointed as any sitting room, and her custom-designed bedclothes were as grand as any evening gowns. Her confinement allowed her to turn down all but the choicest callers, and gaining an invitation to her rooms was almost as sought after as a voucher to Almack's. Yet, despite her confinement, she was more aware of what was happening on the streets of London than most of the people who walked them. It was rumored that she could tell you not only what the regent had for breakfast, but also which merchant sold the kippers and what hens laid the eggs. Over the years, Juliana had developed a healthy respect for her knowledge. She had also found it prudent not to delve too deeply into her sources.

Juliana rose from her chair and made a show of smoothing the skirt of her black crepe dress. Trying to keep her voice light, she stated, "Whoever reads the will, I believe it is a silly waste of time. It is too soon. Only a fortnight. They found the *Anne*'s debris, but they never found any bodies. My father could still be alive."

The woman's mouth curved into a sad smile. "My girl, I lost a father and a husband to the sea. I know exactly how you are feeling, twice over. God knows, I wish there was even a bit of doubt. But the Admiralty agrees that the chances of finding anyone alive in these waters are very slim. You must face the truth, my dear. Your father is gone, and you must go on with your life as he would wish you to."

Juliana bit her lip. "I know. 'Tis just that I miss him so. There is no one who knows me as he did. No one—"

Untrue, her mind whispered. There was one person who had spent almost as many years with her as her father had, one person who knew her almost as well as he did.

One person who had not bothered to send anything more than the most perfunctory note of condolence since her father's death.

She shook off the thought as she realized Mrs. Jolly was talking. ". . . cannot be expected to offer for you now. After all, you are officially in mourning. 'Tis unfortunate that you must miss the better part of the upcoming Season, but by June you will be able to put off your colors and resume your station in society. By this time next year I fully expect that you will have made an advantageous match."

Juliana stared at the usually compassionate woman in shock. "My father has just died. I don't give a fig about finding an advantageous match."

"Which is exactly why *I* must. Your father charged me and the commodore to look after you, a charge that is in no way diminished by his death. Part of that responsibility entails finding you a suitable husband. You must know that is what he hoped for you."

Reluctantly Juliana nodded. Since her father's death, her need for a family had grown stronger. She felt so alone. And yet, the thought of marrying any of the *suitable* men she knew somehow left her feeling even more alone. "I cannot think of such things right now."

"It seems to me that you have not been able to think of 'such things' for a good long while, considering the number of proposals you've turned down this last year." Mrs. Jolly's eyes narrowed cannily. "Tell me, my dear. Is there anything I should know of on this matter?"

The timely knock from the commodore announcing Mr. McGregor's arrival saved Juliana from answering.

The downstairs drawing room was the largest room in the Jolly household, but it was filled to the bursting point. The marquis had been as generous as he was wealthy, and he never forgot a kindness or an obligation. People from all walks of life crowded into the room, from the lowliest kitchen maid, to street merchants, to silk garbed gentry who looked at the rabble in alarm. There was even a sharp-nosed reporter from the *Morning Post*, who had come to chronicle the eminent marquis's final wishes for his readership. It was an unusual sight, and one that might have brought a smile to Juliana's lips under other circumstances. *I hope you are watching this, Father. You would enjoy it.*

The commodore led Juliana to the front of the room to a seat beside Meg. Meg took Juliana's hand and squeezed it tightly. The gesture of comfort brought a lump to Juliana's throat. Self-consciously, she glanced away at the crowd—and caught sight of a dark-haired boy disappearing behind a gaggle of kitchen servants and street vendors. Juliana thought he was probably one of the bootblacks or a child of one of the merchants. Still, she nudged Meg and nodded toward the door to the hall. " 'Tis likely my imagination, but I thought I just saw the boy we met on the docks, the one who knew Con—"

"My dear Lady Juliana, I am inconsolable over your gweat loss."

"Um, thank you, Lord Renquist," Juliana replied as she looked in surprise at the gentleman. Renquist wore an elegant bottle green coat and a nattily powdered wig. He looked as if he'd dressed for a ball, not a will reading. Reluctantly Juliana offered him her hand. "I did not expect to . . . have the pleasure of seeing you."

"Of couwrse not," he oozed as he enveloped her hand in his. "And I should not pwesume to be here, save that I was entweated to attend by your cousin Gwenville."

It *would* be Grenville. Juliana's cousin was still in Sicily, and had replied to the news of her father's death with a terse letter that he would be returning to London as soon as it was convenient. His indifference did not surprise Juliana—the only time her father had heard from Grenville during the past few years was when he wanted an advance on his allowance. The fact that he'd sent someone in his stead did little to mollify Juliana, especially since that someone was the supercilious Renquist. No doubt the man was here to catalog Grenville's inheritance. She was more than a little tempted to say as much, but Meg spoke first.

"I was not aware that you knew Juliana's cousin, Lord Renquist. I believe he has been abroad for years. When did you make his acquaintance?"

Renquist's carefully desolate expression shifted to annoyance. Then, as if remembering where he was, his sympathetic smile returned. "I met Gwenville when we were in school together. Though now I suppose I must begin to call him the mawqwess."

Juliana barely masked a wince. Grenville was her father's closest male relative. As such, he would inherit the title, and likely the marquessate and various other estates that made up her father's holdings. Juliana did not fear for the lands and properties—they were well established enough to run themselves regardless of whether Grenville sold them or no. But he would also inherit the Marquis Line. The thought of Grenville having charge of her father's beloved fleet made her blood run cold. *He will sell every one of my father's ships for the coin they'll bring, I know he will.*

The man behind the desk pounded his gavel for silence. Juliana quickly surmised that this was "the disagreeable Mr. McGregor" Mrs. Jolly had spoken of. He was a thin, unremarkable man with stooped shoulders, and his clothes were as rumpled as an unmade bed. His thatch of white hair was as unkempt as his coat. Juliana frowned, wondering why her father, who could have had his pick of all the solicitors in

Chancery, would have chosen this disheveled person to entrust with his final bequests.

Her thoughts were cut short as the solicitor reached into his wrinkled coat and produced a quill pen, an inkwell, and a roll of papers from what appeared to be a profusion of pockets. He cleared his throat and began reading the will in an emotionless but surprisingly rich, deep brogue.

The first stipends were to the minor servants, page upon page of small bequests. Juliana tried to remain attentive, for these were her father's last wishes, but try as she might, her attention wandered. She glanced to her left, and caught sight of the Han dynasty vase her father had bought for her in a market in Shanghai. She turned to the right, and saw the Indian tapestry he'd given her in Madras.

She twisted her black lace handkerchief into a tortured knot, fighting the overwhelming loneliness inside her. Her father was dead. She would never again hear his booming laugh, never feel his tremendous hug. Never hear him say that he loved her. His property and title would go to an inferior man. It was monstrously unfair, but there was nothing she could do. She'd had the ill luck to be born a woman. As Mrs. Jolly had pointed out, her one purpose in life was to make an "advantageous match." Under the law, she was considered little more than another piece of her father's property. And in the end she would go to the highest bidder, just like his beautiful ships.

A commotion in the back of the room caught her attention. She turned in her chair and saw at least two dozen tars push their way into the room, led by a short, stocky man with button bright eyes and an enormous cauliflower nose.

"Tommy Blue!" Before anyone could stop her Juliana jumped out of her seat and wrapped the man in a huge embrace. "I thought you were bound for Gibraltar."

"I was, but when I put into Plymouth for the last of my cargo I heard about your da. I turned the *Valiant* right around and headed for home."

Mr. McGregor rose from his chair. "Ye must see that this is *most* irregular. Kindly take yourself and your hooligan friends outside at once."

Captain Thomas Aloysius Blue strode up to the solicitor as if he were heading for a fight. "These *hooligans* is some of the finest men what ever sailed the seven seas, and every man jack of 'em sails for the Marquis Line. We got a right to know what 'appens to our ships. And iffen you want us out you'll have to carry us, one by one."

A cheer from the back of the room showed that his mates felt the same.

"Most irregular," Mr. McGregor muttered as he made a note on a scrap of paper and deposited it in one of his many pockets. Then he took his seat and resumed his reading of the will. Juliana also returned to her seat, but she glanced at the sailors who'd mixed in with the rest of the crowd. Tommy Blue stood out in front like a field marshall and gave her a jaunty wink.

For the first time since her father's death, Juliana grinned.

At the very back of the room, one of the sailors pulled his stocking cap down over his blond hair and lifted his pea coat collar to hide his scarred cheek. He pressed against the wall and craned his neck to get a better view of the rest of the room. But while the crowd around him stared at the lawyer, his gaze never strayed from the black-garbed woman seated near the front table.

Zut, you are the biggest fool in England!

Connor winced. Maybe Raoul was right. God knows the room was stuffed with enough people who could recognize the notorious Captain Gabriel—from swells he'd met at Morrow's ball, to Commodore Jolly, to the news reporter who'd interviewed him for the *Times* only three days before. And Tommy Blue, if he got a good look at him, might recognize him as the beggar boy who'd been taken in by the marquis. He'd risked his entire mission to come here, yet he'd come all the same when he'd heard that Tommy was looking for men to come with him to the reading of Albany's will. He had to see her, to know how she was faring. And from what he could see, she wasn't faring well.

She was pale as a sheet. And too thin by half. Pushing his cap up a notch, Connor turned an angry eye at the commodore, who was currently polishing a brass button on his sleeve. God's teeth, what was wrong with the man? Couldn't he see the girl was wasting away—

A quick movement near the door caught his eye. If Connor's cap hadn't been pushed up, he might have missed it, but as it was he saw all he needed. He moved stealthily through the crowd to the door, careful not to attract attention. Then he snatched his prey by the collar, whisked him into the hallway, and landed him in a dark alcove before he could make a sound.

Hunkering down, Connor brought his eyes level with his catch as he whispered, "Jamie, what in blazes are you doing here?"

The boy's eyes were white with fear, but his voice shook only a little as he answered. "Came for her. The lady. Heard she lost her da."

"You know her?"

Jamie nodded and gave him a brief summary of their meeting on the docks. Connor grimaced, knowing now how she'd tracked him to the Bell even though Barnacle had sworn on "Satan's hairy arse" that he'd told her nothing. "You still shouldn't be here," Connor said as he dug a shilling out of his pocket. "This will pay for a cab to the docks. Go back to the ship."

Jamie stared at the coin but he didn't take it. Instead he stuffed his hands in his pockets. "Ain't goin'."

Connor was in no mood to argue. He'd have enough trouble explaining his own presence here, let alone Jamie's. Whether the boy knew it or not, he was putting them both at risk. "You'll go where I tell you," he snapped, his anger more from fear than fury. "That's an order, mister. You know the penalty for disobeying your captain."

Jamie knew, all right. Every sailor did. Disobeying the captain put the whole crew in danger. At sea, it meant irons, flogging, or even keelhauling. In port, it meant immediate dismissal. Jamie risked being turned out from the only family he'd ever known. Yet he stood his ground. "She called me a gentleman. No one's ever done that, not once. Now she's an orphan, like me. She might want a friend. And a gentleman don't . . . doesn't turn his back on a friend."

Connor knew better. Gentlemen turned their back on friends all the time. But in the months since he'd rescued Jamie from the hellhole wharf, the child had barely strung three words together. Now he was chatting like a magpie. An unfamiliar tightness rose in Connor's throat. He'd saved the boy on a whim, because he couldn't have stood seeing a dog treated so cruelly, much less a starving child. But as he knelt in front of the boy and saw the first hints of pride and self-respect stir in his long-empty eyes, he realized Jamie had become much more to him than a charity case. All at once he felt richer than all the grand nobs in Mayfair put together. *I owe you for this at least, Juliana.*

He got to his feet and glanced around, making sure they'd aroused no suspicions. Everyone still hovered around the dining room door, listening as the solicitor read the marquis's will. "All right, boy. We'll both stay. But we'll listen from here. If we have to make a dash for it, we can—"

"Connor Reed," the lawyer read.

Suddenly it seemed to Jamie as if Captain Gabriel had forgotten all his instructions. The captain raced to the doorway, and even partially elbowed his way inside the room. Jamie followed, taking up a position behind a bowlegged footman, where he could see both the lady and his unusually forgetful Captain.

" '. . . dunna know if he is alive or dead," the solicitor continued. "If he is alive, I dunna know if he even thinks of me or my daughter. I know that the circumstances of our last meeting gave him little reason to, and that is a situation I profoundly regret.' "

Above him, the captain mouthed something, but he made no sound, so Jamie couldn't figure it. He looked like a man who'd just swallowed a cupful of jiggered gin. Jamie's gaze shifted to the lady, whose head was turned just enough for him to glimpse her profile. Queerly enough, she looked as if she also had tumbled to some bad liquor.

" 'I had an opportunity to show mercy, but I did not. Instead, I listened to my pride and arrogance, and—though it shames me to admit it—concern for my daughter's future position. My actions were justified, but they were not just. My hasty judgment of Reed is the one moment of my life I wish I could live over.' "

All around Jamie, people were buzzing like bees.

"Oo's this Reed?" a young scullery maid hissed.

"Never 'eard a the bloke," the bowlegged footman answered back. "I weren't with his lordship all that long. But if you ask me, the lord was a bit nodcocked to 'ave wasted ink on a man what might a snuffed it long past."

"Reed," an old cook mused. "My memory's not what it used to be. Still, it seems I recall a boy by that name, who—"

Jamie lost the rest as a bigger boy jostled him aside and took his prime spot. Jamie balled his fist to pummel the bully, then stopped when he remembered he'd promised his captain not to draw notice. Reluctantly giving up a prime fight, he worked his way through the close packed crowd until he reached Captain Gabriel's side.

" '. . . and in closing, I leave him the sum of five hundred pounds, the exact amount of the regrettable circumstances between us, in hopes that he will accept it, along with my heartfelt forgiveness,' " the solicitor read.

Jamie's eyes widened. Five hundred pounds! He couldn't imagine one man having such an amount, much less giving it away. He looked up at the captain, expecting to see the same surprise on his face. But the captain's gaze was fixed on the lady, who looked to be crying. The captain was about to step forward when another man showed up at the lady's side, a lord in a bottle green coat and a powdered wig, who all but enveloped Lady Juliana in an embrace. Frowning, Jamie studied the man, not liking the way he made so free with the lady's shoulders. *She don't like it. I can tell by the way she—*

Captain Gabriel grabbed his arm and pulled him out of the room, down the hallway toward the back door.

Jamie dragged his feet. "You said we could stay."

"I was wrong." He lifted the boy and tucked him under his arm without breaking stride. "There's nothing for us here. There never was. We were only fooling ourselves. And the sooner we get out of this world and back to our own lives, the better."

He opened the door, then paused and looked down the hall toward the dining room, as if he were taking a last look at a port he might never see again. Jamie thought it was mighty queer behavior, and was about to say so when a distant shriek cut him off. The next moment a dozen people poured down the narrow hallway, nearly running the two of them over in their haste to be out the door.

The captain grabbed a hawker by his coat lapel. "What's happened?"

"Leave off. If I can get to Fleet Street before that palsy reporter I can sell the news for a crown easy."

Connor yanked him up to his tiptoes. "You'll be in no shape to sell anything if you don't tell me what's going on."

"Didn't you hear? He left it to the girl. The houses, the lands, the ships, everything. Except for the few hundred pounds he gave to the others, the marquis of Albany left every bleedin' farthing of his fortune to his daughter."

6

—🌿—

Hortensia Jolly sat bolt upright in bed, scattering her carefully arranged pillows everywhere. "He did *what*?"

The bewildered commodore patted his mother's hand. "Now, mother, you mustn't become agitated. The doctor—"

"The doctor can go hang. And the marquis along with him," she cried, her lusty voice booming through the room. She turned her withering gaze on the solicitor. "I blame you, Mr. McGregor. You Scots are supposed to be so practical. How could you allow the marquis to enact such an ill-conceived notion?"

The solicitor appeared not at all intimidated. He retrieved a quizzing glass from one of his many pockets and met her accusing stare head on. "M' dear lady, in this country, 'tis a body's sovereign right to dispose of his property as he chooses."

"I am most certainly *not* your dear lady," Mrs. Jolly fired back. "I am excessively put out with you. And with Frederick. It is *so* like a man. Better to leave the poor girl a pauper than to saddle her with the responsibility of managing his entire shipping empire!"

" 'Twas his final wish."

" 'Twas his final folly! Juliana knows nothing of business, or politics, or anything to do with the world of commerce. Her father never trained her in his company—no gentleman of sense and character would, not unless he wanted his daughter to be gawked at like one of the mangy lions caged at Tower Gate. I'll own that Frederick did not expect to pass on until long after the girl was safely wed to a suitable husband who could run the line for her, but that does not speak to the point. The fact is that he *did* pass on—in a most untimely and ungallant manner—leaving the poor lamb behind to deal with his thoughtlessness. She will be ridiculed by friend and foe alike. I will not stand by and see the child put through that, whatever her father's wishes."

"Am I to have no say in this?" a soft voice queried. Juliana stood on the threshold of the bedchamber, like a leaf paused at the edge of a hurricane. Her eyes were dry, and remarkably clear for a girl who had been through as much turmoil as she had in the last few hours. "If you are discussing my future, I think I should be involved in the decisions."

"There is nothing to decide," Mrs. Jolly stated. "Your father's bequests, however well-meaning, are quite preposterous. They must be rectified. The estates and lands might conceivably be managed without your intervention, but the shipping line is quite another matter. We must dissolve the company and sell off the ships at the earliest opportunity."

Juliana took a step across the threshold. "If father had wanted his ships sold, he would have left them to my cousin Grenville. The Marquis Line was his dream. It will not be sold to the highest bidder."

Mrs. Jolly was rarely surprised, but Juliana's answer struck her momentarily speechless. "Child, think what you are saying. You know nothing of trade, much less the shipping business. Think of what happened to Lady Pease last Season, when she contemplated buying a racehorse. Only her mother's connection to the duke of Edinburgh saved her from becoming the laughingstock of the *ton*."

"Lady Pease was a silly woman who cared nothing for horses, and would have surely made a fool of herself in some other way if not that. You told me so yourself."

"Yes, well, perhaps I said something to that effect, but it don't signify. The shipping business is a good sight more complicated than a racetrack. You will have to deal with"—the matron placed her hand on her heart and gave a deep shudder—"with men of low character."

Juliana crossed her arms. "No lower than that of several members of the gentry I know."

The commodore was suddenly seized by a fit of coughing, and something suspiciously like a smile tugged at Mr. McGregor's austere lips. Mrs. Jolly quelled both with a look. "Honestly, Juliana, you are the most headstrong of children. Is there no turning you from this course?"

"None whatsoever."

Hortensia Jolly was ill used to changing direction once her course was set. She had plans for Juliana, and those plans definitely did not include her making a cake of herself in front of the entire *ton*. But she knew enough of Juliana's stubborn character to realize there was little chance of dissuading the girl once her mind was made up.

"Well, as a young woman under my protection, I insist that you take along a chaperone whenever you visit your father's offices. Someone of stature. Someone of impeccable character. Someone like—" Her brow arched in devilish delight. "Someone like Mr. McGregor."

The Scotsman's confident expression crumbled. "*Me?* Madam, you canna be serious. I have other clients to attend to . . . other responsibilities . . ."

Mrs. Jolly smoothed the lines of her satin bed jacket.

"Now you have one client, and one responsibility. I am sure
your partners will not object—if they wish to continue repre-
senting the late marquis's estate."

"But I have no experience dealing with"—McGregor bent
toward Mrs. Jolly and confessed in a clandestine whisper—
"with young persons of the female persuasion."

"Then it is high time you acquired some. You and your associates helped get Juliana into this predicament, and you
can jolly well get her out of it. Besides, she will have need of
your business acumen—you do have experience with that, do
you not?"

"A great deal, madam," Mr. McGregor replied as he regained what he could of his composure. He turned stiffly to
Juliana. "I'll require a few days to set my schedule to rights. I
shall call for you on—well, let's say, Friday next."

"Let's say *Wednesday* next," Mrs. Jolly interjected. "There
is nothing more to say on the matter."

"Yes, there is," Juliana said as she stepped forward. "I am
not a child, and I do not need a nursemaid. With all due respect, Mr. McGregor, I do not need your assistance."

"Don't you, lass? Are you familiar with the maritime laws,
or the customs requirements in Bombay and the Burmese
territory, or the tax on spirit vending, or the salt monopoly, or
the—"

"Enough!" Mrs. Jolly cried. "You can explain all that to
Lady Juliana on Wednesday. I am sure it will meet with her
pleasure."

Juliana looked as if very little about the situation met with
her pleasure, but she said nothing. Instead she bowed stiffly,
and with a final glance at Mr. McGregor, she left the room.

Hortensia watched her go, noting the defiance in the girl's
eyes. Stubborn. Willful. And, though Hortensia would admit
it to no one but herself, a great deal like herself at Juliana's
age. "Mr. McGregor, in addition to your chaperone duties, I
wish you to write me daily to apprise me of how Lady Juliana

comports herself. Take special care to note her actions and the people she associates with. Can you accomplish that?"

The solicitor's expression was curiously unreadable. "Your wish is my command, my dear woman."

"I am not—oh, blast," Hortensia said, for McGregor had exited the room. "That rumpled Scotsman is excessively annoying."

"Oh, I don't think so," the commodore commented as he sat beside his mother. "I am sure Mr. McGregor will be quite helpful to Juliana."

"Humph. 'Tis more my hope that he shall bore her to death, and that she will tire of the whole affair before she is eaten alive by rascal sea captains and scoundrel merchants. Or before she irrevocably damages her chances at a suitable marriage."

Jolly scratched his chin in thought. "But Mama, don't you think a man would value her pluck in taking on her father's company?"

"Only if that pluck brings with it a substantial dowry and a spotless reputation. Juliana risks both by mixing with business concerns. Let us hope that another scandal of greater proportions rises to eclipse her folly," she added as she picked up the latest copy of the *Tattler*. "Let us see. Whatever is Princess Caroline up to now . . . ?"

Wednesday next dawned unusually bright and cheerful for a midwinter day. The weather matched Juliana's mood as she looked out the coach window at the busy London docks. To the left were the great warehouses, the immense, splendid structures of brick and stone that had been engineered by John Rennie at the beginning of the century. Four stories tall, they towered over the narrow streets like giants, and were packed to the rafters with rice, tea, tobacco, and every other commodity that came from Britain's far-flung kingdom. Almost everything imported into England came through this noisy, bustling city within a city. Carters and laborers swarmed like bees, moving the heavy crates and barrels that held the bounty of the world's greatest empire.

Juliana gripped the edge of the coach window and felt excitement bubble up in her veins. As a child, she'd spent hours gazing out the second-story window of her father's office and made a wonderful game of guessing what mysterious treasures lay hidden inside the mountains of cargo. "Look, Meg, that's a crate of tea from China. And that barrel is from India—do you think it holds silk and spices?"

"Or rubies," Meg said, catching the excitement. "Oh, Julie, the only rubies I ever saw were the paste copies in my mother's old acting trunk. What if that barrel is *stuffed* with rubies?"

"I ken more likely 'tis stuffed with rubber," an unenthusiastic voice from the other side of the coach commented.

Juliana turned to Mr. McGregor, whose glum expression was the only dark spot in an otherwise bright day. "It could be rubies."

"I dunna think so. Rubber is an easily transportable good, like sugar and salt. Rubies and other gemstones require costly protection during transport and, as they are not a necessity, they are difficult to sell. But every man in this city requires a bit of sugar and salt to season his meal. Little risk, dependable return. You'd do well to remember that, Lady Juliana."

"Thank you for the advice," Juliana replied, though her voice lacked the ring of veracity. She had not been pleased when Mrs. Jolly had assigned the glum-faced solicitor as her mentor, and she liked him less with each passing moment. The man had a genius for leaching the excitement out of every circumstance. But even the dour Mr. McGregor could not entirely quench her anticipation for the adventure that lay ahead. For the first time in years she had more to look forward to than attending balls and parties and gossiping about the latest scandal. She was about to take the helm of the mighty Marquis Line, her father's dream. And maybe, by making his dream her own, the terrible ache in her heart would begin to fade. An ache for her father, and for—

"Connor Reed."

Juliana sat bolt upright. "W-what?"

Mr. McGregor produced a handkerchief from one of his numerous pockets and gave his nose a swipe. "Connor Reed was a beneficiary who was left a considerable inheritance by your father, but who has not yet come forward. I dunno why. I put advertisements in all the newspapers, and dropped hints in the local watering holes. But not a blessed soul has come forward to claim the money. It's a poser, and that's the truth."

Not to Juliana. The Admiralty had no wish to associate their heroic privateer with his less-than-honorable former life. Even though the marquis's will absolved Connor of any legal punishment for his larceny, the moral stain would remain. And while the peers, politicians, and power brokers who had invited Connor into their homes might sanction all manner of murder and mayhem in the king's name, they would be sorely unforgiving of a crime perpetrated against one of their own.

In any event, it was none of her affair. "Perhaps this Reed person is out of the country. Or dead," she added with a relishing smile. "In any event, a missing beneficiary is no concern of mine."

"Funny, I thought you might ken something of the fellow's whereabouts."

Juliana's smile died. She turned to the window and affected disinterest. "La, sir, what a curious thought. I never heard of the man before that afternoon."

McGregor produced a tin of snuff from a pocket and took a pinch. "You don't say? Well, that's another poser, considering your da spoke of this man thinking of him *and* of you. Are you certain you've never heard of this man?"

Mr. McGregor's unwavering stare threatened to drain the

truth right out of her. "Perhaps I heard my father speak of this gentleman, but if I did it was long ago."

"Well, I couldna help seeing that you were that torn up when you heard the man's name. Are you absolutely sure you know nothing of this man?"

Juliana read the accusation in Mr. McGregor's gaze. She opened her mouth, half-afraid that the whole sordid truth would come tumbling out of her, but Meg spoke first. "For shame, Mr. McGregor. Juliana had only recently learned of the death of her father. Is it not natural that she would break into tears occasionally, for no reason at all? If she says she has never heard of this Connor Reed, then I am quite certain she hasn't."

Mr. McGregor settled back in his seat. "Forgive me, Lady Juliana. As I told Mrs. Jolly, I am unused to the company of young female persons. I had no wish to offend. I only wanted to ken the whereabouts of the inheritor of a sizable legacy. In any event, I shouldna have troubled ye. In a few minutes you'll have your hands full of more problems than kenning the whereabouts of some old acquaintance of your da's."

Juliana looked out at the towers of crates and boxes that covered the wharf like a movable city. Once she'd imagined them full of fabulous treasures, but McGregor had pointed out that the "treasures" were likely only ordinary and mundane commodities. She should be used to such disappointments by now. Years ago she'd discovered her "one true love" in the arms of another woman. Recently that same man had turned out to be a self-serving privateer who did not even have enough respect for her father's memory to acknowledge his final forgiveness.

The joy she'd felt earlier was gone. She turned from the window and sighed. "I suppose there might be problems, Mr. McGregor. But as you said—this shipping business is really only a matter of moving crates of salt and sugar from one port to another. Truly, how difficult can that be?"

A great deal more difficult than Juliana could have possibly imagined. When she entered her father's offices, she stepped straight into the heart of a hurricane. Merchants and bosuns stuffed the waiting room, all demanding immediate payment of bills and wages. Frantic clerks ran from desk to desk like frightened chickens. Two of the apprentices were having a fistfight in the accounting office. Papers flew, inkwells crashed to the floor, and pandemonium reigned.

It was all Juliana could do to calm the employees and try to solve the worst of the unpaid bills and problems. McGregor handled the legal issues, and Meg proved a gem at soothing the customers' ruffled feathers. Still, no matter how many questions Juliana answered, bills she paid, or decisions she made, the stacks of papers on her father's enormous mahogany desk never seemed to diminish.

"You need this."

Juliana barely glanced at the cup of tea Meg offered as she continued to study the Admiralty report of reefs and shoals in the China Sea. "Not now. I must determine if I should send a shallow or deep-hulled ship on the China run this year. I'll take some tea with my lunch."

"Lunch? 'Tis almost time for dinner!"

This time Juliana did look up. The big bay window behind her father's desk showed a sky laced with the red and orange clouds of the sinking sun. Juliana pressed her hand to her forehead and blinked in surprise. "But it cannot be so late. I have so much left to do. There are the charts to study. And the harbor taxes to assess and pay. And the cargo manifests to read and—"

"Well, you shall have to read them over tomorrow. You look exhausted, my dear."

Juliana rose from the desk and stood by the second-story window, staring at the play of copper light on the gently moving Thames. " 'Tis odd, but I do not feel at all the same girl that I was when I walked in here this morning."

"Nor do I," Meg admitted as she took a gulp of the

unclaimed tea. "In truth, I have not worked so hard since I handled the props in a production of *The Duke's Revenge*, which had seven scene changes in four acts. I must admit that I shall be glad to see the back of this place. It has been a tumultuous day."

It had indeed been a tumultuous day—far more hectic than Juliana had expected. And yet, she felt exhilarated. As if she had just taken a bracing tonic. Or walked a country mile. Or—

Or been kissed by Connor Reed in the moonlight.

"Julie, you should sit down. You are growing pale."

" 'Tis nothing," she replied hastily. It was true enough. Connor Reed was nothing to her now. "In any event, we have done well for our first day, and I think we deserve a celebration. Mrs. Jolly and the commodore will no doubt agree. And"—she paused as Mr. McGregor entered the office, his nose buried in a stack of papers—"I say, Mr. McGregor. Meg and I would be pleased if you could join us for dinner tonight. We are going to celebrate the success of my first day at the helm of the Marquis Line."

The Scotsman glanced at the pages he held and lifted an eyebrow. "Well, there's some who might consider it a success. You lost only a thousand pounds."

Juliana's smile crumbled. "A th-thousand? But how is that possible? We worked so hard."

"Hard work isn't enough, lass. We lost the contracts for Lovejoy and Sons and half a dozen other merchants. They are—well, beggin' your pardon, my lady, but they're not falling over themselves to trust their cargo to a green girl."

"But they have not given me a chance. 'Tis not fair!"

"They aren't interested in fairness, just profits." McGregor stuffed the papers into one of his pockets. "Your da had a history of success in the shipping business, but not you. They're skittish as new colts. In time they might grow to trust you, but till they do, I recommend that you hire a manager.

Someone experienced—and male—who could persuade the merchants that the Marquis Line is still sound as a pound."

Juliana lifted her chin. "My father entrusted his company to me, not some unknown manager. He had faith in me."

"He did. But the merchants do not. You need a manager, lass. And, if you don't take offense to the suggestion, you should find someone proper quick. You've a large fortune, but even the regent himself couldna afford to lose money at this clip."

After the solicitor left, Juliana sank into her father's chair and put her head in her hands. "A thousand pounds lost! After we worked so hard. And now McGregor tells me I have to hire some glorified nursemaid to run the company—*my* company—or risk losing it."

Meg patted her shoulder. " 'Tis only for a little while, until the merchants learn to trust you. Why not ask the commodore to step in?"

"Meg, Jolly is a dear man, but he knows nothing of business, and only slightly more of the sea. No, it must be someone of true authority, not just a token appointment. And I haven't the first idea of who." She looked up and gave her friend a courageous smile. "Well, there is one good thing. At least we know that nothing else can go wrong."

The words had not sooner left her mouth than the door to her office flew open and Captain Blue barreled in. "You got to talk to 'em, Miss Juliana. The other captains. They're refusing to sail for a woman!"

The dozen or so captains of the Marquis Line who were in port had assembled in a semicircle on the steps of the Marquis building. Some of them held torches to fend off the deepening twilight. Beyond the captains stood a growing crowd of midshipmen, masters, bosuns, laborers, fishmongers, and nearly every curiosity seeker in the vicinity. Enterprising hawkers were selling buns and hot chestnuts to the crowd. Blacklegs were taking bets on the outcome of the confrontation. And in the back of the crowd, concealed by the shadows of one of the brick warehouses, stood a man in an expensive coat who watched the proceedings with glee.

The boisterous rabble fell to a hush as Juliana stepped onto the stairs. Half the crowd had not expected her to appear at all. Most of the others thought she would dissolve into womanly vapors. Instead, she stood with her head held high, and calmly surveyed the brawny men in front of her. Outwardly she looked like a queen perusing her court.

Inwardly she was frightened to the edge of her wits.

Of all the things that had gone wrong during the day, this was by far the worst. Only a handful of the assembled captains knew her from the old days. The rest were new blood hired as the Marquis Line expanded. But except for Tommy, that handful could not be counted on for support. They remembered her as a gangly girl—certainly not someone fit to run a worldwide business concern.

If these captains refused to sail for a woman, she could try to recruit others. But sailors worth their salt were hard to come by, and it was likely that she'd face the same prejudice from any other men that she tried to hire. The Marquis ships would lie useless in the harbor with rotting cargoes and missed deliveries. Her father's company would die a slow and ignoble death. Juliana's only chance lay in convincing the captains that she could run the shipping empire as well as any man.

After losing a thousand pounds in one day, Juliana found it difficult to believe in herself, much less convince others to believe in her.

Counterfeiting confidence, she laced her hands together smartly and lifted her chin an inch higher. "Who speaks for you?"

The captains looked among themselves, clearly unprepared for her tone of command. They respected power, Juliana noted silently. That might be her one true weapon.

Showing no quarter, she took another step forward. "Come, I do not have all night. Who speaks for you?"

At the urging of the others, a tall man with a thick neck and a thicker frown stepped forward. "I'm Howick, Miss. Of the *Alexander*."

Juliana recognized the name of her father's fastest schooner, one which she'd heard him talk of many times. "Does she still list to starboard in a brisk headwind?"

Howick blinked in surprise. "That she do, miss. In fact, it weren't just last week that she—" He stopped as another man behind him jostled his elbow. "Uh, that ain't the point. Me and the others—we come to say that we won't be sailing for no woman. Meaning no disrespect, but—"

"No disrespect?" Tommy Blue cried as he stormed past Juliana. "You lily-livered son of a barnacled boil, how can you say you mean her no disrespect? Ya mean her *every* disrespect, and if her da were here he'd—"

"But he ain't here!" Howick fired back. " 'Tis all right for you, Tommy. You've been with the line longer than any of us, and ya got no family to worry over. But I got a wife and two bairns, and I'll not have them widowed and orphaned before their time. I signed up to sail for a man, not a maid."

Juliana drew herself to her full height. "It makes no difference that I am a woman."

Coarse laughter sounded from the crowd gathered to the right of the steps. "Lift up your skirts, darlin', and we'll show ye the diff—"

The heckler's insult ended abruptly. Juliana peered into the crowd, wondering what had suddenly silenced him, but the gloom of twilight and the evening fog rolling in from the Thames made it impossible to see. In any case, she could ill afford to squander attention on anything but the matter at hand. She turned her attention back to the captains and opened her mouth to speak, but stopped as Mr. McGregor stepped unexpectedly to her side.

"I know that you men are suspicious of having a woman in

control of your destinies. I had my doubts too. But after working with Lady Juliana, I can tell you for a fact that she's got what it takes to make this line a success. She's got a remarkably unfeminine head on her shoulders, and she can make a decision as good as any man. Now, I know that lass doesn't know the business, but she knows the difference between a ratline and a gridline—and there's few owners that can say the same. Young as she is, I believe she will make a proper adequate owner for the Marquis Line."

"Proper adequate" may not have been the most flowery compliment Juliana had ever received, but from the circumspect solicitor it was high praise indeed. She reached out and gave the man's hand an appreciative squeeze, then glanced back at the assembled captains. McGregor and the others were whispering among themselves, clearly unsure of their course. Juliana sensed the tide was beginning to turn her way.

"You'll all be wrecked by summer."

The oily words oozed from the darkness beyond the left side of the steps, in the shadows of the warehouses where few people had gathered. Juliana bristled. She'd heard the voice before, though she could not precisely remember where. "Nonsense. I would never jeopardize the lives of these men. I am perfectly capable—"

"Capable of going to balls and nobby parties. Capable of wearing fancy gowns, eatin' fine food, and diddlin' with a randy lord or two. But d'ya think she'll give a damn that you're overloaded with cargo on the Lisbon run with Boney's ships shootin' down your arse?"

"You have no right to accuse me of such immodest and reckless behavior. And you are a coward for making such spurious claims while hiding in the shadows."

"Seems as I remember *you* hiding in the shadows not long past." A man stepped out of the fog with a smile that chilled her blood. "Know your dreams, don't I, dearie?"

"Sikes," Juliana muttered weakly. All too clearly she recalled the scandalous things the man had whispered into her ear at the Bell. All too clearly she recalled how avidly she'd listened. "You have . . . no business with me."

His oily smile deepened. "Don't I now? Made you a promise, I did."

He'd promised revenge for Connor's throttling. Now she realized how wrong she'd been to disregard the threat. She would lay odds that Sikes was behind the captains' dissatisfaction, a belief strengthened by the lack of surprise on Captain Howich's countenance. Like the serpent in the Garden of Eden, Sikes had whispered into the captain's ear—just as he had whispered in hers.

She turned back to Captain Howick. "I am the daughter of the marquis of Albany. I have wealth, position, and an irreproachable character. Whatever insinuations this . . . person has made, I assure you my reputation is spotless."

Sikes smirked. "Spotless, is it? Then how do you explain your visit to the Bell not three weeks past, to make a secret assignation with your lover?"

The crowd gasped as one. Mr. McGregor barely restrained Tommy from charging Sikes. Juliana paled. "That is *not* true. He isn't—"

Her words died. If she denied going to the Bell, Sikes could produce witnesses to say that she had. If she tried to explain that she was meeting an old friend, not a lover, she would betray Connor's past. Whatever she said, she'd appear to be the loose-moraled lady Sikes made her out to be.

Whatever she said, Sikes won.

She faced Captain Howick. "I will not lie to you. I *have* met this man, and under circumstances that might appear less than favorable to my character. To say more would be to betray the confidence of a . . . a friend. But it was not as this man makes it out to be." She looked out over the crowd, searching for a friendly face. But all she saw were the curious and the disbelieving. "Whatever you believe of me, know this. The Marquis Line is the last thing I have of my father. I watched it grow from a handful of ships to a mighty fleet.

"I know the treacheries of the low waters of the Giant's Causeway off the north Irish coast. I've weathered squalls off the Cape St. Roque in Brazil, and welcomed the site of the green jalousies of Bridgetown, Barbados, after long months at sea. I know the wheel of stars, the fickle moon-tides, and the way the sun turns the water to living diamonds in the South Seas. I love the sea, and I love the Marquis Line. I ask only for a chance to prove it."

No one said a word. Even the hecklers in the crowd had fallen silent. Howick and the other captains shifted on their feet, not meeting her gaze. *I've lost,* Juliana thought. The Marquis Line would die, along with her one chance to make something of her life. Her father's beautiful ships would be sold to the highest bidder. And eventually, so would she . . .

"God's teeth, you are the sorriest bunch of jack tars I've ever seen!"

A man vaulted onto the steps. He stood away from the torches, his identity concealed by a heavy black cape and slouch hat. But Juliana would have known his voice among a thousand men.

Connor!

7

Juliana's head spun. Her first thought was that Connor risked too much—his popularity with the *ton* would be ruined if one of the captains who had been with the line from the beginning recognized him as the man who'd stolen from her father. The next was a giddy, heart-stopping thrill that he'd risked so much to save her.

He strode across the steps, keeping just on the edge of the torchlight. "You call yourselves captains, yet you listen to a harp who wouldn't fool a child. 'Tis a wonder you all haven't sold your ships for glass beads and trinkets!"

"Watch yourself, boyo," Howick cautioned. "This is none of your affair."

"Justice is *every* man's affair. You believe the worst of this lady without a shred of real evidence. And you believe she cannot run a business simply because she is a woman."

"Well, she *is* a woman," one of the captains pointed out.

"That's hardly a crime. I have it on good authority that some of your mothers were women."

Laughter rippled through the crowd, but it quickly died as Sikes moved forward. For the briefest instant, his glance darted to the steps behind Juliana, then his gaze focused once more on Connor. "Clever words can't change the truth, and the truth is that this lady had a lover's rendezvous with a man at the Bell."

"I know she met a man at the Bell, but it was not a lover's rendezvous. I know . . . because I was that man."

He pulled off his hat. Juliana gave a strangled cry. He'd publicly revealed his identity to save her. *Oh, Connor, you brave, wonderful fool—*

Her thoughts died as she realized her fears were unfounded. *"Mon Dieu,* it is Captain Gabriel!"

"Archangel!"

The isolated shouts gathered momentum until the whole crowd cheered in one voice for their hero. Juliana stared at the scene, stunned at once by "Captain Gabriel's" mastery in gaining the support of the entire assembly and by the fact that no one seemed to recognize him as the former Connor Reed. True, most of the captains had been hired on after he'd left for the Navy, but surely Tommy Blue would know him. But the face of the Marquis Line's longest serving captain held the same blank astonishment as everyone else's. Puzzled, Juliana turned toward Connor. And in that instant she saw him as the others did.

Standing above the crowd and silhouetted by the torches, his shadowed figure seemed larger than life. The flickering light turned his hair to a fiery halo, while his black cloak and the silver fog swirled around him like a sorcerer's spell. He stood with his legs apart and his fists on his hips, radiating power and ruthless strength. Juliana stared, mesmerized along with the rest of the crowd. His cold, hooded eyes surveyed the crowd with the indifference of an all-powerful god. It was small wonder that no one recognized him. He was not the Connor she had once known.

He hardly seemed human at all.

She was so stunned that at first she didn't realize he was speaking.

". . . find out about her father. She thought I might know how his ship had fared in the Caribbean storms. I had no news to give her at the time. Though, sadly, a few hours later I learned his fate."

It was a lie, told with impressive ease. The crowd quieted. The captains bowed their heads in respect. Connor waited a calculated heartbeat before continuing.

"This lady's only crime was loving her father. She deserves your support, not your censure. Most of you here knew the marquis, and you knew he was a brave and fair man. If he chose his daughter to run his company, does she not deserve a chance to prove her worth? We are Englishmen, privileged to live in the greatest country in the entire world. Does not *every* person in this great empire deserve a chance to prove their worth?"

"Aye!" the crowd cried with patriotic zeal.

A few minutes ago Juliana had been on the verge of losing everything. Now, she watched Howick and the captains huddle again, but the grins they sent her way told her what their decision would be. The Marquis Line was saved. And the man she had to thank for it was heading toward the base of the steps, leaving without so much as a glance in her direction.

"Con—um, Captain!" Juliana hitched up her skirt and ran with unladylike alacrity to his side. "I just wanted—" she began breathlessly. "I mean, I do not know why you . . . that is, you were wonderfully gallant, and I wanted you to know how much I appreciate your regard."

Connor lifted his gaze and gave her a burning look. "I did it for your father, not for you. Never you." And without another word he slipped into the fog and was swallowed up by the night.

The crowd surged around Juliana. Howick doffed his hat and promised the captains' support. An unknown woman who was built like a barge gave her a thump on the shoulders and said, "That's tellin' 'em, dearie." Tommy Blue pumped her hand. Meg's smile blazed brighter than the torches. Sikes had slunk off into the darkness like the rat he was. Everywhere she turned Juliana met with smiles of congratulations from the gently bred and the lowborn alike. It was a victory on all fronts, but inside she felt hollow, with the same words echoing over and over inside her. *Not for you.* Never *you*.

"Lady Juliana, you comported yourself like a . . . well, like a Scotsman," Mr. McGregor commented with his usual lack of aplomb. "And I thought that captain lad did a right fine job, too." He produced a charcoal and scrap of paper out of his rumpled coat. "What was his name again?"

"Gabriel," Juliana said dully. "And I sincerely hope I shall never see him again."

"Oh, no, that will not do at all," the solicitor replied as he made a notation on the paper. "I dunna know your plans, but I suggest you see him before the week is out. Tomorrow, if you can arrange it. 'Twould be best to offer him the job as soon as possible."

"What job?"

"Why, the manager position, of course."

Juliana stared at the Scotsman as if he'd suddenly lost his mind. "You cannot be serious. The man is a privateer. He's the next best thing to a pirate!"

McGregor shrugged. "Pirate or no, he's got the devil's own gift for the art of persuasion. I dunna doubt he could easily convince the merchants to do business with the Marquis Line. And if you want my advice, I'd sign him up as quick as a tick." He scribbled a sizable number on the paper and showed it to Juliana. "This is what you stand to lose before the week is out."

"I am here to see Commodore Jolly."

The undersecretary of the Vice Admiral of the Blue shuffled through his papers, searching for his calendar of appointments. He gave a sidelong glance at the man in front of him, trying to determine if he was someone of importance. The concealing black cloak and the slouch hat that was pulled down over his brow gave little clue to his features, but the fact that his cloak was thoroughly soaked from the freezing afternoon drizzle told the clerk all that he needed to know. Any person of authority would have hired a carriage to travel to the Admiralty office in this inclement weather. The bureaucrat set aside his papers and waved the visitor aside. "Kindly take a seat. I shall attend to you as soon as I am able."

"You shall attend to me *now*," the man growled.

The undersecretary swallowed. He quickly opened his appointment book and thumbed to the appropriate page. "Ah yes, Mr. Smith. The commodore is expecting you. It is the second door at the top of the stairs. Please go right up."

The man started to turn away, but hesitated. He nodded toward the row of junior officers and sailors seated on the long benches that lined the hallways beyond the undersecretary's desk. "I suggest you attend to these good people as well. Otherwise I would be . . . displeased."

The undersecretary could not see much of the man's face, but he could see his smile. He swallowed again, then waved to the nearest man, a young third lieutenant from a fourth-rated gunboat. "Mr. Yeates, I believe you were next."

Connor paused on the crowded stairway and watched with satisfaction as the undersecretary diligently wrote down the concerns of the junior officer. He knew the change of heart was temporary—the minute he was out of sight he had no doubt the petty bureaucrat would go back to his indifferent ways. Even after all these years and all he'd been through, Connor still couldn't manage to rid himself of the habit of championing lost causes.

Like saving the skin of a woman who despised him.

A cadet jostled his shoulder, jarring Connor back to the present. Damn, he was already late for his meeting with Jolly. He yanked his hat down over his brow and worked his way to the top of the crowded stairway, thankful that the officers and clerks were far too consumed with their own concerns to notice a rain-soaked stranger in a worn cloak. Lucky thing, that, for the commodore's short, unexpected note had urged secrecy, just as it had promised Connor that he "would learn something to his advantage." Commodore Jolly was a highly placed official who had access to secrets of national security—secrets the French would pay dearly for. And his cryptic note proved he wasn't quite the good-hearted buffoon that Connor had supposed him to be.

For an instant, Connor felt a stab of anger that Juliana's guardian would sell his country for coin. God's teeth, would he never be rid of the foolish urge to protect the girl? Well, last night was the final time he was playing white knight to her lady in distress. He'd promised Raoul. He'd promised himself. He had his own skin to think about, his own plans—and his own pleasures. Tonight he was taking Baroness Fairvilla up on her offer of a private supper and let nature take its course. Considering the lady's shameless overtures toward him during the past month, Connor had no doubt what that course would be. By tomorrow morning he doubted he'd give a second thought to a spoiled, too-tall chit with nothing to recommend her but a pair of ocean green eyes.

Smiling at the thought of anticipated pleasures, Connor entered Commodore Jolly's office . . . where his gaze collided with a pair of ocean green eyes.

Juliana rose stiffly from the leather chair in the commodore's well-appointed oak-paneled office, trying to tamp down her panic. She'd practiced her speech so many times that she could have recited it in her sleep. Nevertheless, when Connor strode into the office wrapped in the same cloak that he'd worn last night and wearing a smile so sinful that it made her heart somersault, she forgot every one of her carefully rehearsed words. "I . . . that is, I'm so glad . . . I mean, I wanted to—"

His roar cut her short. "What the hell are you doing here?"

Her practical nature restored her wits. She stepped past him and shut the door to the office. "Heavens, keep your voice down. We do not want the whole Admiralty to know our business."

"We don't *have* any business. I came to meet Commodore Jolly, not you. He sent me a note."

Juliana fingered the sable trim of her gray kerseymere walking dress. "Well, it wasn't precisely Jolly who sent the note."

Connor's gaze jumped from her face to the commodore's empty desk and unoccupied chair to the stone-cold brazier on the other side of the room. He pulled off his hat and raked a hand through his damp hair, splattering raindrops across the rug. "Does he know anything of this meeting?"

Juliana lifted her chin. "No. I knew the commodore was called away suddenly to Portsmouth, so I arranged to make use of his office. 'Tis not hard to hoodwink a clerk when I know my guardian's hand as well as well as my own. And I am *not* alone. Meg and our abagails are waiting in a room down the hall."

"Which makes this all entirely proper, naturally."

Juliana stiffened at his patronizing tone. "Of course it is not entirely proper. But if I had asked you to come to the Marquis offices, you would very likely have ignored the invitation."

"You were dead right about that, Princess. Now I'm ignoring this one." He settled his hat back on his head and turned to leave.

"Wait! I have a proposition for you."

Connor hesitated, but only for a moment. He glanced back at her with a wolf's sneer. "Sorry, but it's a bit early in my day to start compromising schoolgirls."

"I am not . . . oh, you are the most *odious* of men! I meant a business proposition. I want you to work for me."

Connor hesitated again. "You haven't been nipping from the commodore's brandy flask, have you?"

"Of course not. I want you to work for me—as manager for the Marquis Line."

Connor started to say something, but Juliana overrode him, speaking at breakneck speed. "The position would not interfere with your own . . . um, enterprises. You could continue to sail under your own command, wherever and whenever you please. But I need a figurehead for my company—someone the merchants and captains can put their faith in until they learn to put their faith in me. After your assistance last night, my solicitor, Mr. McGregor, determined that you are the man for the job."

"And what about you?" he asked quietly. "Do you think I'm the man for the job?"

"I . . . will do whatever is necessary to save the Marquis Line."

Slowly, Connor turned back to her. With his hat pulled down over his brow she could not see his eyes, but it hardly mattered. His smile turned her blood to ice. "Of course. I should have recalled what kind of *man* you think I am. But no matter. I am not interested."

"But it is a good position. You must—"

"*Must?*" he seethed. "Lady, your days of ordering me around like your trained dog are over. If I were destitute, if I were starving, if I were washed up on the shore and rotting like a piece of driftwood, I would *still* not work for you. Never. There is nothing you have that I want."

The words cut deep, but she thrust aside the pain. She sandwiched her slim form between him and the door. "Do you not want a thousand pounds?"

"A thousand . . . God's teeth, woman, how do you expect to turn a profit if you offer every employee that kind of sum?"

"I am not offering it to every employee. Just to you. And I will be paying only half of it. My father left the rest to you in his will. I know you cannot claim it outright without revealing your identity. But I can arrange it so that the money can be paid to you discreetly, with no one save my solicitor knowing the details of the transaction. For a few months' work you will be a thousand pounds richer. Now in truth, can you afford to turn down such an offer?"

In truth? Connor thought. In truth, he would have cut off his left hand before he took a farthing of her father's money and cut off his right before he took a farthing of hers. In truth, he was torn between admiring her courage in making this outrageous offer and throttling her for putting herself in a compromising position with a man of his reputation.

In truth, he'd have given just about anything to be her hero one more time.

He gazed down into her green eyes, wishing like hell that he was still the good and honorable man she'd once known. But that man had died nearly four years ago, in the stink and squalor of a prison ship. With a talent he'd learned during the months of abuse and starvation, he schooled his features into a mask of indifference. "For the last time, I am not the man you need. Now, be so kind as to step aside. I have an appointment with a lady—an appointment I would most particularly hate to miss, as her husband will be returning to London on the morrow."

He watched the truth fall into her green eyes. He watched as a part of her shattered. He told himself it didn't matter. In a moment she would step aside and he'd be out of this office, and out of her life forever.

She did not step aside.

"You *are* the man I need. I cannot save my father's company without you. If a thousand pounds is not enough, I shall make it two thousand. Or three. Name your price and I will pay it."

God, she was glorious. With her chin high and her eyes defiant she looked exactly as she had as a child when she'd climbed up to the crow's nest and stood with her face to the wind. When Connor had climbed up after her and brought her down, her father had given her a hiding that had kept her standing for days, but she'd never showed an ounce of regret. Like her father, Connor had been mad as hell at her for risking her life—and just as proud of her courage. As a child, Juliana had always gone where angels feared to tread. As a woman, she was just as brave and foolhardy.

And she was sorely in need of another hiding.

Connor put his hand against the door and leaned closer. "I am not cheap, but I can be bought. I do not need your money. But there is something you can trade for my services, if you're up for the barter." His gaze skimmed down and lingered wickedly on her lush, ripe lips. "A kiss."

8

"A k-kiss? But that is *preposterous*."

Connor's wolf's smile widened. "Why? Have you no experience with kissing?"

"Of course I have," Juliana stated. Then, with somewhat less veracity, she added, "I have been kissed dozens of times."

"Good. Then one more will be of no consequence."

Her gaze flittered to his lips—sensual lips that promised wicked pleasures. Long ago those lips had barely brushed hers. The memory still rocked her soul. "I c-cannot kiss you."

Connor shrugged. "Then I shall kiss you."

He lowered his mouth toward hers, but she slipped out of his embrace and hurried to the other side of the room. She stood stiffly, with her back securely against the commodore's desk. It took barely five steps, but her heart hammered as if she had just run a mile. Nevertheless, she faced him squarely. "I cannot kiss you. I reserve my embraces for those I have a *tendre* for."

This also was not entirely true. She had allowed Toby Bascomb to kiss her though she was only toying with the idea of returning his affections. His wandering hands and slobbering kisses were more than enough to make up her mind, and the fact that Toby became engaged not a week later showed that his heart was far from broken. Young Fitzroy Pompadour was someone she actually fancied herself in love with—until she'd discovered that kissing him was like kissing a potato. Her final adventure, with the notorious Baronet Blakeney, was the worst by far. Though she'd had no regard for him whatsoever, she'd allowed him to lure her behind a box hedge in Vauxhall garden to see if his kisses were all the "fast" ladies of the *ton* insinuated they were. But Blakeney had been so concerned that her embrace was crushing his elaborately tied French linen cravat that she'd left in disgust.

And then, of course, there had been Connor's kiss.

"I cannot kiss you," she repeated firmly. " 'Twould not be proper."

Connor arched a knowing brow. "And meeting a man in a deserted office is?"

"That is different. It was necessary to—oh bother, you have me flummoxed."

"Do I?" he asked softly as he took a step closer.

Lord, what was it about his voice that made her feel as if she were running on ice? She crossed her arms resolutely in front of her. "I shall not kiss you."

Connor shrugged. "Suit yourself. But that is my price for taking your job. No kiss, no job." He waited a heartbeat before adding. "I believe you said that you would do whatever was necessary to save the Marquis Line."

Blast! She *would* do anything to save the line, and the scoundrel knew it. She worried her lip as she tried to figure a way out of the situation. "Oh, very well. One kiss."

With her arms still crossed in front of her she stuck out her chin, pursed her lips into a tight O, and shut her eyes.

She heard him approach. His tread was strong and sure even on the deep rug. She could smell the rain on his cloak, the lingering scent of shaving lather, and a faint, heady musk that stirred the chord of memory deep inside her. A moonlit conservatory. Strong hands enfolding her own. A beloved face bending so close to her own that his warm, musky scent filled her world.

A soft caress that exploded through her like fireworks.

Her eyes shot open. "I cannot kiss you. I can't—"

But it was too late.

He intended to teach her a lesson. She needed to be reminded that he was no longer the callow young swain who'd been at her beck and call, but a man who was well practiced in the arts of seduction. He wanted—no, he *needed*—to prove that she no longer had any hold over him. With cold calculation, he determined to kiss her thoroughly, completely, and heartlessly, with all the skill he'd learned in a hundred brothels from here to Shanghai. He planned to ignite her senses until she begged for more, then walk away leaving her weak and wanting.

His plan went badly awry.

He covered her mouth, driven by a passion that came out of nowhere. She tasted sweet—God, he'd forgotten how sweet. He cupped her face in both hands and tilted her head to deepen the caress. With the innocence of an unfolding flower, she parted her lips, tantalizing him, intoxicating him. He delved into her softness and was rewarded by a tiny mew of pleasure from the back of her throat. Desire, heavy and urgent, tightened his body.

For years he'd lived on the pale memory of her kiss. He'd tried to forget it a hundred times, but it always came back to him in hopeless dreams and wishes. Even now he could hardly believe this was real. *In a minute I'll wake up in a foreign port, alone in a cold bed, stiff as a pike—*

She reached up and wove her fingers through his hair, moaning his name. Joy knifed through him. This was no dream.

Somewhere in the back of his mind a thread of his all-but-forgotten decency made him start to pull back. That died as she locked her arms around his neck, pulling him into a deeper embrace. He savaged her mouth, suckling and spearing into her lush sweetness like a starving man at a feast. She answered him with an eager innocence. Her untutored pleasure seduced him more quickly than any courtesan's tricks. He pulled her close, fitting her against him as if they were two halves of the same being. For years, dreams of her had been the only thing that had kept him sane. Now the reality drove him mad.

Blood thundered in his ears. It didn't matter where they were, or who they were. It only mattered that she was in his arms at last. Without breaking their embrace, he bent her back across the desk and pressed into the V of her legs. She squirmed wantonly under him. Lust raged through him. He'd wanted this for as long as he could remember. Longer. He'd protected her, nurtured her, cherished her. He'd saved her life. She was his, dammit. He bunched up her skirt to reveal the bare skin of her thigh. *His*. With a feral growl, he stroked the silk glory of her flesh, and felt her shiver with a pleasure that matched his own—

"Oh, my heavens!"

Meg's cry shattered the embrace. Connor pulled back and staggered against the desk like a bottle-witted man. He shook his head, struggling to regain his balance and his sanity.

Meg faced Connor with her hands on her hips, wearing an expression that made him glad she was not carrying a sword. "Sir, how dare you take such liberties? If I were a man, I would call you out."

"My dear, don't make such a fuss," Juliana replied as she calmly arranged her skirt back over her legs. "The captain and I were engaging in a . . . business transaction."

"B-business?" Meg sputtered.

"Yes. Captain Gabriel has agreed to be the new manager for the Marquis Line." She lifted her gaze to meet Connor's. "Is that not so?"

Connor stared back, dumbfounded. Except for her heightened color, there was nothing about her that showed that she'd just been thoroughly kissed—and nearly much more. She'd returned his caress with a virginal sweetness, and he'd been idiot enough to believe she was untouched. But her cool gaze showed that her innocence was an act.

Deep inside him, a hope that even the hell of the prison ship hadn't managed to destroy cracked apart. *But I'll be keelhauled before I'll let her know it.* He met her eyes with a gaze every degree as cool as her own. "You fulfilled your part of our transaction, my lady. Rest assured that I shall fulfill mine."

He strode to the door, pausing only to scoop up his hat. He left the room without a backward glance and took the marble stairs two at a time in his haste to exit the building. Outside, the wind had picked up and the light drizzle had changed to a biting sleet, but it hardly mattered.

The foul weather seemed like a spring day compared to the misery in his heart.

"I cannot *believe* that you kissed him," Meg cried as she paced in Juliana's sitting room. During the carriage ride home, she'd kept silent, reluctant to share recent events with Lucy and her own lady's maid, Henrietta, who would doubtless take it straight to Mrs. Jolly. She'd bitten her tongue so hard that she was amazed it wasn't cleft in two by the time they got home. Now that she was alone with Juliana, all her pent-up admonishments burst out. "Whatever possessed you to do such a thing?"

"I already told you. It was the captain's price for becoming manager of the Marquis Line. Honestly, you are making too much of a little kiss."

"Little kiss? He had his hand up your skirt! If I had not chanced to come in at that moment I don't know what would have happened."

Two spots of color bloomed on Juliana's cheeks, but her demeanor remained untroubled. She pulled a length of royal blue embroidery thread from her basket and bent back to her needlework. "Meg, you are far too parochial. This is the nineteenth century, not the Middle Ages. Besides, he agreed to take the job. That is all that matters."

"That is not all, and you know it." Meg stopped her pacing and came over to the fire. She settled into the gold brocade wing chair opposite Juliana. "My dear, this man has a notorious reputation when it comes to women. How can you be sure he will not tell everyone that—"

"He will not. The captain is an opportunist—he will do whatever is most advantageous to him, and working for the Marquis Line is certain to increase his stature with the shipping community. His greed will keep him silent."

Meg peered at Juliana over the rim of her spectacles. "If he is so greedy, why did he turn down your money?"

Juliana stabbed her needle into the embroidery. "His reasons are not of the least interest to me. Now, if you would be so kind, I should like to take an hour's rest before tea."

Meg left the room, but Juliana did not rest. Instead she threw her embroidery into a tangled heap and began pacing just as her friend had done. As angry as Meg was at Connor, Juliana was ten times more furious. And even more than that at herself.

The moment his lips met hers, all her carefully cultivated poise and virtue had shattered like a dropped Christmas globe. Her blood had turned to hot honey. She'd melted into his arms, aching for the feel of his steel-hard body molding to hers. It was as if she were burning alive from the inside out. She'd pulled him closer, feeding on him with an animal hunger she'd never dreamed she possessed. When he'd bent her back across the desk she'd complied eagerly, yearning for him to claim her body the way he'd claimed her mouth. When Meg cried out, her first emotion had not been one of relief, but of profound disappointment. Luckily, her years of rigorous deportment had helped her to quickly regain her good sense. She realized that Connor's behavior was shameless, ungentlemanly, and thoroughly uncivilized.

And wonderful.

"It was *not* wonderful," she argued aloud. "It was improper and embarrassing and if he tries to kiss me again I shall scratch his eyes out."

Of course, that did not address what would happen if she kissed him.

"This is boorish. I shall put it out of my mind entirely." Resolved, she went to her writing desk and penned a quick note to Mr. McGregor, informing him that she had secured the assistance of Captain Gabriel. It did not sound nearly so scandalous on paper—though she did leave out the details of their negotiations. *Like his fee.*

She put the letter on the silver salver for Lucy to deliver to the afternoon post, than began to open her correspondence. It was a considerable stack, as she had been occupied with other matters for the better part of a week. Most of the letters were perfunctory condolences about her father from people who had never known him, but a few warmed her heart. One badly misspelled missive from an old tar in Liverpool particularly affected her. Her father had made many friends over the years, looking beyond the trappings of wealth and station, believing that people should be respected for their inner worth. *Like raising up a wharf rat who had risked his own life to save mine—*

No. That Connor was dead. The man she knew now had professed to love her, but she'd seen him in the arms of another woman. He'd stolen from her father. He'd turned into a privateer, a ruthless mercenary whose only redemption was that he sailed for the crown. Tonight he was going to have his way with a married woman. And his kiss had awakened a hunger in her, a need for him and no other.

She put her head in her hands. And for the first time that afternoon, Juliana's eyes brimmed with tears.

"Mon Dieu, I cannot *believe* that you kissed her."

"Can we just drop the subject?" Connor growled as he held the nearly shut lantern in front of him. He stooped to avoid a drainpipe that traversed the narrow alley. "You've made it clear that you do not approve of my actions."

"I do not *approve* of flat beer. I do not *approve* of sloppy bootblacks, or poorly tied ratlines, or winning horses that toss shoes in the final furlong. But you, my friend, are the most idiot, slow-witted, imbecilic *Anglais* that ever—"

"So you have said. Incessantly." Connor pulled out his handkerchief and wiped the sleet from his eyes. He scanned the darkness ahead for any hint of trouble. The Admiral usually chose the locations for their secret meetings well, but there was always a chance they might be discovered. Besides, Limehouse held more dangers than an out-of-place Bow Street Runner. "I believe this is the place where we are to wait."

"Good. And while we are waiting I shall tell you again what a fool—"

"One more word, Raoul, and I'll stuff this handkerchief down your throat."

Raoul didn't utter a sound.

Connor turned away and studied the alley. It was a foul place even for the Limehouse slums, with a lacework of rusted pipes and dank ice pooling in the rutted crusts of mud that covered the floor. It stank like a sewer. The memories called up by the stench and the narrow confines set his teeth on edge. 'Twas like being in prison. *Or a grave.*

"Well, one thing's sure. No one is likely to bother us in this hellhole." He sat down on what appeared to be a fairly sturdy barrel and attempted to knock some of the caked mud off his boots. "The Admiral had better show soon. I gave up a private dinner with the baroness for this."

Raoul stroked his mustache. "I recall you sent your regrets before the Admiral's summons arrived."

Connor glowered. St. Juste was too observant by half. He should never have told him that he'd kissed Juliana. But if he had not, how could he have explained why he was suddenly in her employ? And how would he have explained the subtler changes, such as the way his jaw pulled taut whenever someone mentioned her name? Try as he might, he could not wipe the feel of her body from his mind. Or the taste of her from his lips—

A scraping sound caught his ear. He swung the lantern beam and pulled his pistol from his belt. A long, naked tail flicked through the light before disappearing into a filth-edged hole. Rats. Christ, he hated rats. They clawed up memories of a tiny box in the lowest, blackest ship's hold, too small for a man to sit or to stand, too foul for him to breathe. The darkness had had no day or night, and no end. He fingered the scar on his cheek, the visible reminder of that terrifying time. The invisible reminders were just as permanent. All his fine, pretty ideals had been swallowed up in that coffin cell, by the pain, the hunger, the loneliness, and the darkness. The best part of him had died in that torture box. The broken, starving shell that had come out was hardly human at all.

He settled back on the barrel. "Raoul, what are we doing here?"

The viscount gave him a quizzical look. "But of course, we are waiting for the Admiral."

"No, I mean why the hell did we ever get involved in this deception? Why aren't we out at sea, with a clean wind at our backs, instead of skulking around some godforsaken alley waiting for a man who will not tell us his name or even show us his face?"

Raoul sighed. "You know the answer, *mon ami*. This is the only way we can hope to gain our—well, not our souls, perhaps. They are long gone. But we shall have our revenge. You for the *Absalom*. And I for a man who was finer than either you or I can hope to be."

Connor closed his eyes, remembering Daniel St. Juste. He had been a short man, not nearly as tall as his nephew, and an old war wound had left him with a limp. Nevertheless, there had been a fire in his eyes that made any man he met think twice about crossing him. And there had been a kindness in him that was too big for this world.

He had been murdered by a friend.

Another scraping sound brought Connor back to the present. More rats, he thought with a grimace. "God's teeth, Raoul, if the Admiral does arrive I've a mind to tell him what I think of his bloody cloak-and-dagger foolishness."

A voice hissed from the darkness. "My cloak-and-dagger foolishness has kept you alive, boy."

Connor jumped to his feet. He swung the lantern toward the voice, but all he saw was the piled refuse of the crowded alley. "Is that truly you, sir?"

"Of course it is me. Who else would be in a *hellhole* like this at this time of night?"

Connor winced. The Admiral must have been listening to them for several minutes. *Maybe longer.* Thankfully, Connor hadn't mentioned Juliana's name. He set the lantern down on the barrel and took a bold step forward. "What do you have for me?"

The Admiral's voice wheezed out like air from a pig's bladder. "The emperor is marshaling his troops, and plans a major offensive in the next few months. His agents will pay handsomely for any strategic naval information we can send their way. Which is why I am most particularly interested in the friendship you have recently cultivated, Captain Gabriel."

A warning chilled down Connor's spine. "I have cultivated many friendships among the rich and powerful. You will have to be more specific."

"I speak of a lady of your acquaintance—Lady Juliana Dare."

"No!" The word burst out, scattering a flurry of unseen vermin to their nests.

Raoul tugged Connor's sleeve and bent to his ear. "My friend, may I remind you that this man has enough on us to send us to the gallows ten times over?"

"I don't care. I will not make her part of this."

"*I* am the one who says who is part of this, boy," the Admiral hissed. "The girl has inherited dozens of ships—ships that could easily transport our messages to foreign ports. 'Tis a plum ripe for picking."

"Well, you're bloody well going to have to pick another one," Connor growled. "Besides, 'tis hardly likely I'll see her again."

"It was my understanding that you are to see her tomorrow morning, when you start work as her manager."

God's teeth, was there anything this man did not know? "That is true. But I will not involve her in this."

"You have never been reluctant to use the gentry in the past. Why hesitate now?"

Good question. Juliana was as heartless as every other member of the aristocracy. He should have jumped at the chance to use her as her class had so callously used him. He should have—but he could not. The longer he waited to answer, the more damning his silence became. Finally he cleared his throat. "I cannot tell you why, but—"

"He kissed her."

Connor spun to face Raoul, his gaze murderous.

"He would have found out, *mon ami*. He always does."

"You . . . kissed her?"

For the first time the voice from the darkness sounded

startled—and human. But in a heartbeat, the Admiral redisguised his words. "I shall contact you shortly with more details of our operation. Meanwhile, continue your association with the Marquis Line, and keep an eye on the Dare woman. And on her plain little friend."

"She is not *that* plain," Raoul muttered.

"Silence. There has been enough talking back for one night. I am in control of this operation. I *own* you. Never forget that."

Connor stepped forward. "Can you at least tell us when you will give us the information we seek?"

Silence was his only reply.

They started to make their way back down the alley. Raoul kept up a steady one-sided commentary on the unfairness of the tavern game of cups and balls, the politics of Parliament, the dismal state of his Hessians—anything that came to mind. Connor wasn't fooled. Underneath the bright conversation St. Juste was just as worried as he was. The game was not going at all as they'd planned.

I own you.

It was no idle threat. A word from the Admiral could send them to Newman's Hotel in a heartbeat. He could endure the possibility when only he and Raoul were involved. But now other reputations, and maybe lives, were at stake. And the fact that he was mad as hell at one of those lives made the situation no less palatable.

Months ago, when he and Raoul and he had been approached by the Admiral, they had made a devil's pact. The shadowy figure had promised the names of the cowards who had murdered Daniel St. Juste under a flag of truce. Since then, every battle, every victory, every breath they'd taken had brought them closer toward that goal. The Londoners called him a hero, but he was deaf to their acclaim. He did not work for his country's honor, nor for the money he was awarded in the prize courts, nor even for revenge like his friend Raoul. But he had his price, just as the viscount had his. He'd fulfilled his devil's bargain with single-minded calculation—until a freckled nose, ocean eyes, and a courtesan's mouth had melted his indifference to a puddle.

He hunched his shoulders against the sleet, feeling the cold as he hadn't in months. Juliana had reawakened his feelings—for that alone he could damn her. And yet, even now he knew that he would do whatever it took to protect her from the Admiral's plots. She was innocent of the deceit that stained his life. Though that was perhaps the only deceit she was innocent of.

She'd played him for a fool. He was nothing to her. Less than nothing. She'd proved as much when she'd called him a low-born cur, and again this afternoon when she'd been so unaffected by his caress. Only an idiot would want a woman who felt so little for him.

But he did want her. God's teeth, he *ached* for her. Even now he'd have sold his soul for another chance to hold her in his arms. But he could not have done so, even if he'd wanted to.

His soul was no longer his to barter.

9

The next few weeks were ones of intense activity for Juliana. For a girl who had spent her days sleeping until noon and dancing until dawn, the experience of doing something useful was new, different, and exhilarating. She got up every morning at a very unfashionable hour and went to the offices of the Marquis Line, often not returning home until well after dark. She spent the days learning the shipping business from the ground up, or from stem to stern, as McGregor put it. At the end of the day she fell into bed, often fully clothed because she was too exhausted to wait for her abigail to undress her, with her head aching from the facts and figures that had been stuffed into it during the day. More than once, she swore to herself that she'd had enough and that the Marquis Line was just going to have to get by with another owner. But every morning she woke up at dawn, and rang for the coach to take her to the London docks.

Meg was by her side almost constantly, providing moral

support and a sympathetic ear whenever the pressure became too great. Mr. McGregor was somewhat light on sympathy, but he was full of short-worded advice that did more to increase her knowledge than any long-winded diatribe. Even Commodore Jolly visited the office almost daily, trying to lift her spirits, even though it was quite clear he had only the vaguest idea of the complexities of running a business.

And then there was Connor.

She saw very little of him at first. He spent his time tracking down the local merchants and shipping agents. He'd visit their haunts and hideouts, and almost invariably return with a commitment for a shipment. But gradually he spent more time at the office, getting to know her employees, from the most seasoned captains to the lowliest clerks. His knowledge of the sea was impressive. He often corrected the nautical maps with information from his own experience—and had saved more than one of her ships from ending up on uncharted shoals. He had a way with people, of making them feel important and worthwhile no matter what their circumstances. And his dry wit had a way of coaxing grins from even the most recalcitrant expressions. Even Mr. McGregor had been seen to crack a smile in his presence.

Everyone in the office looked forward to Connor's colorful stories, but whenever Juliana entered the room, his tales would end abruptly and his easy manner would be replaced by one of coolly civil deference. Juliana told herself that this was how it should be—after all, she'd struck a bargain for his services as her manager, nothing more. But sometimes she purposely hid behind her office door, just so she could listen to him tell his outrageous tales. His rich, colorful stories wrapped around her like a magic spell, reminding her of the adventures they'd shared as children. And though he usually had the rest of his listeners reeling with laughter, she often had to bite her lip and fight back tears. Her father had said it was no use to regret the past. *But sometimes it is hard not to, Papa. Monstrous hard.*

Of course, it was nothing compared to her regret for the future.

Juliana had been in charge of the line less than three weeks when some of her gentry friends stopped by for afternoon tea and to give her the latest news of the beau monde. At first she took it as a compliment—after all, they had braved the incivility of the London docks to see her. But gradually she began to sense that something else might be afoot.

"Well, I vow, the girl was a goosecap and no mistake," Mrs. Chapman-Bowes commented as she reached for another cake.

"Indeed," Millicent Peak sniffed. "Everyone knows that shade of blue has been right out since last Season. Quite shatterbrained to wear such a travesty. *Très* not the thing."

"I heard that her father lost a fortune at cards," Meg offered from her seat at the edge of the room. "If she is forced to wear the green bonnet, perhaps she could not afford a new gown."

"Then she should have stayed at home rather than foisting such a spectacle on her friends," Mr. Hamilton intoned.

"Dashedly inconsidewate," Lord Renquist agreed. "Yes, just a touch more tea, my deawr."

Juliana dutifully filled Renquist's teacup and tried her best to take interest in the conversation. These people had come here to offer their support, but she could not help thinking that their conversation seemed a bit trifling. True, a few months ago she could have easily spent hours discussing the "travesty" of an unfortunate fashion choice, but the depth of the affront paled besides the much greater disasters that had come across her desk.

Out of the corner of her eye, she caught Meg stifling a yawn. "I fear Meg and I are both sadly out of step. But do you not think that we might be better served by turning our minds to a far greater affront?"

Mr. Hamilton took a pinch of snuff. "Greater than that fright of a gown? Gad, what could be worse than that?"

Juliana set down the pot, wondering if the gentleman was jesting with her. "The *war*, sir. I know from my shipping reports that Napoleon's forces are growing in strength daily. He attacks us on land and sea, and if the tide does not turn soon, I fear—"

"Fiddle," Mrs. Chapman-Bowes commented as she waved her lace handkerchief in disinterest. "You give too much credence to that French upstart. He is of no consequential breeding."

"I believe the defeated noblemen of Spain and Italy would differ in their opinion," Juliana muttered.

"Lady Juwiana has a point," Lord Renquist offered. "Napoleon may be low-born, but he knows the business end of a sword. He is qwite clever, for a fwog. And then, there is the spy."

"What spy?" Juliana and Meg asked in unison.

"Why, *the* spy, my dears," Mrs. Chapman-Bowes intoned as she stirred a third spoonful of sugar into her cup. "The spy in the Admiralty. Lord Renquist has told us all about him. 'Tis rumored that he is passing all manner of secrets to Bonaparte right under their noses. I have it on good authority that he even absconded with the Majorca papers."

" 'Tis true," Mr. Hamilton echoed. "Lord Renquist and I are attached to the Admiral of the White, and his office talks of nothing else. Demmed tedious, that."

"Tedious?" Juliana said incredulously.

"But is it not vastly romantic?" Millicent giggled. "Imagine—a cunning spy risking life and limb to thwart the Admiralty. 'Tis like a novel."

" 'Tis nothing of the sort! You speak of a villain who has given our country's secrets to the foulest madman the world has ever known."

"Fiddle," Mrs. Chapman-Bowes said. "Napoleon is a

low-bred cur, and his troops are no better. Hardly worth our attention."

Juliana bit her tongue. After all, they were not privy to the same reports that she was. Even Mr. Hamilton and Lord Renquist, who held positions at the Admiralty, might not have a clear view of what was truly going on. " 'Tis possible that you do not fully comprehend the threat this monster poses. But reports of Napoleon's victories cross my desk every day. He is eating up countries like a child eats pudding. The only thing that is holding him at bay is our brave sailors and soldiers, who are giving their lives for our freedom. Surely *they* are worth your attention?"

"Quite," Mrs. Chapman-Bowes sniffed.

"Most assuredly," Millicent Peak agreed as she stroked the trim of her ermine muff back into place.

"Goes without saying," Mr. Hamilton sniffed.

Lord Renquist asked, "Have you any more of these spwendid cakes?"

Juliana stared at the guests as if they'd lost their senses. "But men are *dying*!"

"There, there," Mrs. Chapman-Bowes soothed her. "You must not work yourself into the vapors over this. It is quite understandable that you should feel so violently about this. After all," she added as she cast a sly look at her companions, "I am sure you are feeling the influence of working so closely with your tame pirate."

"My *what*?"

Miss Peak lifted her gloved hand to her face and twittered affectedly. "Oh, Juliana, surely you know that is what they call your Captain Gabriel. It must be vastly entertaining to have a notorious privateer at your beck and call. Quite a hum."

"Capital jest," Hamilton added.

"It has made you all the rage," Mrs. Chapman-Bowes agreed with a judicious nod of her ostrich-plumed head. "I must admit, when I first heard of your scheme to enter into business, I thought the act *outré*." But you have conquered, my dear. Everyone is in awe of your cleverness in gaining such a coup—even Lady Jersey cannot touch your popularity. I vow, you shall be the be the talk of the Season without even taking the first step at Almack's."

"Without compare," Miss Peak agreed. "And now, we were hoping—as we are such good friends—if you would allow us to view the captain. Up close, I mean. We have seen him at parties, at a respectable distance. But to talk directly with a man of such ruthless reputation—what a lark that would be! Could you arrange it?"

For a long while, Juliana did nothing but stare at her tightly clucked knuckles. Then she spoke in a voice as calm as the sea before a squall. "Am I to understand that you all have come here to—now, how exactly did you put it—to *view* the captain? As if he were on display, like those poor madmen at Bedlam?"

Lord Renquist fluffed his cravat. "Well, I should not put it exactly like that."

"And how would you put it? That you are a self-centered fop who has not a thought in his head but for his own amusement?"

"I say!" Hamilton started. "That was a bit uncalled-for. Not at all the thing."

"Completely," Miss Peak echoed. "You should not say such things about dear Lord Renquist. Why, the regent is considering him for a knighthood."

"I don't care if he's being considered for sainthood!" Juliana rose to her feet, her temper rising with her. "While you sit here in your silks and satin, brave men like Captain Gabriel are dying for our country. He is worth ten of your kind—a hundred."

Mrs. Chapman-Bowes fluttered her fan in alarm. "Lady Juliana, you are becoming a spectacle yourself. And over a man of no breeding."

"His courage gives him breeding. He has more honor in

his finger than you have in your whole powdered and patched body. And if any of you had an ounce of sense, you would consider it an honor to shake his hand, instead of treating him like some sort of carnival oddity—"

She paused as she became aware that all three of her visitors were staring past her shoulder at her office door.

"I have the ship's manifests you were waiting for," rumbled a voice like quiet thunder.

Juliana turned and saw Connor standing in the doorway. Had he overheard their inconsiderate words? Worse, had he been listening during her impassioned defense? Emotions far too tangled to sort out brought a furious blush to her cheek. "Tha-thank you, Captain. My visitors were just—"

"—just leaving," Mrs. Chapman-Bowes finished as she rose grandly to her feet. "The lady has made it quite clear that she prefers other classes of company. We shall not trouble you again. Come, Lord Renquist, Mr. Hamilton, Miss Peak."

Mr. Hamilton did not have to be told twice. He skirted Connor like a wary mouse skittering past a resting lion. Miss Peak was less eager to leave. She gazed at Connor like a starstruck debutante. "But he is here, madam. Could we not just stay awhile and—"

"We are leaving!" Mrs. Chapman-Bowes hustled the girl past the captain, then turned to give Juliana a final scathing glance. "I am the soul of forgiveness, but you have behaved most uncivilly to me, Lady Juliana. You have not heard the end of this. Now, be so good as to have someone escort us out."

Meg jumped to her feet. "I'll do it," she stated. And, as she passed Juliana, she added quietly, " 'Twill be a pleasure to close the door behind these prattle-boxes."

After they left, Juliana sat on the edge of her desk and crossed her arms in front of her. She glanced at Connor, who had not moved from the doorway. "I am sorry if you heard what they were saying. It was unconscionable."

"I have endured far worse," he said simply. "But I'll admit—I did not expect our fighting men to be so well defended."

His expression never changed, and yet she felt a warmth curl through her at the compliment, a pleasure she hadn't felt since her days at sea, when her only judges were the waves and wind and her only goal a steady course.

She shook her head. "Mrs. Chapman-Bowes is a powerful woman. Her word in the right ear can make or break a reputation—and I do not think she was mightily impressed by my behavior. 'Tis possible she could damage my position in society . . . and Father was so proud of what I'd accomplished. He would be mightily disappointed in me."

For a long while Connor said nothing. Then he walked over to the office window, and looked out at the busy Thames. "I believe you are right. Your father would have been disappointed in you. After all, if you were a truly savvy businesswoman, you would have promoted me as a carnival oddity, and charged a penny for the viewing. Your father was never one to miss a chance at easy profit."

Connor turned around and looked at her, his eyes gleaming. And for the first time in years, the two shared a smile.

These were good days for Juliana. Long days, to be sure, for she worked harder than she ever had in her life. But being near Connor made the time fly by. After the day she defended him against her peers, he no longer avoided her office and often stopped by to discuss the cargo shipments and trade routes. When they sat down across the desk from each other, they were no longer the great lady and the notorious privateer—they were simply two people who shared the same dream, to make the Marquis Line a success. And because neither was the kind to change course without a fight, that shared dream sometimes resulted in an argument that could be heard by the whole of Wapping.

"No, no, no," Connor stated as he paced Juliana's office one afternoon in early March. "You cannot give Captain Jamison the *Reliant*. The ship is bound for India, and Jamison has barely got his sea legs."

"But he has a sharp mind and a brave heart," Juliana argued as she sat at the desk and grabbed a sheet of paper. "Here, look at this. Jamison's first request for command is dated over a year ago. He deserves a chance to prove his worth."

"God's teeth, woman, we are not running a charity! Jamison is a fine man, but he lacks seasoning. Now, there is a command—" He shuffled through the papers on Juliana's desk as if it were his own. "Here. The Lisbon convoy. It leaves in a week's time with three of our ships. He can pilot the *Pelican*."

Juliana rolled her eyes. "Connor, *I* could pilot the *Pelican* on the Lisbon route. 'Tis a biscuit run."

" 'Tis a biscuit run past the coast of France. I agree that nothing is likely to happen—Bonaparte is after ordnance, not tea and sugar. But the winds off the Bay of Biscay can be challenging in this season, and it will be a good test of his mettle. If he performs well on the run, we can consider him for a command on the next long voyage." He sat on the edge of her desk and crossed his arms across his chest, grinning. "You *know* that I am right."

He was. Dammit. During the past month Connor's advice had been unerringly right. He had an almost uncanny sense of matching man and ship and of ensuring that the merchant cargo arrived on time. His knowledge of the trade routes, his familiarity with the ports—and his considerable skills at persuasion—had convinced even recalcitrant merchants such as Atticus Lovejoy of the powerful Lovejoy and Sons to continue to ship with the line. Juliana could not help but be grateful for his assistance. Any more than she could help being swayed by his infectious charm.

Of course, according to the *Morning Post*'s society column,

Connor had been using that infectious charm with great success on several of the *haute ton*'s sophisticates.

She told herself that the irritation she felt was not jealousy, just an owner's justifiable concern for the safety of her ships. All right. I shall assign Jamison to convoy duty. And to make sure of his success I shall assign Tommy Blue as mate, to assist him if he runs into trouble."

"You could—if Blue were here. He took off two days ago leaving a note that he was needed on personal business."

Juliana frowned. "That does not sound at all like Tommy. Do you think it had something to do with . . . well, with Connor Reed?"

Connor shrugged. "Tommy never gave any hint he recognized me from the old days. And if he did, leaving for parts unknown wouldn't be the course he'd set. But he's a good man, and there's no doubt he deserves some time on his own. He'll be back when he's finished his business. After all," he said, flashing his devilish grin, "even a man Tommy's age has a right to sow some wild oats."

When it came to charm, Connor had an arsenal of weapons, and his disarming grin was as deadly as a quarterdeck canon. But caution reminded her that behind that grin was a man who'd asked her to marry him—just before she saw him in another woman's arms. Juliana bent to her desk and made a show of organizing her papers. "Very well, I'll assign Billy Pike as mate to Jamison for the Lisbon convoy. I believe that will be all for this afternoon."

Connor arched an eyebrow in surprise. "Did I do something to offend you, my lady?"

She schooled her features into her most pleasantly disinterested society smile. "La, sir, what could you have done that would offend me—or indeed, which would interest me one way or another?"

His grin didn't waver, but there was a quick flash of vulnerability in his eyes. "Forgive me for my forwardness," he commented evenly as he left the desk and went to the wall

peg to retrieve his coat and hat. "I'll trouble you no mo
today."

His smooth voice gave no hint that she'd wounded hi
but she knew she'd hurt him, and she'd done it out of spit
She rose from the desk, propping her arms on it as s
said, "Connor, wait. I . . . I am the one who should apologiz
'Twas a mean-spirited comment, one I should never ha
said. 'Tis just . . ." Humphing, she brought her palm down o
the desk. "Good heavens, Connor. What could you possib
see in Kitty Shacklesford?"

He frowned. "Who is—? Oh, you must mean the lady
met at Almack's."

"The lady you danced with for four straight sets at A
mack's! Not that it is any of my business, but—"

"No" he interrupted, his voice low. "It is not your business

"The blazes it isn't. Connor, that little cat may look pri
and proper, but she is an outrageous flirt and mean as tl
devil. She cares more for her hats than she does for h
suitors. She will break your heart."

"And what, my lady, makes you think that Kitty Shackle
ford holds my heart?"

Juliana's heart pulled taut. During their weeks togethe
she had managed to fight down her attraction to Connor. B
when he used that voice—that same, low, honey-smoo
voice that he'd used on the night he'd asked her to mar
him—her resolve melted like wax. She gripped the edge
her desk, reminding herself that they were employee a
employer, that he'd once betrayed her for another, that the
were a thousand reasons she should feel nothing for hi
"Nevertheless, I must warn you against her society. She h
no true regard for you."

Connor adjusted his cuffs, apparently more interested
them than her advice. "If I were you, I would not be so d
paraging to Miss Shacklesford. By appearing to have me
her beck and call, she draws the attention of more socia

rominent swains. She is only endeavoring to find a suitable usband—like any well-bred society miss."

Like you. Juliana heard the condemning words as clearly s if he'd spoken them aloud. Truthfully, she too had encouraged men to dangle after her for the sole purpose of appearing more popular. The fact that she regretted her actions ow did little to make up her callousness. "You are right. In he past I have encouraged men for whom I had little affection, and the goal was to increase my social standing. It was eartless, and I regret my actions sorely. But it was the only vay I knew to procure a good marriage. I wanted a family, Connor. I wished children of my own to love and cherish. Is hat such a terrible thing to wish for?"

"No, my lady," he said, his voice suddenly as old as the sea. It is all any of us wish for."

Juliana opened her mouth to reply, but no words came. he was bound in the strange, uncanny spell that happened vhenever she looked into his eyes and saw the hint of heart eneath his ice-cool facade, the shadow of the boy she'd once nown. And loved.

In all the weeks they'd been together, he had never con-ded in her about his past. She knew no more of what had appened to him after he left her father's house than she had n the day he had appeared in Lord Morrow's ballroom. She ad kept her questions to herself—considering the woman he'd seen in his arms on the night he left, she wasn't sure she vanted to know the answers. Still, they had worked side by ide for months, and shared a camaraderie that she had rarely njoyed with any other man. And there was a part of her that vas mightily afraid that one day he would disappear just as uddenly as he had arrived.

Her gaze skimmed to his sensuous lips, recalling the kiss hat neither of them had spoken of since that day. He'd never inted that the kiss in the commodore's office meant any-hing to him other than a bargain fulfilled. And since then he'd never touched her. While she appreciated the respect he accorded her, there was a part of her that wished like the devil that he would forget she was his employer and take her in his arms for one more scandalous kiss.

He didn't, of course. He turned away and started for the office door. "You need not concern yourself over Miss Shacklesford. I am quite aware that I am nothing more than a novelty to her, as I am to the rest of your class. I even believe they are laying odds at White's as to how I received my scar."

"How did you receive it?" she asked quietly.

For a moment she saw the wariness in his eyes thaw. "I disagreed with the captain of a ship I worked on shortly after—well, shortly after I left London. He thought to teach me a lesson. He . . . succeeded."

" 'Twas a cruel lesson," she replied, suddenly furious at the unknown captain. "You were so young. Surely your crime could not have warranted such punishment." Unable to restrain herself, she lifted her hand and brushed his ruined cheek.

He jerked away.

"My crime was in trusting too much in the goodness of my fellow man," he said as the ice returned to his eyes. "I have never made that mistake again. In any event, there will soon be little interest in my scar or in anything else about me. The members of your class already begin to tire of my company. I suppose I shall have to defend another besieged island like Sicily to win back their affections."

"You shall do no such thing! You should not take such a chance. Especially now that there is the added danger of a spy about."

Connor froze. "Spy?"

"Yes, a spy in the Admiralty. Lord Renquist and his friends told me about him. Apparently the villain is selling secrets to Napoleon."

Connor stood so still that she wondered if he'd heard her

"Did he . . . um . . . happen to mention if they had any idea who the man was?"

Juliana shook her head. "I gathered not. Which makes it even more imperative that you keep out of sea battles for the time being. It would be too great a risk."

"I am first and foremost a privateer. I make my living taking such risks."

"You do not have to." She gripped her hands together, and confessed an idea that had been forming in her mind for over a fortnight. "I know our bargain was that you could sail whenever you wished, but such a profession is no longer necessary. I can make you my manager permanently, at a generous salary. Just please, please promise you will give up your letter of marque and stay safely in port."

For a moment, doubt clouded Connor's gaze. Then his mouth pulled up in his cynical, all-too-familiar grin. "Careful, my lady. Continue with such displays of emotions and you are likely to replace Miss Shacklesford in the scandal column. And what would your fine friends make of that?"

"I don't give a snap for their opinions. And you are trying to change the subject."

"I *have* changed the subject," Connor replied as he headed for the door. "I will inform the clerk to draw up a commission for Jamison to captain the *Pelican* with Pike as his mate."

"Don't you dare leave. I am not finished with our discussion. I want you to stay. I *order* you to stay."

Connor halted, then turned to her with the slow stealth of a jungle cat. "Do not test me, my lady. You will lose."

She lifted her chin defiantly. "I am not testing you. I am trying to help you. Can you not get that through your thick skull?"

For a moment she again caught a glimpse of the boy who had been her second soul. "Recommend Jamison to captain the *Pelican*. And as for Miss Shacklesford . . ." His mouth turned up in a wolfish grin. "I should think that you of all women would be glad that I am not the sort of gentleman to kiss and tell."

He ducked out of her office just in time to miss the paperweight Juliana launched at his head.

10

—❧—

You know I am not one to carry tales, Hortensia. In fact, I hesitated weeks before telling you this. I should rather go to Almack's dressed in last year's fashion than speak ill of our beloved Juliana. But I can keep silent no longer. During our tea she behaved in a most unseemly manner, and I fear 'tis all due to the très ungenteel influence of that ill-bred Captain Gabriel . . .

Mrs. Jolly set down Mrs. Chapman-Bowes's letter and took a thoughtful sip of her afternoon tea. Lydia Chapman-Bowes had tongue enough for two sets of teeth, but there was usually a grain of truth in what she said. Of course, Hortensia was well aware that Juliana had hired the privateer as her manager—most of the fashionable salons of London were buzzing with the news. But she had deliberately instructed Mr. McGregor to keep the rakish captain at a distance from Juliana. Until now, she had believed her orders were being obeyed.

Frowning, she glanced over the rim of her teacup to the

other occupant of the room. "Dearest, what can you tell me of Juliana's relationship with Captain Gabriel?"

Commodore Jolly shrugged. "Relationship? I should have thought Mr. McGregor would have told you all about him. I know that he writes you every day."

Hortensia Jolly looked over at the stack of letters from Mr. McGregor. The solicitor wrote terse letters that told her nothing beyond the business news. "McGregor is as tight with his words as he is with a pound. I know that he encouraged Juliana to hire the captain soon after she took over the Marquis Line, but I was under the impression they saw little of each other. However, if I am to believe anything about this missive of Mrs. Chapman-Bowes, it is possible that the captain might have considerable dealings with our Juliana. Since you returned from your visit to Portsmouth you have frequently visited the offices of the Marquis Line. What can you tell me of this man?"

The Commodore scratched his chin in thought. "Well, he is a captain."

"I was fairly certain of that, my dear. What do you know of his character?"

"Oh, 'tis of the first water. At least, that is what the officers of the Admirality who have spent time with him have told me. Sir Humphrey invited him to dinner and served capons—and capons, mind you, are dashed difficult to eat. According to Humphrey, the captain handled his cutlery with aplomb. Then Lord Boggins took him to White's, where he claimed that the fellow played a capital hand of whist, which ain't easy to do with Lord Boggins. The blighter is always forgetting who played the last card—"

"Horatio, I am not interested in how the captain handles cards. How does he handle gently bred young ladies?"

The commodore fiddled with his cravat. "Uh, I could not presume to say."

"Try, my darling," his mother said as she rubbed a spot between her brows.

"He is . . . a well-featured man. Except for his scar, of course."

Mrs. Jolly went still. She'd forgotten that the captain had a scar. Now the newspaper accounts came back to her. *Scarred cheek. Notorious reputation. Handsome as the devil.*

And, apparently, spending a great deal of time with Juliana.

"Let me see if I understand this correctly. From your observation, Juliana spends considerable time with Captain Gabriel."

"Just so," her son stated with a nod as he collected his teacup.

"A man with a scar? Who is a notorius privateer?"

"That's it to a cow's thumb."

"And Mr. McGregor has done nothing to prevent this association?"

"Most certainly not, for it is my impression that Juliana has learned a great deal from the captain."

"Perhaps more than we know," she said dryly. "From this moment on I am entirely resolved to *murder* Mr. McGregor."

"W-what?"

"You heard me. I instructed him to keep the captain and Juliana apart, but that fool has delivered my sweet lamb into the hands of a handsome, notorious rake. With a scar! Heavens, no gently bred Bath miss could resist such a challenge. A greater recipe for disaster I have never heard. And to think I was the one who arranged for that addlepated Scotsman to help her!"

"Mr. McGregor has been a help to her, Mother. So has Captain Gabriel." Jolly hurried to his mother's side and began patting her hand. "You should not upset yourself so. The doctor warned you against unusual exertion. In any case, if you are worried about a *tendre* forming between the captain and Lady Juliana, you may set your mind at rest. The two spent the first few weeks barely speaking to each other. Now they can barely spend a moment together without arguing."

"That concerns me more than anything else!" Instinctively, she started to rise and immediately winced. *Damn,* she thought as she glared at her useless legs. Sometimes she still forgot, even after all these years. She closed her eyes and felt the long-ago memory of terrifying helplessness wash over her. She would not allow it happen. Not to her Juliana. "Horatio, I want to speak with this Captain Gabriel. You shall bring him to my rooms. This evening."

"But Mother, he might have a previous engagement."

"See to it that he does not," she commanded as she settled back against her pillows. "And make sure that you take Juliana out for a drive or to the theatre or some such nonsense. I want her to be engaged elsewhere when I meet the captain. Meg is unwell and will keep to her rooms, but I do not want either of them to know of this meeting."

The commodore's confusion showed that he had little understanding of his mother's concerns, but he nodded and left the bedchamber to do her bidding. Hortensia loved him with the full measure of her heart, but she wished he was not such a muttonhead when it came to matters requiring any degree of cleverness. And he had been such a promising young man. . . .

Still, her son's failings were nothing compared to the distress she felt over Juliana. Hortensia had assumed that, when Juliana's period of mourning was over, the girl would reclaim her position in polite society—and her title as one of the most sought after ladies in London. Even now, the butler's silver salver was piled high with the calling cards of beaux still seeking the girl's hand. Hortensia had no doubt that a bevy of ardent admirers would quickly steer the girl's thoughts away from this shipping line foolishness. But if the child's good name became embroiled in scandal . . .

The haute *ton* could forgive many things—ladies of rank with several children, none of whom resembled their husbands, stylish rakes like Beau Brummel whose extravagant tastes were always paid for with other people's money, and a loutish, self-centered regent who cared more for his cuff links than he did for his subjects. They might even forgive a valiant young miss who honored her father's dying wish to take over his shipping line.

But if that same young miss were linked even by rumor to a man of no social standing, whose notorious profession was nothing compared to his notorious reputation with the ladies . . . well, one only had to recall the terrible social fate of the once wildly popular Lady Caroline Lamb to know what Juliana's future might hold. Every door in Mayfair would be closed to her. Every former friend would disown her. She would lose all the popularity she now enjoyed—along with any hope of an acceptable match and a happy future.

Pen in hand, Mrs. Jolly scratched out a terse note. But even as she wrote, other images from long ago filled her mind. A stormy night. A mad carriage chase. A dreadful crash that robbed her of the use of her legs—and so very, very much more.

She bit her lip and signed the missive, then folded it tightly and handed it to her abigail. "See that this letter is delivered to the evening post. Pay the messenger extra for special delivery. I only pray that I am in time."

"Time for what, Madame?"

Later at tea in the servant's hall, Mrs. Jolly's abigail related to her friends that the older lady had made no attempt to answer her question. "She just stared out the window like I weren't even in the room, and muttered something that sounded like 'heavens, a scar.'"

"The den of the lioness," Raoul commented as he looked across the cobbled street at Number 42 Berkeley Square. Candlelight poured out through the manor's great front windows, lighting the street in front of it as bright as day. "*Mon Dieu,* the place is lit like a church on Twelfth Night. A bad spot from which to make a quick getaway."

"I doubt that will be necessary," Connor replied as he

adjusted the knot in his expensive silk cravat, hastily purchased only a few hours ago after he'd received the unexpected summons. "Mrs. Jolly may have the reputation of a termagant, but she is still a woman. And I have yet to fail in charming a member of the fairer sex."

"Including Lady Juliana?"

Connor's confident smile lost a bit of its luster. "I am handling the lady quite well."

Raoul stroked his mustache. "Ah yes, I think perhaps the entire coast of Normandy has heard how well you handle her."

Connor grimaced. He did argue with Juliana constantly and loudly about almost everything. The woman knew the sea, but she had a great deal to learn about the business of commerce. Still, she was a remarkably quick study, and recently she had begun making imaginative, clever, and profitable decisions on a regular basis. It would not be too long before Connor ran out of reasons to argue with her.

He did not want to think about that.

Raoul's words brought him back to the present. "It is rumored that this very afternoon she threw an andiron at you."

" 'Twas a paperweight. A *small* paperweight. And she has a bloody poor aim."

"Ah. That was a stroke of luck," Raoul commented without much conviction.

"Well, we might soon have more problems than a paperweight. She . . . mentioned that she had heard rumors of a spy in the Admiralty."

Raoul shrugged. "Rumors are not proof. I myself have heard rumors of sea serpents and mermaids."

"Yes, but this rumor is *true*. It can only be a matter of time before we are discovered. And when that happens, I do not want to be anywhere near Juliana or the Marquis Line."

Rauol shrugged again. "Then leave."

Connor wanted to. God, he'd intended to leave weeks before. Members of his crew were beginning to whisper that he'd become a landlubber. Truly, like them, there was a part of him that yearned for the wide-open freedom of the sea. But every morning when he rose, his first thoughts were of Juliana. And every morning, his steps turned toward the offices of the Marquis Line, as if drawn by an invisible, irresistible force, like the tides to the moon.

"*Zut alors*, your cravat lists like a drunkard. Here." Raoul efficiently retied Connor's stock into a natty four-in-hand. "All right, my friend, you are on your own. Good luck in bearding the lioness. And as for the Lady Juliana, just remember there are other fish in the sea. And most of them are *très content* to assault men with kisses rather than paperweights."

Connor shook his head. "Don't you ever think of anything but sex?"

The Frenchman considered for a moment. "*Mais oui*, but nothing else I like so much."

Connor strode across the street, grinning in spite of himself. God, he envied the bastard. Raoul had more women than spots on a Billy Blue neckcloth, but his heart was true to none of them. As opposed to Connor, who could not seem to get his mind off of one vexing, spoiled miss . . . who had stood up to him with a bravery he'd rarely seen equaled. And who had a kiss that could take a man to heaven in a heartbeat.

Raoul stood in the darkness, watching his friend enter the brightly lit manor house. Memories assailed him. A country chateau blazing with light. Lush vineyards, secret forests, and green, fertile hillsides. His mother's beautiful voice singing him to sleep. His early years had been a golden haze of uncomplicated happiness—until the night his mother had woken him from a deep sleep and told him he was to leave the house with an uncle he barely knew. Confused, tired, and irritated, Raoul had purposely not returned his mother's kiss. He hadn't known it was the last time he would ever see her alive. . . .

A knife-edge of light from the basement door caught Raoul's eye. A cloak-wrapped figure carrying a small satchel stepped cautiously out of the house and glanced both ways before starting down the fog-shrouded street. The cloak concealed the person's features, but it could do nothing to disguise the graceful cadence of the walk or the subtle sway of hips as the figure hurried across the cobbles. Raoul knew that walk. He'd watched her from a distance on the London docks more times than he could count.

What was Mademoiselle Evans doing out alone at this time of night?

Only one answer came to mind. She was meeting a lover. A curious disappointment stung his heart. In his travels he'd known dozen of women he'd believed to be virtuous but who turned out to be false as paste jewels. Why should he waste a second thought on this one? He turned in the opposite direction, telling himself it did not matter that it was a moonless night, or that she was alone and unchaperoned, or that mayhem could befall an unvirtuous woman as easily as it could a virtuous one—

"Merde!" He turned on his heel and started after the girl.

11

Meg adjusted her spectacles and peered down Half-Moon Street. In the distance, a hired coach clattered its way toward the busy thoroughfare of Piccadilly, but the rest of the street was deserted. The gentry were all inside their warm, well-appointed homes, primping and preening for the start of the Season. Meg pulled her cloak closer against the damp winter wind, wondering if any of them ever spared a thought for the souls who did not have homes to go to.

She clutched her bundle tighter and darted across the street, then continued her way down Curzon toward Shepherd's Market. During the day, this business district was a beehive of activity, but at night the shops were shut tight and deserted. Huge glass shop windows stared out at her like blind eyes, reflecting her faint, ghostly image in their surfaces.

A shiver crept down her spine. She heard a muffled foot-fall behind her and whirled around, nearly overbalancing herself in the process. But the only thing there was the curling fog and the blackness of the empty, staring windows. *Margaret Evans, you are being a goose.*

A thin figure detached itself from the shadows. "Miss?"

"Lettie!" Meg hurried across the street, more relieved than she cared to admit at the presence of another soul. "How are you? Are the children well?"

"Alice is ever so much better, thanks to you, miss. And you wouldn't recognize my Josh. That mutton stew you gave me last fortnight made him grow a foot taller. And those sweetmeats you sent were a glorious treat. You're an angel from heaven to send them, and that's a fact," Lettie said, bobbing a shaky curtsy. The reason for her awkwardness was all too apparent. The girl's thin body was several months gone with child.

Lettie was only nineteen, little more than a child herself, and yet she had given birth to three children, including a stillborn daughter. Now there was another on the way. Meg handed over the bundle of clothes and food. "I don't know if I can come again. I had to cry sick tonight to get away, and I cannot keep doing that. I do wish that you could come to the house. I could give you so much more if I didn't have to carry—"

The distant jangle of reins silenced her. Lettie glanced down a nearby alley, then turned back to Meg, her eyes wide with fright. "I got to go, miss. My man's waitin'."

The girl turned to leave, but Meg caught her hand. "Ask him if he'll bring you to my house, Lettie."

"He won't. You know he won't. My man can't show his face."

"Then *you* come. Lettie, I have friends. You and the children don't have to stay with that—"

"I got to go, Miss," Lettie cried, pulling out of Meg's grasp. She ran into the shadows, clutching the bundle to her chest. A few moments later Meg heard the shrill creak of a dogcart's rusty wheel—followed by the sound of a brutal slap.

Meg hugged her middle, fighting an almost overwhelming sense of futility. Girls like Lettie knew only one means of staying alive, and that way broke their spirit a little more every day. And there were hundreds of Letties in this city. Thousands.

"Aye, what a we got 'ere?"

She whirled around, and came face to face with a large man in a laborer's coat and a polka dot neckcloth. He looked as if he'd been carved from a block of granite—with very little cut away.

"I come to check that my shop's locked good and proper, and find myself a not-so-good and not-so-proper miss. This is turning out to be a right fine night."

He took a step closer. Meg took a step back. "My good man, you have mistaken me for . . . well, I am not who you believe me to be. However, I can understand how you could make such an error, and I forgive you for it. Now, if you will be so good as to step out of my way—"

"Ooh, pretty manners, too. Like she was a real lady. Well, I can play His Nibs as good as any." He swept off his hat and made an elaborate, mocking bow. "Would her ladyship cares to join me for a cup of the creature at the Pulteney 'otel, afore we retire to my rooms for a bit a sport?"

"Sir, you compound your error! Pray do not further embarrass yourself." With a huff of exasperation Meg pushed by the man and stepped into the street.

His arm snaked out, yanking her against him so hard that it drove the air from her lungs. "I 'ad enough of your games, ducks. Now if you don't want to go to my rooms, that's jack with me. My shop's right here."

She struggled against his punishing hold. "Let me go. You've made a mistake!"

"The only mistake I made is wastin' time on your games. Now stop your wiggling—at least until we get insi—"

The man's words ended midsentence. Meg pushed herself out of his arms, not understanding his sudden silence—

until she spied a darker shadow behind the man, and the fain
glint of light off the edge of a knife.

"My friend, you appear to be hard of hearing. The lady ha
said she is not interested in your advances. You shall apolo
gize to her at once."

"Apologize? To a bleeding whor—" The man grunted a
the dagger poked into his ribs. "Er, I'm sorry."

"*Très bien.* Now, I advise you to find your way out of thi
street . . . for I fear this blade has a taste for blood."

The man didn't need to be asked twice.

Meg could not see her rescuer's face in the shadows, bu
there was something vaguely familiar about his accent. "I an
in your debt, sir."

"The man was a pig, fit only for the roasting spit,
the Frenchman commented as he returned his blade to it
sheath. "Did he hurt you?"

"No," she said thoughtfully. She had *definitely* heard hi
voice before. "Are we acquainted?"

"*Mais non. Certainement,* I should have remembered
meeting so charming and valiant a mademoiselle."

Meg looked down, glad that the night shadows hid he
blush. "I fear that I am neither charming nor valiant. And
feel like an utter cake for letting that man sneak up on me."

"*Un cochon.* Such a man takes pleasure in fear," th
stranger replied, barely hiding his disgust. He bowed and
nodded down the street. "If you would do me the honor,
should be pleased to accompany you to safety."

She took his offered arm and started down Curzon Street
feeling unaccountably at ease with him. In substance, he
situation had not changed. She was still alone on a deserted
street with a complete stranger—a stranger who wielded
dagger as if it were his own hand. It made no sense, and ye
she trusted him as she trusted her own heart—a heart tha
was beating unusually fast at the moment. Away from th
shadows of the market, she could see more of his profile, in

:luding his handsome, striking features and his impressive mustache. That too triggered a memory.

As if sensing her perusal, the man pulled up his collar and urned away. Meg blushed anew. It was quite not the thing or a girl to stare at a gentleman, even in such particular cir-:umstances as these. Especially when the girl was as relent-essly plain as she was.

The Frenchman put his hand over hers. "But you slow your walk. Are you sure the bully did not—"

"No, he did nothing," she said, praying that she did not ound as breathless as she felt. "I was just . . . thinking of Lettie. She and her children are in such a desperate state."

"Ah, *la malheureuse*. You are kind to help such an unfortunate."

They were nearing the end of Curzon Street, where it :rossed Bolton and turned up toward the well-lighted Berkeley Square. In a few minutes she would be at the Jollys' Aouse. And it was quite possible that she would never see this Aandsome stranger again. Perhaps it was that prospect that made her tell him things of her past that she would never Aave dreamed of sharing with a gentleman to whom she had Aot been properly introduced.

"Lettie is not just any unfortunate. We grew up together—Aer mother was the wardrobe mistress for my father's acting Aroupe. Several years ago her mother remarried and Lettie's stepfather took them to London. We lost touch, but when I Arrived here I made it a point to look her up. She was . . . well Aer mother had died and her worthless stepfather had cast Aer off. She lives a wretched and desperate life."

The gentleman shrugged. "*Un conte tragique*. And sadly :ommon. But there are places for such unfortunates—:harities and workhouses. A lady such as you should not rouble her lovely head over such matters."

"A lady such as myself," Meg repeated with a humorless mile. "Sir, you mistake me for someone of consequence. I have no family, no fortune, and—despite your kind compliments—I have no beauty to recommend me. In truth, if not for the kindness of Commodore Jolly and his family, it is quite likely that I would have suffered the same fate as Lettie."

The man stopped dead in his tracks and looked at her in horror. *"C'est impossible!"*

Lord, what had she done! She had foolishly revealed the truth of her pitiful circumstances to a gentleman she barely knew. A gentleman of obvious breeding and sensibility. A gentleman who was easily the most handsome she had ever laid eyes on.

Such a man might call on a gently bred miss, but he would never deign to associate with a woman who had narrowly escaped the poorhouse, even if she was the ward of a commodore. Hopes she did not even know she was nurturing crumbled to dust.

Embarrassed at her idiotic confession, she turned on her heel and dashed across the square. Unfortunately, her exit suffered as she slipped on a patch of ice and stumbled forward, an awkward move that sent her spectacles clattering to the cobbles. A new blush suffused her cheeks as she knelt down and began to feel blindly across the stones.

She felt him kneel down beside her. He took her hand in his gentle grasp, handling her as if she were made of china. Without a word he scooped up her glasses and placed them in her palm, his caring touch lingering for moments longer than necessary before he rose and slipped behind the concealing curtain of fog.

And then she knew.

Connor had faced ruthless pirates, bloodthirsty corsairs, South Seas savages, French cannons, and a host of other dangers. He would have gladly taken on any one of them over Mrs. Jolly.

"You have sat there for nearly three-quarters of an hour," the lady said as she gave him a glance that drilled him more sharply than any pistol. "And yet you have told me nothing except some business events that could not be of any possible interest to me. And you have told me nothing of yourself but some fairy tale that even the most backward child could not believe."

Connor had worked long and hard on "Captain Gabriel's" history, but under Mrs. Jolly's scrutiny it seemed as false as— well, as false as the fabricated tale it was. "Madam, I can only tell you the Admiralty has complete faith in my word."

"Yes, and we know what towering intellects they are. Most of them are more interested in earning a voucher to Almack's than earning medals, and the rest are sunk in a game so deep that even I have trouble divining it. I wonder," she mused as her eyes narrowed with sharp scrutiny, "into which camp you fall."

"Perhaps into the camp that cares only for an end to this bloody war."

If Mrs. Jolly regarded his answer, she made scant show of it. Instead, she smoothed her lace cap and pointed to a porcelain ewer and pitcher on her cherrywood dresser. "All this nonsense has parched my throat. Be so good as to pour me a cup of water before we continue."

Connor wondered what the woman was up to. In all his travels, he'd rarely come across a more astute mind, and she was far too clever to waste their time together on a frivolous gesture. Nevertheless, he gave a gentleman's nod and went to the pitcher.

"Hmm. It takes a bit of walking to show the cut of a man's livery," she remarked as she accepted the glass. "That coat is the work of Weston's in Conduit, is it not?"

"I believe so," Connor replied as he retook his chair. He vaguely remembered the shop where he'd been measured and poked for what had seemed like an eternity. "I don't recall."

"A proper gentlemen would recall not only the tailor, but the day and the hour of his latest fitting. The *ton* have a spanking fine memory for details—except when it comes to the bill, of course."

Connor's expression edged into a smile. He realized that he liked Mrs. Jolly and that in another time and place they might have been friends. "We were talking about my fitness as a manager—"

"We were *talking* about your spending so much time with my lamb," she countered sharply. " 'Tis said that well-cut clothes can hide any fault, and that's true enough when it comes to a plump belly or narrow shoulders. There's some who call a tailor's shop a 'court of miracles' for all the wonders done with sawdust padding and whalebone corsets. But they can't disguise a man's stance, or the subtle shift of his weight when he walks." She leaned forward and peered shrewdly at Connor. "I've seen only a few others who shift their weight as you do, as if the irons were still on your legs. What were you in prison for?"

Connor felt as if he'd taken a punch to his gut. "Madam, I fear you are mistaken—"

"No, *you* are mistaken if you think you can flummox me. Tell me the truth, or I assure you that by tomorrow evening every member of the Upper Ten Thousand will know that your whole tale is Banbury."

Connor raked his fingers through his hair. His only recourse was the truth. Or at least, as much of it as he dared. "You are correct, madam. I did serve time, but 'twas on a ship, not in a cell. She was named the *Absalom*."

Mrs. Jolly raised her hand to her throat. "Heavens, that filthy scow was decommissioned fifteen years past, and her brutish captain drummed out of the service along with her. I thought both had long since gone to Davy Jones's locker. How could you have taken up with such a wretched man?"

Connor fingered his scarred cheek, recalling the wretched bar in Kingstown where the *Absalom*'s mate had plied a lonely, heartbroken boy with cup after cup of grog. The next afternoon he'd woken in the stinking belly of a ship already under way, with iron shackles around his legs. "I had little choice, madam."

The woman gasped. "Shanghaied! 'Tis our country's shame that some still sanction that deplorable practice. But as a rule, only criminals and malcontents are taken, not stalwart men and boys. You are too young to be a quota-man. The captain had no right—"

"The captain had no right to do any of the things he did," Connor stated in an emotionless voice. "But there was no one to speak for me, no one to miss me. I was on that ship for ten months."

"You are fortunate to be alive."

Fortunate? Connor was not so sure. During those months he had been treated like an animal, and he had become an animal in order to survive. He closed his eyes and felt the horror of those months rise in him like a choking wave. No matter how many years passed, he would never be free of the memories. "You are correct about one thing, madam. Both the ship and the captain are no more. The ship sank in a battle off the coast of Patagonia. The captain . . . drowned."

Mrs. Jolly searched his face, expecting more. He gave her nothing. The silence stretched between them like a rigging line, pulling tauter with each passing minute. In the end Mrs. Jolly had looked away, though not before he thought he caught a shadow of regret in her eyes.

"You have weathered a hard life, boy. It is to your credit that you have risen up from such desperate circumstances to the position you now enjoy. But do not mistake my respect for my acceptance." She reached over to her nightstand and extracted a package of letters. "Mr. McGregor has written me everyday of the progress of the Marquis Line. It appears that Juliana's progress has been quite remarkable. It strikes me that she no longer requires a manager. I think it is high time you secured yourself another position."

Connor had thought the same, but having someone else tell him raised his hackles. "Madam, I make my own decisions."

"Captain, almost no one makes their own decisions, even when they believe they do. We are all slaves to the circumstances of our pasts and the limited choices in our present. And your best choice is to leave the Marquis Line and allow Lady Juliana to renew her friendship with her peers."

Her peers. Of which Connor would never be one. His eyes narrowed to a dangerous gleam. "And if I refuse?"

"I do not believe you shall. During my observation, I noticed something else about you, something not so obvious as your scarred face, but just as much a part of your character. You may play the ruthless privateer in public, but underneath you have a noble heart. And I would be willing to wager my husband's pension that that heart beats only for Juliana."

Connor's confidence crumbled. "That is . . . absurd."

Mrs. Jolly waved away his protests. "Oh, stop trying to gammon me. But do not worry. I doubt anyone besides myself has the least suspicion, including the lady. Yet we both know it is true."

Connor shifted uneasily in his chair. "If such a thing were true . . . and I am not saying it is. But if it were—why would you think I would willingly leave the lady?"

"Because you love her. Because you know in your heart that, as much as you love her, you could never be the man that a girl as fine and true as she is deserves."

With one well-aimed thrust she had cut his dreams to shreds. For the first time in years he had looked forward to the sunrise, because it meant another day with Juliana. He reveled in their battles, he enjoyed her neat parries and her quick intelligence, and he treasured the occasions when she gave him a rare, glorious smile. Helping her to realize her father's dream had brought more pleasure to the wreck of his life than he'd thought possible. But until that moment, he honestly hadn't realized that his pleasure had slipped quietly, irrevocably, and hopelessly into being in love. *You're a fool, Connor. A bloody, idiot fool.*

He rose from the chair and gave Mrs. Jolly the efficient nod of a man facing a firing squad. "You have made your point, madam."

"I never doubted it. Now, I suggest you sever your relationship as quickly and painlessly as possible. A note of resignation delivered to the Marquis Line on the morrow should take care of the matter."

Connor's mouth ticked up. "If you think that, then you do not know Juliana. She'll want answers."

"Then give them to her. You are a privateer, and have stayed in port for over two months. You can say that you wasted enough time with the Marquis Line when there is profit to be made elsewhere. You can say that you missed the open sea. You can say that you had a monstrous craving for deep-water mackerel. Say anything you like, but leave the girl behind. 'Tis the course you would have taken eventually anyway, is it not?"

Eventually. But not while he could still plunder a few more precious hours with Juliana. He would have traded a year of his life for every day spent with her and counted himself lucky in the bargain. But the lady was right. He was just delaying the inevitable. And possibly damning Juliana's reputation beyond repair.

He rose from his chair and walked to the window, peering out into the empty night. "There is a convoy—a supply run to Lisbon. It leaves within the week. I am confident that I could arrange for my snow to sail along as protection."

"It might be harder to arrange than you suppose. Such a task is fit more for a fourth-rate brig than a yar schooner. The Admiralty is loath to put war heroes in biscuit runs."

"Have no fear, madam. I have resources at my disposal that can secure me whatever voyage I wish—even ones fit for a fourth-rate brig. Who knows—it might even have the added advantage of casting me as a coward in Juliana's eyes."

Mrs. Jolly's expression softened. She reached out and took Connor's hand as a sad, delicate sorrow shadowed her eyes. "No doubt you consider me a deplorable termagant. No, do not argue. I am. But there was a time—long ago to be sure— but there was still a time when I was just as determined and headstrong as Lady Juliana. And because of my foolishness, I lost—" She glanced at her legs and closed her eyes, as if reliving a painful memory. But when she opened them again, her resolute expression was back in place.

"If it is any consolation, I believe you are a finer man than most of the preening popinjays who call themselves gentlemen. But we live in a world of rules, boy. Not fair rules, but rules nonetheless. Juliana's best chance of happiness lies in making an acceptable marriage. You must see that a man of your notorious reputation and uncertain future can never offer her that chance."

But Mrs. Jolly was wrong. There was a chance—one slim, hazard chance that he might see daylight at the end of this nightmare. But the reality was that he'd probably be dead before the year was out. He couldn't offer Juliana a future. Hell, he could barely offer her tomorrow.

He left the room and headed down the stairs into the night. For the second time in his life, he was leaving Juliana behind without an explanation, but he had no choice. Even if he could have extricated himself from the Admiral's plots, even if he wasn't killed in this endless war, even if by some miracle he could again win Juliana's love, he could never give her any kind of happiness.

The captain of the *Absalom* had indeed perished on the night his ship sank, but not from drowning. He'd died with Connor's hands wrapped around his throat.

12

"... along with seventy barrels of prime indigo. Now, as to the tea shipments—" Mr. McGregor glanced up from his ream of papers. "My lady, have ya heard a single word that I've said?"

Juliana looked up from the carpet pattern she had been studying with such diligence. "Of course I have. You were speaking of the penny increase in sugar taxes."

"I was—five minutes ago."

"Oh. Yes, I remember now. You had gone on to the reports on the weather conditions in Pangopango—"

"Ten minutes ago." He sighed, and got up from his chair. "We can speak of this later, my lady. I can see that you have other things on your mind."

He lifted his gaze past Juliana's shoulder, to the window and its view of the river, where the bannerless masts of Connor's ship were still visible in the dying light. "I hear that Captain Gabriel sails for Lisbon with the morning tide."

Juliana shuffled through the papers on her desk. "I

wouldn't know. And if I did, I wouldn't care, except that our ship the *Pelican* sails with him. Besides, he made no secret of the fact that he would leave someday. All he was truly interested in was making a profit."

"Hmm, I suppose that is why he stayed on for close to two months with no pay," the solicitor mused. He stroked his chin and gave Juliana a canny look. "Well, I suppose we shoulda kenned it long ago. After all, he's only a blue-water privateer, a henhearted rascal who makes easy money on convoy duty while other brave men face their deaths."

"That's not true! The captain has proved his bravery a hundred times over. He ran the blockade near Malaga and delivered badly needed supplies to our Peninsula forces. He faced the French guns at Toulon and rescued two dozen wounded officers who would have surely died if he had not—" Juliana bit her lip and resumed shuffling her papers. "I am a bit fatigued, Mr. McGregor. We can resume our business in the morning."

Sighing, the solicitor deposited his pen into one of his many pockets. "If that is your wish, my lady. But . . . well, you and the captain—ya make a bonny team. It couldna hurt to speak with him before he leaves. We could go together and—"

Juliana waved her hand indifferently. "La, sir, even with your company 'twould be unthinkable for a woman of my position to approach a man of his in anything but a business arena."

McGregor frowned in puzzlement. "Even though he is your employee?"

Juliana sighed, realizing it would take time and patience to explain the complex intricacies of the social order to the solicitor. Currently she was in short supply of both.

"The voyage to Lisbon and back will take Captain Gabriel a little over a month. By the time he returns, I intend to make the Marquis Line so successful there will be no doubt that his services are no longer needed." She also intended to make sure she was being courted by at least three beaux by the time Connor returned. "In any event, we have a great deal of work to do in little time, and I believe the sooner we start, the better. Good afternoon, Mr. McGregor."

At the threshold, Mr. McGregor paused, and looked back. "You've a rare head for business, and no mistake. I just hope you've the sense to use it outside of this office as well."

Juliana watched him go and again reminded herself that she was doing the right thing. She would never shame herself by running after a man who had turned his back on her.

Even if his leaving left a hole in her heart that even the wide salt sea couldn't fill.

"Shatterbrained," she muttered as she turned once more to her desk. Heavens, if this kept up she'd be as useless as Meg. Her once-sensible friend couldn't hold a rational thought in her head since she'd met her mysterious Frenchman. Grimacing, Juliana thought back to their morning conversation.

"Honestly, Julie, you cannot imagine how brave he was. He risked his very life to save my honor. Did I tell you how fearless he was?"

"Three times, dearest. But I'm not entirely certain his life was in danger. After all, he had a knife, while the other man—"

"And so gallant. He walked me home, even though he might have been discovered. He must have been in disguise at the Morrow's ball. Oh, it is too thrilling—a gentleman posing as a servant. 'Tis just like a play. Perhaps he is a nobleman running from an evil relative who seeks to kill him for his inheritance. Oh, I could not bear it if he were in such constant danger . . ."

Halfway through her kipper, Juliana had suggested that Meg spend her day riding in Hyde Park with the commodore, where she might catch a glimpse of her servant/nobleman/Frenchman. The thought of enduring another day of Meg's starry-eyed prattling over her mustachioed savior was too frightful to contemplate. After all, Juliana had a business to run, a business that required all her attention and acumen. Her annoyance had nothing to do with the fact that Meg's lovelorn sighs grated on her nerves like a badly played violin. Nothing at all.

Liar, her mind whispered.

A commotion in the hallway outside brought her thoughts abruptly back on course. One of the junior clerks stuck his head around the edge of the door. Juliana picked up a quill and strove to look busy. "What is it, Mr. O'Brian?"

"Beggin' your pardon, miss, but it's that merchant, Mr. Lovejoy, and he's mad as blazes. Wants his goods off the *Pelican* this minute and no mistake."

Slowly Juliana put down her pen. Lovejoy was one of the most powerful and influential merchants in the city. He had shipped almost exclusively with her father, but since she had taken over the line she'd had the devil's own time persuading him to continue his contract. Just two weeks ago he'd agreed to give the Marquis Line another chance, and the Lisbon-bound *Pelican* was his first new cargo. Or at least, it was supposed to be. "Did he give a reason?"

"No reason. Just sputtering like a steam kettle left too long on the boil. Wants to talk to Mr. McGregor double-sharp."

"Mr. McGregor is not here. I will speak with him."

Mr. O'Brian looked sheepishly at his instep. "Well, you see—he said he don't want to talk to you. 'Won't talk to any bleedin' woman,' if you'll excuse the language. But I don't think he'll wait for Mr. McGregor. Wants his cargo off the *Pelican* this minute. Says he'll call the authorities on us if we don't do it proper quick."

McGregor had said she had a rare head for business. It was time she put it to use. She took a deep breath. "Show him in, Mr. O'Brian."

"Didn't ya hear me? He won't talk with no woman—"

"He will—if you tell him that this woman thinks he is the lowest kind of coward for not speaking to her face to face."

A few minutes later, Atticus Lovejoy barreled into her office. "I ain't no coward."

"Apparently I was mistaken. I apologize," Juliana said with unruffled calm as she pointed to the chair across from her. "Please sit down."

Mr. Lovejoy looked skeptical, but he settled into the chair. "You might as well know right off, miss, that my mind's made up. I want my goods off the *Pelican* this instant."

"Of course you do, and I would not dream of stopping you," Juliana said graciously. "I only ask to know the reason. Surely that is a reasonable request?"

Lovejoy was built like a brick house. He'd come up from nothing on the docks, and was used to dealing with men as tough as he was. This supremely unflustered woman flustered him mightily. "Well, it's the Admiral, ain't it?"

"Admiral who?"

"The spy in the admiralty. It's all over the docks that he's stolen a satchel of papers from the War Office. Ain't you heard?"

No, she hadn't. Being a woman, she was excluded from much of the gossip that circulated on the docks. And being currently out of favor with the *ton*, she received no news from that quarter. For a moment she felt the lonely weight of her position—a loneliness she had never felt when Connor had been by her side. "I had heard of the spy, but not of his recent theft. I hope it is nothing too valuable."

"Nothing—save the whole bleedin' plan for the Valencia campaign."

The region of Valencia and its well-protected harbor was one of the bloodiest battlefields in the whole Peninsula. If England's plans fell into Napoleon's hands, it would mean the death of countless men. Years ago on her father's ship, they had come upon the remains of a sea battle where the French had sent a trio of fire-ships into a supposedly secret and poorly armed resupply mission. She could still remember the putrid smell of the men and animals dying from their wounds. She could still remember their screams.

"This foul traitor must be apprehended before he delivers the papers to Napoleon. They cannot be allowed to fall into enemy hands."

Lovejoy rubbed his chin. "Well, ya got spirit, I'll say that much for you. Odds are I'd still be shipping my goods with you—if Captain Gabriel hadn't cut and run like he did."

Juliana's temper flared. "He did not cut and run! The captain left my employ because he took a more profitable offer."

"I thought the same—until I found out he's sailing with the convoy for nothing."

Juliana felt as if she'd been punched by a prizefighter. "N-nothing?"

"Not a brass farthing. And if it weren't for profit he left for, it had to be another reason. And what reason could there be excepting that he thinks you ain't got the ball—well, um, that you ain't got the ballast to run this company?"

Juliana gripped the edge of her desk, momentarily too stunned for words. She had thought Connor had meant it when he praised her work, and said that she would have made her father proud. Now she saw that he had never thought she had a chance of managing the line. Just like everyone else.

". . . can see why I have no choice but to weigh anchor and ship my cargo with another company. I ain't saying you're not a good lass, or that your heart's not in the right place. But I can't afford to risk my cargo to a girl who don't know the difference between a shroud and a ratline."

"The shrouds run vertical, the ratlines horizontal," she muttered automatically.

Lovejoy rubbed his chin, clearly impressed. "Well, you know your rigging. And you've a bold spirit. You'd have made a fine ship's captain if you'd been born a man. My course is still set on takin' my cargo elsewhere, but there's still a chance we could strike a deal—specially if you were to see your way clear to reducing my costs by half. . . ."

"We sail within the hour. You can't come aboard."

Juliana paused on the swaying gangway of Connor's ship. Glancing up at the top of the plank, she recognized the same tobacco-chawing brute who'd turned her away the night she'd come to the docks to apologize to Connor. In the evening twilight, the hulking tar looked even larger than she remembered. Nevertheless, she took another step up the gangway..

"Are ya deaf? Didn't ya hear me—"

"I heard," Juliana said. "And if you try to stop me I shall scream so shrilly that every constable in the city will come running. They'll swarm this ship like wasps, and keep it in dock for hours while they sort it out. You'll miss the tide. You'll fall behind in your schedule. There will be dock fees, tardiness taxes, extra wages for the sailors, and overdue payments to the merchants. Is that *really* what you want?"

The tar looked as if he'd swallowed his tobacco. "Blimey, the captain don't want . . . now see here, you can't do all that."

"Try me," she promised. "Where is the captain?"

"He's in the wardroom with the mates. And he don't want to be disturbed. I gots my orders. I gots my—"

"Oh, to hell with this," Juliana said, elbowing the man aside. She stormed down the deck, ignoring the stunned looks of the hard-bitten sailors as she made her way to the lower deck. Pausing for just a moment, she caught the sounds of voices coming from the wardroom. Connor. And the bastard was laughing! Her anger renewed, she thrust open the door and barreled in. "How dare you? How dare—"

Her words died as she caught sight of him. Since he'd come to London he'd dressed like proper gentlemen, but on his ship Connor clearly tossed those conventions aside. Bent intently over his charts, his ragged hair untamed by a queue and falling loose across his forehead, he wore a pair of worn leather breeches, plain high boots that had not seen polish in a year—and nothing else.

He straightened slowly, his intense gaze pinning her like a butterfly on a child's display board. "Gentlemen . . . it appears we must continue this discussion later."

Juliana was only vaguely aware of the men who slipped out the door behind her. She drank in the sight of Connor's chiseled face, his bright hair, the poorly healed scar that had wounded so much more than his cheek. She swallowed, realizing too late just how desperately she'd missed seeing him this past week. Of course, she hadn't counted on seeing quite this much of him. . . .

With an almost deliberate slowness, he turned his back to her and pulled down a linen shirt hung on a nearby peg. "What are you doing here?"

For a several seconds she couldn't remember. The sight of his muscles rippling across his broad, tanned back drove the thoughts from her head and the air from her lungs. *He's beautiful,* she thought with an astonished wonder. It wasn't the first time she'd seen him without a shirt. But the powerful, hard-muscled man who casually tucked his shirt into his belt was very different from the boy she remembered . . . just as the innocent adoration she'd felt for him as a child was far different from the not-so-innocent heat that thrummed in her center.

With his back still to her he demanded, "Well, have you lost your tongue along with all regard for your reputation?"

"Reputation?" Juliana's temper flared. "You are a *fine* one to talk about my reputation. I just spent the better part of an hour talking that miser Lovejoy into leaving his cargo on the *Pelican*—for three-quarters the normal rate. And I was lucky to get that. He said that you left my employ because you had lost faith in me—that you were so desperate to leave that you took this job of convoy guard duty for nothing. Is it true?"

Connor's hand stilled. "I never lost faith in you. That's not . . . why I was desperate to leave."

"Then why?" she cried. "For once in your life deal honestly with me. I believed in you. I thought you believed in me. You made me see that there might be a future for me beyond the social whirl and a carefully arranged mar—" She bit her lip, and tried valiantly to retain her composure. "But it was all a lie, wasn't it? Your praises, your encouragement—all cruel, heartless lies."

"That's not true!" He strode across the room and took her shoulders in an almost punishing grip. "No owner could have done better for the line—not even your father. I never lied to you about that."

"Then why did you leave me?"

His eyes pierced her with hypnotic intensity, like a hawk searching for prey. His gaze absorbed her, driving the thoughts from her mind and the air from her lungs. His hastily tucked-in shirt gaped open, revealing far more of his powerful chest and its dusting of tight blond curls than decency prescribed. The narrow room made her overwhelmingly aware of his size, of his strength, of the way his sun-colored hair fell rakishly across his brow. But most of all she felt his power—the raw, barely restrained energy that seethed beneath his stone-hard expression.

Childhood memories and his gentleman's veneer had given her a false sense of security and made her forget his notorious reputation as a privateer. But she remembered the time in the hallway in the Morrow house when she'd realized that his big hands could have easily broken her ankle in two. She recalled the time in Jolly's office when his ruthlessly carnal caress had threatened to break much more than her ankle. Connor Reed was a dangerous man. And yet she still saw the shadow of the boy she'd loved . . . would always love—

He released her with a suddenness that made her stagger.

'Tis the tide, she thought as she steadied herself against the captain's table. *It* must *be the tide.*

"Do not trouble yourself about Lovejoy," Connor said as he moved to the cabinet and poured himself a glass of whiskey. "I will write him from Lisbon, and assure him that I have the utmost faith in you and the Marquis Line."

"A . . . letter?" Juliana breathed, still feeling unaccountably weak. "Why a letter? Why not see him when you return?"

Connor rolled the glass in his hand, then he threw back his head and downed it in a single swallow. "I am not coming back. After Lisbon I make for Gibraltar. By this time next month I shall be with the fleet in the Mediterranean."

The Mediterranean! "You cannot. This snow is no match for a well-armed frigate."

"Perhaps. But England needs all the ships she can get at the moment. Besides," he added as he raked his hand through his hair, "it is not as if anyone here will miss me."

"I . . . will," she confessed softly. The thought of Connor facing Napoleon's deadly cannons left no room for lies. "Please, do not go."

He hung his head. "Juliana, you don't understand. I must leave—"

"No!" The cry came from her soul, deeper than convention, deeper than honor. The thought of not seeing him for weeks devastated her. But the thought of not seeing him for months, maybe never again—she could not bear it. "You must not go. Lovejoy told me papers were stolen from the War Office last night, detailing the Spanish campaign. If they reach Napoleon, our ships will be sitting ducks for the French fleet. I could not bear for you to be in such danger. Stay, Connor. Please."

He lifted his hand to her cheek. "Juliana . . . Princess . . . I cannot."

The ache in his voice echoed the ache in her heart. Her pride weighed little compared to the emptiness her life would be without him. They were bound together in a way that made no sense. And yet nothing in her life made sense without him.

She wound her arms around his neck and pressed herself against him. "Stay," she whispered.

His whole body went rigid. "For God's sake, I'm not made of stone!"

"You don't have to be my manager. You can be anything you want. *I'll* be anything you want. Just don't leave me. I cannot bear losing you aga—"

A roll of the tide slapped against the ship, momentarily unbalancing the pair. To keep them both from toppling Connor twisted and fell heavily against a cabinet, sending a small chest crashing to the floor. The chest flew open, spewing its contents of letters haphazardly across the room.

It took Juliana a moment to realize that all the correspondence bore the seal of the War Office.

13

⚜

"Steady as she goes, pilot," Connor commanded as he stood on the quarterdeck of his ship with his hands clasped behind his back and surveyed the vast blue kingdom that stretched around him as far as the eye could see. Fair weather had borne them beyond the chops of the channel in record time, and the remains of a long easy southern swell had urged them westward with steady determination. The morning sun rose behind him, scattering diamonds across the gently rippling surface. Ahead, the low-riding merchant ships dipped and swayed like fat, contented ducks, while overhead the sails billowed and fluttered like angels' wings.

Connor breathed deeply, relishing the clean, lonely peace of the ocean dawn. On mornings like these he could almost believe that he was still a boy on the Marquis's schooner, with the wide world before him.

The sound of breaking china from the deck below shattered the illusion.

"I imagine that would be breakfast," Raoul commented as

he climbed to the quarterdeck. "If the mademoiselle keeps this up, we will have no dishes left."

During the two days they'd been at sea, Juliana had decimated a startling amount of pottery. Not to mention what she had done to Connor's cabin. "She's got to eat sometime," he growled.

"I am not so sure. This one has a will of iron, and we will not reach Portugal for ten days." He gazed out to sea. "*Mon ami*, you must talk with her. She will listen to you."

"Trust me, she'd rather walk the plank," Connor scoffed, ignoring the stab of pain through his heart. God's teeth, why did that chest have to break open? In another minute he'd have had her off the ship. She would have been safe. She'd have remembered him with honor—perhaps even with love. But instead, that bloody box had spilled its treasonous contents all over the floor of the wardroom. He'd had no choice but to lock Juliana in his quarters and sail with the tide. Delay would have cost him his mission. Kidnapping cost him only his heart.

At the time it had seemed a wise bargain.

Another crash brought his thoughts back to the present. Raoul was right. He had to do something. Before he lost every dish on the ship. Before her hunger strike truly endangered her life.

Sighing, he leaned on the rail and stared into the open water. A school of dolphins surfaced nearby, including several cows and their spirited calves. Despite his glum mood, he could not help smiling as he watched the playful animals. "I envy you, friends. No wars. No heartache. Just endless freedom, and no responsibilities save the love of your mothers for their young . . ."

A thought stirred in his mind. "Raoul, how many men have we assigned to stand watch on Lady Juliana?"

"Three. But she drove them all away with bruised shins and blistered ears. The rest of the crew refuses to go near her door—save to deliver the dishes she breaks and the food she will not eat. Besides, 'tis hardly necessary. Unless she has a taste for cold salt water, the *demoiselle* cannot escape this ship."

"Nevertheless, I believe there is one crew member who can guard her in complete safety," Connor mused as he rubbed his chin. "And if my plan plays out as I think it will, she will also be dining with the manners of the queen."

"Do that, and I shall truly call you the Archangel," Raoul replied. "We cannot afford any more distractions from our mission to deliver the letters to the Spanish courier. I hope you know what you are doing."

So did Connor. Delivering the War Office letters was their most dangerous mission to date, and failure would mean not only his life but the lives of many others as well. Their safety was in his hands—and now, so was Juliana's. The treason that damned his name was perilously close to damning hers. He was once again her protector, just as he had been when they were children.

Only this time the danger he was protecting her from was himself.

Juliana cast her gaze around the room, searching for something, anything, that might aid her escape. But the spacious captain's quarters had been stripped of everything but the bedclothes before she was locked in. And while she could have wrapped her fist in the sheets and broken the glass panes of the large aft window, it was still a long, cold drop to the water below. She would certainly drown. And yet death seemed almost preferable to enduring the terrible ache in her heart. *He betrayed me. He betrayed all of England. How could I have let myself fall in l—?*

She heard the metal scrape of the door's outer bolt sliding back. She reached around and picked up one of the two remaining waterglasses from the room's huge sea chest. Drawing back her arm, she launched it toward the door at head level, only to watch it shatter against the wall.

"Damn. That was my best crystal."

Connor stepped into the room wearing much the same clothes that he'd worn the last time she'd seen him. His white shirt was still tucked haphazardly into his belt. His leather breeches still clung to his thighs like a second skin. She closed her eyes, hating the traitorous heat that burned inside her. Hating him. "Please leave."

"Gladly. As soon as you promise to take something to eat."

"Never!"

She twisted around and reached for the last glass, but Connor grabbed her waist and dumped her into one of his massive oak and leather chairs. He gripped the arms and bent down, trapping her like a cornered fox.

"You will eat, Princess. I do not intend to arrive in Lisbon harbor with a corpse."

"Sir, that is the only way you will keep me from telling of your despicable deed. I can assure you that you will not get away with your crime. By now my family has discovered that you have taken me. They will hunt you down and hang you like the dog you are."

His hard mouth edged up in a humorless smile. "Hate to disappoint you, but your family hasn't the least idea of where you are. Nor are they likely to any time soon. No one saw you come aboard. My men even planted rumors that you had been seen heading in the direction of the Temple." He bent so close that she could feel his heat. "It will be days before your family unravels the deception."

Days. Alone with him. She should have hated the thought. Instead, her heart began to pound like ocean waves against a cliff. "My family . . . will come."

"Face it, Princess, no one is sailing to your rescue. But if the wind holds we shall reach Lisbon in ten days and I will see that you are safely delivered to the magistrate. I give you my word that no harm will come to you—"

She gave a harsh laugh. "Your *word*. And what good is that? You are without honor."

He arched a cynical brow. "I recall you being without it too, just before we sailed."

She'd revealed her most secret heart to him, the cherished, yearning passion that years of separation, pride, social convention, and even betrayal had not been able to kill. She loved him with all the worship of the child she'd been, and all the desire of the woman she'd become. The horror of losing him forever had made her confess that love. The horror of his treason made her curse it.

She glared at him with all the pain and fury in her soul. "I despise you."

He winced as the barb struck home. Surprisingly, she took no pleasure in it.

The pain in his eyes lasted barely a heartbeat. He stared down at her, his eyes glittering like ice shards, his hard, ruthless features carved in unforgiving stone. "As I said, I do not intend to deliver a corpse to the Portuguese magistrate. You must eat. So I have arranged for you to have a companion to share your meals." Unhurriedly, he straightened and turned toward the cabin door. "Sir, you may come in now."

"He can share those meals with the devil," Juliana cried as she bolted from the chair. "I have no intention of—"

She stopped as a dark-haired child entered the room carrying a tray of food. "You—you are the boy from the docks. The one who told me to look for the captain at the Bell." Her gaze flew to Connor's. "Have you sunk so low that you would kidnap a child?"

"I ain't been kidnapped and I ain't no child," the boy stated huffily as he set down the tray. "Name's Jamie and I'm the cabin boy. Least I was until the captain promoted me to be your new 'watch.' "

Juliana stared at the boy. She'd driven away the men Connor had sent to guard her who were three times his size. "Is this some sort of jest?"

"No jest, Princess. I have promoted Jamie to 'acting lieutenant of the watch' for our prisoners. Since you are currently our only prisoner, you are his sole responsibility. He is charged to watch you day and night. He is also charged to take his meals with you, and to eat only when you do. If you eat, he eats. If you starve . . ." He shrugged.

"But that is barbaric!"

"Barbaric or not, Jamie has his orders. Like any member of my crew he will obey them to the death. Is that not so, sir?"

"Aye, captain," Jamie said, though his gaze remained fixed on the food-laden tray.

Juliana turned to Connor and saw him watching her with calculation. *Check and mate,* she thought grimly. She had no doubt that the devil would let the child starve—just as she had no doubt that he would never willingly let her leave this ship alive. He had no choice but to kill her, since she'd rather die than allow him to sell out his entire country.

But he had not killed her yet. And while she was alive, there was a chance she might find a way to steal the Admiralty letters, signal one of the other ships in the convoy, and escape. She might even be able to use her wealth to buy the allegiance of some of his men. Possibilities spun through her mind, but practicality persevered. Bribery would have to wait until after breakfast.

She turned her back on Connor and sat down at the table, inviting the weary boy to sit beside her. "If we are to dine as one, my fine young lieutenant, I must know what you are partial to. So which would you prefer—the ham or the kippers?"

Juliana had steeled her courage for all manner of terrors on Connor's ship, but in truth the next few days proved to be almost pleasant. Though still confined to the aft quarters, she had access to Connor's surprisingly extensive library to help pass the time. On the evening of the third day, she was brought a collapsible tub, and was able to take a much welcome bath. To her surprise, a clean dress was miraculously provided, a blue flowered muslin with a velvet jacket and Spanish cap sleeves that was very nearly her size. When she put it on, she twirled around in front of the floor length mirror, realizing just how much she enjoyed wearing colorful clothing after the drab mourning garb she'd been confined to for the past two and a half months.

She saw nothing of Connor. She was relieved, of course. No man on earth was more loathsome to her. And yet every time the cabin door opened, she found her heart beating faster with anticipation, until she saw it was only Jamie or one of the other men. She told herself that she wished to see him only so that she might convince him to return the stolen Admiralty dispatches. But in the dark of the night, when she lay on the bed that had so recently been his and buried her face in the pillow that still held his scent, she could not deny her broken heart—or ignore the hot, damning dreams that left her body aching.

But in the midst of her peril, she found a diamond. Jamie was the joy of her days. Though wary at first, the young boy gradually gave her his trust, until by the end of her fifth day on the ship he was chattering through their meals incessantly. His language was sometimes less than elegant, but Juliana preferred his lively conversation to the stilted rhetoric of her own class. He talked with surprising comprehension about everything from poetry to the points of the compass, and Juliana found herself wondering about his education. "Your parents must have taught you well, sir," she commented one day over tea.

Jamie grew still. "Never knew my parents. Never knew much about anything till the captain picked me up on the Moroccan wharf. No one had given spit about me afore then. Captain taught me everything I know. Saved my life, he did. Can I have more cake?"

Juliana handed the boy another slice, but her mind was still trying to make sense of what he'd just said. Connor was a treasonous privateer. And yet as she took in the picture of the chattering, contented child and compared it to the horror of life in the stinking Middle Eastern slums, her opinion of her captor's villainy turned to dust. Connor had acted with the same selfless charity as her father, when the marquis had taken an orphaned wharf rat and raised him as his own. It was a kindness she hadn't expected of the ruthless man Connor had become. It was a kindness that for some supremely contrary reason, made her eyes pool with tears.

"Are you blubbering, lady?"

"The polite term is 'crying,' " Juliana corrected gently as she dabbed away a tear. "I assure you, 'tis nothing. Just a mote in my eye."

The boy frowned, obviously concerned over the welfare of his charge. "I dunno. Knew a lady once who took to blub— that is, to cryin', and she fell down dead before the week was out. 'Course, she was going on eighty, but the 'pothecary said she woulda fared better if she'd had some fresh air now 'n' then."

Jamie paused for a moment and rubbed his chin, looking for a moment so much like Connor that Juliana's heart skipped a beat. "Tell you what. If you give me your parole, I can fix it so you can take a spin topside."

A "spin topside" would seem like heaven after days in the cabin. And it might afford her an opportunity to reclaim the purloined dispatches. She hated using the boy, but if she was to save her country, she could ill afford to pass up any chance at escape. She took Jamie's offered hand, and gifted him with her sincerest smile. "I would be very grateful for a walk around the deck. And I promise that, while I am in your company, I will do nothing to dishonor your faith in me."

"She is up to something," Connor growled as he stood on the forecastle and watched Juliana pause on the quarterdeck and gaze out at the sea. "I know that walk. She's plotting."

"Well, she would be a fool if she wasn't," Raoul replied. "She is a prisoner of war who is in peril of her life. And forgive me, *mon ami,* but you have done nothing to dispel that belief."

Connor looked away and watched the light of the dying sun unfurl its colors across the dark sea. Normally he loved this time of day, the moment of vast peace that settled over a vessel just before the evening watch. But there was no peace in his heart that night—or any night since they'd started this voyage. They were still a week out of Lisbon—a week that promised to hold more misery and torture than any man could endure. She was on his ship. Hell, she was in his bed! And if he acted on any of the sinful appetites that raged through his body, he'd ruin them both beyond redemption. " 'Tis better that she hates me."

"Ah yes. I forgot about your damn English honor," the Frenchman replied laconically. "*Alors,* it is astonishing that there are so many children in your country, considering the way your men keep their distance from the *jeune filles.*"

"I have done enough damage to the girl's reputation. The only thing I can do for her now is to make sure she is returned to her family untouched."

"And perhaps to give her a kind word or two—all right," Raoul said, backing away from Connor's murderous glance. "Very well, *mon ami. I* will seek out what the lady is up to. And *you* may linger here with the cold comfort of your English honor." He turned away and headed for the ship's stern muttering, "*Mon Dieu,* 'tis astonishing that there are any children at all."

Connor gazed past the bow at the half dozen merchant vessels of the convoy. So far the ruse had worked, and no ships had appeared on the horizon to threaten his plans. But luck was as fickle as the weather—and as unforgiving as a woman's heart. Frowning, he lifted his face to the wind, sensing the change in the pit of his soul.

A week to Lisbon, even if the weather held. And somewhere, out in the vast emptiness of the ocean, a storm was brewing.

14

Too far, Juliana thought as she leaned out over the quarter-deck railing and mentally measured the distance to the water below. Oh, she would survive the drop, but the shock of hitting the cold water would disorient her, and she would lose several of the precious minutes she would need to make for the convoy ships. Perhaps if she waited for the warmer currents of the south, the shock would be less taxing. Or if she had a rope—

"I would not advise it, *ma petite*. The sea is very wide, and you are very small."

Juliana scooted back from the railing and started to recite her carefully devised explanation. "I fancied I saw a whale, and was leaning out to get a closer—" She stopped as she looked into his face. He no longer wore the ridiculous white wig and gaudy livery of the Morrows' footmen, but she would have recognized him anywhere. "Why, you are Meg's Frenchman!"

The gentleman's confident smile disintegrated in surprise. "Mademoiselle Evans spoke of me?"

"Incessantly," she assured him. "I cannot say that I am pleased to find you in this circumstance, sir. However, for what you did for Meg, I owe you my heartfelt thanks."

The Frenchman gave her a courteous bow. "Any gentleman would have done as much."

Juliana's gaze traveled to the forecastle, to where Connor's dark form carved a piece from the setting sun. "If you think that, monsieur, then you do not know much of your treasonous captain. I can understand that you are part of this for your country's sake, but he has no such excuse. A more dishonorable man never drew breath."

"Not so dishonorable. He has given you his cabin, and he has allowed you the use of Rose's dresses."

"Who is Rose?"

For a moment the Frenchman bent his head and shook it. "To not even tell her of . . . *zut*, he is the fool of the world!"

"I heartily agree," she huffed.

"Lady, I urge you not to be so quick to paint your world in the colors of *blanc et noir*. The shade of truth lies somewhere in between. If you but knew the circumstances that had brought him to this point—"

"I *know* the circumstances. He is a deceitful dog, and has been ever since he stole from my father, and ran off with—" She swallowed, and turned her face to the wind, relishing the sobering cold. "If you mean do I know how he came by this ship, I must say I do not. But I would bet my fortune that he attained it by nefarious means."

"Then you would now be a pauper, mademoiselle, because he—"

A young voice interrupted her. "Hey, heave to," Jamie cried as he climbed to the quarterdeck like a knight charging to his lady's side. He stepped between Juliana and the Frenchman, brandishing the shawl she'd sent him for like a weapon. "She's my prisoner—Captain said so. You shouldn't be talking with her without asking me first, Viscount."

Juliana's eyes widened. "You are a viscount?"

"Raoul St. Juste, vicomte d'Aubigny-sur-mer," he replied, giving the child a grimace of annoyance. "Unfortunately, my ancestors had the ill luck to lose our chateau and lands in the Revolution."

"Along with their heads," Jamie added with cheerful honesty. "Now the viscount is just a sailor, same as me."

A shadow crossed St. Juste's face, gone too quickly for Juliana to name it. He reached down and gave Jamie's hair a playful mussing. "And there is no finer thing on this earth to be than 'just a sailor,' is there, *mon frère*?"

Juliana looked on, feeling a stark, sudden envy for the easy companionship between the two. Years ago on her father's ship, she too had shared that uncomplicated camaraderie with the sailors. Finishing schools, extravagant balls, court presentations, and social maneuvering had made her discount the contentment of those early years. She'd convinced herself that success was measured by Prinny's good opinion, and that a voucher to Almack's was a passport to heaven. But after several seasons as the pink of London society, with scores of acquaintances and nearly as many admirers, Meg, the Jollys, and recalcitrant Mr. McGregor were the only people she could truly count as her friends. *Though, until a few days ago, I had counted one more. . . .*

"Are you all right, mademoiselle? You look as if you suffer a touch of the *mal de mer*."

"I'm f-fine," Juliana stuttered. 'Twas the salt in the air, no doubt. "Just a bit fatigued, I imagine."

"You look fair wagged out," Jamie pronounced as he frowned with proprietary concern at his charge. "You need supper. If the viscount'll take the prisoner watch, I'll see it's sent to your cabin smart quick."

"It would be a pleasure," St. Juste answered as he gallantly offered Juliana his arm.

As they strolled the twilight deck, the viscount told pleasant, entertaining tales about the sea, the weather, and other neutral subjects. Under other circumstances Juliana would have enjoyed the conversation, but now she could barely manage an interested nod. Her attention was fixed on a point just past the port bow, to where the silhouettes of the *Pelican* and the other merchant vessels could be seen striking half canvas for the night. Slowed to a veritable standstill by the gathering fog and approaching night, the vessels and their guard ship were not nearly as far apart as they had been hours before. If she could lower a boat, or at least find a way to signal the ships to send one . . .

But to do either of these things, she would need the help of at least one member of Connor's crew. And she needed a man who had some measure of authority who would be able to order away the evening watch. She needed a man who retained some of his honor, despite his present treasonous circumstance. Most of all, she needed a man who had a use for her coin—such as someone who had come from privileged circumstances and who might be tempted to see her wealth as a way to buy back some of his family's former glory.

She turned to the viscount and schooled her expression into her most dazzling "belle of the ball" smile. "La, sir, 'tis frightfully pleasant to find a gallant on this vessel. I vow that I was in danger of growing quite buffle-headed for lack of any genteel conversation. . . ."

From that evening on, Juliana's hours on deck were spent in the company of both Jamie and St. Juste. The genial Frenchman took it upon himself to introduce her to the crew members, and she learned that they were all decent, good-hearted men underneath. Even the hulking Barnacle, who had been so intimidating that long ago night when she had first approached Connor's ship, had a little daughter in Surrey whom he missed like the devil and whose very name could bring him close to blubbering. She found it remarkably easy to fall back into the easy cadence of sea slang, like slipping on a pair of comfortable shoes after standing too long in pinched high boots.

She no longer believed that her life was in danger and under other circumstances, she would have found the voyage quite enjoyable. But she could not allow herself to forget that the wardroom contained a box of stolen dispatches or that Connor was still a kidnapper who had betrayed his country. Not to mention the fact that she was wearing the dresses of a mysterious woman named Rose, who knew Connor intimately enough to keep her clothing in the captain's quarters. His light-skirt, no doubt. Not that the fact that Connor had a mistress meant anything to her . . .

"Why so glum, mademoiselle?" St. Juste asked one evening as she stood leaning against the poop deck railing,

Juliana faltered, unwilling to admit that she had been speculating on Connor's love life. "I-I suppose I am concerned for the weather."

Raoul patted her hand. "Do not trouble yourself. The storm could pass us by. In any event, we shall be in Lisbon in three days' time."

Inwardly Juliana cursed herself for letting the time slip by. Now she had only three days to come up with a plan to retrieve the stolen dispatches, reach one of the convoy ships, and make her escape. There was no time to waste.

She glanced around, noting that Jamie was busy playing cat's cradle with the bosun and the rest of the sailors were safely out of earshot. Surreptitiously she bent close to St. Juste's ear. "My lord, you know that I am a wealthy woman. I can offer you a great deal of money—enough to buy back your chateau and lands. All you need do is help me to signal one of the convoy ships. We could lower a longboat tonight, and—sir, tell me that you are not laughing!"

" 'Tis impossible not to," Raoul said, trying nobly to douse his amusement. "Oh, it was a grand effort, and not entirely untempting, but you are wasting your breath. Neither I nor any man on this ship would betray our captain."

Juliana gripped the rail in profound disappointment. St. Juste was her best hope. To know that he was not even remotely interested put paid to nearly all of her plans. "You fear him that much, then?"

"Fear? Lady, look around." He made a sweeping gesture around the deck of the snow. "Do these look like frightened men?"

The motley assembly of hard-bitten men seemed as contented as well-fed babes as they performed their evening tasks. A wiry man scaled the ratlines to the crow's nest like an eager monkey. A portly gent she'd come to know by the nickname of Powder polished one of the ship's arsenal of cannons with the pride of a papa for his bairn. Near the mainmast, a group of tars joined in for a lusty sailing ditty, though she noticed the main bellower was given a silencing look by Connor before the lyrics turned too ribald.

All in all, it was one of the most well-managed, contented vessels she'd ever been on. And it disconcerted her mightily that a man as duplicitous as Connor could enjoy such loyalty from his men. "All right. I shall admit that the captain runs a yar ship. But that does not excuse the fact that he is a treasonous brigand who thought nothing of kidnapping a defenseless woman."

"No woman with eyes like yours could ever be defenseless," Raoul replied with a thoughtful smile. "As I have said before, the captain had no wish to kidnap you, until your untimely discovery forced his hand. And as for his treason—well, I warned you that the world is not always a place of black and white. If you would but give the man a chance—"

"To do what? To betray my country? To deliver secrets into enemy hands, which might cost hundreds of soldiers and sailors their lives? To thrust even greater sorrow and despair on my dear family, who must be crazed with worry by now?" She lifted her chin proudly. "No, monsieur. The captain will receive no quarter from me. Once he was a man of honor, but those days are long past. Were it in my power, I would send him straight to Hades."

Raoul pressed his finger to his brow. "*Alors,* 'tis amazing there are *any* children."

"What?"

"Nothing. In any event, we cannot change the past, and it is sometimes almost as difficult to change our futures. It is likely that all on this ship will be dead before the year is out. Because I shall probably never see you again, I desire to speak with you on an entirely different matter. Something that has been much on my mind."

Juliana watched in surprise as the suave Frenchman glanced down and started to kick the instep of his boot like an uncertain schoolboy.

"In days you shall be returned to the bosom of your loving family. This unpleasant episode shall fade as an unsavory nightmare. But before you put the memory entirely out of your mind, I would ask you—*mais non,* I would *implore* you—to speak with some charity of me to Mademoiselle Evans. Though I shall never see that good lady again, I should like to think that somewhere in this world there is someone who remembers me as a man of noble honor, rather than as the penniless rascal that I truly am."

I am a block of wood, Juliana thought. In all the days she had spent in Raoul's company, she had never regarded his few but telling mentions of Meg, never taken note of the cautious questions and heartbeat pauses when he spoke her name. Completely absorbed by her own predicament, she had given little thought to anyone else's concerns. She reached up and cupped his cheek. "My lord, whatever ill-luck set me on this voyage, you have shown me nothing but kindness during it. I shall be pleased to relate the particulars of your gallant behavior to Miss Evans. And who can say? Perhaps someday you shall have the opportunity to tell her face to—"

Connor's roar split the quiet evening like cannon fire. "Mr. St. Juste, return to your duties at once!"

Raoul drew himself up to his full height as he replied, "But I am not presently on duty—"

"You are now. Beat to the forecastle. At once!"

Raoul gave Juliana an apologetic glance, then strode off toward the bow. Juliana watched him go, her courage sinking lower by the second. For a week she had barely seen Connor's shadow. Now he loomed over her like an angry god, the twilight gathering round him like a cloak, his eyes blazing. "Sir, there was no cause to—"

He ignored her. "Jamie, see to the lady's quarters. She is to remain in the cabin for the rest of the voyage."

"But that is three whole days!" Juliana cried. "I have not broken my parole. 'Tis unjust to confine me. I will not have it."

All activity on the ship came to a dead stop. For several moments the only sounds were the creak of the rocking hull and the occasional flap of the evening wind in the sails. Every sailor stared transfixed at the raised deck, at the woman who had dared to talk back to the captain.

Juliana had faced Connor's anger, but she had never weathered the full force of his cold fury. She stared into the depths of his eyes, into a soul as remote and unforgiving as the rocky slopes of hell. But even under the damning gaze she felt the unseen chain that stretched between them. She felt the power radiating from him like a dark sun. She caught his heady, masculine scent on the wind. She remembered her dreams, the shameless fantasies that conquered her in his bed. Against her will, she felt her traitorous body start to ache with unsated need. In the heart of the ice, she burned.

"You will do as I say, my lady," he threatened, his jagged voice strained to the edge of control. "Obey me, or I will make you regret your insubordination in ways you cannot even imagine."

Juliana swallowed, her heart thundering. Terror rose in her like a wave. Still, she kept her chin high. The Connor she'd once cared for was dead, but the man he'd become was

still humane enough to earn the respect of his men. Somewhere behind the ice wall of his unforgiving countenance
there had to be a spark of human decency. And that man deserved a last chance to clear himself.

She licked her lips, and tried one final time to reach him.
"Connor, for the sake of your country, for the sake of the officer you once were and who I . . . cared for, please give up
this traitorous scheme."

For an instant she saw a spark of vulnerability in his eyes.
"If you wish to live, I suggest you never mention our pasts
again."

He turned to leave, but she spoke first, her words tumbling out like jackstraws. "I'm sorry for what happened between us. Perhaps if I had known that you needed the money,
I could have arranged something . . . but Raoul said I cannot
change the past."

He turned back to her slowly. "Raoul? You use his *Chris-
tian* name?"

She pressed on with her heartfelt words. She had failed to
save him in the past, but she still had a chance to save him
now. "It is not yet too late. You still have time to return the
dispatches and regain some measure of your honor."

"Honor?" He spat the word like a curse. "You are a fine
one to talk of honor, when you just tried to seduce St. Juste."

Seduce! Her eyes widened as she recalled how she taken
Raoul's face in her hands, a gesture of friendship that had
been completely misinterpreted. "That was not the way of
it. I was only trying—"

"I know bloody well what you were trying," he answered,
his chilling gaze impossibly becoming colder. "God knows,
I'd expected you'd changed since we were children, Juliana. But I never thought you'd stoop so low that you'd barter
your body."

He turned and started to stride away. But she could not let
him leave—not while he believed that she would . . . that she
could . . . Her mind could not even fashion the words for

what he believed she'd done. She ran after him and caught his sleeve. "Connor, listen to me. I would never do such a thing. I could never—"

He gripped her wrist and spun her around, pinning her arm painfully against her back. He leaned forward, pressing so close that his body molded to the length of her back. "Do not, for one instant, mistake me for one of your palsied admirers, or for a man of character like Raoul. I could strip you of whatever's left of your precious honor in a heartbeat. And," he growled, bending so close that his hot breath seared her ear, "I could make you beg for more."

He released her so quickly she staggered against the railing for support. She watched him stride off until the twilight swallowed him up. Only then did she find the strength to breathe again.

She had to escape. She had to retrieve the dispatches and leave this ship. Before England's plans fell into enemy hands. Before she lost courage. Before it was too late.

Before she gave in to her shameful desires and sought out his bed.

15

The midnight bell tolled to silence.

Beneath the deck in the aft cabin, Juliana craned her neck as she listened to the footsteps of the changing watch. With her gaze fixed on the ceiling, she followed the sound of the footfalls across the deck above. *He stops at the aft railing. Then a slow turn to the left. Nine measured steps across the deck, and down the ladder to the quarterdeck . . .*

Since the beginning of her imprisonment, she'd listened to the midnight watch. She knew she had some fifteen minutes before the footfalls of the watch returned, minutes that would spell the difference between defeat and disaster. She slipped out of bed and hurried to the aft bay window, where some hours earlier she had carefully broken out a glass pane. She reached outside and felt the hull until her hand found the knotted rope that she had dropped over the side a few days past.

St. Juste had been her best plan for escape, but he had not been her only plan.

Gripping the rope, she cautiously eased herself backwar
out of the window, trying not to look at the churning blac
water far below. The night wind hit her bare shoulders, fo
she'd stripped down to her shift for the climb, but sh
clenched her teeth and continued to work her way out of th
small opening. A sudden roll of the ship yanked her rough
from her perch, and for a terrified moment she swung ou
over the emptiness with only her grip on the rope saving he
from falling. Then her feet found purchase on one of th
knots. She laid her cheek against the coarse hemp while he
heart slowed to a manageable beat. Then, hand over hand
she climbed the hull to the aft deck of the ship.

Once topside, Juliana hurried to the midship, steerin
clear of the signal lanterns hung at the corners of the deck
The masts, rigging lines, and lowered canvas provided ampl
cover, and she was easily able to crouch behind a moonsa
under repair as the watch passed by. She glanced across th
bow and saw the stern lights of one of the convoy ship
straight ahead, barely a hundred feet off the port bow. No
that they were virtually at a standstill she could climb dow
the bowline and swim to the nearest ship. The water woul
be cold, but if she lowered herself into it slowly, she could er
dure it for that short distance, and the storm current woul
help drive her toward the convoy vessel. At least, she hoped
would.

Once she was on the ship, they could slip away in the fo
and lay on sail before Connor realized they'd gone. By th
time the sun rose, they'd be well on their way to Lisbon, to
many hours ahead for him catch up with them before the
reached the harbor and its naval fleet. Faced with th
prospect of fighting English warships instead of unarme
merchant vessels, Juliana had no doubt that the Archange
would turn tail and run back to his frog masters.

All she had to do to foil Connor's treasonous plot wa
to swim over to the nearest convoy ship. That—and on
thing more.

Once again she waited for the watch to pass by. Then she
urried through the shadows and climbed through the hatch
own to the lower deck. Tiptoeing through the narrow
allway, she paused in front of the door to the wardroom.
ardly daring to breathe, she gingerly slid back the door bolt
d slipped inside.

After a moment, her eyes grew accustomed to the faint
ght gleaming through the porthole from the deck above. It
asn't much—most of the room was in complete darkness—
t it was enough to make out the shape of the cupboard, and
the small chest that rested on top.

Juliana snatched the chest from its perch and headed for
e door. But her steps slowed. The evidence inside the chest
ould send Connor to the gallows if he were captured. She
ew she should jump at the chance to send a traitor to his
ath. And yet the thought of Connor being put to death—
d by her hand—filled her with an anguish so great that the
in of it nearly robbed her of breath.

A light flared in the darkness as the man in the room's far
rner lit a single candle. "Hello, Princess."

"Connor. Wh . . . what are you doing here?"

His smile gleamed in the flickering light. "Waiting for you.
new you'd try to escape tonight. Saw it in your eyes. And I
ew that whatever you tried, you'd never leave the dis-
tches behind. Of course, I didn't know you'd come for
em in such a—now, how would your fashionable friends
t it?" He paused as his gaze ran over her from head to toe.
h, I have it. In a such a topping rig."

She swallowed, shamed by his mockery—and by the
rnal heat that coursed through her. She clutched the chest
dispatches as if it were a shield. "You will not get away with
is. I've . . . I've already signaled the nearest ship."

"You've signaled no one," he said, taking a step closer.
ou would never risk their lives to save your own. Besides,
u've been watched since you climbed that rope to the aft
ck—which, by the way, was a damned fool thing to do. If

I'd known you meant to pull such a cork-brained stunt, I'
have locked you up in irons for your own safety. The wind
have kicked up hellish crosscurrents and that water's cold a
death. You might have been killed."

"And deprived you of the pleasure of performing that tas
yourself," she finished, her voice as brittle as corn husks.

He reached up and brushed his knuckles across her chee
so tenderly that she could barely suppress a quiver of desire
"I already told you—I will not harm you. How many times d
I have to say it?"

"A thousand times would not be enough. I could neve
trust a man who could betray his country."

"There are many kinds of betrayal." He stroked her face
carving the path of his scar on her untouched cheek. "Whe
your father banished me, you turned your back on me like a
the rest of your class. I doubt you remembered me an hou
after I was gone."

An hour after he was gone, she was striding through th
winter night after him. " 'Tis not true," she breathed in word
barely above a whisper. "I loved you."

He bent so close that she could feel the warm caress of h
breath on her cheek. She wanted him—God, she ached fo
him! It would be so easy to take a step closer, and offer he
lips to his caress. She remembered the kiss in Jolly's office-
the burning glory she'd become in his arms. It would be s
easy to give in to the need throbbing within her. All it re
quired was that she give up her family, her country, he
honor. . . .

"Lie or no lie, you were my savior, Princess. Though a
the dark days and darker nights, your memory was the on
thing that kept me sane. I'll never hurt you. Never."

"Then let me go," she pleaded.

He paused a heartbeat before repeating, "Never."

He dropped his hand and stepped toward the door. '
shall have someone take you back to your cabin. At the m
ment I would not trust myself with that task."

She closed her eyes, her cheeks blossoming with shame as she realized how close she had come to betraying her country for his caress. He had to be stopped, and she was the only one who could do it.

Taking a deep breath, she uttered what she hoped would sound like a come-hither sigh. "Connor, I would be pleased if you would accompany me to my cabin."

His eyes widened.

"When I think that I shall never see you again, well, I—" she wiped away a tear that was not there.

He gave her a shrewd glance. "What are you up to, minx?"

Still holding the chest, she sidled closer. "If you cannot figure it out, then I am doing it wrong. I am only a woman, Connor," she breathed as she lifted her lips to his.

His look was wary. Nevertheless, her offered mouth proved too much of temptation. "Dammit, Juliana, you don't know how much I've wanted this. How I've dreamed of—"

She shoved the dispatch chest soundly into his unmentionables.

He bent double and cursed impossible combinations of anatomy. But before he drew a second breath Juliana had already sprinted down the hallway and up to the deck, with the chest securely tucked under her arm. She sped down the length of the ship, jumping ropes and canvas. She made for the forecastle, her gaze fixed on the distant light of the convoy ship and freedom—until at the last moment a hulking sailor stepped from behind the mainmast and blocked her path.

"Sorry, miss, but ya can't pass," Barnacle apologized. "I gots my orders."

She turned to the left and found her way blocked by another sailor. Spinning around, she came face to face with a sympathetically smiling Raoul. She backed against the railing and stared at an unbreachable wall of sheepish but resolute sailors. Her horror increased as she caught sight of Jamie and the bosun on the forecastle, signaling the convoy ships to back away.

The wall of sailors parted and Connor stepped forward his tender expression replaced by one of pure murder. "I've had enough of this, Juliana. You've taken your best shot. Several," he admitted with a grimace. "But it's over. Time to heave to and admit defeat. Come, give me your hand."

"Never," she cried. She heaved the chest into the sea then she glared at Connor in triumph. "If you still want Napoleon's gold, you'll have to fish for it!"

"Only if Bonaparte wants our old larder bills," Connor replied as he reached into his shirt and pulled out a thick packet of dispatches. "I switched them the day after you found the dispatches."

The day after . . . and all this time she'd been planning to steal them. All this time she thought she'd had a chance. But Connor had already figured all her plans, and ruined every one. From the beginning the deck was stacked in his favor.

"Give me your hand, Juliana. I've won."

She backed away until she pressed against the railing and she had to grip a shroud line to keep from falling. Connor had the dispatches. But if she escaped there was still a chance she could let the Lisbon magistrate know of his plot. If she could just reach the convoy ship.

"You haven't won. Not entirely." Then she let go of the rigging line and plummeted backward into the sea.

The water hit her like a sledgehammer, driving nearly all the air from her lungs. It was freezing cold, like a thousand knives stabbing into every part of her body. Blackness stretched in all directions and she flailed wildly, unable to tell which way was up. A final kick sent her through the surface and she grabbed a lungful of air. Then she started to pull for the nearest convoy ship.

But the waves pushed her backward, the cold, rough water leaching the strength from her limbs. Try as she might she was no match for the ocean. The cold drove through her numbing her arms and legs. Waves battered her body, and the hungry water closed over her again.

She was going to die. Oddly, she felt no fear at the thought. Years ago when she'd almost drowned, she'd fought for life with all her strength. But years ago she hadn't had her heart cut out by a man who'd used her love and trust to betray her country. She loved him and hated him, and the agony was more than she could endure. Growing still, she let herself sink deeper into to depths. No more pain. No more betrayal. She drifted down, her thoughts on the Connor she'd loved. *Dear Lord, he was a good man once. Remember what he was, not what he's become. And if you can, forgive him—*

A hand grabbed her arm and yanked her painfully to the surface. The peace of death shattered—the agony of living returned. Sputtering and coughing she tried to wrench away from her rescuer.

"Lie still, idiot, or I'll knock you senseless."

She froze. Her rescuer was behind her, pulling her toward the ship with long strokes, but she didn't need to see his face to know it would be creased by a livid scar. Salt tears mixed with salt water as she pleaded one last time. "Please, let me go."

"Never," he growled, his low words a promise and a threat. "You're mine. Forever."

"Is he gonna kill her?" Jamie asked quietly.

"C'est possible," Raoul acknowledged with a shrug. It lacked an hour until dawn, and since Connor had brought the girl back on board they'd heard nothing but roars and curses coming from behind the closed door of the captain's cabin. He knew Juliana was all right—at least, she had been all right when he'd wrapped her in thick wool blankets and carried her into the cabin. She'd been spent in body and spirit, but she'd still gifted him with a smile so luminous that it almost outshone Mademoiselle Evans's—a smile that had turned to ash when Connor stormed into the room and ordered him out. "I must admit that I have never seen the captain looking quite so—how you say—bubbling."

"Boiling," the Barnacle supplied from the hatch, where he stood with a group of anxious tars. "The cap'n looked fair ready to spit the little lady for 'is supper. But that might not be such a rum thing. My missus says a man can do with a bit a stirring up once in a while."

Thoughtfully, Raoul twisted his mustache. "Your good wife must have a touch of French in her. But enough. We have a ship to sail, and the dawn will be here too soon. To your hammocks, my friends. *Allons-y!*"

As the men reluctantly shuffled away, Jamie tugged on Raoul's sleeve. "But I should stay here. I'm her watch. What if she tries to escape again?"

"She will not escape tonight. Neither, I think, will our good captain."

Jamie scratched his chin. "I don't understand."

"You will. In a few years." He lifted the child in his arms and carried him down the hallway. Behind them another roar erupted from the room, but Raoul wasn't concerned. Instead, his broad grin grew noticeably wider. "Multitudes of *l'enfants*, I think."

For Connor, seeing Juliana fall into the black waves, knowing that the sea could swallow her in a heartbeat, had given a new meaning to terror. Having her alive—even if she despised him—was the only thing that made his own life worth living. The worst moments of his life had been the frantic, searching minutes when he'd thought he'd lost her forever. The best had been when he dragged her sputtering, kicking, furious body into the longboat and knew she was going to live.

Of course, since that treasured moment, he'd come close to throwing the ungrateful chit right back over the side.

"And another thing," Connor bellowed as he paced the room. "A dozen of my best men jumped into the water to save you. A dozen! You put every one of those men's lives in danger with your foolish act!"

From her strategic beachhead at the end of his bed, Juliana pulled one of the woolen blankets closer around her bare shoulders. In the lonely light of the room's single candle, she gave Connor a murderous glare. "I'm sorry that I endangered your *men*," she stated, clearly not at all sorry that she had endangered him. "But it was not a foolish act. I was trying to escape. As a prisoner it was my duty to—"

"To hell with duty. You could have been killed!"

Juliana raised her chin disdainfully, her aristocratic hauteur somewhat impaired by the fact that at the moment she closely resembled a bedraggled water rat. " 'Twas my duty—something a blackguard like you knows nothing about."

"Don't talk to me of duty, lady. I spent years dutifully keeping your sweet little behind safe from harm—too many years to let you waste your life on an idiot attempt to reach one of the convoy ships. You must have seen they were out of range. God's teeth, I thought you had more sense than that."

"I thought you had better sense, sir. My drowning would have silenced my tongue and spared you a trip to the gallows."

He stopped pacing. Hell, what was he doing? She was on the edge of exhaustion, and he could think of nothing to do but rant at her like an angry fishwife. He went to the bed and reached out to comfort her, stifling the pain that struck him as she shrank away from his touch. "I am not going to hurt you."

Her unaristocratic sailor's oath showed that she didn't trust his veracity.

"I am not going to hurt you," he repeated carefully, trying to school his voice into gentleness. 'Twas like trying to turn a hoary-hided humpback into an angelfish. "You're chilled to the bone. I only want to remove these wet blankets so that you will not catch your death of cold."

" 'Tis your fault. You made me wet."

He let out a long breath, knowing she couldn't possibly understand the licentious images that statement brought to mind. Drawing on his nearly exhausted supply of decency, he clenched his teeth and continued. "I'm taking the blankets. That's an order."

Her suspicious glare showed that she doubted him entirely, but she did allow him to remove the blankets. Without the heavy wrap she looked impossibly fragile, with her still-damp shift plastered to her slender form. For a moment the years rolled back, and he saw her again as the child he'd rescued from the Thames, the lace-and-satin miracle whose green eyes had looked past his filthy appearance and made him remember that he was still a human being. He'd saved her life that day, but she'd saved his soul. She'd become his friend, his joy, his guiding star, and he'd worshiped her with all the fire in his young heart—

His memories disintegrated as his gaze skimmed her front and saw the dark nipple beneath her wet shift. She was no child. He was no innocent boy. And the fire seething in his gut wasn't one of worship. With clumsy haste he tucked the bedsheets around her and practically bolted for the door. *I will return her to her family untouched, even if I have to take a bath in the Arctic Ocean. Every day. Every hour.*

"Connor."

Sweet Lord, she could make him hard just by saying his name. He stopped, but did not turn around. "Aye?"

He heard her slip from the bed and felt her approach. Lust tore through him as he imagined her padding toward him with innocent, coltish grace. Arctic baths. *Every minute.*

She drew in a hesitant breath. "I know you have chosen . . . an ungallant path. I know you have chosen gold over honor. But I have seen the respect in your men's eyes, and I have watched your kindness toward Jamie. And you showed . . . well, surprisingly selfless bravery in rescuing me. There is still—there must be—some goodness in your heart."

Her uncertain voice brushed like silk against his ruined soul. He gripped the door handle, sinking into a torture greater than any he'd experienced on the *Absalom*. "You are mistaken, my lady."

He heard her huff of annoyance and could almost see her planting her hands on her hips. Despite his torture, the image brought a smile to his lips.

"You are monstrously pigheaded. Listen to me. It is not too late. There is still time for you to make amends. When we sail into Lisbon harbor you can hand the dispatches over to the magistrate. If you confess your crime and throw yourself on the mercy of the court, you might escape with your life."

And the sea would lose its salt. " 'Tis not likely. Laws are for the heavy funded or high friended. Who would stand for me in this Lisbon court?"

"I would."

He wished he'd starved on the London docks. He wished he'd drowned with the *Absolom*. Anything would be better than this killing sweetness stabbing through his heart. Bitterness for what could never be rose in his throat. His words came out in shattered pieces. "I . . . thank you. But it is too late. It was too late years ago."

He started to press down on the door handle, but stopped. He heard nothing, felt nothing, yet every instinct in his body went on alert. He spun around and raised his arm—and caught her wrist inches before she brought the last of his crystal glasses crashing down on his head. He easily twisted her arm, ignoring her cry of pain as the heavy glass thumped to the wooden floor and rolled into a corner. Then he yanked her ruthlessly against him so that he could stare down into her luminous, traitorous eyes. "So this is how you meant to stand up for me."

"I did not. I would have helped you, but you chose— Please, you are hurting me."

"I haven't even begun." His eyes glittering with lethal promise. "You called me a betrayer—well, Lady High and Mighty, it seems you're a traitor too. But of course, my kind

doesn't matter to the likes of you. Your breeding is too refined for dirt like me."

"That's not true," she cried. "I . . . I cared for you. Very
much."

He circled her waist and pulled her against him, grinning
wickedly at her shocked gasp when she felt the hard evidence
of his lust. "I care for you, too. *Very* much," he mocked. "But
I draw the line at trading my body for favors. I sell secrets for
gold—but I'm not a professional like you high-born dells,
who are ready to do any randy fop for a lofty title and a—"

Her fierce slap knocked him silent—for a moment. He
rubbed the livid welt and smiled with malice. "That . . . was a
mistake."

"You are a shameless cur," she cried, struggling against his
hold. "You have no decency, no honor. I shall be glad when
they hang you. I hate you. I despise you. I—"

His mouth fused to hers in a crushing kiss.

16

—🌿—

His kiss was as ruthless as his grip. There was no love in it, not a trace of regard they'd once shared. It was a bold, carnal seduction, nothing more. But it was Connor who was doing the seducing, and Juliana couldn't have stopped wanting it any more than she could have stopped her heart from beating.

Desire that had been building inside her for weeks raged in her like a furnace. She didn't want this. She couldn't want this. But as Connor's hot, thorough caress moved from her lips to the sensitive lobe of her ear, she knew he'd already won the battle that had barely begun.

"I hate you," she breathed weakly.

"Yes I know," he growled as he laved moist, searing kisses down the column of her throat.

"I mean it. I despise—oh, Connor!" She sank her fingers in his hair and brought his mouth to hers, eager for more.

For a thousand lonely nights Connor had dreamed of having her in his arms, savaging her with all the aching hunger in his damned, burning soul. His tongue spiraled down into the sweet, wet heat of her mouth. He buried his fingers in the abundance of her hair and held her fast for the plundering assault of his kiss. He feasted on her lips, eyelids, and chin before lingering in the pounding hollow of her throat. He could taste the salt on her skin, a remembrance of the death he'd narrowly saved her from. The naked fear of that moment returned, stoking the already white-hot flames of his desire. *If she'd died . . . if I'd lost her forever . . .*

His mouth took hers, drowning her in a caress far darker and hungrier than the ocean beneath them.

She was fire. In all her dreams, she'd never imagined the deep, coiling heat that pulsed from her core. It was nothing like the tepid fondlings of her admirers. She buried her fingers in his chest hair, loving the way he was made, gorging on his strength and power. For the first time she knew what a woman was made for—what she was made for. Pleasure. Seduction. *Connor.*

"Juliana," he whispered against her throat, his husky voice seducing her every bit as much as his hungry caress. "I need you. God, how I need you."

Her blood bubbled like molten lava. His hands were everywhere, coaxing and fondling her yielding body with the same brutal mastery as his wicked kiss. He was a villain and a traitor, and she wanted to hate him with every fiber of her being. But he was also Connor—her Connor—the man she loved with every broken piece of her heart. Her duty to her country vied with her love of the man, the two forces warring in her soul. She leaned against his chest, exhausted by war and passion. "Connor . . . you are tearing me . . . apart."

His caresses ceased. Slowly, as if every muscle in his body ached, he raised his head and stared down into her eyes. The pain in them ripped her soul. He dropped his arms and turned away. "Forgive me, my lady. I will not trouble you again."

"Connor. Please . . . I want to . . . but how can I love you when you have given me every reason to distrust you? How can I believe in you?"

"You did once," he offered quietly. "Without thought or reason, you believed in me without question, and trusted me with your heart."

"Yes, and you shattered it! You asked me to marry you when you already had another *lover*."

Connor froze. "What are you talking about?"

"You heard me," she stated as she went back to the bed, and slumped down on to the edge with barely contained misery. "I know you loved another."

"Juliana, I fully admit that I've done a number of despicable things in my life, but when I offered for you I was pure."

He'd meant to allay her doubts. Instead the misery in her eyes increased. "Save your pretty speeches. After you left the house that night, I followed you to your rooms. I was . . . was going to run away with you."

It had taken him years to construct the high, unbreachable ice wall that guarded his heart. It took her a heartbeat to melt it. He stared at her, experiencing the giddy, innocent wonder he hadn't felt since the night she had pledged to be his wife. "You were going to give up your life of privilege, your entire fortune, for me?"

She nodded. "It was foolish, but I did not discover how foolish until I reached your courtyard. I looked up at your window, and I saw . . . There was a shadow on the curtains, on the curtains *I'd* made for you . . . You were in her arms . . . and I knew you'd never truly loved me. Never."

He told himself it was better this way. He had already cost her so much—her trust, her honor, almost her life. He could not take more. The best thing he could do for her was to walk out of her life forever, leaving her with the belief that he'd never been worthy of her love. What was one more lie on top of so many?

Swallowing his misery, he walked to the door and reached for the handle, knowing he was doing the right thing, the best thing, the honorable thing . . .

A thing he could no more do than he could stop loving her.

"Juliana, the woman you saw that night. She was my sister."

For a long time, there was no sound in the cabin save for the creak and groan of the ship's timbers. Then Connor went to the window and stared out at what was left of the night. "I told you that my mother died, but I never told you how. 'Twas in childbirth. A baby girl, fragile as a bud. My mother died within hours of her birth. But before she died she made me swear to take care of the babe. As if I needed urging—to me she was perfect, the one good thing in the filth and squalor that was my life."

He wiped his hand over his face, recalling the horror of those dark days after his mother's death. "During that winter, keeping her alive was what kept me alive. I stole everything I could lay my hands on—not proud of it, but it was all I could do to keep food in our bellies. By some miracle we survived through spring, and I found an innkeeper's wife willing to take her in for a few pennies. Over the years I sent them every piece of blunt that came my way, and saw her whenever I was in port. I never told your father—he had already done so much for me that I had no right to burden him further. My sister was my responsibility.

"I thought she was safe and well, but as my own life became busier, and my own hopes for a future with you began to absorb my attention, I started to see her less and less. I relied on her letters as truth. It proved to be a disastrous error on my part.

"On New Year's Day, the very morning after I offered for you, she appeared at my door in a deplorable state. She had to leave the city at once, and the only way I could think to get

ιe money to help her was to take it from your father's
rongbox. 'Twas the rash act of a desperate young man, but
. the time I saw no other way. Her honor was at stake. In-
eed, perhaps her life."

Behind him, Connor heard the ropes creak under the
ιattress as Juliana moved off the bed, but she said nothing.
'er silence cut his heart. He'd hoped for a word of under-
anding, acknowledgment, anything. But she had gone
ιrough a lifetime of changes that night, and this final revela-
on might have been just too much for her gently bred soul
ɔ endure. "Whatever the reason, I still stole the money from
ɔur father, a man who had shown me nothing but kindness. I
ɔ not expect your forgiveness any more today than I did
ears ago. All that I can offer is that I have paid a thousand
ιmes over for my dishonor, because I lost you. And I hope
ιat, someday, you might find it in you to—"

"You *idiot*!" Juliana stood behind him, transformed from a
eartbroken waif to a furious warrior whose eyes blazed with
ιre murder from the depths of her "gently bred soul." "Do
ɔu know the agony I suffered over you, the years of . . . Why
id you never tell me that you had a *sister*?"

"I told you. My sister was my responsibility. You and
ɔur father had already done so much for me. I planned to
•ll you after we were wed, but as a man of honor, I couldn't
xpect—"

Juliana hit him on his shoulder.

Connor rubbed the stinging spot. She'd never best
Villiam Mace, but when her blood was up, she could deliver
prime mendozy. "Quit this foolishness."

"I only wish I had a cannon! Man of honor, my barnacled
ull! Your idiotic gallantry broke my heart."

"I was trying to protect you. I was—oh no you don't!"

As Juliana hauled back for another strike, Connor's hand
ruck out and captured her wrist. Deprived of the use of her
sts, the still-furious woman attempted to kick him in the
ιin. Cursing roundly, Connor gathered up the struggling

hellcat and dumped her back on the bed, where he pinned down her flailing fists and legs before he continued. "Listen to me! My sister was badly abused. The man who'd seduced her was a powerful peer, one of your cousin Grenville's set, and he was obsessed with her beyond reason. He'd already set men to track her. She pleaded with me not to tell the marquis or your cousin for fear the fiend might catch wind of it."

"You could have told *me*. My mother's jewels—"

"—were not mine to take. I loved you too much to ask. He laid his forehead against hers and breathed a sigh of heartache. "Maybe I did make foolish choices, but I was one-and-twenty, and still more boy than man. And my sister was only fourteen."

Fourteen, Juliana thought, her anger fading. Two years younger than she'd been at the time. She turned her head to the side, sickened. "That poor girl. Who was the man?"

"I know not. He never gave his name, and they met in a secluded apartment. She knew he was nobility from his manners and the names he mentioned—including Grenville's. At first I'd intended to return and see that the devil paid for his infamy, but I was . . . prevented. By the time I was able to return, the trail had long since grown cold."

"You should have told me."

"I'd have moved heaven and earth not to," he murmured as he brushed cherishing kisses across her brow. "I wanted to save you from the knowledge that such animals existed. I was my duty to protect you."

"I wasn't a child," she protested softly as his lips moved to her throat.

"You were a babe. So was I." Lord, she was pure temptation. Unable to resist, he feasted on the sweet flesh behind her ear, and felt her breath catch in response. "I need you, Princess."

"We need each other," she breathed, bound up in a love neither could resist. "We always have. But between my stubborn pride and your foolish honor—"

She went absolutely still. Alarmed, Connor raised himself and gazed down into her troubled eyes. "Juliana?"

"Connor, these past months at the line have taught me something of human nature. And it is hard for me to fathom that a man who once gave up everything he had or hoped to have—including marriage to a wealthy heiress—to save his sister would turn around and sell out his country for a few pieces of brass." She paused, her beautiful eyes narrowing with a businesswoman's shrewdness as she asked, "So what is *really* going on here?"

He opened his mouth, but instead of words, the sound of thunder rocked the cabin. Connor sat up, wrapping Juliana protectively in his arms. The thunder sounded again.

"It's getting closer," she said, instinctively pressing closer. " 'Tis a spindrift gale, sure."

"That is no storm," he stated in a funereal voice. "That's cannon fire."

"What's the situation, Mr. St. Juste?"

"French corvettes," Raoul said as he handed Connor the spyglass and pointed to the grim brightening in the storm-gray east. "We did not see them in the rain. Two, I think."

"Make it three." Connor lowered the glass and gripped the rail. "Dammit, why send that kind of firepower after a supply convoy?"

"Perhaps they are not after the convoy?"

Connor's jaw pulled tight. "Then they are in for a disappointment."

He started to stride down the deck, taking a quick survey of the ship. "The lads have beat to quarters, but even they'll have a time of it against three armed—Mr. Barnacle!" he bellowed, "keep your ham-fisted assistant away from that cannon block, or we'll all be meeting Davy Jones."

"Aye, sir," Barnacle said sheepishly.

Connor approached the assistant. "Remember, 'tis not the first shot that matters, but the last."

"Aye," the lad said as he returned to his cannon, clearly elated at the thought of the approaching battle.

Connor watched him, a grim smile crossing his face. He'd seen the face of war too often to feel any thrill at the prospect. Men would die today. Maybe he would die today. And by God, he wanted to live, now more than ever.

For a precious instant he allowed himself to savor the memory of Juliana's sweet declaration of love, of the impossible, unexpected wonder that she had been willing to give up her life of privilege for him all those years ago. At that moment nothing could have dragged him from her side—except the volley of French guns.

He marched the deck to the forecastle, to where Raoul stood against the bow railing. "Three against one," he said shrugging. "Hardly seems sporting."

" 'Tis a canter in the park," Connor agreed, knowing neither of them meant it. "Signal the convoy ships to run like the devil. 'Tis the only way we can ensure their safety. We'll give them as much time as we can, but tell the captains to lay on all sail. And signal the *Pelican* to wait. I've got a job—God's teeth, what is that idiot doing?"

Connor watched as one of the merchant ships broke away from the pack and started for the corvettes. He jumped to the forecastle and rubbed the rain from his eyes. " 'Tis the *Pelican*. That young idiot Jamison must be seeking a medal. Tell him to return and lay alongside, Mr. St. Juste. I have passengers for him to collect."

"If you mean me," a quiet voice behind him commented, "you had best tell him to sail on. I am not leaving."

Connor spun around, and came face to face Juliana in an oversized oilskin and a listing sou'wester. "I ordered you to stay below."

"I am not afraid of a fight."

"Well, I am." Connor gripped her arm, and pulled her nose to nose as he continued. "This isn't some *Gazette* article about an antiseptic battle. There are two hundred cannons on those ships, and in a little while all of them will be trained on this vessel. Not to mention the sharpshooters in the rigging, ready to pick off anything that moves, or the flaming brands they could shoot at our sails, or the rifles and bayonets we'll face if we're boarded. There's death in every quarter, Princess."

"Then I want to face it with you. I don't care if it is right or honorable. I lost you once, I could not bear to lose you again."

Her shining eyes scored truer hits than any cannon shot. There were a hundred things he wanted to say to her, and a hundred more things he wanted to do to her—and not a bloody one of them was appropriate for a water-drenched deck at the start of a battle with nearly two hundred curious sailors looking on. *Bad time for a war,* he thought as he handed her roughly to Raoul. "Take charge of her, Mr. St. Juste. And see that she and Jamie get on that ship!"

Raoul glanced Connor's back, then returned his gaze to Lady Juliana. "It would appear things have changed," he offered. "You no longer wish to kill our captain?"

"No," she admitted. "But I understand none of this. You are supposed to be spies. Connor has stolen vital dispatches. But you are fighting French ships—your own countrymen—"

"Not my countrymen, lady," Raoul said darkly. "I am French, yes, but I do not serve the despot Bonaparte. His murdering dogs killed my uncle, the best man who ever walked this earth. This was his ship, *Le Rêve*, the Dream. He had a dream of peace. At first—after the terror of the Revolution—he thought Napoleon would bring that peace. My uncle served him, as did I. But power corrupted the emperor's once noble intentions, and my uncle left France rather than fight for a madman.

"But Napoleon, he could not let such a man leave his court and live. He sent men to hunt him down, and slaughtered him under a flag of truce. If not for Connor, I and many of the men on this ship would be dead as well. He sailed us through a narrow passage where the larger ships could not follow, staying at the helm though he was badly wounded himself."

"But why did you not tell me this before?"

"*Ma petite*, would you have listened?"

No, she would not have. Until that night she would have believed almost nothing good about Connor. She'd let her pride and pain over Connor's long-ago betrayal blind her to the man he'd become. Now she realized how badly she'd misjudged him. Now, when it might be too late.

Another cannon volley sounded, followed by the crack of lumber. Juliana ran to the rail and peered through the rain. "The *Pelican*! They've split her mainmast."

"She is lost to us. Even now she lowers her colors in surrender. They will take her as a prize, but at least her sailors shall be safe—"

His words ended as the nearest corvette fired again. The ball smashed into the *Pelican*, splitting the ship in two. She sank in minutes. Juliana gripped the rail, unable to believe the horror she'd just witnessed. "They've hulled her. With her colors down. . . . All those men . . . my men . . ."

She didn't even know Connor was behind her until he took her in his arms. "Take the helm, Mr. St. Juste. I'll be there shortly."

"They killed her, Connor. With her colors down."

"There's no honor in war, whatever the poets say." Connor cradled her against him. "I know what it is to face treachery in battle."

"Raoul told me," she said, lifting her gaze to his. "He told me about his uncle's ship, and how it was attacked by the French. He told me how you saved them."

"Not all of them. Daniel died, and so did many others— brave men who deserved death no more than young Jamison on the *Pelican*. But I'll make those corvettes pay for what they've done. I swear it."

"No," she cried softly. "I want you to run. I don't care about duty, or honor, or anything else. I want you safe."

He smoothed back a strand of her damp hair and tucked it behind her ear. "The course is set, and there is nothing either of us can do to change it. I've got a battle to fight, and you— ah, here's the fellow now."

Barnacle walked up, carrying the struggling Jamie under his arm. "Found him on orlop deck, hiding beneath the water casks. Harder to catch than a rat, he is."

"Put me down," the boy cried. "I'm not going."

"Neither am I," Juliana declared, with less struggle but no less certainty. "Not unless you truss me up like a Christmas goose and send me over the side."

"An interesting image." Connor grinned. "But not necessary."

He signaled Barnacle to release the boy, then knelt down and took his shoulders. "Sir, you shall accompany Lady Juliana because she is still in grave danger, and you are still assigned to protect her. 'Tis your duty, sir, and you shall continue to perform it until"—he glanced up at Juliana—"until I release you from that charge."

Jamie worried his lip, struggling between doing his duty and sticking with his mates. In the end he nodded. "Aye, captain," he said as he saluted and headed for the longboat.

Juliana watched him go, crossing her hands resolutely in front of her. "I am not yours to order, sir. Jamie can go, but I am staying."

Connor's mouth ticked up. "I thought you might say something like that. So I brought this." He took an oilskin-wrapped packet out of his coat and stuffed it securely into her belt. "See that they get to the proper authorities."

Juliana's eyes filled with tears as the last piece of Connor's supposed treachery fell out of place. "The dispatches. Oh,

Connor, I knew in my heart that you were an honorable man. If only I had listened to my heart all those years ago . . ."

"No time for regrets, lady. No time for anything, except—"

He swept off her hat and pulled her into his arms, capturing her mouth in one last caress. He tasted of smoke and battle and courage, and she returned his kiss with all the fury of the corvette's cannons. For a moment there was no war, no danger, just two people who'd found their hearts in each other's arms. Then he groaned and swept her up, lifting her into the longboat.

"I love you," she cried as the cables creaked and the boat lowered to the waves.

"Then trust me," he bellowed back. "I love you, no matter what happens—God's teeth, Mr. Markham, will you shore up that mizzenline? The prince regent could tie a better rigging knot—"

The oarsmen pulled away, rowing the longboat toward the merchant ship St. Juste had signaled when the *Pelican* went down. Juliana sat huddled in the center, hardly aware of Jamie's arms around her as she watched the corvettes open fire on Connor's ship. The shots streamed like red fireballs over the bow and stern, striking no wood but tearing through the main canvas. Juliana saw Connor standing on the forecastle, silhouetted against the smoke and flames like the devil himself. He lifted his sword, and brought it down in a sharp command.

Then the snow's cannons thundered in one voice and turned the top deck of the nearest corvette to kindling.

"She's scored a hit," Jamie cried. "I knew the captain would beat them. I knew—"

His triumph died as another corvette took aim and splintered the snow's topgallant, raining shards of fire on the deck below.

"Connor!" Juliana jumped to her feet. Dispatches or no dispatches, she couldn't leave him. Her duty to her country was nothing compared to her duty to him. Her place was at his side, even if it meant her death. Turning, she cried to the oarsmen. "We must go back! I can't leave—"

The longboat bobbed on a high wave and she lost her balance. Her last sight of the snow was of Connor lifting his sword for another volley. Then her head hit the edge of the hull and she knew no more.

17

—🌿—

Pine and foxglove. Juliana twitched her nose, wondering how the ocean could suddenly smell like a mountain forest. She slit her eyes open, blinking against the light. She was lying on her side on homespun sheets that smelled of soap, dressed in a nightrail made of much the same material. Beside her, a clapboard window was open to the afternoon sun, which poured in like thick, bright butterscotch. Most definitely not the ocean. She started to rub the sleep from her eyes, but paused as her fingers met a bandage that appeared to be wrapped around her forehead. Fragments of memory began to fit together in her mind. The longboat. The smoke and flames. The thundering cannons firing on Connor's ship.

She'd lost consciousness in the thick of a lopsided battle. Her last vision of Connor had been of him standing on the deck with his sword raised, in the direct line of fire of the enemy cannons. He could be wounded. He could be—

An unfamiliar sawing sound behind her caught her attention. She looked behind her to the other side of the bed and saw a man slumped in a corner chair. His white shirt was soiled with the soot and smoke of the battle, he badly needed a shave, and his blond hair fell across his forehead in a most unseemly tangle. And he was snoring.

He looked almost as ill-kempt as he had on the day when she had first met him. And to Juliana's eyes, that made him the most handsome, most magnificent, most wonderful sight in the world.

She shook his knee. "Connor. Darling, wake up."

He jerked awake, almost falling out of the chair. For a moment he glanced around in confusion, as if he too expected to still be on the open sea. Then his gaze fell on her and his face burst into a grin of relief and joy. "God, Princess, I thought I'd lost you."

"Fa, from a little knock on the head?" she said nonchalantly, glowing at his confession. But her thoughts quickly turned to those who might have worse injuries. "Connor, all your men—?"

"The men are fine and so is the snow," he assured her as he took her hand. "When we shattered the deck of the first corvette the others lost their nerve. One ran like a yellow dog. The other stayed for one last volley before turning tail. My ship lost her topgallant and a few sails need mending, but otherwise she's as yar as ever. Raoul has taken her on to Lisbon with the rest of the convoy."

Juliana glanced around the room. "This . . . is not Lisbon?"

Connor laughed, a lusty sound that did more to repair her wounded head than an ocean of salve. "Nay. We're in a fishing village just north of the Douro River. 'Twas the closest port I could make after the battle, and with the way your head was bleeding I couldn't chance the extra days it would take to reach Lisbon. Jamie and I stayed behind to see you safe."

"Jamie! He is not hurt?"

"Not unless you count his pride. He felt I should have trusted him to look after you alone, since that is his charge.

But he was as much in need of rest as you were. And besides, I was not certain he was up to defending you against the formidable Senhora Esmerelda Maria de Varzim."

"Who?"

Before Connor could answer, the door burst open and an elderly matron bustled in, her dark eyes blazing with all the fire of the French cannons. She lodged herself between the two and began to efficiently tuck the covers around Juliana, all the while prattling on in breakneck Portuguese.

"Senhora, please, I do not understand you."

" 'Tis me she is talking to," Connor supplied. "She thinks I am an insensitive lout for disturbing your sleep. She is the most accomplished healer I know, far superior to those powdered quacks in the Lisbon court. But she has the passion of a tigress when it comes to her patient's welfare. I have been ordered out."

"Don't go!" Juliana bit her lip, mortified that she sounded like all the desperate females she so despised. But she could not help it. She was horribly afraid that Connor would disappear from her life as suddenly as he'd appeared. "Please, I want you to stay with me."

"That . . . would not be a good idea." Connor's gaze skimmed to the bedclothes and to her nightrail. In the depths of his eyes something elemental changed. For a moment their gazes met, and Juliana felt the burning that he'd fired in her last night return with a vengeance. Then the senhora gave Connor a determined shove and again began to berate him in her native tongue.

Sighing, he gave Juliana a resigned shrug. "As you see, French warships are nothing compared to this termagant. But she is right. You do need rest."

"I need—" She stopped the words, shocked at the unmaidenly turn of her thoughts. Swallowing, she chose a safer course. "I need to know that you will get some rest also."

He smiled, the same boyish grin that had completely conquered her young heart. "As you wish, my lady."

He left the room, closely followed by the chastising Senhora de Varzim. Even after the door had closed, she could hear the woman's voice carrying down the hall. As she drifted back to sleep she heard the senhora's voice in her head, repeating a phrase she'd used over and over again during her berating. *Esposa.*

Wife.

"And what are those boats called?" Jamie asked. He and Connor stood on the hills overlooking the small harbor of the village.

"Bean-cods," Connor supplied, grimacing at the ridiculous name for a remarkable ship. "The fishermen of Portugal have used them for centuries. The slanted front sail gives them speed and maneuverability, while the broad hull gives them plenty of room to store their catch. They can outrun a ship as fast as our snow."

Jamie's eyes widened. "Could we try it? Have a race, I mean, when our ship comes back for us. We could win a king's ransom."

Connor fought down a grin. Even in the midst of a war, the boy was up for a wager. *There must be some nobleman's blood in him somewhere.* "I do not think so," he admitted. Then, at the boy's crestfallen appearance, he added, "But we will see. Perhaps when Raoul returns with the snow we can see if—"

He stopped as he heard the crunch of loose gravel behind him. He spun around with his hand already on his dagger hilt in a fighting stance. But the intruder was unarmed—or armed to the teeth, depending on how one looked at it.

Juliana was on the path behind them, carefully making her way toward them with that coltish grace that never failed to fascinate him. Her bandage was gone, revealing an unbound fall of hair. Instead of the homespun nightrail, she was now wearing what could only be one of Senhora de Varzim's dresses, for it was far too large for her. But even in the atrocious outfit, she looked as poised as a queen.

Jamie propelled himself into her arms and started a tirade. "Glad you're fine and told captain you would be, even though you bled like a—did you know the corvettes ran away when we fired on—cowards and wished we'd gone after 'em but captain said—that's an ugly dress—"

"Jamie, I think the lady would appreciate it if you finished at least one sentence."

Juliana laughed and gave the boy a hug. "The lady is pleased to hear whatever you have to say. But I think, perhaps, you might want to see the special treat the senhora is cooking up for your dinner. It is called *paseis de nata*."

Jamie was obviously torn between the wish to stay with his charge and his curiosity about the food. In the end, curiosity won. "All right, but promise to come back before it gets dark. It's dangerous up here at night."

Connor's gaze strayed to Juliana, whose hair shone with the light of the first evening stars. *Dangerous* didn't even begin to describe it.

He clamped his hands resolutely behind him. "Jamie is right, my lady. It is not safe to be up here at night, especially when you are still recovering from your head wound."

"I am recovered enough to want some answers." She reached into the voluminous skirt and pulled out an oilskin-wrapped packet. "I found these dispatches with my shoes and hose and the remains of my soot-covered dress. If you truly had any intention of handing them over to the enemy, you would have done so by now. So I ask you again—what is really going on here?"

He'd known from the first she would want to know the truth—just as he knew he could not tell her without further endangering her life. He rubbed his eyes, suddenly feeling tired beyond all measure. "Believe me, it is better that you do not know—"

"The devil it isn't! Connor, in the last few days I have been kidnapped, held prisoner, almost drowned, and survived a

a battle. I think the least you could do is give me the cour-
esy of telling me what I have stepped into the middle of."

"Courtesy?" He threw up his arms. "My lady, this is not an
fternoon tea party. I am trying to keep you safe by shielding
ou from things you are not part of."

"I am part of this because I love you. And unless every-
ing you told me last night about your sister was a lie, then I
elieve you love me, too."

He stared out at the sea and formed words that tasted like
and in his mouth. "Everything I told you was a lie. I do not
ve you."

Her laughter put paid to any faith he had in his acting
bility. "You are such a cake, Connor. 'Tis like it was when we
ere young, and you claimed that you didn't give a fig for me
nd wouldn't care if I walked the ship's railing. Before I took
arely three steps you pulled me down to safety."

"And spanked you soundly," he recalled darkly, remem-
ering the day the twelve-year-old Juliana had dared him to
rove his love. When Connor, an earnest seventeen-year-old
r more aware of his feelings for her than she was, had told
er to suck an egg, she'd hopped up on the midship railing
nd almost tumbled overboard before he yanked her back.
'Twas a damned fool thing to do. You could have been
lled."

"Perhaps. But it was worth it to me to prove that you
ared." She looked over the edge of the cliff at the rocky
each below. "I would say this cliff is quite as treacherous as
at railing. If I were to walk along the edge . . . like this . . . I
onder if you would—"

Her sentence was cut short as the loose rocks slid away be-
eath her, and she started to pitch toward the edge. But be-
re she was in any true danger, Connor grabbed her dress
nd yanked her back, pulling her so forcefully that they tum-
led to the ground. They fell into a stand of heather that
irted the path, with Connor twisting beneath her so that he

broke her fall. He fell with an awkward "umph," which he repeated when she landed on top of him.

"Idiot woman!" he growled. "I could have cracked my
skull."

"Well, perhaps that might have knocked some sense into
it." She pulled herself up his chest so that she was nose-to-
nose with him.

"You are still a spoiled brat."

"And you are still an overbearing bully."

"Selfish chit."

"Pompous know-it-all."

"Minx!"

"Scoundrel!"

They stared at each other, four years of fury and frustration boiling within them. Then they poured that frustration
into a burning caress, sating a need that could only be filled in
each other's arms. They tangled and rolled in the sweet
heather, feasting on the carnal joys of taste and touch. For
endless minutes they gave in to the love that had bound them
as one beyond time, distance, and even truth. Then, groaning
as if with the sound of one soul being ripped in half, Connor
forced himself out of her arms and sat up, gazing out at the
darkening sea. "This . . . cannot happen."

"It already has," she said softly. "It happened years ago.
And you told the senhora that I was your *esposa*."

"I did that—" Connor glanced back, then sharply turned
his eyes again to the sea. The vision of Juliana lying in the
twilit heather with a sprig of it in her hair was not a sight to
cool a man's blood. He thought resolutely of icy winds and
arctic waters. "I did that to protect your reputation. The
senora would have known you were more to me than a pas-
senger when I insisted on staying in the room while you were
recovering. I did not want her to think that you were . . ."

"Your lover?"

"My doxie. This is no romantic midnight tryst in your father's conservatory, and I am no honorable suitor. We're

middle of a war, Juliana. Any hope we might have had of a
ure died years ago.

"In a week's time Raoul will return with my ship. A day or
o afterward, officials will be arriving from Lisbon to take
u home. You will go back to your life of wealth and privi-
e. I will go back to a life of—well, something less. We shall
ly never see each other again."

Juliana sat up and curled against his back, resting her
eek on his shoulder. "Then 'tis sensible that we spend what
le time we have left together."

Sensible? A sensible move like that would get her ruined
d put him in torment. He was already going to have to
end the rest of his arguably short life doing his best to
get her sweet kisses. Anything more would drive him mad.
Stiffly he rose to his feet and pulled her up after him. "From
s moment on I am going to do my best to avoid you. I sug-
t you do the same. Now, head back down the path, Juliana.
 follow a few paces behind. And God's teeth, if you so
ch as try to look back at me I'll see that the senhora locks
 in your room until I'm gone."

Juliana did as he asked. She walked down the path with
 gaze dutifully ahead, never looking back. But though she
eared to follow his orders, her mind was whirling. She
ed Connor, and he loved her, and unless something drastic
pened, he would be gone forever in a week.

Years ago she'd let him walk out of her life, and nothing
 been right since. She did not know what intrigues he was
t of. She did not even really know which side he was
king for. But she was certain of one thing. She was not let-
 the man she loved walk out of her life without a fight.
 was going to make it as impossible for him to imagine
ng without her as it was for her to imagine living with-
 him.

By the time she had reached the bottom of the path,
 had firmly decided that she was going to seduce Con-
 Reed.

18

—❧—

The trouble with seduction, Juliana thought bleakly as s
walked along the beach several days later, is that if one we
not familiar with the particulars, it's damned difficult to fi
out about. Mrs. Jolly had taught her about the mores
London society. McGregor had taught her about running t
Marquis Line. But when it came to making a man take her
his bed, she was definitely at sixes and sevens. There were
books to be had on the subject. The women in the village w
might answer her questions did not speak her language.
fact, the only certain knowledge she had about the act w
the rather cryptic suggestion of one of her finishing scho
teachers, who had advised her to close her eyes and think
England.

As she walked past the wharf, a few of the fisherma
wives who were busy mending nets called out a greeting
her. She waved her hand in reply, returning their simple he
with honest appreciation. After the tangled intrigues of t
ton and the equally complex maneuverings of the shippi

siness, the uncomplicated friendship of these people
emed like a gift from heaven. They lived in harmony with
e ocean, marking their lives not by balls and parties but by
e ebb and flow of the tide. It was a hard life, but it filled
liana with a peace and satisfaction she'd never felt in the
ll-appointed salons of Mayfair. In a way she could not
derstand, a part of her life would always be bound up in
e sea. Just as a part of her soul would always be bound
in loving Connor.

Juliana's thoughts ended abruptly as someone jostled her
ow. She looked over into the broad, grinning face of Sen-
ra de Varzim. Still grinning, she pointed at the water.
arido."

Juliana shook her head. "Pardon, Senhora. I do not
derstand."

"Conn-air," the lady replied, still pointing at the sea.
arido."

"Oh, my, er, husband," Juliana acknowledged. "Yes, he
d Jamie went out with the other fishermen this morning to
lp with the catch." *And to avoid me.*

The older woman nodded toward the ocean and began
eaking in breakneck Portuguese. Juliana waved her hands.
Tis no good, senhora. I cannot understand you."

Hmphing, the signora tried again. With her right hand she
pped Juliana's shoulder. *"Esposa."* Then with her left hand
e made a fist. *"Marido."* She flung her two hands apart.

Juliana grimaced. "Yes, I suppose that is as good a way to
plain it as any. We've had a bit of a spat."

"Spat." The senhora tasted the word, clearly finding it
appetizing. Once again she shook her right hand and
en her left. *"Esposa. Marido."* Smiling, she brought her
o hands together in a motion so blatantly sexual that it
de Juliana blush.

"Yes, well, that is all well and good. But Connor—my
rido—is set against it."

Senhora de Varzim looked out at the sea, clearly surprised.

Juliana gathered that the smart money in the village had be
on the suspicion that she was the one responsible for causi
Connor to spend his nights with the senhora's bachelor so
She raised her hands and made a bold, if embarrassed
tempt at repeating the senhora's coarse gesture. "My *mari*
is . . ." She lifted her shoulders and glanced forlornly at t
ocean. "He is set against it, senhora. And I wish I could ma
you understand, because I haven't the first idea of how
change his mind."

The senhora laid a finger to her cheek, then let out a bo
laugh. Taking Juliana's arm she hustled the girl back do
the beach, all the while calling out the other women. By t
time they had reached the senhora's house, Juliana was su
rounded by most of the village wives, all of them talking a
laughing at a frantic pace. Juliana could still not understa
their words, but their gestures and encouraging looks ma
their meaning clear.

Apparently Senhora de Varzim had made her and Conn
reconciliation her pet project.

Something was going on. Connor sensed it the minute
stepped off the bean-cod and started unloading the da
catch. The wives of the some of the men came to help w
the nets, and paused to whisper in their husband's ea
Soon the entire beach was buzzing with clandestine wh
pers, whispers that became noticeably silent whenever
approached. If he hadn't known better, he'd have suspect
the villagers of plotting with the French. But these fisherm
were loyal Portuguese, and the tenacious people had spe
too many centuries fighting to keep their little country f
of Spain's long shadow to lose it to a foreign tyrant. No, t
plotting going on had nothing to do with Napoleon. A
probably, he thought as he lifted the last of the heavy nets
of the boat and spread them on the frames to dry, it l
nothing to do with him.

Tomorrow he would complete his mission. A few d

ter that, his ship would return and he would leave this vil-
ge. He'd say good-bye to the cheerful fishermen, the fra-
ant hills, the colorfully tiled houses, the savory food, the
h port . . . and Juliana.

During the day the hard, rewarding work of spreading and
rvesting the wide nets had kept him too busy to think about
r. But when the twilight fell and the stars came out, his
art and body would start to work against him, filling his
nd with dreams of things that could never be. *If our lives
d gone differently we'd be married by now, maybe even
ve a little girl like Pedro and his pretty wife. We'd be
owing old together.*

Jamie's cry cut through the regrets. "Captain, ya gotta
me. There's a party!"

Connor followed Jamie's gaze down the beach and saw a
nfire being built at the edge of the sea. He frowned, trying
recall what saint's day fell at the end of March, but none
me to mind. Still, as he and Jamie walked toward the blaze
ere was no denying that some sort of celebration was going
. There was food everywhere, and glasses of *aloirado*, the
ely aged port wine that was the treasure of this region.
e'd smuggled a case or two of it in his time. A glass was
rust in his hand. He took a sip of the amber liquid, letting
seductive sweetness curl over his tongue. It was some of
e finest he'd ever tasted, as heady as lust and potent as sin,
t it had nothing on Juliana's kisses. Where the devil was
e, anyway?

On the other side of the blaze, the unmarried girls served
od and flirted with the young men. In their traditional
lorful skirts and bare feet, they made an appealing picture,
d Connor's glum mood didn't stop him from admiring the
at turn of ankle of one girl. Her face was turned away with
r hair bound up in a scarf, but her crimson skirt swayed
ainst her slender hips with an enticing grace, and her en-
anting step almost reminded him of—

Connor dropped his half-full glass to the sand and

stormed to the other side of the bonfire. He gripped the re
skirted girl's wrist and turned her to face him. "What th
blazes do you think you are doing?"

"I was serving dinner, until you manhandled me," Julia
answered as she shrugged off his grasp and moved to the ne
table. "There's no need for rudeness. Take a seat and I'm su
that one of the women will serve you—eventually."

"I'm not interested in the bloody food," he stated, fo
lowing after her. "I want to know why you're dressed up .
like this. 'Tis unseemly for a woman of your station."

"Well, perhaps next time you kidnap me you will have th
foresight to bring along a ballgown." She turned away, h
angry expression becoming a bewitching smile as she ladl
some savory lamb stew onto the plate of a grinning you
man. "Enjoy your meal, senhor."

The young man's grin crumbled to ash when he m
Connor's murderous glare.

Juliana moved to serve the next man, but Connor grabb
the dish from her hands and plunked it on the wood
table. "Will you listen? You cannot do this. Serving meals is
task for the unmarried women, and we're supposed to I
married."

"Well, you are not acting as if we are!" She placed her fis
on her hips, her expression every bit as stormy as his. "Yo
obvious indifference has caused a positive scandal in this v
lage. Senhora de Varzim thinks we've quarreled. She was th
one who organized this affair."

Experience had taught Connor to smell Juliana's plots
mile away. "And you had nothing to do with it?"

She lifted her chin haughtily. "Sir, you presume a gre
deal. Besides, *you* were the one who fabricated the story th
we were married."

"Yes, but *I* am not the one prancing about with bare fe
and ankles. Nor am I wearing an outfit that shows . . . we
that barely covers . . . God's teeth, Juliana, a woman of yo

breeding should not be strutting around half-naked in front of all these men."

"At least they are not acting like an overbearing, boorish husband. Honestly, Connor. If I did not know better, I'd vow you were jealous."

Jealous? Hell, he was going to wring the neck of the next man who so much as looked at her. "Senhora de Varzim thinks we've quarreled? Fine." He gave Juliana a swift peck on the cheek. "We've made up. Now go back to your room and change into something more—"

A tap on the shoulder drew his attention. He turned around and met the unamused gaze of Senhora de Varzim. "No, Signor. *Beijo.*"

Kiss. "But I just did—"

She shook her head. *"Beijo."* And with that, the whole crowd started pounding on the tables and chanting in unison. *"Beijo. Beijo. Beijo."*

Juliana tapped her toes impatiently against the sand. "Unless you wish to stand here all night, I suggest we get this over with."

With the whole village conspiring against him, he hadn't much choice but to play out his role of conciliatory husband. Grimacing, he tilted her chin toward his, intending to give her a perfunctorily ardent buss and leave it at that. Surely he could restrain his passion for her for one little kiss.

Some women's eyes were the windows of their souls, but for Juliana it was her mouth, and when he brushed her firmly closed lips he tasted all the anger, uncertainty, and pain bound up in her heart. Unable to resist, he brushed them again, savoring the sweetness that was headier than any port wine, aching with the pain that was the foundation of both their souls. The crowd around him had quieted, and he knew that the kiss had satisfied them. He could walk away now without regrets, knowing that he had behaved honorably toward her. He had not defiled her beyond repair. He had not robbed her of her innocence. He could walk away now. He needed to walk away now.

And the sea would turn to desert before he could willingly leave her. He lowered his mouth for a third time and her lips parted beneath his, and from that instant they were both lost.

She could never remember exactly how she ended up in her bedroom, or exactly what became of Connor's shirt or her blouse, but it hardly mattered. What she did recall was Connor's kiss, an endless, savaging caress that turned her knees to water and her blood to fire. She clung to him like a leaf in a whirlpool, spinning faster and faster as she was sucked into the center, driven by his heat, his power, and her own building need.

They fell together into the covers, an awkward move that only increased their desire. He tasted her deeply, lavishly, exploring her most tender recesses and enticing her to do the same. She felt places inside her that she hadn't even known existed blossom into lush, throbbing life. She buried her face in his hair, breathing in his hot, musky smell. Breathing *him*.

She stroked his back, loving the way he was made, the coiled strength of his muscles, the soft thunder of the groans that he uttered whenever she touched him. He needed her as much as she needed him, and the knowledge filled her with a hunger that grew fiercer with every frantic beat of her heart.

"God, I've wanted this," he growled against the edge of her mouth.

"Me, too," she said, or tried to. The words seemed lodged somewhere in her throat. She tried to free them, but her effort ended in a gasp as his hand stroked the side of her breast. A bolt of pleasure shot through her, igniting a scorching fire in her center, but even in the midst of her passion a prick of conscience needled her. "Connor, I confess. I . . . I did plot to seduce you."

His teeth and tongue savaged the tender lobe of her ear. "You don't say."

"Yes, 'tis true," she admitted, though her shallow breaths made coherent words difficult. "It was calculated, duplicitous, and—oh, yes," she groaned as his hand covered her breast, and mercilessly kneaded the sensitive bud into a taut peak. Lightning shot through her, turning her inner flame into an aching, hungry beast.

"Please," she breathed. "This is . . . not honest. I seduced you most . . . ah, please, now the other . . . most dishonorably. Will understand if . . . God, you feel like heaven . . . will understand if you want to end this."

Slowly he lifted his head, and gazed down at her with tender, burning eyes. "The only dishonor is mine, Princess. I'm going to ruin you. And God forgive me, I don't care."

She lifted her fingers and gently caressed his scarred cheek. "You could never ruin me. I'm yours. You're mine." She ran her nails down the tight, coarse curls of his chest, as if to prove her ownership. "I was made for you."

She didn't know if the sound he made was a laugh or a cry. He lifted himself off her, his gaze stark with all the uncertainty and loneliness she'd seen in him on the first day they'd met. "I vowed to protect you. Always. But instead, I've torn you from your life, destroying your past and your present, and probably your future. I've taken so much from you." He traced his fingers along the length of her arm, as if he could not prevent himself from touching her, and said in a voice rife with self-loathing. "Now I'm taking your innocence from you, too."

For months after her father had taken him in, she'd found Connor sitting alone on deck, staring off at the horizon with eyes like open wounds. He fought off everyone else's help, but when she sat beside him and took his hand, he didn't pull away. She lost count of the number of hours they'd sat that way, still and silent, two hurting children finding their healing in each other.

Deep down, they were still searching for the healing they could only find in each other.

Connor had not made any promises about the future. She'd asked for none. They might never have more than tonight. She knew she was taking the scraps of the feast, but a starving woman did not ask questions. Tenderly she took his face between her hands.

"Shall I tell you of my future? In a few days I will return to London, to a terrific scandal that will fade as soon as another indiscretion comes along. I will go back to the line, but in time I'll be sucked back into the world of routs, balls, and the giddy pleasures of the upper class. I'll fill the hollowness inside with a whirl of activities, until I'm wed to a man I will not love, but who can give me a family and children to fill the emptiness. No, don't protest—you know it to be true. 'Tis the fate of women of my position, the brood mares for the titled class. I was born to it and I face it as I must. But—" She bit her lip, her voice wavering for the first time since she started. " 'Tis a terrible cold life, Connor. I need the memory of our love to keep me warm. . . ."

"Hush," he said as he brushed away tears she didn't even know she was crying. He lowered his mouth to her cheek and kissed away her tears one by one. "The past and future are nothing to us. This night is all that matters. This night, when we belong to no one but each other."

He drew her into his arms. Once again she was caught in the magic, the mystical binding that fused them together like two halves of a single sun. His mouth and hands were everywhere, coaxing and caressing, claiming every part of her as his own. She was warm, hot, burning like a living flame. He caressed her into a frenzy, stripping away the last of her clothing and the last of her fears. His mouth moved lower, possessing first her breast and then her stomach. Unsated hunger drove groans of passion from her throat, groans he covered with a renewed, ravenous caress. Then he stroked his hand down her body, delving into her throbbing, intimate center as his mouth claimed her animal moans.

"You're so sweet. So tight. Give yourself to me," he whispered urgently. "For this one night, Princess, pretend you're only mine."

She wanted to say it was not pretend—that she *was* only his, and always would be. But she was past words. She rode his hand, bucking and writhing in the passion that burned for him, only him. She gave herself up to his caresses, opening herself to him with a joy so rich that she thought she'd die from the beauty of it. And without even a thought of maidenly modesty, she stripped down his breeches and caressed his fullness with the same ruthless tenderness that he'd shown her.

He groaned, gripping her wrists and pinning her wanton hands to the sheets. "Do that again and this will be over before it begins."

"It will never be over. Not for us. Take what is yours. What's always been yours."

They looked into each other's eyes, hearts revealed without shame or shadows. In a dance as old as Eden, she raised her hips and he moved over her.

"God, you're small," he groaned, his voice ragged with need. He entered her just an inch, holding himself in check with iron control. "So innocent. Pure. Have no right—"

"Love gives you the right. I love you, Connor. I love—"

She gasped as he penetrated her, claiming her body as his love had claimed her soul. The quick pain was a small price to pay for the joy of having him inside her. Clinging to his shoulders, she felt a shudder pass through him, and thought what a miracle it was that a world-weary man could find peace in her body. She fell back on the pillows and sighed contentedly, knowing that she'd finally reached the pinnacle of a woman's fulfillment. "That was wonderful," she breathed.

His low chuckle rumbled through her like thunder. "Trust me, Princess. *Wonderful* is just beginning."

He moved inside her, slowly at first, but building in speed with each powerful stroke. He drove into her, sending sheets of white-hot energy crashing through her with the force of a tidal wave. Her world became a red haze. Her body accepted him again and again, caressing him intimately, firing his passion by drawing him deeper with every thrust. Tenderness was discarded. Gentleness was a memory. She arched wildly beneath him, destroyed and remade with every thrust. The only thing keeping her from breaking apart was the burning intensity of Connor's ice-and-fire eyes.

They moved together, two bodies and one heart, forged together in their love. She clung to his sweat-sleek body, knowing that this was what she was made for, what they'd been made for. He pushed her to the edge of madness, driving her into the oblivion where nothing existed but her love for him. Then, after he'd watched her fulfillment blaze and die in her eyes, he shattered her again with the power of his own release.

19

"You are damn lucky," Connor growled as he toyed with a strand of her wildly disheveled hair. "If I'd had any idea what that body of yours could do, I'd have had you locked away in a convent school, with nuns, and high walls, and large dogs."

Juliana sighed and snuggled against his chest. "Yes, and you'd have had as much luck at that as you did ordering me not to climb the volcano on that South Sea island. You were always such a bully. But I might have gone to the convent, if"—she peeped up as him, her voice laced with wicked mischief as she added—"if you had kept a key."

He threw back his head and gave a lusty laugh. God's teeth, he couldn't remember the last time he'd felt this content. Cradling Juliana against him, tenderly stroking her hair and laughing with her, pleasured him almost as much as taking her. *Almost,* he thought, closing his eyes as he savored the memory of being inside her. In his vagabond life he'd known dozens of women in countless ports, and had foolishly believed that he was experienced in love. But nothing had prepared him for what he'd found in her arms.

What had previously been a simple act of physical release became an act of worship and discovery. For the first time in his life he had made love instead of just having sex, the difference as vast as the ocean to a drop of rain. She'd been heaven in his arms, paradise to his soul, so giving, so sweet, so pure . . . and, if her hand on a strategic part of his anatomy was any indication, she was also one hell of a fast learner.

Gathering his wits, he reluctantly pushed her away. "Be still. We have already done it twice."

Silvered moonlight slanted through the window, illuminating her expression of disappointment. "So two is the usual number?"

Usual? *Nothing* was usual when it come to Juliana. If he'd allowed her clever fingers to work their magic a moment longer she'd have discovered that his body was more than willing to make her his a third time. But he was still captain of their course, and right now he needed to think with his mind, not his body. "Juliana, I want to make love to you the way I want my next breath, but I can't because—" He gritted his teeth, wishing like the devil that he didn't have to say the words. But someone had to say them, and he was still her pledged protector. "We cannot make love again because it is very nearly dawn, and I have to . . . well, the particulars do not matter. What does matter is that in a few days I will have to leave you."

The killing truth cut deep into his soul. However, it did not seem to bother Juliana one bit. Instead of dissolving into tears, she tilted her head and laid a finger alongside her cheek. Connor knew the look, and it filled him with almost as much dread as the coming morning. *Christ, she's plotting again.*

"Yes, I have been pondering this situation," she said thoughtfully. "You stole the dispatches because you wanted money. Well, I have a way for you to gain a fortune and not

reak a single law in the process." She lifted her chin, obvi-
usly vastly pleased with herself as she pronounced, "I am
ning with you."

"The hell you are."

"Don't take that patronizing tone with me, Connor. I have
nade up my mind. I am going with you because I belong by
our side. We shall be married at once."

Connor gaped at her, her words catapulting him into
neaven and hell at once. "That is . . . impossible."

"Of course it isn't. I love you. You love me. And when I
narry, my entire fortune, including the Marquis Line, be-
omes the property of my husband. 'Tis not a law I've previ-
usly favored, but now I see a use for it. By marrying me you
ould gain more money than you could ever make as a priva-
er. So it makes perfect sense that we should be wed at the
arliest opportunity." Once again she laid a thoughtful finger
 her cheek. "Hmm, I suspect there is a priest somewhere
earby. Or perhaps a local magistrate of some sort. And
 could borrow a wedding dress from one of the village
omen. One should really be married in a proper dress, don't
ou think—of course, I should have to come up with some
rt of a reason to—"

He gripped her arms. "Juliana, we cannot marry. I am . . ."
e cast his mind about for something to dissuade her. "I am a
owardly, dishonorable traitor."

He might as well have told her that he'd stained his shirt
r all the effect it had on her. "You will have to do better than
at. You would not have given me the dispatches if you were
 traitor. You would not have saved Raoul and the rest of the
en on his uncle's ship from the French if you were cow-
dly. And you would not have given up your naval career for
our sister if you were not honorable—"

"Peace," he cried. He bolted out of bed and paced the
oor in consternation. "We cannot marry. I will not dishonor
ou in such a fashion."

She stretched on the moon-bright sheets like a contented

cat. "Tonight you've dishonored me in a number of fashion
I rather like it."

He closed his eyes against the vision of her enticing bod
displayed in wanton glory in the moonlight. God's teeth, sh
could make a saint hard, and he was no saint. "I cannot marr
you. I am not free."

She went still. "You are married?"

He was a consummate liar, but even he could not manag
that one. "No."

She let out an audible sigh. "Well, that is fortunate," sh
replied as she scooted off the bed and padded to his side. "
you were married, I would have had to become your mis
tress. And while I do not personally mind the notion of
carte blanche, I fear Meg and Mrs. Jolly would be quite scan
dalized, and the poor commodore might be forced to call yo
out."

"Sweet heaven, will you be serious?"

"Believe me, I am perfectly serious. I am no blushin
schoolgirl, or starry-eyed debutante. I know you are mixe
up in some sort of intrigue, but I also know that you woul
never do anything to betray me or our country. You are ne
capable of such a thing."

He turned to the window and muttered, "Trust me
Princess. You have no idea of what I am capable of."

She smoothed a shock of hair from his forehead. "Da
ling, I cannot pretend to know what you have been throug
during the past few years, but I know the hell that I wer
through when you left. There is no life for me without you.
you face danger, I mean to face it with you. If you go, I g
with you. For better or for worse, for richer or poorer, t
death us do—"

He stopped her words with a kiss so passionate that it le
them both trembling. He wrapped her in his arms and burie
his face in her hair, drinking in her intoxicating scent as h
groaned, "Beloved, I can't damn you to my life. Tell m
something, anything, that I can say to make you leave me."

She rubbed her cheek against his chest. "Tell me you
e a liar."

He seared a cherishing kiss against her temple. "I am
iar."

"Tell me you do not desire me."

He cupped his hands around her backside and pressed
r belly against his fully aroused manhood. "I don't desire
u."

She sank her fingers in his hair and brought his mouth
ose to hers as she whispered, "Tell me you have never
ved me."

"I never . . . God forgive me, I love you more than life."
ith a feral growl he devoured her in a firestorm that burned
em both alive. Tongues and teeth feasted together in a des-
rate, lavish banquet that echoed the hunger in their souls,
e yearning of one heart for its mate. He started to move
ward the bed, but they didn't reach it. Instead, they fell to
e braided rug with Juliana straddling his body.

He stroked into her and she arched back, reaching her
vn fulfillment in a few powerful thrusts. He watched as the
ory broke her in pieces, knowing that he alone could give
r this wonder, this loving madness that was theirs alone.
e delved his finger into their joining, coaxing her into a new
lfillment before he sated his own need in her welcoming
dy. And when the storm was over and he cradled her
ainst him with cherishing tenderness, he brushed a soft
ss against her brow and murmured, "I love you. Whatever
ppens, believe that I love you."

Someone was knocking on the door. Juliana raised her
ad from the pillow, blinking against the unexpectedly
ight light pouring in the bedroom window. The last thing
e recalled was Connor carrying her to the bed just as dawn
s breaking. From the sun's height now it must be nearly
d-morning. Still groggy, she turned over. "Darling, we've
erslep—"

The bed was empty.

The knocking started again, and she heard Senhora d
Varzim's voice from the other side. She could not make ou
what the lady was saying, but the agitation in her voice, an
the fact that Connor was missing, propelled her out of bed
She grabbed the first thing at hand—the senhora's oversize
dress—and struggled it over her head as she went to th
door. "I'm awake, senhora. What is the matter? And where
Con—?"

Senhora de Varzim covered the girl's mouth with he
hand. "Con-air," she warned, shaking her head firmly. "N
Con-air." And with that she took the girl's hand and drew he
along the narrow hallway.

"Yes, I can see that. But where is he? Are you taking me t
him? Oh blast, I wish you could understand—"

She stopped as they came out into the sunshine of the sen
hora's courtyard. Decorated in the brightly glazed azuleje
tiles of the country and blooming with a hundred spring blos
soms, the place was like a little piece of paradise. But Julian
felt as if she'd entered Hades the moment she stepped into i
Next to the corner shrine to São Goncalo stood two Englis
soldiers bearing muskets. And between the redcoats stood
man she recognized instantly. She had not seen him in year
but there was no mistaking the finely styled dark hair an
well-cut clothes or the classic lines of a face that had grow
even more handsome over the years. He swept off his ha
with an elegance that Connor could never hope to matc
"Hello, Cousin."

"Grenville? What are you doing here?"

He started to speak, then glanced at the glaring senhor
" 'Tis a long tale, my dear, and one best not told with pryir
ears, even ones that understand so little of our language. W
had best leave this peasant to her own devices."

"This *peasant* was uncommonly kind to me," Julian
replied tartly. "To me, and to—" She bit her tongue. "In ar

ase, 'tis fortunate you arrived. I . . . fell overboard. In a
attle. I was washed up on shore, and—"

The new marquis of Albany smiled grimly. "You needn't
e, cousin. We know what has been going on here. We pro-
ably know more than you do." He nodded to the soldiers
nd asked them to step out of the courtyard for a moment.
Then he spoke to Senhora de Varzim in her native tongue,
pparently asking her to do the same. The woman let go of
uliana's hand reluctantly, then backed out of the courtyard,
nouthing a final silent "No Con-air" as she left.

"Juliana, would you take a seat?"

She lifted her chin defiantly. "No Rollo, I should rather
ke to stand, I think."

Grenville gave a smile. "Well, you've got spirit, I will give
ou that. I expected to find a terrified debutante. Instead, I
nd a bold woman who believes she knows her own mind."

"I *do* know my own mind," she fired back. "I had to dis-
over it when my father died, and my only living relative
ould not even bother to leave his own selfish pursuits to
omfort me in my grief."

Her cousin had the grace to look sheepish. "I had my
easons."

"Fine. Then you will understand *my* reasons for not being
ll that pleased to see you." She walked stiffly past Grenville
nd glanced surreptitiously out the courtyard entrance at the
ills beyond. If Connor knew of the soldiers' arrival, why had
e left her behind?

"You look for him in vain, Juliana. He is gone."

She spun around. "I . . . do not know who you mean."

Grenville's mouth ticked up in grudging respect. "You've
pirit, and you are loyal. 'Tis a rare combination in a woman.
nfortunately, your loyalty is sorely misplaced. I told you
aat we know what has been going on here. You have been
aying here in this village for the past few days in the com-
any of one Captain Gabriel."

Juliana swallowed, remembering the senhora's warning. "You are mistaken. True, I have been here several days recovering from wounds, but I have been here alone—"

"Oh, enough of this." Grenville snapped his fingers. Immediately one of the redcoats appeared at the courtyard door, holding a small, flailing boy in his arms.

"Jamie!"

The soldier released the struggling child and the boy ran into her open arms. "I didn't tell 'em nothing about the captain. Nothin', I swear."

"I know. It's all right, sweetheart," she said, smoothing the trembling boy's hair. She looked at Grenville, seething with fury. "How dare you? He's only a defenseless child."

"Defenseless? He nearly broke the shins of two of my best men."

"That does not give you the right to arrest innocent children!"

"No," he agreed smoothly. "But this does."

He reached into his coat and pulled out a letter. Unfolding it, he handed it to Juliana. "You will recognize Wellington's personal seal and signature. However, if you have any remaining doubts, the dozen men under my command would be able to vouchsafe its authenticity."

Juliana stared at the commission, stunned by what she read. It stated that Grenville was with the Horse Guards, a network of agents working in secret in the Peninsula under the direct command of the duke of Wellington. It was an important and dangerous position—one that fit her image of her wastrel cousin not at all. "I do not understand. How can you have a commission? You always gave more thought to your cravat than to your country."

"Men change, Juliana," he replied with something that sounded surprisingly like honesty. "Some change for the better, others . . ." He let his words trail off as he folded the letter and stuffed it back into his coat. Then he waved to one of the soldiers. "The lady and I have matters that are best discussed in private. Take the boy. And see that you have more care with him. He is, as my cousin rightly points out, only a child."

Jamie, however, had other ideas. He planted himself squarely between Juliana and her cousin. "I ain't goin'. Told the captain I'd protect her. Got my orders."

Juliana reached out to defend the boy, but halted in astonishment as Grenville hunkered down before the child. "I, too, am following orders. Doing my job, just like you. But you have my assurance that I will not harm Lady Juliana. Here is my hand on it."

Jamie eyed him warily, but he accepted the marquis's hand. Then, with a final encouraging glance at Juliana, he let the soldier take him from the yard.

"That was kind of you," Juliana acknowledged.

"I told you that a man can change, cousin." He rose to his feet, and faced Juliana squarely. "Unfortunately, others only appear to change their nature. So when I received Mrs. Jolly's most recent letter, I—"

"Mrs. Jolly has been writing to you?"

"Regularly. I asked her to keep me informed of your circumstances while I was away. I had hoped . . . well, it is no matter what I hoped. The point is that the letter that arrived a week past related that you had hired a new manager, Captain Gabriel, who might have designs on you. A few well-placed inquiries told me that Gabriel was none other than the baseborn cur who betrayed your father's trust. And when I heard that half the fleet was searching for the traitorous dog—"

Juliana's hands balled to fists. "Connor is not a traitor. You always were ready to believe the worst of him."

"True enough. I always hated him for taking the lion's share of my uncle's affection—and an equal portion of yours. But I am not a liar. Connor Reed has been in league with Napoleon for months."

"But he was fired on by French ships. They . . . sank the *Pelican*. Connor fought bravely to save us. I saw him."

"You saw what he wanted you to see. But the truth is that he kidnapped you, seduced you, and then abandoned you in order to fulfill his mission of delivering stolen Admiralty dispatches to Napoleon's troops."

"You know nothing of the truth! He loves me. And as for stolen dispatches—" She patted the oilskin packet hidden in the folds of the senhora's voluminous skirt. "I have not the first idea of what you are talking about."

Grenville shook his head. "You are a poor liar, cousin. I can only guess at the tales the man told to you to win your affection. Did he perchance mention the battle in which he gained his ship?"

"I heard how French dogs fell upon them under a flag of truce."

"There was no truce. And the ships he fired on were English—his own country. I have read the eyewitness report myself. You, my poor, trusting innocent, have been played for a fool by a duplicitous traitor."

" 'Tis not true," she stated, though her words carried less force than before. Where was Connor? Why was he not here to counter these vile accusations?

What if Grenville was right?

"No," she cried, as much for herself as for him. "I do not believe your accusations. He is a good and honorable man. Whatever he has done, I am sure there is a noble reason for it."

"And what noble reason would there be, cousin, for the fact that your merchant ships have been transporting stolen documents to French foreign agents for the past three months?"

For a long while, nothing moved in the courtyard save a lone bottle green fly that skipped from flower to flower. But in Juliana's mind, thoughts whirled. Connor's words of last night came back to her. *You have no idea what I am capable of.* As her manager, he would have had access to her cargo shipments and could have easily hidden documents inside them. What if the Admiralty dispatches were not the first secret papers he had stolen? What if he really was—? "No, I will not believe it. He would never abuse my trust in that way. Your information is false."

"No lass, 'tis all too true."

Startled, Juliana spun around, and saw a familiar rumpled figure at the courtyard entrance. "Mr. McGregor?"

"I swear I dinna know, not until you'd gone missing. We searched through all the office papers, trying to find out some clue of why you'd disappeared. It wasn't long before we came across the evidence of the captain's dealings. Betrayed us all, he did. Since the first day. And it's myself I blame for ever suggestin' you bring that foul traitor into our fold."

"No, I am the one to blame," admitted a large man who ambled to McGregor's side. Commodore Jolly took off his naval hat, and fiddled dejectedly with the brim as he continued. "When McGregor brought me the proof, I could not believe it either. But there's no doubt—the Admiralty's put out warrants for the man's arrest. He's been in Boney's back pocket for longer than anyone suspected. And when it became clear he'd kidnapped you—oh, my dear, we've been so worried."

The commodore folded her into his arms, but even his supporting embrace barely kept her from sinking to the ground. She might have her doubts about Grenville, but these men were her trusted friends. They would not lie to her. And if they were telling the truth, then Connor—

"This is a mistake. A terrible mistake."

"I only wish it were," Grenville answered, with something like real regret in his eyes. "But the charges against the man are mounting by the day. Larceny, transport of illegal goods, treason. There is even some evidence that he may be a murderer. . . ."

"No!" She pushed out of Jolly's embrace and backed into a corner of the courtyard. They had to be wrong, yet everything they said made sense—horrible, damning sense. How could she believe Connor in the face of all this evidence? Larceny. Treason. *Murder.* And yet, she had to believe in him. She must. *I love you. Whatever happens, believe that I love you.*

His last words came back to her, lending her strength. "You are wrong. Connor is no hardened criminal, and I can prove it." She reached into her skirt and pulled out the oilskin pouch. "He did steal the dispatches, but he gave them to me. He could not go through with handing them over to the French. 'Tis hardly the action of a seasoned villain."

Jolly blanched. McGregor gasped. Even Grenville's confident expression lost some of its luster. Her cousin took the packet and began to unwrap it. "I do not understand this. But, if this is true, then it will go a long way toward proving his innoce—" His words died as he held the papers in front of her and thumbed through them one by one.

They were nothing but blank sheets of parchment.

Juliana spent most of the voyage home alone in her cabin, crying herself empty until there was nothing left inside her, not even sorrow. The constant concern of the commodore, Mr. McGregor, and her young protector Jamie, whom she had arranged to come with her to London, did nothing to ease her pain. When she reached London, she threw herself into the Marquis Line, working long hours with few meals and little sleep. She drove herself to the limit, filling her days and nights with work, fighting off the sleep that brought wonderful, terrible dreams of Connor's smile, Connor's touch, Connor's kiss. . . .

Not a fortnight had gone by before she collapsed to the ground.

Despair and exhaustion had taken its toll on her. For weeks afterward she could barely leave her bed, and more than one physician doubted she would ever rise from it again. There was a part of her that wished she wouldn't. But, just as it had after Connor's first betrayal, her young body proved traitorously resilient. Gradually she began to improve, until even the most pessimistic doctors declared her out of danger. After a month in bed, she took her first tentative step across her bedroom carpet. And the man assisting her was the same one who had been at her side almost constantly since she had first fallen ill—her cousin, Rollo Grenville.

On the first day of July in the year of our Lord eighteen hundred and twelve, Commodore Sir Horatio Jolly and his mother, the honorable Mrs. Robert Jolly, will have the pleasure of bestowing the hand of their ward, the Lady Juliana Dare, in honorable marriage to Lord Rollo Grenville, the Sixth Marquis of Albany, in All Saints' Church in Knightsbridge at noon . . .

Juliana put down the *Morning Post* and stirred her morning chocolate. Odd. She genuinely thought that she would feel something when she finally saw the wedding banns in print. It was, after all, the most important step in a young woman's life. Instead, she felt the same numbing emptiness that had filled her for the past three months.

A young voice caught her attention. "But she told me I could see her first thing!"

An instant later the door burst open and Jamie ran in, with Juliana's agitated abigail close at his heels. "I'm sorry, my lady. I know the doctor said your were still to get rest in the morning, but the boy would not take no for an answer."

"It is all right, Lucy. I did tell him he could come in," Juliana said as the boy wrapped his arms around her. In the months since she'd brought Jamie back from Portugal to live with her, he'd added a great deal of joy to the Jolly household. Though at first there were objections to a single young woman's adopting an orphan, Juliana had held her ground. Now it was impossible to imagine the house without him.

The commodore frequently took Jamie to his office at the Admiralty, and Mrs. Jolly, for all her grumblings about his "tar's manners," was quite taken with his scampish spirit and quick mind. Meg had begun giving him acting lessons. Already names of fine schools were being discussed. For his part, Jamie seemed as content to live on dry land as he was at sea. Apparently he was young enough to forget easily, though Juliana was somewhat surprised at how easily. Still, she was thankful that he never mentioned his former life on the privateer vessel, and seemed to have entirely forgotten the fact that his former mates and captain had deserted him.

Unfortunately, Juliana could not seem to master that skill.

"Are you coming to the park today? I want you to see how well I ride."

According to Meg, the boy sat a horse about as well as an upright sack of potatoes, but that was hardly important. In the last few months, Juliana had watched him begin to blossom into a confident young man, and she could not have been prouder of him if he'd ridden like a Corinthian. She brushed a rakish shock of hair off his forehead, trying not to see another's face as she did so. *I must learn to do this without thinking of him. I must.*

"So will you come?"

"Dearest, I cannot. Today Aunt Meg and I must go to the mantuamaker to see about my wedding dress."

Jamie's bright expression soured. "So you're really gonna marry him."

" '*Going to* marry him,' sweetheart," Juliana corrected. "And yes, I am. He is a fine gentleman, and he has been very kind to both you and to me."

"He wasn't at first."

Juliana paused just a heartbeat before continuing. "No, he wasn't. But a man can change. He was very attentive during my illness, and visited me almost every day. He gave up his commission and took over my duties at the shipping line. And since I have begun to get well again, he has taken me to balls and card parties, and done everything he can to make me forget . . . that is, to make my life pleasant. And he has promised to be a good father to you, and has already set aside a substantial amount for your education."

"I would rather have a pony," Jamie grumbled.

Juliana hugged him tightly, wishing her own needs were as simple. "You shall have ponies by the score. But right now I must dress, or I shall miss my appointment. Now, one last hug and off with you."

Jamie complied, darting out of the door as quickly as he'd come in. Juliana watched him go, a bittersweet smile on her lips. The only time she'd felt alive in the last few months was when Jamie wrapped his arms around her. *Surely it will not always be so. Once I am truly married, I will learn to feel something more than gratitude for Rollo. Then my life would at least be bearable—*

Her thoughts ended as a slim figure opened her door and stormed in with almost as much bluster as Jamie. "I cannot believe it. You are really going to go through with it."

"I would be a fool not to," Juliana said as she slipped out of bed, avoiding Meg's direct gaze. She sat at her dressing table and picked up her silver hairbrush. "My cousin is handsome, well respected by the War Office and his peers," she commented as she began to brush her hair. "He has asked several times for my hand, even though he knows . . . well, even though he knows what I have been through. He has made it clear that he is devoted to me. I can think of no reason why I should not marry him."

"None, except that you do not love him."

Juliana gave an elegant laugh. "My dear, you prattle like a school chit. Our tastes and ideas march together, and I've no doubt we will make a superior couple. Love has nothing to do with making a suitable match."

"It does—when you are still in love with Connor."

Juliana's hand stilled. "You promised never to mention his name."

"I kept silent for as long as I could. But now—" She bent

over Juliana's shoulder and met her friend's gaze in the mirror. "Julie, ever since your illness I have watched you, and you are only going through the motions of living. Oh, no one else has noticed—you laugh at the appropriate times, and say all the right things. As far as your society friends are concerned, you are more popular than ever. But there is no spark of life in you. You have even lost interest in the Marquis Line."

Juliana's hand tightened on her brush. Meg was right; she was no longer the girl who had left London. When she had returned from Portugal, news of 'Captain Gabriel's' treachery had been the talk of every salon in Mayfair. All the friends he had once had turned their backs on him—indeed, it was almost impossible to find anyone who admitted knowing him. Her own behavior was the subject of nearly as much speculation, but her prolonged illness after her homecoming did much to sway public sentiment in her favor, and the Jollys' unwavering support and her cousin's constant attention did the rest. In time, several ripe scandals had replaced her own, and Grenville's honorable marriage proposal had firmly relegated her questionable behavior to the realm of old news. As for Captain Gabriel—his name was never mentioned in polite society at all, except when the occasional report surfaced of some captain claiming to have sunk the notorious Archangel's ship.

She died a little every time she read one.

"I do not know whether he is alive or dead," Juliana said in a voice like brittle leaves. "If he is alive, and has not come for me by now—well, that is proof enough that I was nothing more to him than a pawn in his game of treachery. And if he is dead . . ." She bit her lip, fighting back the tears that she vowed she would never cry. "In any case, I must marry."

Meg knelt down beside her and put her hand on her arm. "But why so soon? It has been only three months since your ordeal, and only six since your father died. I will admit that I am not entirely unfond of Rollo—he has been most kind to you. But I cannot but feel that you deserve better than a marriage of convenience. At least give your heart some time to heal before you make such an important decision."

"I would, had I the time to spare." She laid down her brush and covered her friend's hand with her own. "I did not tell you before, but the truth will be apparent soon enough. The reason I was so ill, the reason I must marry so quickly . . . Meg, I am going to have Connor's baby."

20

— 🌿 —

Meg's grip tightened on Juliana's arm. "Oh, my poor darling. What you must have endured . . . oh, the fiend! I wish him at the bottom of the ocean for using you so horribly!"

"Nay, it was not like that. I knew what I was doing. I wanted—" She closed her eyes, unable to find the words that could make her friend understand. Those moments in Connor's arms had been a lie on his part, but not on hers, and the babe they had made together was very real. She placed her hand over her still-flat stomach, cherishing the tiny life inside her with all the love that Connor had callously cast aside. "It does not matter what I wanted then. But I do want this child, Meg—more than I have ever wanted anything in my life. I know it is not what you expected of me, and I shall understand if you turn away—"

"Do not be a nodcock, this changes nothing between us. But, I must ask . . . do the Jollys know?"

Juliana shook her head. "No, and I will do all I can to keep my predicament from them. They have been too kind to me

r me to let my shameful behavior stain their reputations.
ıe only one who knows the truth is Grenville. I could not
cept his offer of marriage without telling him. He has
omised to give me his name and protection, and I have
omised to give him full control of the Marquis Line and the
st of my fortune. 'Tis a fair bargain. It is just—"

Her voice broke as she once again skated dangerously
ıse to tears. "I am sorry, my dear. I've struck a bargain, and
now it to be a good one. 'Tis just . . . well, I thought my life
ɔuld turn out very differently."

"I know," Meg whispered. "Much as I try not to, I still oc-
sionally think about St. Juste." Actually, it was more than
casionally. When Juliana had returned, she'd told Meg all
ɔout the vicomte d' Aubigny-sur-mer, including the words
ɛ'd spoken about his feelings for Meg. Since then not a
ght had gone by when Meg didn't dream of the brave and
ɔnorable Frenchman taking her hand and leading her down
łower-strewn aisle to a church altar. But the wonderful vi-
ɔn died as soon as she woke and remembered that her
ɛenchman was neither brave nor honorable, just one of the
ȧthsome villains who had kidnapped her dearest friend.
ıd her future, as always, was to be lived as a penniless,
łloved old maid. She blinked, coming perilously close to
ying herself.

Juliana got up from the dressing table, shaking herself
undly. "Look at the pair of us! Blubbering like a pair of
ıe-footed boobies. My father used to say that regrets were
waste of time. He would have had us keelhauled for be-
ving in this manner, and he'd have been quite right."

She turned to the window and pushed aside the curtain,
ɔking out at the crowded, lushly planted park across the
eet. "A few days after my father's death, I stared out at this
ry park. It was all skeleton trees and gloom, not a hint of life
ywhere. Now look at it—filled with people and overflow-
g with green leaves and blossoms. Life is always changing
urse, Meg, and we must do our best to change with it. But

our future is not so very unpleasant. I have asked Rollo
allow me to raise the children in the country, away from th
rumors and prying questions of the *haute ton*. And you, m
dear Meg, will you come and live with us?"

"You will not miss the social whirl of London? Or runnin
the Marquis Line?"

For a moment, Juliana's confident smile wavered. "I d
love the line, and wish I could continue with father's dream
but that future is not to be. Rollo has promised that he wi
not sell off the ships, and I believe he will honor that pledg
And as for missing the society of the Upper Ten Thousand
you are worth more than the whole of the silly lot put t
gether. We shall be as happy as larks. In fact, I quite suspe
the larks will be jealous."

"Perhaps we shall," Meg answered, almost believing it.

"Depend on it. In the meantime—oh heavens, look at th
time on the mantel clock. It lacks but an hour until we me
the dressmaker and you *know* what Madame Bovier is like
one is late. In all likelihood I should end up being married
a proper stylish potato sack! Then we have lunch with th
countess of Arlington, an 'at home' with Lady Sterling, t
with Mrs. Jolly to discuss the wedding plans, dinner at th
Woolriches', the new play at Covent Garden—and som
where in the midst of this I must buy Jamie a new ridin
crop. . . ."

"Julie, you could make a whirlwind seem lazy. We shall n
have a moment to breathe."

"Or to regret. Father was right—life is too short to was
on lamenting. I have a boy who needs me, a baby who'll nee
me soon, and the world's most wonderful friend. And if ei
ther of us wastes another precious minute thinking abo
those traitorous privateers again, we should pledge to—" S
formed her fingers into an inexpert fist. "Well, we should d
liver each other a handy bunch of fives!"

Laughing, the women stepped away from the windo

h silently vowing that the dangerous and despicable nnor Reed and Raoul St. Juste were absolutely and com- tely out of their lives forever.

Below in the crowded park, under the spreading branches ɔne of the large oak trees, two men in cloaks watched the tain fall back in place over the bedroom window. They l nothing, but the clean-shaven one dropped his half- ɔked cigar to the pavement and ground it ruthlessly under heel.

The wedding day drew near. With her period of mourning rly at an end, and curiosity about her unexpected engage- nt the talk of every scandal broth in Mayfair, Juliana once in found herself at the heart of London society. Balls were considered entirely successful unless she made an ap- rance. Speculation about the design of her wedding dress nmandeered more space in the papers than the war with poleon. And her intended Lord Albany, the former En- h spy and acting head of the Marquis Line, was rumored ɔe in the running for a position of some considerable influ- e with the War Office.

Juliana was again the reigning queen of the Season, but ry passing day felt like another tug of the noose around ' neck. She had made her decision—the only decision she was possible in her position. Yet every night she dreamed a privateer with pale, wounded eyes, accusing her of be- ving his love by marrying another.

A week before the wedding, the Jollys hosted a dinner ty of some twenty-odd friends. The perpetually wrinkled . McGregor was seated beside Grenville's groomsman, rd Renquist, who appeared afraid to even glance in the so- tor's direction for fear he would somehow damage his ɪdy image. The commodore sat at the head of the table, his al rig gleaming like a spit-polished vessel, though it could argued that his smile outshone even his brass buttons.

Even Jamie had secured a place at the table beside Meg, ▮
bright grin closely resembling the expression of a cat who h▮
eaten a canary.

The other end of the table was commandeered by M▮
Jolly, whose unprecedented appearance would no dou▮
be the talk of every Mayfair salon for weeks to come. Lo▮
and Lady Marchmont were there discussing, as alwa▮
the weather, and also in attendance was the ever glum ▮
Feathergill, who had recently been passed over for yet a▮
other promotion. Rice and Caldwell were there from the A▮
miralty, along with Mr. Hamilton and his newly affianc▮
Miss Peak. The two were certainly a match for each other, ▮
liana thought as she watched the pair discuss in detail the i▮
portance of the latest dance step. But then, that was what h▮
future held as well. Dance steps, the latest fashion magazi▮
the newest society scandal . . . and the war and the fate of t▮
brave soldiers, sailors and merchant captains were of no co▮
sequence whatsoever.

By and large, it was a warm and companionable gatheri▮
but Juliana could not seem to keep her mind on the conv▮
sation. The group of friends reminded her so completely ▮
the day in January when Connor had come to the Joll▮
house, when she had treated him so rudely, then follow▮
him to the docks to apologize. So much had changed in h▮
life, and yet nothing had changed at all. She was still the p▮
nacle of London society, still one of the wealthiest wom▮
in the country. And she was still hopelessly in love w▮
Connor. . . .

"A toast," Grenville said as he rose from his seat, smili▮
his impeccably handsome grin. "To my bride-to-be, t▮
loveliest woman in London."

Glasses were raised and cheers were made. Julia▮
schooled her features into a look of sincere pleasure, t▮
same one she'd counterfeited at countless interminable ca▮
parties and soirees.

Lord Renquist pushed back his chair and stood up. "▮

dy Juliana, successful in society, in business, and now in
e."

Juliana's smile wavered, but she pasted it back in place and
e Renquist an appreciative nod.

Mr. McGregor rose as well. "I'm not one for speeches, but
lass were as good an employer as ever there was. The lads
ss you to a man. You're a yar schooner in a fair wind, and
t's a fact. And I wish the same bonny success with yer mar-
ze that you had with your business."

The cheers were a little less strong, but Juliana's smile
w wider, and for the first time that evening she felt genu-
tears in her eyes.

Jolly bounded up, and hoisted his glass so rigorously that it
rly spilled. "Capital toast, McGregor. Here's to Juliana.
re's to the king. And while we're at it, here's to whoever
ches that villain who's been smuggling guns to Bonaparte."

A groan suffused the table at the sight of Jolly making yet
other social blunder. The gathering might have shared his
timent, but a party was hardly the place for a political
tement. At least, that's what everyone thought—except
iana. Until that moment, she had not realized that the no-
ious spy was still at large. "Guns? But I thought that when
nn—I mean, I thought the spy was put out of commission
nths ago."

"Not likely," McGregor quipped. "The cad's as slippery as
a snake and has men everywhere. It is rumored that he is
ng ships to smuggle English guns to France."

"But that is heinous!"

"Most certainly," Grenville intoned as he casually but-
ed a roll. "But hardly unique. With the volume of ships
sing through the ports a few plans are bound to slip
ough."

"This cannot be allowed to continue," she fired back, hor-
ed at his indifference. "Perhaps I can help. I could review
shipping manifests, and help make certain that nothing
gular occurs—"

Her fiancé raised his hand, silencing her. "This would
entirely inappropriate. Such behavior would be unseemly
a woman of your station."

"Unseemly? Our country is being compromised, and i
up to all of us to do our part. I know the business, and t
people on the docks are my friends. And I know everyone
the Marquis Line. We worked together for months—"

"Now they work for me," Grenville interjected smootl
"And I fear it would be . . . confusing for them if you came
the offices. Now, Mr. Feathergill, I believe you had a toast.

Mr. Feathergill might have, but Juliana did not stay
hear it. Claiming fatigue, she rose from the table, wavi
Meg to remain seated as she left the dining room and went
the sitting room, where she sank to the couch. Frustrati
that had been building in her for weeks came to a head.

She'd made a bargain to protect her child, but now s
saw what that bargain would truly cost. Pride. Self-respe
And, most of all, her birthright. Her father had left his bu
ness to her. But she had given up that responsibility to bu
name for her child. And given up her future to a man s
could never love.

The creak of a wheelchair alerted her to Mrs. Jolly's
proach. "I thought I might find you . . . yes, Henry, just lea
me here, and please shut the door behind you. I would like
speak with Lady Juliana. Alone."

Juliana wiped the sheen of tears from her eyes. As far
Mrs. Jolly was concerned, she was a happy bride-to-be, w
knew nothing of her dire circumstances. "Forgive me
leaving so abruptly. I was feeling somewhat tired, and I—"

"Is it the babe?"

Juliana paled. "But how—?"

"Honestly, my dear, did you really think you could h
such a thing from me?"

"I am not . . . I cannot . . . oh, Mrs. Jolly." Juliana thr
herself into her arms and sobbed out the tears she'd be

ttling for months. "I'm sorry . . . wanted to tell you, but I
s afraid you would hate me."

"Nonsense," the woman soothed, stroking the girl's hair.
ou are as dear to me as any daughter. That is why I made a
int of writing to your cousin, and why I was so pleased
en you said that he had offered for you. I have always
ped for you to make a marriage with a gentleman as fine
d upstanding as he is."

Juliana shook her head. "He is fine and upstanding. But I
not love him. I thought I could, but . . . no, it is not pos-
le. He cares more for social convention than he does for
safety of our country . . . or for me. He will have me boxed
d banded like some fancy hat, and keep me in his cupboard
display. How could I endure such a life . . ." She closed her
s and bit back another rising sob. "I know Connor is a vil-
and a traitor—perhaps even a murderer. But I love him
I cannot possibly marry another."

"I am afraid it is the only thing that *is* possible. My dear, I
Il tell you a story—something I have told to no one, not
n my son." She glanced at the door to the sitting room, as
o make certain it was securely shut. "Years ago I fell in
e. The man was far beneath my station, but that hardly
ttered. I believed everything he told me, and allowed him
arry me off to Gretna Green."

Surprise dried Juliana's tears. "You, Mrs. Jolly? But you
so proper."

"I was seventeen, my dear, and twice as willful as you. But
aid for my indiscretion tenfold. On the way to the anvil
re was a terrible carriage accident. When I woke days
r I found that I'd lost the use of my legs, and the man
o'd sworn to love me all his life had taken the first mail
ch back to London."

Juliana's own distress paled beside what Mrs. Jolly had
lured. "The monster. He should have been drawn and
artered."

The woman's mouth ticked up. "He married a shrew̶i̶ heiress from Surrey, which I believe was a worse fate. But ̶ own reputation was in great jeopardy. I would have been ̶ ined, except for a few valiant friends who stood by my si̶ The most noble of these was my dear Robert, Horatio's ̶ ther. I'd always thought him a buffoon, but by giving me ̶ name and protection he silenced the rumors. He might ha̶ been a bit buffle-headed, but he had a heart as big as t̶ world. And, in time, I came to have a true and abiding aff̶ tion for him."

Juliana folded her hands in her lap, sitting very still. "Y̶ think that my situation is the same—that I will eventua̶ develop feelings for Grenville, and that . . . Connor nev̶ loved me."

Hortensia Jolly covered the girl's tightly clasped han̶ "I've no crystal ball, my girl. I cannot tell what the futu̶ holds for your feelings or your heart. But, for what it is wor̶ I believe that the captain did care for you. I spoke to him o̶ night about you . . . yes, I know you weren't aware of it, bu̶ happened all the same. In fact, I must admit to be quite s̶ prised when I found that he was a traitor. I am rarely wrong in my judgments . . . but it's of no consequence. If h̶ alive at all, he is nowhere near England. And even if he we̶ he could never offer you an honorable marriage. Grenvill̶ offer is the only thing that can redeem your reputation. Y̶ must think of what would be best for your child."

Slowly, Juliana nodded. "Of course you are right. That̶ the only thing that truly matters."

"In years to come you will see that you've made a wise ̶ cision. You will come to care for your husband as deeply a̶ cared for Robert, I am sure of it," Mrs. Jolly proclaim̶ "Now, go and dry those pretty eyes and come back to ̶ party."

The two left the sitting room. For a moment the room̶ mained empty. Then a side door that had been ajar ̶ pushed open, and an elegant, dark-haired gentleman stepp̶

hrough. "You see, I told you there was nothing to worry about.
"he will stay clear of the docks. And she will go through with
he marriage."

The man beside him stroked his chin, saying nothing.

"She will," the first man insisted as he nervously raked
back his hair. "She has no choice. The line will be ours, as we
ntended from the first."

"See that it is. Time is running short, and we need ab-
olute control of the line. Either the chit marries, or I will
eal with her as I dealt with her father. And you, my lord, will
ot be far behind."

And with that the man known as the Admiral made his
vay out of the room and rejoined the Jollys' dinner party.

21

—🍃—

.

"Are you sure we should be doing this again?" Meg asked as she pulled her cloak closer and hurried after Juliana along the banks of the Thames. "We had bad luck when we came to the docks alone before. And Grenville made it clear that he considered it unseemly for you to visit the Marquis Line offices."

"Yes, well, that is why we hired a coach instead of taking one of our own, so that there would be no servants to report back to him. Besides, Grenville does not own me or the line. At least, not for three more days. In any case, he is at Mrs. Pemberton's recital this evening, listening to the lady massacre Mozart. He will never even know that we went to the offices."

"And why exactly are we going to the offices?"

Why indeed? It seemed that she had fewer and fewer answers these days. Since her talk with Mrs. Jolly she'd tried to resign herself to her fate. Yet it was important that she make the right choice for her future—for herself, for the Marquis

Line, and, most important, for her child. "Perhaps if I see my old office, I shall be able to give it up more easily. Perhaps all I require is a chance to say good-bye."

The offices were locked up tight for the night, but Juliana knew the clerk's secret of jiggling the side door handle in such a way that the latch dropped. Inside, she walked through the deserted offices, savoring the memories of the days she had spent at the helm of this company, helping to continue her father's legacy. She'd been respected. She'd had her dreams. And she had not yet discovered that the man she loved with all her heart was nothing but a vile traitor.

While Meg searched for a light, Juliana stood next to the wide window in the owner's office. She could see the clouds building in the distance, foretelling that a storm was on its way. Her gaze wandered to the ships anchored in the Thames, a forest of masts rising and falling in the gentle tide. She felt as if a part of her was coming back to life. She recognized the silhouettes of the Marquis Line ships even in the deepening twilight. The *Silver*, the *Lysander*, the *Jennie Fagin*, and more . . . she knew them the way she knew the fingers on her hand, and loved each and every one of them.

And already she could see that Grenville was making decisions for them that neither she nor her father would have approved of.

Many of the ships were in port—too many for this time of the season. Her cousin was missing the best trade winds of the year. Perhaps Grenville was waiting on cargo shipments from the north, but it was still pure folly to keep what amounted to half the Marquis fleet in the port at once. Grenville should have had more care with the business, but she was unsurprised that he had not. Ever since his speech at dinner, she'd known he was far more interested in making political connections at the War Office than he was in the shipping business.

The line had been her father's legacy to her, but she had given it up to an indifferent owner in a time of great danger and strife. For too long she had been avoiding taking responsibility for her own mistakes and triumphs. She had been letting others steer her course. If decisions were to be made about her life, she was the one who had to make them. Good or bad, right or wrong, socially approved or beyond the pale.

She placed her hand on her stomach, thinking about the baby inside her. She wanted to give her baby an honorable name and a decent life, but what kind of decency was based on a lie? Her father had given her a legacy of courage and honor, of facing life head-on whatever the consequences. Did her child deserve any less?

The first huge drops of rain began to splatter against the window, but she barely noticed. Turning her back on the society she'd always known was a frightening prospect, yet she believed in her heart that it was the right thing. Somehow she knew it was what her father would have wanted her to do. And for the first time in weeks she was charting her own course.

"Meg, you will likely think me the greatest fool in the world. But I cannot turn my back on my Father's dream for the price of social acceptance, anymore than I can turn my back on my ch—Meg?"

There was no answer.

Honestly, that girl must get her spectacles checked if she has gotten lost in these offices. Using the remains of the twilight, Juliana felt along the bookshelves. "It is all right Meg," she called out. "I remember keeping a phosphorous box on the shelves . . . yes, here it is."

She struck the spark and lit a nearby candle, placing it on the corner of Grenville's desk. *My desk, soon. And likely to be the only place I'm welcome in a long, long time.* Still, she could feel her spirits rising by the second. The prospect of never attending another of Mrs. Pemberton's boring soirees or drinking another glass of warm lemonade at Almack's, or making polite, vapid conversation with Lord Renquist vastly appealed to her. She'd made the right choice, she was sure of t. She was—

Her thoughts veered in another direction as she spied a piece of paper on the top of the desk. Curious, she lifted it up to the flickering candlelight. It was a cargo invoice for the *Silver*, one of her father's largest ships. According to the manifest, Grenville intended to send it out only half full of cargo. Monstrous waste of cargo space, and a foolish move even for the most foolish of businessmen. She was taking back the line none too soon. Curious at what other blunders her cousin was making, she sifted through the rest of the correspondence on his desk. After all, it was still hers by right, and she would be back in this chair as soon as she told him the wedding was off—

Her hand still as she picked up a letter that had been secreted at the bottom of the pile. It bore the signature of Viscount Melville, the First Lord of the Admiralty. It was hard to make out in the dim light, but it appeared to be some sort of naval plan. "Meg, come here at once. I've found something very curious on Grenville's desk, and I—"

Lightning split the sky outside, throwing a man's shadow on the wall in front of her. Before she could even think to scream, she was grabbed from behind and a cloth was clamped over her mouth and nose. She struggled valiantly, but a gagging scent sucked her down like numbing quicksand. She tumbled into unconsciousness, but just before as the blackness closed around her, she heard a voice speaking as if from a great distance away.

"Hell, Princess, can't you just once keep your pretty neck out of trouble?"

She felt Connor wrap her in a thick cloak to protect her from the rain and cradle her against him as if she were the most precious thing in the world. She snuggled into the warmth of his embrace, the black despair of the last few months clearing like smoke in the wind. Everything would be all right now. Connor would make it all right. She wanted to tell him that she was only half-alive without him, that she knew in her heart that none of the things they said about him were true, that they were going to have a child, that she had never stopped believing in him, or wanting him, or loving him . . . She tried and tried to say the words, fighting against the strange lethargy when she finally broke free—minutes, hours or days later, she couldn't tell which—her eyes fluttered open and she blinked, expecting to gaze into Connor's brilliant, loving eyes . . .

But Connor was not there.

Warm lantern light illuminated the cozy bedchamber, while the relentless night storm still raged outside a window. Juliana groaned, feeling woozy and achy, as if she had just consumed a great quantity of wine. But even more painful was the disappointment. It had been a dream. Nothing but another foolish dream. Swallowing her despair, she started to push herself up from the pillows, but froze as she sensed that something was amiss. The curtains on the nearby window were sunny yellow instead of her bedchamber's royal blue. Unless someone had dramatically redecorated her room while she was sleeping—and shrunk it to half its size—she was no longer at the Jollys'.

"Meg, what is going—" Her words died as she caught sight of the thick cloak that was still wrapped around her body—a cloak that did not belong to her. Memory flooded back. The office . . . the terrifying shadow . . . the overpowering scent that still lingered in the back of her throat. She struggled to sit upright on the bed, disturbing the blanket that had been carefully tucked around her. "Meg! Where—?"

"Hush now," a soft voice nearby said calmly. A young woman moved into view, a pretty blond girl wearing a blue dress that matched her eyes. Juliana blinked, trying to focus her still-blurred vision. She didn't recognize the girl, but there was something vaguely familiar about her.

"Do not try to rise yet," the young woman cautioned as she laid a gentle hand on Juliana's shoulder. "You must give yourself a few minutes to clear your head, and regain your strength."

"Like . . . hell," Juliana bit out as her mind cleared along with her vision. The soft-spoken girl might seem harmless, but she must be part of the kidnapping. Juliana struggled to rise, fighting against the lingering effect of the drug. "Where am I? Where's Meg?"

"You are in a building near the wharf, in apartments over an old sailmaker. No, do not try to stand yet. Your friend is sleeping in the room next door. She is fine, I assure you."

"You *assure* me? I've been *kidnapped*! I want to see Meg. I want—"

"Lie still."

The quiet command from the other side of the room brought Juliana to a dead stop. Slowly she turned her head, her heart pounding so hard that she thought it would crack her ribs.

"Hello, Princess."

A man stepped out of the room's shadows. His ragged hair was damp and tangled, his face was in want of a razor, and his worn greatcoat and mud-spattered boots would have drummed him out of any gentlemen's club. Fear and joy flooded through her. He was alive. He was safe. And he had kidnapped her. She gripped the covers, hating him, loving him, wanting him to hold her so hard that it hurt.

"Bastard!"

He wrapped his gloved hand around the bedpost. "Well, I see the drug did not affect your memory."

"The magistrate will clap you in irons for kidnapping me," she proclaimed as she struggled to a sitting position.

She opened her mouth to scream, but he spoke first. In the past these rooms were used by press-gangers, and they have been well equipped to muffle any sound. But please, yell if you like." He bent closer, his smile hovering dangerously close to a grin. "God's teeth, you're beautiful when you're angry."

Oh, he was despicable! She started to reply, but the girl stepped between them. "Connor, it is not fair to tease her. She needs to recover her wits."

Juliana had wit enough to see the look that passed between them. Such a look happened only between old friends—or lovers. *He's brought me to the house of his mistress,* Juliana thought, fury tempering the misery in her heart. *Could any man be more loathsome?*

"Rose is right. I'm sorry for this, but you left me no choice. I could not have you going to the authorities with what you'd found in the office. I promise you will not be harmed—"

"You *promise.*" Impassioned, Juliana rose to her feet—and dropped like a stone.

Connor caught her up inches before she hit the floor. "God's teeth, will you never listen to me?"

She barely heard him. The feel of his arms around her was more intoxicating than any drug. Memories filled her, of the night in Portugal, when he'd held her, loved her, and promised not to leave her. But those words had been a lie, just like everything else. She pushed herself out of his arms and slapped him.

Lucky to the last, Connor thought as he watched her sink to the bed. If she'd put her full strength behind that punch, she would have likely decked him. He stripped off his leather riding gloves and worked his bruised jaw, knowing it was going to ache like hell in a little while.

Like his heart.

"I know you've no reason to trust me. God knows I don't blame you, but you must listen to me, for your own safety. The truth is—"

She glared up at him, her eyes ablaze with indignation. "The truth? I will tell you the truth. You kidnapped us. And before that, you kidnapped me. At best you are a despicable py, at worst a murderer. You lied to me about your past. You ised my friendship and regard to further your plots, you deerted me and Jamie in Portugal. Tell me, is that not the ruth?"

"Most of it," he answered honestly.

He saw the pain in her eyes, and knew she'd been hoping or a different answer. For a moment he'd considered giving to her, of lying to her one more time. But he couldn't do it, ot now.

"Rose, will you see to Miss Evans, and make sure that she s all right?"

"But Raoul is with her."

Connor snorted. "That is what I meant. See to her. Beides, I have some things to . . . discuss with Lady Juliana."

"There is nothing I wish to discuss with you," she replied aughtily as the girl slipped out of the door. "Except possibly ie dimensions of your coffin, for they shall surely hang you or what you have done. You are a black-hearted, traitorous, respassing, kidnapping scoundrel!"

"I won't deny that I am all those things, and more besides. God knows I've made mistakes in my life—too many for any hance at redemption. But there's one thing I'll not do, even ' it buys me a prime seat on Newman's lift." His eyes narowed and took on a deadly sheen. "I will not watch the oman I love sail a course that is likely to get her a prime iew of the Thames from the bottom up."

22

—🍃—

The woman he loved. For a moment Juliana forgot how to breathe. Joy raged through her like wildfire, bringing life back to all the cold, hurting places inside . . . until her common sense returned. He could say that he loved her until judgment day, but the facts proved him a liar.

She stood up and balled her hands into tight fists, seething with fury and shame. "The only danger I am in is from *you*. If you think that you will gain my trust with more of your lies you are sadly mistaken. I know what you are. Traitor. Kidnapper. *Murderer.* The authorities will track you down and justice will prevail."

"I only hope it does," he replied cryptically. "You will never know how hard it was for me to stay away from you. All those weeks . . . when you were so very ill, and Dr. Fairchild feared for your life."

"How did you know—?" She closed her eyes, the answer coming in a flash. "Jamie. No wonder he never seemed to miss you. You used him to spy on me."

"To make sure you were safe," Connor corrected. He stepped nearer, so close she could smell the scent of rain on his skin. "God, I've missed you. I've thought of you every day, every hour."

With her vision fully cleared she could see the drawn, haunted shadows under his eyes. He looked on the edge of exhaustion, and it was all she could do not to reach out and cradle his weary head against her breast. But his words a lie, like all his others. "You are a black-hearted scoundrel of the worst sort. And as soon as the commodore and Grenville find that you have kidnapped me, they will—"

"Grenville." Connor's shadowed jaw pulled taut. "Your fiancé."

"Y-yes, my fiancé," she stated. She had already decided not to marry her cousin, but she had no intention of telling Connor that, or of confessing anything that might give him any hint that she was still monstrously in love with him. "Gren—that is, my dearest, darling Grenville, whom I love with all my heart, will come to my rescue. We're going to be married in three days, you know. Three days—"

"Enough!"

Connor's roar shook the room. He grabbed her shoulders with all the wounded hunger she'd imagined a hundred times in her dreams. For a moment she thought he might throttle her. Instead he cursed, and began to stalk the room like a caged animal. "God's teeth, why did you have to blunder into his office, tonight of all nights? You could have ruined everything."

"I hope I did. I hope I ruined all your fiendish plots. And when the authorities catch you, I hope they throw you in prison for a thousand years."

"Well, you might just get your wish. I suppose I should be pleased. You are the one person who once had complete faith in me, and now you think I am the blackest scoundrel in the world. Apparently Melville's plan worked."

"Vi-Viscount Melville, the first Lord of the Admiralty?"

His low chuckle rumbled through the room. "You never expected that card, did you? A posh lord seeking out a blackguard like me. But he did. He needed my help."

He leaned closer and wrapped his fingers around one of the bedposts as he continued. "For years Whitehall's secrets have been compromised by the Admiral's spies. His duplicity has cost the country dozens of battles and the lives of hundreds of men. He keeps to the shadows, never showing his true face, letting his network of criminals and villains do his work for him. Few have heard his voice, and almost no one has seen his face. And everyone the War Office sent after him ended up dead.

"England was losing the war, so Whitehall decided on a new plan. Instead of risking their own men, they decided to use someone from the Admiral's own class—someone who could walk into a den of thieves and call it home. They needed a man with a disreputable past—and God knows I had trouble to spare. Raoul and I were already privateers. We were already skirting the law—the Admiralty just arranged for our reputations to become a little more . . . colorful. It was the perfect solution by their standards—set a criminal to catch a criminal. Besides"—he gripped the bedpost so hard that his knuckles turned white—"no one would miss either of us if we ended up in the gutter with a knife through the ribs."

Juliana's hand flew to her throat, unable to hide her true feelings in the face of the vivid image. "I cannot believe the Admiralty would send two men into such danger."

"Can't you? To the members of your class I will never be anything but a wharf rat—" He winced, then shook his head. "Hell, you didn't deserve that."

He ran his hand over his tired face, and breathed a sigh that seemed dredged from the heart of his soul. "In any event, the plot worked. The Admiral took the bait and recruited us. All it cost me was what remained of my reputation and honor. A bargain by anyone's standards."

Connor a hero instead of a traitor? "But how can you expect me to believe you are working for the War Office? You are a wanted traitor. You stole Admiralty dispatches!"

"My orders were to *deliver* the dispatches to our operatives in northern Portugal. They were crucial to our forces in the Peninsula, and the only way to ensure their safety was to transport them on the ship of the one captain the Admiral trusted completely. That is why I could not let you leave my ship. If you'd gone to the authorities, the Admiral would have found out I was working against him, and the dispatches might never have reached their destination in time. You would have blown the plan to high heaven and cost countless soldiers their lives—not to mention getting both you and me killed in the bargain. The Admiral doesn't like loose ends."

"If this is true, then why did you not tell me when I saw the dispatches?"

Connor reached out and tucked a finger under her chin. Gently, he brushed the rough pad of his thumb across her cheek. "Because you would not have believed me, Princess. Any more than you believe me now."

She jerked away from his hand, condemned by his words and seared by his touch. His eyes captured hers, ice-hard and wild, but clear of any duplicity. "And did the Admiral also order you to desert me?"

He winced as the barb struck home. She was surprised to feel his pain stab her own heart. "He learned that I was working against him. I suspected it when the French ships attacked so viciously, but I was not certain that the plan had gone sour until . . ."

He swallowed, taking a moment's pause. "That morning in Portugal, I went up in the hills and delivered the dispatches to the Spanish guerrillas who were to smuggle them across the border. When I returned I saw the soldiers . . . and Grenville. I knew that I'd been betrayed. There was no way to help you and Jamie, and I knew your ignorance of my connection to the Admiral would keep you safe. Even then, it took two of the Spaniards to hold me back—"

"But the false dispatches. If you didn't know the soldiers were coming, why did you put the blank paper in my pocket?"

Connor looked sheepish. "You *never* had the real dispatches. I gave you that packet to get you into the longboat when the French attacked. It was the only way I could think to get you off the ship. I would have done anything to keep you safe."

Safe? He'd left her with her heart in shreds. But, if any part of what he was saying was true . . . She walked slowly to the other side of the room, her mind reeling. "If that is true, why did you not come to me after you had returned to London?"

"Because for the past few months Raoul and I have been one step ahead of the hangman. We've been setting traps for the Admiral's men, gathering evidence against them, but it's been a slippery task. The Admiral has set his entire organization against us. And since the War Office cannot acknowledge us without tipping their hand, the law is after us as well. Involving you in any way would have put you in danger. I couldn't risk that—not again. It was hell not to be with you, especially when I heard you were so ill. Once I even started to go to your front door, but Grenville showed up—God's teeth, of all the men in the world, how could you make such an idiotic choice for a husband?"

Because I am having your child. But she dared not confess it. He could be lying. So she gave the rote answer she had spoken so many times at so many social gatherings before. "Grenville is a fine and honorable man. It is a privilege to have engendered his affection."

Connor's eyes narrowed to a dangerous gleam. "Are you so in love with him that you believe that? Yes, I suppose you must love him. Otherwise, you would have never agreed to marry him so soon after we—" Cursing, he turned away. "Whatever you believe of him, it is a lie. He's been using the Marquis Line to smuggle secrets and munitions to the

French. And I'm all but certain that he's the Admiral's right-hand man."

Juliana gasped. Grenville working for the Admiral? The notion was absurd beyond belief! And yet . . . of all the things Connor had told her, this one rang truest in her heart. It explained the dispatches she had found on Grenville's desk, and why he sent the ships out with what appeared to be a less than full loads of cargo. And she had always wondered why her cousin was so reluctant to have her visit the Marquis Line offices, and why he'd been so quick to give up his commission and take over the business, and why he'd kept proposing to her, even after he knew that she was carrying another man's child—

Perhaps Connor was telling her the truth. Perhaps he had never betrayed her at all, but was trying all along to keep her safe.

She bit her lip, finally beginning to trust the ashes of hope that stirred in her heart. "Have you proof of this? Anything that shows that you are working for the War Office?"

"Well, I did not expect I would have need of presenting it tonight," he growled. "Besides, if the Admiral's men found a commission on me, I'd have been dead in two minutes. And Lord Melville wasn't about to put anything in writing. He'd deny me even now, to avoid revealing himself to the Admiral. If I'm caught now I'll go straight to prison—if I'm lucky."

"Then have you proof of Grenville's duplicity?"

"I believe that proof exists on the *Silver*. I found papers in his office that show she's set to sail in two days, even though her cargo hold is only half full. If I can board her in secret tomorrow night and if I find that the extra cargo space is full of—but no," he admitted, hanging his head. "I have nothing that I can show you now."

She wrapped her arms around her middle, feeling the same sickening devastation that she'd experienced in Portugal when she'd first learned he'd deserted her. "Then why should I believe that you are not trying to use my feelings for you to convince me not to go to the authorities?"

His ragged words seemed torn from his soul. "I had hoped you would know I could never use you in such a way."

"And how could I know that? You yourself told me I had no idea what you were capable of. You said as much that night in Portugal—" She swallowed a sob, realizing too late that she'd let her lifelong love for him cloud her judgment. When she looked at him, she still saw a shadow of the boy who had been her protector, the young lieutenant who'd won her heart, and the privateer captain she'd fallen in love with all over again. Even now she was willing to believe him, against all logic and reason.

But facts were facts, and all the hope in her heart couldn't change them. "Can you show me nothing to prove you've spoken the truth?"

He swallowed, his eyes filled with misery. "After what I've put you through, you'd be a fool to believe me. I see that now. I'm sorry, Princess."

I'm sorry, Princess. Another time he'd spoken those words came back to her, on the night he'd left the house after admitting to stealing her father's money. Since then, nothing had been right in her life, nothing had made sense. She'd been half of a whole, enduring her life instead of living it, until Connor had taken her in his arms in Portugal and reminded her what being alive meant.

Liar. Villain. Traitor. She had ample proof that he was all these things. Yet when she looked in his eyes, she saw the ghost of the half-starved wharf rat who had jumped into the freezing Thames to save her. Men changed—but not that much. Connor had risked his life for her that day. He'd been her friend and protector, her champion in all things. He would have walked into hell to save her.

Perhaps it was time she walked into hell to save him.

She took a deep breath. "Connor, I believe—" She stopped as a flash of lightning illuminated the wall behind im, a place thick in shadows. Stunned, she barreled past Connor as if he wasn't there. She stood in front of the wall, staring at the squares of fabric mounted with great care in a picture frame. Hardly daring to breathe, she lifted her hand and touched the glass. "My curtains. You kept them."

"Foolish, I suppose," Connor said as he came to stand behind her. "Went against my ruthless privateer image. But they were the one proof I had that you'd once loved me. For years I had my sister keep them on her farm, but I asked Rose to bring them here when I—Juliana, are you crying?"

"She's your sister! Rose . . . I thought . . . but she's your sister!"

"Of course she is," Connor agreed, looking at the Juliana with growing concern. "Perhaps you should sit down."

"I don't want to sit down," she cried, her words choking out between laughter and tears. "We're both idiots, Connor. Hopeless, bloody idiots. How do you think our poor baby is going to fare, with two such foolish parents?"

"Our *baby*?"

"Well don't look so shocked, Captain Gabriel," she said as she wound her arms around his neck. "You're not the only one who can keep a secret. I'm not half bad at it my—"

Her words died as he swept down on her mouth, and ravished her with a joy and hunger that made his caresses in Portugal seem tame.

23

—❧—

Connor cradled Juliana against his chest and traced slow figure eights on her naked back, savoring the sweet afterglow of their lovemaking. He'd thought he was not capable of feeling any more love for her, but the idea of her carrying their child made him cherish her with a fineness he'd never believed possible in his rough and ragged soul. "Our child," he mused in wonder as he splayed his hand over her stomach. "So that is why you were going to marry. You wanted to give our babe a name."

"Um, but I had already decided not to go through with it even before you kidnapped me."

"You'd already decided—" Connor leaned back against the pillows and threw his arm over his eyes. "I wish you had told me that to start with. I was half-mad believing you'd fallen in love with another. And with Grenville, of all people. Not that I would have allowed you to go through with it. Raoul and I were already concocting plans to stop the wedding. Who knows," he added, grinning. "I might have had to kidnap you."

"Sir, you have quite used up your credit on that score. In any event, when I walk down the aisle, I have already determined it will be with a notorious privateer."

His grin faded. "Not just a privateer, Juliana. There's something you need to know. Something I need to tell you. They informed you that I was a murderer. Well . . . I am.

"I told you of the infernal captain who gave me this scar. What I did not tell you is that I was one of the lucky ones. He would lock men in the hold for days, even weeks at a time. Sometimes for no reason at all.

"One night he picked a battle with Raoul's uncle's ship. It was an ill choice—the snow outgunned him on all fronts. With his ship sinking, the captain ordered several of his men, including me, to launch the longboat and row him to shore. It would have meant safety for me, but I knew he was leaving the men in the hold behind to drown like rats. I demanded he give me the key. I can still remember his laugh, how it mingled with the screams of the men below. That's when I wrapped my hands around his throat. I don't remember much of anything after that, not until I found myself in the hold with key in hand—"

Juliana's fingers stopped his mouth. "Hush. That foul captain was the murderer, not you. You saved those poor men."

"Unfortunately, the lords of the Admiralty might not see it that way. If a witness comes forward, I'll hang for mutiny instead of treason—if the Admiral does not get me first. Either way, 'tis likely to be a short marriage. You'll be a widow almost before you're a bride."

"You are not to talk like that. We will search the *Silver* and unmask the Admiral, and we will live happily ever after. I have decided on it."

"Have you?" he commented softly as he curled a strand of her silken hair around his fingers. "Well, if there is anyone who can make miracles happen, it is . . ." He paused, realizing what she'd said. "What do you mean, *we* will search the ship? I'm not risking you or our child. You are not going to be anywhere near the *Silver*."

"But it is a big ship, and I know it like the back of my hand. And you and Raoul could use my help, you know you could."

"Maybe so, but that doesn't mean I intend to take it. I have already put you at risk by telling you the truth about Grenville. You and Meg are going back to the Jollys' house and stay safely put until this whole affair is over."

"La, talk all you please." She waved away his concerns. "You can not order me and Meg to our rooms as if we were children. If you will not take me with you to search the *Silver*, I will simply go on my own. Of course, 'twould be more prudent if we went together instead of stumbling over each other, but if you insist . . ."

Connor rammed his hand through his hair. "You are the most confounded woman! This is not a garden party you are crashing—'tis a dangerous espionage operation. If we land in the suds over this one, you'll lose more than your reputation."

"All the more reason for me to come." She wound her arms around his neck. "You know there is no life for me without you. If trouble comes, I want to be at your side when you meet it. 'Tis where I belong—the only place I have ever belonged."

"I will not—ah, hell!" He turned her beneath him and took her mouth in a crushing kiss. She was his love and his life, the one sweet, true thing in his tarnished existence. In her eyes he saw the reflection of a hero, a better man than he was, but a man he might some day become with her help and the help of their child. She was right—there was no life for her without him, any more than there was life for him without her. He'd spent enough desolate years without her to know that. "All right. Triumph or defeat, we'll face the future together. Besides, I have never been able to change that determined mind of yours once it is made up."

"Wise decision. Of course, it could not hurt you to try—"

A knock on the door interrupted her. "*Mon ami*, it is time."

"Blast," Connor said as he rolled to the side of the bed. "It's past midnight. If we are to get you and Meg home before the servants report that you've been out all night, we must leave now."

"But we've had so little time."

"Soon we'll have all the time in the world," he promised, kissing her. "Get dressed. And tomorrow you must keep to your rooms and refuse to see anyone, so that Grenville has no opportunity to discover that you are on to him. Then, at midnight tomorrow, Raoul and I will meet you at the end of your alleyway."

"All right, though I do not believe the lying in is necessary," she said as she slipped her gown over her head. "Meg is a grand actress, and though I am not up to her mark, I can be convincing enough when I have to be. But I must ask—are you certain that Grenville is the man you seek? He is an inept businessman, but he is still of our family, and he has been most kind to Jamie. It is hard for me to believe that he is as evil as you say. Could you not be letting your childhood dislike of him color your opinion?"

Connor cursed as he fastened his belt. "Hell yes, I despise the man. When I was a boy he never treated me as anything other than a filthy guttersnipe. But he is a traitor, all right. The Admiral has always coveted the Marquis Line. Now Grenville has delivered it to him, lock, stock, and barrel."

Juliana swallowed and sat back on the bed. "If the Marquis ships are being used to transport munitions, the reputation of the Line would be ruined."

Her expression showed that she felt as if she'd just lost her father all over again. Connor wrapped her in his arms and smoothed her hair, but another knock stopped him from any further comfort. Damn, he hated this job, this war, this whole bloody mess. Most of all, he hated that it hurt *her*. "Years from now, when we are very old and sitting by a fire, with two dozen grandchildren playing at our feet, we'll have forgotten all about this dark business."

"Yes, we will," she said, her voice wavering. "And who knows—by then you might have won an argument or two."

He gave her a fierce hug. "Ah, Princess, I do not believe in miracles."

But he silently sent up a prayer to whatever angel was listening, knowing they would likely have need of a few miracles before this game was played out.

The obsidian water lapped against the curve of the *Silver*'s hull as the longboat pulled alongside. Juliana ran her hand lovingly over the smooth wooden surface, feeling it rise and settle with a rhythm as steady as a beating heart. Ships had souls, and this one's was fine and true as the bright metal for which it was named. And if Grenville and the Admiral had misused her or any of her other ships for their nefarious deeds, Juliana vowed she would make them pay for every pound of contraband cargo.

Connor and Raoul took a final pull toward the ship. With no more sound than the slap of a wave, they lifted the heavy oars from the water and stowed them in the locks. Connor took up the claw and knotted line, and lobbed it up and over the side of the ship. He yanked it twice to make sure it was firmly hooked into the railing, then hunkered down.

"Right. You all know the plan. We board her here at the forecastle, away from the watchman on the waist and quarterdeck. Keep to the shadows. It is the last night of shore leave, so she'll only be manned by a skeleton crew. Get below as quick as you can. St. Juste and Meg take the upper decks and the stores, while Juliana and I head down to the orlop deck. At the first sign of suspicious cargo, get back to the longboat and signal Rose on the docks. She'll alert the harbormaster. Any questions?"

"Just one last plea," Raoul said. "That these women will come to their senses, and stay here until we return."

Meg and Juliana shared a knowing look, then casually ucked their oversized shirts into the boy's breeches they'd fted from the Jollys' youngest footmen for the occasion. The nen may be notorious privateers who were feared all along ne Barbary Coast, but they were quite helpless when it came o dissuading a pair of determined women. "We are coming nd that is settled," Juliana stated. "We'd best get to it."

As Connor surmised, the deck was nearly empty. The mid-ight watch strolled along, apparently more interested in olishing the buttons on his coat than in looking for tres-assers. Juliana and Connor slipped by the guards and down ne main hatch. It looked as if the tide of their luck was finally tarting to turn.

They came to the main hallway. Connor signaled her to tay flush against the wall while he checked to make certain ne corridor was empty. In the wavering light of the hallway's aint lantern, Juliana saw the glint of the pistol barrel stuck in Connor's belt. She swallowed, realizing again how much anger they were in. And yet, for the first time in months she asn't afraid. They were together, and whether their time asted fifty minutes or fifty years, it was the only life worth ving.

Low voices captured her attention. Someone was talking ehind the closed door of the officer's mess. She leaned closer, nd thought she caught the refined timber of a gentleman's ultured laugh. Grenville! But no, that was impossible. The ommodore had taken him to their gentlemen's club for a arewell celebration to his bachelorhood. The coachmen had eported that he had watched them walk into the entrance, here they were greeted by a dozen friends. Jolly was fever-hly proud of the party he had organized, and she knew he ould not let the guest of honor leave until the last glass had een raised. They would likely not return home until well ast dawn.

"Juliana!"

Connor motioned her to follow him down the steep stairs

to the lowest deck of the ship. The air was close and black as pitch.

" 'Tis like entering a tomb," she whispered.

"Aye. Too much like the hold of the stinking *Absalom* for my taste." He struck a light, then handed her the small, shielded signal lantern he'd fixed to his belt. "I'll search the bow section, while you take the aft. And remember, if you even smell trouble, call to me."

"I am not afraid," she assured him.

Connor's lips edged up. "You never could lie worth a damn." He placed a soft kiss on her forehead. "Now keep sharp, and keep safe. Remember we have fifty years and a dozen grandchildren ahead of us."

"Two dozen," she corrected, but he'd already disappeared into the darkness.

Juliana lifted her lantern high. She was surrounded by towers of grain sacks, all of them looking unsuspicious. From where she stood, the most dishonest thing about this cargo was the price stamped on the sacks. Honestly, it was criminal what merchants are charging for their grain these days.

A mouse skittered across the floor in front of her. Startled, she shinnied up the sacks, nearly reaching the top before she winced at her own folly. Sighing, she climbed over the top of the pile and started hand over hand down the other side. *I've far more to worry about than an undergrown rode—*

Her thoughts jarred to a halt as she surveyed the area hidden behind the wall of grain sacks. Rifles. Cannon barrels lying alongside pyramids stacks of balls. Kegs of gunpowder. Crates of cartridges. Guns, bayonets, and ordnance by the hundredfold. It was a valley of death that stretched almost from one end of the ship to another.

"C-Connor," she cried weakly. "Con—"

"I see it," he said, appearing at her side. "God's teeth. There's enough here to arm a fort for a month."

"And kill a thousand Englishmen," she whispered hoarsely. "We must get back to the longboat and—"

"That will not be necessary."

A figure stepped out from behind the sacks. Juliana stiff-
ed, but her fright turned to relief the moment she saw who
was. "Thank heaven you are here. Grenville has been using
e Line—"

"It was not Grenville," the man said.

Connor pulled on her arm, his gaze locked to the man's.
uliana, get behind me."

"Why? And of course it is Grenville. He is the only one
10 could have arranged a shipment like this—Connor, why
e you so pale?"

"I know that voice," he said, never taking his eyes off
e man.

"Well, of course." Juliana turned back to the man. "What
s happened to your accent?"

"I am devilishly afwaid he affected it, my deawr. Just as I
fected my lisp," Lord Renquist said as he came from be-
nd the sacks, flanked by two massive tars. "Regretted
issing Grenville's send-off tonight, but nothing to be done
out it. When the Admiral calls, I jump to it. Especially
1en there is a lady involved."

Juliana hardly listened. She was staring at the man who
uld have easily arranged this cargo but whom she'd never
spected because of his unassuming appearance and caring
vice. She'd let a viper into her doors and given him all the
wer he needed to work his traitorous schemes against her
1g and country. Because she'd trusted him. Because he'd
en her father's solicitor. Because he'd been her friend.

The man known as the Admiral, Silas McGregor.

24

— ❧ —

The boat shifted and the lantern swung in Juliana's hand, casting blades of light across the faces of the men in front of her. "How could you? You cared about the Marquis Line. You cared about *me*."

"And I *do*, my dear," McGregor said. "Transport has become a dreadful trouble to me of late—with new regulations, stricter security, and young, sharp-eyed customs officials. When I learned through my law firm of your father's plan to leave his shipping concern to a green girl, it was an opportunity I could not ignore. His death was easily arranged."

"My . . . father." Juliana's voice cracked as she realized the full extent of the evil plot that surrounded her. Only Connor's steadying hand on her arm kept her from sinking to her knees.

"Regrettable," McGregor agreed. "But necessary. I hope you know me well enough to know that I am not a cruel man. It was simply business. If Mrs. Jolly had not so obliging arranged for me to join your firm, rest assured that I shoul

ve found some other method of entering into it. 'Twas an
portunity I could not allow to let pass. It was little risk
—"

"For a dependable return," Juliana muttered, recalling the
icitor's long-ago adage to her. In his mind he was nothing
re than an ordinary businessman—except that he traded
 death and deception rather than salt and sugar. That
y ordinariness made him all the more chilling. "You—
nster!"

Amazingly, McGregor looked affronted. "Now that is
called-for. I was never so rude to you. In fact, I was quite
pressed by your business sense, so much so that I feared at
es you might find me or Renquist out. He was my contact
 the Admiralty, you know. Has been for years. And you
ved to be a great deal more resilient than either of us an-
pated. When I had my man Sikes stir up the captains
inst you, I expected you to faint like a dove. Likewise,
en the work at the line became so grueling, I expected you
and more of the responsibility to me. Instead, you were a
dit to the line, and to my tutelage."

McGregor's gaze skimmed to Connor. "You, my boy, are
. . disappointment to me. I was pleased when Juliana's
ection for you kept her off balance. And I had hoped to put
 in charge of my operation when I retired. Instead, you
rayed me most grievously."

Connor grimaced. "And I'm all broken up about it."

McGregor's eyes narrowed. "Enjoy your defiance, boy. It
n't last. In a short while you will be begging to die, just like
the others who were foolish enough to try to cross me. You
y think that you have destroyed my operation, but I can
uild it—I always do. But neither of you will live to see it."

"No!" Connor stepped between Juliana and the men and
pped her arm. "I am the one who betrayed you, not her.
t her go. In any case, she is only a girl. No one will listen to
. Surely you—"

His words were cut short by a commotion near the ladder. Another hulking seaman came down the rope steps and tossed down the flailing Meg Evans, followed by the limp form of Raoul.

"Meg!" Juliana cried.

"I am all right," Meg answered as she knelt beside Raoul's unconscious body. "But Mr. St. Juste . . . Raoul . . . he is badly wounded."

"Next time he will think twice before he crosses swords with me," Lord Renquist commented as he took out his snuffbox and applied a pinch to his hand. "Hardly a sporting match."

Juliana felt Connor's fingers tighten on her arm. She saw something flare in his eyes—something she did not like.

"You are right," Connor said, his charming smile returning like a full force gale. "St. Juste is no match for your skill. But I am. I've bested dozens of men, and every man jack of them was better than a tulip like you—"

"Connor!" Juliana cried. "Renquist is one of the finest swordsmen in all England."

"Finest coward, I'd say. I won't be killed by this dandy, too-soft hands. Not afraid to challenge an amateur, but terrified to face a proficient swordsman."

"Enough!" Renquist stalked forward, his face livid. "Under those gentleman's clothes you are nothing but the wharf rat you always were, and you need a lesson in how to speak to your betters. Someone get him a sword."

"Renquist, don't be an ass," McGregor said calmly as he took out his watch. "I wanted this hold secured before the crew returns. We haven't the time for silly games—"

"This is no game. 'Tis a matter of honor," the lord cried as he stripped off his elegant coat. "This low-born cur is no match for a gentleman. A fight to the death it is."

"Suits me fine," Connor replied as he shrugged out of his laborer's jacket.

McGregor glanced at his watch again, and shrugged. "Oh, ry well, Renquist. Have your sport. But I've work to do top- le." He glanced once more at his watch, then turned to the pe ladder. "I will return in a quarter of an hour. See that is business is dispatched by then. And Renquist, do be re to clean up the mess. Blood tends to distress the cus- ms officers."

Juliana watched as a chalk circle was drawn on the deck, d the sailors lined the perimeter like gawkers at a prize- ht, sizing up the odds. Unfortunately, Juliana had already ne so. Renquist was fit and well fed. Connor had been dging both the Admiral and the law for months. Despite skill, he was on the edge of exhaustion.

"Connor, don't do this," Juliana pleaded as she came to his le. "Renquist will cut you to ribbons."

"Hell, I'm dead anyway," Connor replied as he rolled up e sleeves of his shirt and studied his opponent. "God's eth, who'd have thought those fancy coats hid muscles like a—" Connor stopped musing, as if recalling who was lis- ning. Feigning confidence, he chucked her under the chin e way he used to when they were children. "Don't worry. I n best him. Meanwhile," he said as his voice dropped to a iisper, "you and Meg make for the ladder. If I distract the ards long enough, you might be able to slip out."

"Not without you," Juliana gripped his arm, fighting down e panic in her voice.

He gazed at her, his eyes saying more than words ever uld. "You must try to escape. For yourself, for me . . . and r baby."

Their baby. Yes, of course she had to try, for their child's ke. She spoke, trying to sound bold, but her voice came out a whisper. "I shall go on, for our child's sake. But we need u. Both of us. You must not die."

His mouth ticked up in a ghost of his trademark cockiness. till ordering me around, are you, Princess?"

She reached up and traced his scar, knowing that a lifetime would never be enough to say all the things she wanted
to say to him. But they hadn't a lifetime. They hadn't even a
moment. Before her next breath, Connor was pulled from
her arms and pushed into the center of the chalk circle, to
face the confident, cruel-eyed Renquist.

It was a lousy place for a fight. The ship pitched and rolled
with the rising tide, and the lanterns hung near the circle's
edge swayed so badly they nearly made him seasick. Most of
all, it was in a hold—a dark, close hold that reminded him too
much of the *Absalom*. Memories swirled though his mind,
making him every bit as nauseated as the shifting light. And
at the center of it all was Renquist, stalking the circle like a
sleek, well-fed panther, his haughty eyes looking down at
Connor as if he were not human at all, just a mongrel dog that
had to be destroyed. Wharf rat. Bastard. Dockside garbage.
Nothing.

But he wasn't nothing. Not to Juliana. Unable to resist,
his gaze strayed to where she and Meg cradled Raoul's unconscious form. Her face was white with fear, but she held
her chin high and glanced meaningfully at the nearby rope
ladder. She even gave him the wisp of an encouraging smile.
Her love had given him a nobility far beyond that of blood
or birth. In her eyes he was her shining, noble knight,
her hero—

Renquist lunged.

Connor twisted. Luck rather than skill made the blade
pass through his shirt, missing his chest by an inch. Juliana gasped. He spared a second to give her a jaunty smile,
then turned back to Renquist. "You appear to have missed,
m' lord."

"A lucky turn. But luck is no match for blood and breeding."

"Tell me, how much *blood and breeding* does it take to sell
out your country?"

"Shut your mouth. You know nothing of my reasons."

"Yes, but I can guess. High-stakes wagering. Fancy car-ges. A few opera dancers to maintain in the expected style. s an old story. One might even say—*common*."

Renquist lunged again. Connor parried the blade and un around, delivering a quick hit to the lord's sword arm. It s not deep, but it was enough to draw blood. Renquist cked away, looking stunned. "No one has ever drawn first od on me."

"Yes, well, I'm full of surprises," Connor growled as he sed his sword. "*En garde.*"

The fight began in earnest. Steel clashed on steel, again d again until the hold rang with the sound. The two men acked and parried, lunged and feinted. For endless min-es neither gained an advantage, but as the seconds ticked

Connor felt the strength of his thrusts ebbing, while nquist's seemed to grow stronger. He glanced at the men, and saw them edging closer to the stairs. But their y was still blocked by one of the sailors. *More time. I need re time.*

They came together, swords locked at the hilt in a move at brought them nose to nose.

"You cannot win," Renquist sneered. "But you've fought ll—give up now and I promise you a quick death."

"Tempting offer," Connor scoffed. "I'll hold out for a tter one."

Renquist brought down his sword, glancing his oppo-nt's shoulder. Connor winced at the pain, but his smile ver wavered. With his good arm he gripped Renquist's ord hand and deftly twisted it behind him. Then he ought the stunned lord against his chest, his sword at the bleman's throat.

With the blade at his neck, Renquist began to tremble. lease, do not kill me."

"I won't—if you order the guards to let the women pass."

Renquist's trembling grew stronger. "I cannot. The Admiral will kill me."

Connor brought the blade closer to the noble's throat and breathed into his ear, "And I'll kill you if you don't. So which will it be, my fine lord?"

Renquist swallowed. "Yes. I promise. Anything." He signaled to the two remaining guards. "You men. I'll pay you twice what the Admiral is giving you. Let the women pa—"

A roar like thunder split the air. Renquist went limp, his shoulder blossoming with a bright crimson stain. Shocked, Connor let him slide to the ground. McGregor stepped out o the shadows, flanked by his guards. "I was afraid of some thing like this," he said as he handed the empty pistol to a guard and received another. "I always suspected you woul betray me, Renquist. Your honor was all for show."

"I . . . wasn't," the lord said as he held his bleedin shoulder. "I would never—"

"Oh, be still. I left you alive so that the captain could finis the job. Though he paid me well to conceal the indiscre tion from his peers, Renquist is the lord who seduced you sister."

"What?" Connor turned and saw the terror in Renquist eyes. There could be no doubt. This cowardly dog was th man who had cruelly used and beaten his young sister. H twisted the sword that he still held in his hand, giving it bette purchase. It would be easy to cut the helpless man's throa satisfying the revenge that had burned in his blood every m ment of the months he spent on the *Absalom*, and the lor years he'd spent in disgrace and despair. *So very easy.*

A gentle hand stayed his arm. "No, Connor," Juliana sa softly as she came to his side. "To kill him like this, it would cold-blooded murder. It is what the Admiral wants."

Connor's chin shot up. He caught the gleam in McGrego eyes, the savoring the pleasure of watching another so warped by sin. God's teeth, it *was* what he wanted. D gusted, Connor threw down the blade. "She's right. He is n orth it. Neither are you. You're not a great man of business all, McGregor, but a sad, twisted puppeteer. And the sadest thing of all is that you don't even realize that you are a uppet too, that it is your avarice that pulls your strings—"

"Silence!" McGregor's calm veneer stripped away. "Nothing ontrols me. Nothing and no one! You will both be dead in econds. I'd planned a slow death for you, but having your dy watch you die, and knowing that she will die a moment ter, is more exquisite than any torture I could devise." He ocked the gun, and brought it level with Connor's chest. f you have any prayers, Captain, I suggest you say them ow—"

Again thunder roared through the air. Connor stopped reathing, waiting for the pain of a bullet tearing his gut. But e pain didn't come. Instead, he watched the light fade from cGregor's eyes. The gun slipped from his hand and he rumpled to the ground, revealing the man at the top of the ope ladder.

"My dear boy," Commodore Jolly said to Connor as he almly handed his smoking pistol to one of the multitude of eutenants and constables streaming down into the hold. This whole business would have been so much simpler if ou had shared your little plots with Lord Melville."

"I still cannot believe it," Connor said as he sat in the ollys' parlor while Juliana gave a final inspection to the banage the doctor had applied to his shoulder. "You have been atching Raoul and me for months, working under the direct rders of Lord Melville?"

"Just so," the commodore said as he took a sip of tea. "He ispected that you might need some support, even though ou insisted on putting as few people in danger as possible. ut I must tell you it is not so very easy for a man of my size to ass unnoticed in these narrow streets. That is why I played e buffoon. It is a ruse I have used quite successfully on any an occasion."

From the commodore's side, Hortensia Jolly gave an affronted huff. "Well you could have had the civility to tell your own mother."

Jolly bowed his head sheepishly. "I was under orders, Mama."

"Orders be jigged. I was mortally afraid that I'd raised a buffle-head," she stated, her expression growing glum. "Honestly, to think I was responsible for asking that horrid man to help our dear girl—"

"Madam, it is not your fault," the dear girl supplied. "We all believed him. In any case, if you had not asked him to assist me, he would have found another way to become indispensable to me. He said as much when Connor and I—"

"Were in that awful ship, facing that *devil*," Mrs. Jolly finished with a shiver. "You poor lambs. My first instinct was not to trust that man. I should have followed it. On the other hand," she added as her gaze swung to Connor, "my first instinct was not to trust you either, as far as Juliana's virtue was concerned. So—how soon is the wedding?"

"Mrs. Jolly," Juliana cried, blushing crimson. "Give us some time. We have only just escaped from certain death."

A heavily accented voice from the doorway chimed in "Then all the more reason to marry at once, my friends, for you are now used to precarious situations. And marriage, I have heard, is precarious indeed."

"Raoul!" Juliana ran to the door as the Frenchman hobbled in, followed closely by Meg, Rose, and Jamie. "But I thought you were not to leave your bed."

St. Juste waved his hand. "What is a broken leg? I am fit as—how do you say—a drum."

"Fiddle," Meg corrected. "The man terrorized poor Dr. Fairchild. Someone should keep an eye on him."

St. Juste cast a smile in her direction, indicating that he might not mind at all if that someone were she. Then his smile dimmed. "But it is important that I get well quickly

The fiend McGregor died without revealing who killed my uncle. As soon as I am able, I intend to hunt down the last of the Admiral's men to see if they know anything of my uncle's betrayer."

Connor nodded. For years, the thought of finding Daniel's murderer had been the driving force in his life. But now he had a new dream, and new responsibilities. He reached out his hand to Juliana. But she wasn't looking at him. Her gaze was fixed on the doorway behind him.

Grenville stood in the door, hat in hand. He fiddled the brim of it as he entered the room. "I have heard from the officers what transpired this night. And I—well, curse it." He walked over to Connor and stood before him, carefully avoiding Juliana's glance as he did so. "I have never been a saint, but I have always considered myself to be a fair man. But I have allowed our old—um, situation to cloud my judgment and to convince me that you were the Admiralty traitor. Looking back, I can see that Lord Renquist had access to many of the stolen documents, but I never thought to suspect him because he was a peer. I misjudged you sorely, Captain, and not for the first time. I can do nothing to change our past, but I can offer you my heartfelt apology and appreciation for your willingness to risk your life for our country. You have the bravery and honor of a gentleman, and I would count it an honor to shake your hand."

For a long while, Connor stared at the offered hand. Once Grenville's insults had lashed his young ego like a whip, and Connor had hated him for it. Grenville had misjudged him— but Connor had to own that he had done the same. He'd let his old hatred of Juliana's cousin convince him that Grenville was the person smuggling secrets through the Marquis Line, instead of looking at all the possible suspects. Swallowing, he clasped the hand of his old enemy. "We cannot change our past, but perhaps we can change our future."

Grenville gave a quick nod. Then, with an equally quick

glance between Connor and Juliana, he muttered something about having to be at the Admiralty at the crack of dawn, and left the room.

Juliana hurried after him. "Grenville," she said as she caught up with him in the foyer. "Please, I have to speak to you. About the wedding—"

"There is no need," her cousin replied as he took his coat from the footman. "The commodore explained everything to me. You may break our betrothal without censure, and without any stain on your name. In any event, the War Office has been urging me to return to my former operations on the Peninsula. I believe I shall take them up on their request."

"There is no need for you to leave. You are still a part of this family. And you shall always have a place in my heart for the kindness you showed to me."

"*Kindness?* My dear, there was nothing kind about it. I fell in love with you. Even after the commodore told me of Connor's heroic return, I'd hoped you might still . . . but the moment I saw you together, I knew. It is as it was between you when you were growing up—as it always will be."

"I am . . . so sorry. If Connor had not come back—"

"Then we would have endured a tepid marriage, of not much use to anyone. It is better this way. For both of us." He settled his hat on his head and turned toward the front door before adding softly, "I wish you well, Juliana."

For several minutes Juliana stood in the empty hallway, staring at the closed front door. Behind her she could hear the voices of her family through the open door to the parlor—Raoul's smooth accent as he charmed a laughing Meg, Jolly's repeated assurances to his mother that he would never, ever deceive her again, and Rose's soft but insistent attempts to convince Jamie that it was indeed time for him to go to bed. Yet she needed no sound or voice to tell her when he came to stand behind her.

"Are you all right?"

"No," she admitted honestly. "Connor, I never meant to hurt him."

He turned her to him. "Not all endings can be happy ones. But who can tell? Perhaps he will be lucky enough to find a—" His mouth pulled up in a grin. He lifted her lips to his as he punctuated every word with a lingering kiss. "A bossy . . . stubborn . . . pigheaded . . ."

"You missed 'improper,'" she breathed against his mouth.

"I was getting to that. 'Tis the best part."

He lowered his mouth for a deeper caress, a lavish, heady embrace that held all the love of their past and all the promise of their future. Sighing with contentment, Juliana wondered at the miracle that this brave, good man had chosen to love her. Not that there had been much choice in the matter. As Grenville had said, the seed of love had begun to grow between them even while they were children. And no amount of pain, despair, separation, or heartache had been able to kill it.

As a girl she had worshiped him as her shining knight. Now she saw him as a man, full of strengths and weaknesses, victories and doubts. The perfect hero of her youth had been replaced by the reality of a flesh-and-blood man, striving to live with courage and honor in a world that valued those commodities too little. Somehow, that only made his armor shine brighter—

A too-loud cough behind them broke the embrace. Commodore Jolly advanced from the shadows, his self-conscious expression reminding Juliana that a part of him was still very much the blundering buffle-head she'd come to love. "Eh, I must be off to the Admiralty. There are papers to file, reports to fill out. 'Tis a bother, but there is nothing for it. Even clandestine operations require exhaustive documentation. Still, I wanted to make certain that I presented you with this," he said as he handed Connor a scroll of paper. "It contains a good deal of eloquent bluff and bluster, but to get straight to it—Melville has offered you and your men a place in the fleet. Your commission will be reinstated, awarding you the full rank of captain of the Royal Navy, if you wish it."

"If I wish—?" Connor turned the scroll over in his hand, staring at it as if it were made of solid gold. "You cannot imagine how much I have wanted . . .

Abruptly, the hope died in his eyes. Reluctantly, he held the paper back out to Jolly. "I cannot accept this honor. There are events that transpired during my years away . . . events that make it impossible for me to ever to be worthy of this—"

"Are you referring to the *Absalom*?"

Connor's jaw dropped. "You know?"

"By jingo, boy, we're not completely witless. Before he decided to entrust you with the security of our entire country, Melville had you checked out thoroughly. We tracked down several of your shipmates, and every one of them sings the same tune. Those poor beggars in the hold would have died if you hadn't done what you did. You're a hero, not a criminal. Now, if you are done with your self-chastisement, I suggest you send a message to whatever smuggler's harbor you've got your ship anchored in and get it here smart quick. In case you hadn't heard, there's a war on."

The commodore delivered a quick bow and a wink to Juliana, then bustled out the door. But even after he left, Connor continued to stare at the scroll, unable to believe it. "I'm an officer again, Princess," he said in wonder. "A man of position and honor."

"You always were." She wrapped her arms around his neck. "Bilgewater and barnacles, Connor. When are you going to start accepting the fact that you are a good and decent man? Or you will be, as soon as you ask me to marry you."

His brow arched up. "As I recall, you did all the asking. Quite convincingly, too."

"Yes, but I do not recall an answer. I should like one soon, if you do not mind. Otherwise, I shall have to consider the proposal of one of my other suitors. Perhaps Sidney Richmond. Or Fitzwilliam—"

She gasped as he pulled her flush against him. "Connor, your shoulder. You'll tear the dressing."

"Hang the dressing. You're mine, Juliana. We'll make our vows together all right and proper, but even without them you belong to me. We belong to each other, forever and always. And I—now what is the matter?"

" 'Tis just—" She swallowed, knowing tears were not appropriate for such a moment. "I am happy—happier than I ever thought possible. But when I pictured our wedding day, I always imagined my father standing with us. I know he is gone, but there is a part of me that still continues to hope—"

A knock sounded on the front door. Frowning, Juliana followed the butler to the door. "Who could be calling before daw—Tommy Blue? Where have you been? You disappeared so suddenly, and we have heard nothing of you for months—"

"Yes, well, it had to be sudden-like. I had a fish on the line, so to speak, and I had to reel it in before I lost the hook. You follow?"

"No," Connor and Juliana said in unison.

Tommy stroked his scraggly chin. "I don't want it to be a shock, but I don't sees how it can't be. I caught wind of a rumor down Barbados way—a tale of men shipwrecked on an island. Wasn't sure it would pan out. Didn't want to get our hopes up. So I took off quick as Jack Sprite. Did the deed and came back near as quick. Beat the packet ships, we did, so's no sense in sending a letter."

Connor rubbed his temples. They'd had a night of surprises all ready, and one more was putting him past his limit. "Tommy, what in blazes are you going on about? And who is we—?"

A figure stood just outside the doorway. The man was

shrouded in the fog and ghostly light of the sky just before dawn. Yet there was something in his bold stance, something that reminded him of—

Minutes later Jamie snuck out of the parlor, trying to delay the inevitable bedtime as long as possible. He saw his captain standing in the hallway, and went to stand beside him. He rubbed his eyes, sleepy yet curious as he followed his captain's gaze. "Why's the lady hugging that man and crying? She shouldn't be crying, should she?"

Connor reached down and rested his hand on his young lieutenant's shoulders. "She is crying because she is happy, sir. That man is her father."

EPILOGUE

ondon January 1, 1813

t's been too long. God's teeth, why is it taking so long?" His
ajesty's Captain Connor Reed demanded as he paced the
g of his parlor. His usually immaculate naval uniform was
rinkled and askew, and the black ribbon barely contained
e reckless tangle of hair that had once been a neat officer's
ueue. He looked more like a ragamuffin than a decorated
aval officer, but that was hardly surprising. He'd ridden hell-
r-leather through the night from the North Downs the
inute he'd heard that his wife had gone into labor. "Some-
ing is wrong."

"My boy, nothing is wrong," the marquis of Albany as-
red him for the dozenth time. "Babies come into this world
 their own time, and there is not a blessed thing any of us
n do about it."

"Your father-in-law is quite correct. And if my son and that
rogant Frenchman friend of yours were here instead of
vay at sea, they'd no doubt say the same," Mrs. Jolly stated
 she entered the room leaning heavily on her cane. Both

Connor and Albany moved to help her, but she batted them away. For the past several months she had worked diligently to conquer her infirmity, determined to reenter the world she had only been reading about for so long.

She settled regally into an armchair and proclaimed, "You've no cause to fear. Juliana is a strong, healthy, and very determined young woman. And as I tell those addled-witted doctors who insist on proclaiming my recovery a miracle— there is *nothing* a determined woman cannot do when she sets her mind to it."

"True enough," Albany agreed. "She's got the line captains and merchants singing as sweetly as choirboys. I never considered having her work with me in the shipping business. Now I wonder how I ever got along without her." He put his hand on Connor's shoulder and gave it a fatherly shake. "And I know my dear girl would not be what she is today without your love and support while I was lost at sea. Your methods were a bit"—his brow arched—"let us just call them unorthodox. But you saved her, just as surely as you saved her when she fell into the Thames. You saw her for the woman she could be, not the one I and everyone else expected her to be."

"That is how she always saw me," Connor mused, recalling the New Year's Day thirteen years before when he'd first set eyes on her. She'd seen beyond his filthy exterior to the heart within. Now he had a position of honor and purpose and a home of his own, things he'd dared not even dream of on that long-ago day. But most of all he had a wife he loved with all his heart and who loved him in return. And that was a prize far more valuable than any of the riches and honor he'd won in battle—

Meg burst into the room. "'Tis a girl! They are both well and you can see her if—"

Connor did not hear the rest. He streaked out of the room like a fired cannonball and took the stairs two at a time. Heedless to her tsking, he maneuvered around the midwife and fell to his knees at the side of the bed where his wife la

er sunset hair was matted against her forehead and she
oked spent beyond measure, but to Connor she had never
oked more beautiful. And when she turned to the small,
e-wrapped bundle at her side, her smile outshone the sun.

"Oh, Connor, look at our daughter. Our Margaret Rose.
e is so lovely," Juliana whispered.

"How could she not be, with so lovely a mother?" he an-
ered as he gazed in awe at their daughter. She stared at
m with the biggest, bluest eyes he had ever seen. Gingerly
reached out a finger, afraid that even the slightest touch
ght shatter such a delicate creature.

Her tiny, flailing fist punched him soundly.

Connor grinned like a schoolboy. "Ha, well she's certainly
t your spirit."

"And your nerve. Scoundrel."

"Brat."

"Villain."

"My love," Connor breathed, taking her in his arms.

Still tsking, the midwife removed the babe from the em-
acing couple and placed her in a bassinet at the other end
the room, then bustled off to get a new stack of linen.

No one saw the boy slip into the room.

Jamie frowned at the embracing couple. Much as he liked
e lady, there had been entirely too much kissing going
since the captain's marriage. Sighing, he turned to the
ssinet, curious to see what all the fuss was about. It was
all. And wrinkled. And it was beginning to have a decided
or. Shrugging, he started to turn away, but then the baby
ned. She stared up at him with eyes that seemed like twin
eces of the bluest heaven. Then she smiled.

Jamie felt something strange happen inside him, as if he'd
allowed a bit of bad beef. Except—this felt nice. Won-
rful. The baby started to scowl, so he reached down and
sped her tiny fist between his fingers. "Don't cry, little girl.
on't let anything hurt you. You'll see. I'll look after you. I'll
otect you. That's a promise. . . ."

© Colin Simmons

ABOUT THE AUTHOR

RUTH OWEN is the author of many highly praised Loveswepts, including the Maggie Award-winning *Taming the Pirate*. She has been writing ever since she could pick up a pen. Though she loves writing contemporaries, a secret part of her is living out adventures in Regency England. This is her first historical, and she hopes that you enjoy reading it as much as she enjoyed writing it.

Ms. Owen loves to hear from her fans. Write her at P.O. Box 432, Winter Park, Florida 32790-0432, or e-mail her at rmowen@mindspring.com.

Look for these other books in the
MEET ME AT MIDNIGHT series

A Kiss at Midnight by Shana Abe,
on sale February 2000

Just Before Midnight by Suzanne Robinson,
on sale March 2000

Turn the page for sneak peeks at these
enthralling romances.

A KISS AT MIDNIGHT
by Shana Abé
On sale February 2000

Ancient law proclaims that, as the year 999 draws to a close, the land of Alderich will be wrested from the Rune family by the clan of Leonhart. But when Rafael Leonhart kidnaps the beautiful Serath Rune for ransom, he falls under her spell . . . and the conquest he desires most of all is the heart of his alluring captive.

He had been waiting for her too long.

To anyone else, the passing time had been no more than a day and a night, camped out in the woods surrounding the convent, a quiet scrutiny of the situation before the attack. Just a day and a night, and then suddenly the girl was there, and she was theirs.

But to Rafael of Leonhart, the waiting time had been years—thirty-two of them to be exact, the sum of his entire life.

Thirty-two years of waiting to gain access to this girl and steal her away to suit his needs.

Thirty-two years waiting for the turn of this century, when the land of Alderich and the castle, and the wealth they represented, would become his. And now this granddaughter of his enemy would ensure it for him.

So while his soldiers had remained in the woods with him for that day and night, had met with him and discussed how best to breach the walls of a holy sanctuary, most of them felt mere hours slip by. But Rafe had felt his lifetime come sliding to a sudden and final countdown, each second bringing sharp anticipation.

He had Serath. Rafael broke into a fierce smile that no one could see, unable to help himself. He had her. And so he had Alderich.

"This way, my lord." His cousin Abram took the lead momentarily, showing Rafe the correct path amid the autumn grasses.

The woman in front of him started at the words. She turned her head to see Abram, who spared her only one quick look before turning away.

Rafe followed the faint trail, pushing his mount to a gallop as they entered the smoothness of a valley. Serath's black hair flew up with the new wind, brushing against his chest, curling along his neck with surprising softness. Rafe ignored the sensation, concentrating on the land ahead of them.

Rafe slowed his steed, waiting for the rest of his men to catch up, and the figure in his arms shifted and then somehow there was nothing but empty space where a warm woman had been. It happened so quickly that it took him several seconds to comprehend it—as if she had transformed into the very air before him.

Dammit! Rafe reined in completely, looking left and right before catching sight of her running through the trees, swift and nearly gone already.

"Where did she go?" one of the men asked, dumbfounded.

He didn't bother to answer, though several others did, shouting and pointing at the diminishing shape. Rafe was already lunging after her, his stallion picking his way through the trunks of the trees with surety. She would not be able to outrun a horse.

At last Rafael dismounted, walking away from his soldiers his steps slow and sure on the mossy ground.

He stopped, closing his eyes, listening. The obvious came to him first: men behind him, completely silent now but for the creaking of saddles . . . the bare, metallic clinks of shields and swords against chain mail. Horses, a few shifting with impatience. Wind through pine needles, a ghostly murmur of sound. . . .

. . . faint breathing. Muted, nearly imperceptible. Off to his left.

Pure relief made him release his own breath, close to a sigh. Rafe opened his eyes and found her immediately—or rather, found the spot he had figured to be just another bramble of bushes, exactly the same as the multitude of others that dotted the forest floor. He walked past it, the relief becoming close to exhilaration, then stopped again.

"Serath," he said, not raising his voice. "It was a good effort, my lady, but now it is done. Come back. My patience is ended."

And since she did not move, he reached through the brush and grabbed what was there—a mass of cloth, the woman beneath it erupting from the branches and dead leaves with complete and sudden fury, striking at him, struggling as he wrapped his arms around her and tried to contain the unexpected strength of her. It was a strangely silent battle, no sound from her other than the raggedness of her breathing, and his own harsh gasp as she landed a blow to his cheekbone.

"Enough!" Finally he had her restrained in front of him, her arms pinned, her tousled head held just below his.

"Enough," Rafe said again, more subdued, and held her there until she was still at last, that blanket of silence about her shrouding them both.

There were leaves in her hair. They stood out against the black even in this dim light, papery ovals, a few twigs enmeshed in otherwise glossy locks. Her panting was slowing but the heat of her body seemed to grow against him, uncomfortably warm.

Rafael scowled again, fighting the unexpected appeal of this, a soft woman so near.

"Will you obey me, Serath Rune?" he asked her, his voice rough.

Slowly, slowly, he felt the tension from her body begin to fade, begin to melt, ever so slightly, against him. His own body responded with a completely unwelcome rush of hunger for her, for the sweet curves and ebony hair and the scent of some unknown spice that haunted her.

This was bad. He could not allow himself to feel for her, not even this basic, overwhelming lust. He could not allow anything so petty as passion for a woman to disrupt his plans, no matter how fair or enthralling she was.

"Will you obey?" he asked again, gritting his teeth.

And at last she nodded her head, just once, a short jerk. He turned her around in his arms, not releasing her completely, because he didn't trust a nod.

Her head lifted; she shook away the curling strands of hair. Rafael found himself staring into a pair of blue eyes pale with moonlight, a face of such delicate and unlikely beauty that it left him winded for a moment, mute himself.

I know you, Rafe thought, shock running through him.

Aye, there was a profound and telling recognition in him at the full sight of her, those eyes, that look. It was as if he had just discovered a part of himself in this person, a missing part that only now pained him for its loss.

He stood there gaping at her, knowing how inept it seemed, unable to help himself. She was a vision from a forgotten youth, a young woman with a face of timeless sorcery, dark brows, perfect nose, full lips, eyes surrounded by thick, black lashes. Her skin was utterly colorless in this light, her gaze the color of silver on heaven. She was the sun and the moon together, she was smoke and desire made real.

She had the face of an enchantress, yes, but the blue of her gaze told him something more: she had pride, and spirit—and what might have been fear. Rafe fought his reaction to that, the desire to comfort her.

He became suddenly, acutely aware of his hands on her,

the burning heat of his palms against her upper arms, where he held her. The firm but giving flesh of her, so close her body nearly brushed his. He felt a kind of insanity from it, realizing all at once that here in his grip was more than a prize he had won; this was a woman, warmth and familiar succor, and he wanted nothing more than to pull her the rest of the way to him, to feel the whole of her pressed to his body. To bury himself in her.

It *was* a spell—a mortal spell to be sure, but a terrible and disastrous one, and Rafael of Leonhart was, for the first time in his adulthood, helpless to combat the emotions that raged through him.

JUST BEFORE MIDNIGHT
by Suzanne Robinson
On sale March 2000

A blackmailer is on the loose in 1899 London, and the sting is on: A handsome private inquiry agent convinces an American heiress to help him catch a thief by sending counterfeit love letters. To make it seem authentic, he volunteers to play the correspondent. The only problem is, their passion is genuine . . . and time is running out.

London, 1899

If she didn't escape before dawn, she wouldn't get away at all. Mattie Bright tiptoed through the darkened house, her boots clutched in one hand, her skirts lifted in the other. If she were discovered, the consequences would be terrible—another morning of lessons in elocution, manners and the peerage from Mademoiselle Elise; more fittings for her new Worth gowns; and after that, more calls. If she had to sit through another afternoon listening to society ladies and their daughters gush about gowns and lace, calling them 'deevie," which was their private word for divine, she'd squall like a bobcat in a pickle barrel.

"Deevie indeed," she muttered.

Such affectations irritated her intensely, causing her to slip in her determination to improve her character. For Mattie was engaged in a great endeavor to reform, to become more tolerant, more even-tempered, calm, and above all, sweet-natured. These were the qualities of the great lady Papa had always wanted her to become. Sadly, she lacked most of them. Closest to her heart was the desire to be like other young women. Other young ladies seemed to glide along with sweet smiles and kind words, never growing angry at things like women not being allowed to vote, never losing their tempers or wishing they could take charge because some man was making an all-fired mess of things.

Mattie hurried downstairs, through the drawing room and past a table on which were scattered her mother's books on conduct. Her resolve to improve vanished. Glaring at Mama's copy of *Titled Americans*, Mattie cursed every girl in it who had married an English lord. Ever since her parents' efforts to conquer New York society had failed so embarrassingly, their hopes of establishing social preeminence had fastened on their twenty-three-year-old daughter.

Ordinarily she would have refused to have anything to do with such carryings-on, but just before he died Papa had asked Mattie to do just one thing for him. Marry a titled Englishman. It would make all his hard work, all his efforts to give them a better life, worth it. And he and Mama hadn't been satisfied with low standards like the Jeromes, whose daughter Jennie married Lord Randolph Churchill. Papa and Mama aimed high, and Mattie must set her cap for the best, like Consuelo Yznaga, who became Duchess of Manchester, or her goddaughter, Consuelo Vanderbilt, the new Duchess of Marlborough.

The path to gentility had been a rough and long one for Mattie. It had begun as soon as Papa grew wealthy, with many a rebellion along the way. But over the last few years Mattie had come to realize how different she was from most girls, and after a while she'd begun to suspect there was something wrong with her. Otherwise she wouldn't find inventions and new ideas more fascinating than Paris fashions and marriage offers. Her character was flawed, or she would long to be as sweet, loving and giving as her mother and her friend Narcissa. Just when she thought she'd turned herself into a lady she'd forget to control her tongue or her temper, or both.

With a sigh Mattie shut the door to the drawing room. Avoiding the kitchen, where the maids would be starting fires and heating water, Mattie left the house through the conservatory. She stopped to pull on her boots, wiggling her foot into the aged leather. These were her old boots, the ones she wasn't supposed to wear because they were Texas trail boots rather than fine English riding ones. But why wear anything fancy when no one was going to see her?

Mattie stood and luxuriated for a moment in the soft, wrinkled and scratched leather. Then she stamped her boots to settle her feet in them comfortably, and set off for the stables. With every step away from the house her spirits rose. She was wearing her long, loose coat that covered her from neck to boots and fastened tightly at the cuffs. Her hair was covered by a hat and veil, and goggles hung about her neck. Letting herself out the garden gate, she crossed an alley with eager steps and met Trimble, the coachman, on his way to feed the horses.

"Good morning, Miss."

"Mornin', Trimble. You haven't seen me."

"No, Miss. I never do."

Trimble opened the stable doors, and Mattie went to a canvas-covered mound opposite the stalls. The coach horses stuck their heads out and nickered at her. Mattie waved at them as she hauled the canvas off her new motor car. The gray hue of dawn lit the black metal body and polished brass headlamps of the Panhard-Lavassor. A shiver of excitement whipped through her as she reached over and flipped the lever on the steering wheel to retard the spark. Hurrying to the front, she gripped the crank and turned it once. The engine burst to life with a steady metallic hum. It was unlike anything else heard on the road, those tiny, muffled, rapid-fire explosions that blurred into one continuous purr. The brass carriage lamps rattled against their glass. Mattie grinned over her shoulder at the horses, who had become used to the noise of the car.

"One crank every time, fellas. It's a caution." Equine ears pricked. One of them snorted and kicked his stall.

"Dang, Trimble. I think they're jealous."

The coachman was filling a bucket with oats. "More like they wish that foul machine to perdition, begging your pardon, Miss."

Pulling her goggles into place, Mattie jumped into the Panhard and released the brake. "Don't worry, we're leaving. Come on, Pannie, before the poor creatures have conniption fits."

Mattie drove out of the alley at a sedate pace. No sense in waking Mama with engine noise. These drives served as a refuge from the trials of being in Society and trying to catch a titled husband. Essentially American in her outlook, Mattie had trouble giving up her ideals regarding men, women and marriage. She didn't want to get married at all, but if she was going to do it, she wanted to marry someone she loved. Of course, that was no longer an option. Among the English aristocracy, marriage was an alliance between families for financial and social advantage. Love had nothing to do with it. Love was what happened after an heir had been provided— then the partners went their separate ways to find it, the husband sometimes getting a head start on his search.

"Mattie Bright," she said to herself as she turned a corner. "You got as much chance of finding a lovable man in Society as an armadillo does of going to a tea party."

Exhilaration pumped through Mattie's veins with the speed of fuel through the engine. She laughed and whooped, keeping her eyes on the road. Ahead loomed Hyde Park Corner and Wellington Arch. Slowing only a bit, she turned the wheel and accelerated into the curve. The Panhard hugged the pavement and spun onto Park Lane.

startling a chimney sweep and a maid cleaning a wrought iron gate. The maid shrieked and covered her ears, but Mattie zoomed by, her eye on Marble Arch at the end of Park Lane. She would race around the arch, down Bayswater and into Hyde Park by The Ring. There she could circle the park via Rotten Row.

As she sped past Stanhope Gate, Mattie fed the engine more gas. The ends of her scarf flapped wildly, and she gulped in deep breaths. She was going to make this stretch in record time! She was approaching Grosvenor Gate, her pedal foot almost on the floor, when a dark flash appeared in the corner of her eye. Her foot came off the gas pedal, and she grabbed the outside break with one hand. Mattie and the Panhard swerved, barely missing a chestnut thoroughbred as its rider hauled on the reins. She heard the horse scream as the motor car continued its careening circle, jumped a curb and stopped. Mattie was thrown against the steering wheel. Her hat and veil slipped over her face, and the engine stalled.

Mattie fell back in the seat while she caught her breath and her vision cleared. Her shaking hands pushed her hat back and pulled the knot in her veil loose. Behind her she heard shouting and the clatter of hooves on pavement. Somewhat recovered, Mattie tore her hat from her head and jumped out of the Panhard. A continuous stream of curses greeted her. She was relieved at the sight of a costermonger rushing after the Thoroughbred. The horse was dancing down the street with alarm, but was unhurt. The cursing rider, however, was buried under a cascade of lettuce, squash, melons, and tomatoes—lots of tomatoes.

What she could see of the man seemed whole. She must have missed him completely, if only by an inch or two. Mattie folded her arms over her chest and watched him flail a rain of peaches and strawberries that were sliding from the top of the costermonger's cart onto his head.

Had his hair not been seeping with squashed tomatoes, the stranger would have been blond. His riding outfit had the elegant cut of Saville Row, but the effect was marred somewhat by lettuce-leaf epaulets while tomato pulp stained the starched purity of his shirt. Mattie forgot her outrage at the man's carelessness and chuckled. The swearing stopped. The rider paused in the act of wiping his face and gave her a look of outrage that belonged on Banquo's ghost when confronting Macbeth.

"Bloody hell, woman, you should look where you're going. You almost killed me. You must be a blithering fool." Mattie opened her mouth, but the rider held up a hand, noticed it was holding a squash and dropped the vegetable. "No, don't answer. I can see you're one of those ghastly New Women. Driving infernal motor cars, screeching about the vote and other absolute rot. It's obvious you're a blithering fool."

Tossing a lock of jet-colored hair over her shoulder, Mattie drew her brows together. "What are you so all-fired huffy about? You're the one who doesn't look where he's going. You must be blind as a post hole not to have seen me coming, and I'm not fixin' to let you cuss at me for something that your own blamed fault."

The rider was staring at her, openmouthed.

"Dear God, what kind of beastly accent is that?"

"I don't have an accent. You're the one with the accent. You sound like you been eating lemons for breakfast, all pinched and tart."

At this the rider lunged to his feet only to slip on a melon rind and crash to the ground on his posterior. Mattie clapped her hands together and laughed, which elicited another colorful blasphemy from him.

"You look like a piglet in a mud hole!" Mattie chuckled again, but her mirth ended abruptly when something wet and cold smashed her in the face. "Ugh!" She wiped her eyes and looked at her hands. They were covered with tomato. "Why you ornery priss-pants, I'll—" Words failed, but Mattie took action. She scooped up a handful of red melon pulp and hurled it at the rider's newly cleaned face. He ducked, but

Mattie followed with the contents of her other hand. This time the melon hit him in the ear.

The rider lunged at her, this time keeping his footing. He would have had her if the costermonger hadn't rushed up with the Thoroughbred in tow.

"Sir, I caught him, I did. He's all right."

Mattie's opponent clenched his fists, gave Mattie an acid glare and took the reins. His face lost its harsh lines the moment he turned to the horse. His voice took on the quality of a father soothing a lost child.

"There old chap, you're all right. Yes you are. You're just fine. Pay no attention to the harpy and her infernal machine."

"Harpy!"

The horse tossed his head and widened his eyes while the rider turned on Mattie.

"Damn it, woman. Will you be quiet? Only a savage spooks a horse like that."

"What in Sam Hill do you mean calling me a harpy, you no-account skunk?" Mattie scooped up a tomato and aimed.

"Here!" The costermonger rushed to her and snatched the tomato. "Who's going to pay for me cart and vegetables? Look at it. There ain't a whole piece of fruit nor nothing in the whole lot."

"The harpy will pay," said the rider as he led his horse round the cart.

"Ha! The accident was your fault, not mine," Mattie said. She glanced at the costermonger. "The dude will pay."

The vendor looked from Mattie to the rider. "Someone's got to pay, or I'll be getting a copper, I will."

"An excellent idea," the rider said as he mounted his horse. "When he comes just explain to him that the harpy was motoring on Park Lane over thirty miles an hour and caused the whole thing."

"Why you—"

Elegant brows raised. "Do you deny you were going too fast?"

"I'm not in the habit of telling tales, dude. I know how fast I was going, but you just trotted right into the street without looking, dang it."

Ignoring her, the rider leaned down and handed the costermonger a card. "Cheyne Tennant is my name. Should you need my testimony, you can reach me at that address."

"Where are you going?" Mattie demanded. "Come back here!"

She sprang across the space that separated them and grabbed the reins. The horse shied, but she hung on. Tennant swore and grabbed her upper arms. Hauling her against his leg, he steadied the horse and bent down to spit out each word.

"My dear young lady, I have no intention of allowing you to shriek at me in the middle of Park Lane. If I were you I'd pay this poor man and go home where you belong."

For a frozen second they stared at each other—a Montague and Capulet stare. Then something changed. His gaze faltered, darted to her mouth, her neck, lower. When his glance lifted to her eyes, Mattie felt a strange warmth kindle in her chest and spread through the rest of her body. Never in her born days had she seen eyes like that. If a magic spell took shape it would take the form of those eyes—a sapphire charm, one moment blazing, the next freezing. Then Cheyne Tennant blinked rapidly, as if coming to his senses from unconsciousness. Mattie felt his hands loosen their grip, and she plummeted to the ground. She landed on her ass, her skirts flying up to her knees.

"Ow! You idiot, that hurt."

"Then I would suggest we're even."

Bestselling Historical Women's Fiction

❧ AMANDA QUICK ❧

____28354-5 SEDUCTION . . .$6.99/$9.99 Canada

____28932-2 SCANDAL . . . .$6.99/$9.99

____28594-7 SURRENDER . . . .$6.99/$9.99

____29325-7 RENDEZVOUS . . . .$6.99/$9.99

____29315-X RECKLESS . . . .$6.99/$9.99

____29316-8 RAVISHED . . . .$6.99/$9.99

____29317-6 DANGEROUS . . . .$6.99/$9.99

____56506-0 DECEPTION . . . .$6.99/$9.99

____56153-7 DESIRE . . . .$6.99/$9.99

____56940-6 MISTRESS . . . .$6.99/$9.99

____57159-1 MYSTIQUE . . . .$6.99/$9.99

____57190-7 MISCHIEF . . . .$6.50/$8.99

____57407-8 AFFAIR . . . .$6.99/$8.99

____57409-4 WITH THIS RING . . . . . .$6.99/$9.99

❧ IRIS JOHANSEN ❧

____29871-2 LAST BRIDGE HOME . . .$5.99/$8.99

____29604-3 THE GOLDEN
                BARBARIAN . . . .$6.99/$8.99

____29244-7 REAP THE WIND . . . . . .$6.99/$9.99

____29032-0 STORM WINDS . . . .$6.99/$8.99

Ask for these books at your local bookstore or use this page to order.

ase send me the books I have checked above. I am enclosing $____ (add $2.50 to
ver postage and handling). Send check or money order, no cash or C.O.D.'s, please.

me _____

dress _____

y/State/Zip _____

d order to: Bantam Books, Dept. FN 16, 2451 S. Wolf Rd., Des Plaines, IL 60018
ow four to six weeks for delivery.
es and availability subject to change without notice.   FN 16 4/99

Bestselling Historical Women's Fiction

⅜ IRIS JOHANSEN ⅜

____28855-5 THE WIND DANCER . . . $6.99/$9.99
____29968-9 THE TIGER PRINCE . . . $6.99/$8.99
____29944-1 THE MAGNIFICENT
            ROGUE . . . . $6.99/$8.99
____29945-X BELOVED SCOUNDREL . $6.99/$8.99
____29946-8 MIDNIGHT WARRIOR . . $6.99/$8.99
____29947-6 DARK RIDER . . . . $6.99/$8.99
____56990-2 LION'S BRIDE . . . . $6.99/$8.99
____56991-0 THE UGLY DUCKLING. . . $6.99/$8.99
____57181-8 LONG AFTER MIDNIGHT.$6.99/$8.99
____57998-3 AND THEN YOU DIE. . . . $6.99/$8.99
____57802-2 THE FACE OF DECEPTION. $6.99/$9.99

⅜ TERESA MEDEIROS ⅜

____29407-5 HEATHER AND VELVET . .$5.99/$7.50
____29409-1 ONCE AN ANGEL . . . . . $5.99/$7.99
____29408-3 A WHISPER OF ROSES . . $5.99/$7.99
____56332-7 THIEF OF HEARTS . . . . . $5.99/$7.99
____56333-5 FAIREST OF THEM ALL . $5.99/$7.50
____56334-3 BREATH OF MAGIC . . . $5.99/$7.99
____57623-2 SHADOWS AND LACE . . $5.99/$7.99
____57500-7 TOUCH OF ENCHANTMENT. $5.99/$7.99
____57501-5 NOBODY'S DARLING . . . $5.99/$7.99
____57502-3 CHARMING THE PRINCE . $5.99/$8.99

Ask for these books at your local bookstore or use this page to order.

Please send me the books I have checked above. I am enclosing $_____ (add $2.50 t
cover postage and handling). Send check or money order, no cash or C.O.D.'s, pleas

Name_____

Address_____

City/State/Zip_____

Send order to: Bantam Books, Dept. FN 16, 2451 S. Wolf Rd., Des Plaines, IL 600
Allow four to six weeks for delivery.
Prices and availability subject to change without notice.   FN 16 4.